THE
SIX RIVERS
KILLER

M. L. Edson

(Based, unfortunately, on a true story)

Bett,
Thanks for
your support —
Happy reading
Love you —
Mary Lou

ISBN: ISBN-13: 978-1478161776

ISBN-10: 1478161779

First Edition: 2012

Cover by K.W. Anderson

Preface

This book was written to meet a need – to get this story out of my head, onto paper and electronic format, and into the hands of readers.

The evil represented by the perpetrator still exists in the world and threatens everyone, even those who believe that innocence can prevail. There is a warning embedded within this story to those who think they can overcome a power much stronger than themselves. Sometimes that just doesn't happen, and evil dominates.

My sorrow and regret go to the family of the victim of this story. He was a real person with great potential, and I am sure his family has missed him terribly.

Appreciation

Members of my critique group were invaluable to telling this story. Ron Smith (aka Bryson Kilmer), Tom Hessler, Mort Rumberg, Westley Turner, Roberta Davis, and Eva Wise all contributed their time and talents. Thanks also to friends Lee Bowman and Ruth Fricker for their support. I thank them all.

My brother and fellow author, Charles F. Edson (*The Baldwin Negatives)*, also assisted in the editing and critiquing, sometimes *strongly* critiquing, but that's a brother's prerogative.

In writing this story, I had help from many people, including Brenda Goodsey, Public Information Officer with the Humboldt County Sheriff's Office, and other personnel there who still remember this case.

Thanks to the innumerable Peanut M&Ms, which I too frequently devoured while sitting at the computer. However, over the years I perfected the art of peeling off the hard candy coating, saving it, then sucking off the chocolate and eating it and the peanut before retrieving the sugary shell to eat.

Thanks to my husband who passed away before I could get this experience onto paper and to my three children who had to deal with their mother's idiosyncrasies, only some of which came from my involvement with this case.

And, thanks to you for reading this story.

Prologue

The area in and around the Six Rivers National Forest is beautiful, full of towering redwood trees and verdant ferns. Though the weather is often cold and foggy in Northern California, the people there are generally warm and friendly. The area is also remote.

Three hundred miles and six hours north of either San Francisco or Sacramento, it is accessible only by leaving the security of broad freeways and venturing onto a two-lane, twisting highway, dodging soaring redwoods and arriving in a different world. Rainstorms, fog, and rock slides can block highways and restrict access for days. Train passenger service stopped years ago after repeated washouts near the Scotia Bluffs.

Separated from the rest of the world geographically, physically, and even psychologically and emotionally, California's Pacific Northwest was more like the rest of the country fifty years earlier in morals, family values, and culture. The drug of choice has been home-grown marijuana—not necessarily a good thing, but far better than many other choices. "EUREKA! I've found it" is more than the state's motto here. "The grass *is* greener in Humboldt County."

Young adults move away because the economy will not support a lifestyle they would like to achieve. Others stay to live and work peaceably, raise their children, or retire. The vistas, redwoods, parks, beaches, ocean, rivers, people, the peace, and some really terrific restaurants (to say nothing of the best locally-made ravioli in the world), make it God's country—nearly a Utopia far removed from the stereotypes of fast-paced, workaholic, smog-covered Southern California.

Unfortunately, this type of lifestyle could not continue unscathed. The price for Utopia must be paid. Timber trade has fallen; fisheries have closed; county, city, and state bureaucracies are the biggest, most reliable employers. The unemployment rate typically hovers over fourteen percent, recently hitting close to eighteen percent.

For some, reality sucks. And reality, when you are stuck at the bottom of the human pile, has a certain stench that can be tolerated only by giving in to your baser instincts—actions brought on by lust, greed, and unconscionable acts. Your belief that the world is your enemy is supported by your selective vision. Temptation corrupts the weaker souls. You believe everyone else has more than you, and you only have less because the world is against you. Anything that others have is there for the taking.

Someone may be born to this station and choose to remain. Someone might be physically and emotionally beaten into accepting the lifestyle. Or, someone may enter it because the temptations are so great with easy dividends.

Who knows what ills of society create this attitude? Can society even be blamed? Chances to succeed proliferate, opportunities exist, education is available, choices are made. However, these are invisible if eyes and minds are not open. People choose to suckle on the woes, the sludge that propagates more disease. People, even here in Utopia, can fall into patterns of evil.

The Six Rivers Killer

By M. L. Edson

Chapter 1

Thursday, early evening

Phillip Dunne blew warm air into his cupped hands then rubbed them together. He stomped his cold feet into the damp gravel beside Highway 199. The thickening Northern California fog clung to the soaring redwoods, and the moisture matted his brown hair to his forehead. His toes were growing numb; the thin soles of his old Converse tennis shoes were little help. His faded jeans were damp and provided no insulation. Fewer and fewer headlights penetrated the solitude, and every driver ignored his extended thumb.

The tall, muscular man drew his arms close to his body as another car sped past. He let the camouflage-patterned backpack drop to the ground then pulled futilely at the zipper of the worn, gray jacket once more before shoving his hands deep into the pockets. He shivered. *Damn it's cold!* he said to himself.

The hitchhiker fumbled through his pockets, pulled out a pack of Camels and lit up. He stomped again and tried to revive the circulation in his feet as he blew out a long stream of smoke.

He had planned to put more distance between himself and the Pacific Coast long before now, but his luck had not been good. Another car passed. *Typical,* he thought. *None of these shit-heads will stop.* He glared up and down the two-lane highway, looking and listening for an approaching car.

Dunne traveled light. He kept only the bare necessities in his "borrowed" backpack, stolen last week from another hitchhiker. If clothes, cigarettes, and a bit of food didn't fit in it or in his pockets, he didn't need it.

He liked the body he had built. *Coulda' been a football player—a really good one* he told himself. *Could've afforded better clothes.* He tugged at the tight jacket, trying to pull it closed. Again he gave up. He took another long drag on the cigarette and pulled in the warm air. *Shit! I'm freezing!*

He stuck his thumb out as another pair of headlights approached, then flipped the driver the bird as the car sped past. Dunne brushed his damp hair away from his eyes, and swore. *Screw 'em! Fuckin' pricks! I don't give a shit. I'll walk to Oregon … again.*

Headlights glimmered through the dark, penetrated the dampness, and reflected off the wet fronds of the ferns and fallen needles of the surrounding redwoods.

Check this out. Stand straight; now step toward the roadway. Fake 'em out.

The headlights caught him in their beam, and the approaching car slid on the wet pavement. The tires hit the gravel, and the car skidded to a stop.

Dunne didn't have to move to avoid getting hit but slapped the hood of the car and jumped back anyway. *That'll shake 'em up.* He glared into the car then grinned. *A broad's driving! Alone! A real looker, the bitch!*

The passenger-side window of the red Mustang lowered a couple of inches.

"My God, you scared me! Did I hit you?" the woman asked, and she reached over and turned the window knob to lower the window another inch.

"What? I'm okay. Hey, I'm heading north, across the border into Oregon. Could you …?" Dunne said as he reached for the handle. It was locked. *Damn.*

"No, I don't pick—"

"What? I can't hear you." He said and chuckled to himself.

The passenger window went down another inch.

"Just wanted to make sure you were okay. I don't pick up hitch—"

He tilted his head like he still couldn't understand, and with one swift motion, reached into the half-opened window, popped the lock, and opened the door.

"What? No!" the woman yelled.

Dunne jumped into the seat, smiled at her, and pushed a leather bag onto the console, making no move to look into it but judging its weight and bulk. *Maybe something interesting in there.*

She grabbed her purse and pulled it close.

"Hey, I'm okay. Harmless. Really."

The woman leaned away.

"I'm tired. Probably'll fall asleep in a minute," Dunne said and tossed his backpack into the rear seat and tried to stretch his six-foot body. He reached between his legs and released the lever to push the seat back as far as it would go so his legs wouldn't be cramped. *She's not as good lucking up close.* Her dark hair was pulled into a clip at the nape of her neck; her clothes hung on her giving an illusion of shapelessness. *In fact, she's not cute at all.*

"I'm safe. Wouldn't harm a fly. What's your name?"

"Uh, Glenda," she said with a shiver. "What's yours?"

Phillip Dunne ignored her question and asked, "Where are you going?" *Got to get her to relax and trust me. That's the key.* "What's up north for you?"

Glenda coughed and shoved her purse into the back seat. She looked at the intruder trying to size him up, then said, "I start a new job in a couple of weeks. Just graduated college and moving to Portland."

"What's the job?" he asked. *Come on, relax, bitch. Let's get moving.*

"Social work. I want to help people get off welfare and make a success of themselves," she said, looked at him once more, and took a deep breath before shifting into drive and gently pushing on the gas pedal.

Another bleeding-heart, liberal bitch that talks too much. At least we're finally moving. "I really appreciate the ride. What's in Portland? Family?"

"No, I thought I'd get an early start apartment hunting and get settled in. Name's Glenda Shore. What's yours?"

"Name? Oh, sorry. I'm … Glen, Glen Short." Lying was easy. Fun too, to see if anyone would catch him. He stretched his right hand across to shake hers. He was glad to see she automatically reached and grasped his hand. *Weak grip, too. Not much of a fighter. A wimpy bitch.*

"That's really something."

"What?" Dunne glared at her for a moment before he looked away. *Did I fuck up?*

"Our names. They're similar. What are the odds?"

Philip Dunne took a deep breath. "Yeah, what're the odds?" he repeated.

"Where are you heading?" Glenda asked.

"Back to school." *Too damn many questions. Shut the fuck up!* "I took a few days off. My mama got sick, and I had to help her out." Dunne was proud of that "mama" line; it brought the same sympathetic response every time.

"That's really sweet of you. Where does she live? Eureka? Arcata?"

None of your F'n business. I got to shut the bitch up! "Hey, sorry, but I'm really tired. Would you mind if I shut my eyes for a bit?" He adjusted his body, leaned the seat back, stretched his legs, and faked a yawn.

"Sure, I'll leave you alone. Everyone needs his rest."

"Wake me when we reach the tunnel and rest stop up ahead, okay?"

"Sure."

This bitch is taking it too slow. Nice car, though. Probably awesome to drive. Phillip Dunne knew his clothes were drying, and his sense of touch was returning to his extremities. He closed his eyes and pretended to sleep. He smiled at his own competence; he knew how to say what people wanted to hear.

He awoke with a start when Glenda slowed to turn off the main road. *Shit. I didn't want to really fall asleep.*

Glenda pulled into the rest stop and shut off the engine. "Here we are—potty stop."

Cute! "Thanks, glad you woke me," he said aloud. "I need to stretch. I'll watch the car while you run take care of business." He noticed that she had taken the clip out of her hair and the curls fell to the middle of her back, swaying rhythmically over the Humboldt State University logo of her sweatshirt as she turned and walked away. She looked younger now, almost pretty. He felt the need rise inside.

"Sure, Glen." And she was gone.

Dunne climbed out of the car and glanced around, shifting his eyes to make sure he didn't miss anything or anyone. *Good, no one else here.*

He unzipped his pants and relieved himself on the front, driver's side tire. Then he climbed in behind the steering wheel and slid the seat back as far as it would go.

Hmm. Cool car. Good lines. Bet if I rev it up, it'll hit a hundred, he thought and poked at the buttons. *A real car ... almost too easy. Cool.*

Glenda was suddenly at the window glaring at him, tugging at the door handle. Dunne opened the door open a crack but held the handle tight.

"What're you—?"

"Hey, you looked tired," he interrupted. "Thought I'd take over the driving since I'm well rested, and we're still a long way from Grants Pass. No accidents in the last ten years, honest." He smiled broadly at that last touch—"honest." *Of course no accidents ... I just paroled last month.*

Glenda looked around for another human—no one else anywhere. Alone and without options, Glenda quivered, walked around the car, got into the passenger seat, and handed Phillip Dunne, aka Glen Short, her key ring.

He smiled at her. Glenda smiled back and felt reassured at his composure and relaxed features. She buckled her seat belt.

Yep, wimpy. Not much of a fighter.

"Ready for a real ride?" he snarled, shoved the car into reverse, then shifted again and roared out of the parking lot, tires smoking on the damp pavement, and headed for the tunnel just ahead.

Chapter 2

Same evening

Jeffrey Madison opened the front door of the apartment and paused. "It's still raining," he said over his shoulder. "I thought California was the land of sunshine."

"Maybe we made a wrong turn back in Georgia. You won't dissolve," his sister Sherrill answered from the hall and stuffed another towel into the linen closet. "Ukiah is close enough to the coast to get this wet stuff once in a while. Just check the car. Check the trunk, too. I think I'm missing a bag of sheets."

Jeffrey ran through the rain and glanced into the silver Impala parked in the lot. He pulled on each door handle to make sure they were locked and grabbed the bag of sheets from the trunk. He slammed it shut then ran back through the still-opened apartment door.

Sherrill and Jeffrey had spent two weeks driving across the country. It had been a leisurely trip, stopping at national parks and historic sites. They had taken an extra day to see Bryce Canyon then drove to the Great Salt Lake and played tourist for another day.

They had been born barely two years apart and had remained close growing up. Competition and sibling rivalries only made them appreciate each other more now they had reached adulthood.

"Your car is secure," Jeffrey called out. He double-checked his duffel bag, jewelry display box, and suitcases. His manuscript was there. His samples of hand-made silver necklaces and earrings were safely packed. He set the cartons and suitcases beside the front door and made sure its deadbolt was secure.

"You want me to stay another day or two? We could go back to San Francisco. I wouldn't mind spending some time at Fisherman's Wharf. I could—"

"What? Babysit me? Stop worrying."

"I'll worry about you if I want to. You're a long way from home. This is the wild west, after all." Jeffrey gave his sister a wink as he went into the bathroom to brush his teeth. "You saw that motel in Vegas."

"Yeah, the neon lights spelled out 'Wild, Wild West.' You've been reading too many comic books. This isn't the wilderness."

"Well, you have a nice apartment, anyway," he said through a mouth full of bubbles. "Really, are you going to be okay here alone? You promise to keep in touch, right? You just went through a lot back home."

"Yeah, I'll be fine. That part of my life is over, and I'm making a new start." She shoved the stopper into the kitchen sink, turned the water on, and squirted in too much dish soap.

"About time. You spent how many years with that jerk?" he asked and dropped his toothbrush into the plastic holder then stuffed it into his ditty bag near his suitcase.

"I don't want to talk about that now," she said and turned the water off. "Paul's three thousand miles away. I doubt he knows I left." *Hope not, anyway*. She dunked her hand into the water and jerked it back out then turned on the cold faucet and stuck her fingers under the cooling water. Looking around the corner into the living room, she called out, "Hey, get in here! There's a mess to clean up."

"I'm coming, but remember I'm the one who suggested take-out." Jeffrey paused and looked at his sister who was gathering the silverware from the table. She had been hurt by that bum; he knew she was still vulnerable. "Take-out wasn't good enough for your new place," he said as he picked up two glasses from the table and followed her. "You had to eat on china, use real glasses, cook in your wok. I'd say you get to clean up after the meal, *woman*!" Luckily Jeffrey got a start at a hearty laugh before Sherrill punched him, pulling her swing in time to soften the blow.

"*Woman*? Look, kid. I *am* your big sister, remember? I let you tag along for the ride—a long, free ride. Clear across country, I might add." Sherrill secured her long, dark hair into a ponytail, grabbed the last bowl from the table, and headed for the kitchen. A single tear rolled down her cheek. She wiped it away.

Jeffrey noticed the change in her tone of voice when she said, "Leave the dishes. I'll do them in the morning." She sniffed hard and turned. "I checked in at school today, and classroom set-up won't start for a week. The principal knows I'm here." She took a deep breath and added, "I know you want to get an early start. Oregon's a long way off."

"Thanks, Sis. And the redwood trees are beckoning. I'll be sure to be back before you start work. And, no dents in your car, I promise." He grinned but noticed she was still quiet. "I'll sleep in my sleeping bag tonight. Save the sheets." Jeffrey took a long look at his sister puttering around the kitchen. His voice took on a serious tone. "Do you really think Paul doesn't know where you are? He seemed to know your every move back home."

Sherrill stared at her brother. "I told him to get out of my life, and I meant it. I don't want to see him again. It's over."

"After everything he did, he said he was sorry and that he loves you. I'll bet he shows up and tells you everything'll be fine."

"Only fine for him. Not fine for every girl he ever took out. Not fine for me."

"Did you ever love him? At least before Paul started playing arou—"

Silence. Sherrill didn't respond and draped the dishtowel over the oven door handle then smoothed the towel, removed it and shook it with a snap, and re-hung it. She stood by the stove and stared out the window into the darkness.

"Hey, do you think it's too late to call Mom?" Jeffrey asked.

"No. She'll be up," Sherrill whispered. She turned off the kitchen light, followed her brother into the living room, and settled onto the sofa. "It's three hours later back home, but she'd love to hear from us again. It's been two days since we called."

She shifted her weight and tugged at the knit afghan beside her. "Oops, you forgot your journal." She pulled the book out from under the blanket then stood and shoved it into his stomach as he passed by.

"Ooh, thanks," he said and pretended to double over in pain then stuffed it into his monogrammed case. He latched it shut then took his leather jacket out of the guest closet and tossed it over his suitcase. "Can't forget this," he said, then added, "Everything's set. Just have to throw the bags and boxes into the car in the morning and I'm off."

Sherrill dug under the afghan again. "How'd this get here? Don't forget your toothpaste," Sherrill called out as she tossed the red tube of Crystal White with Baking Soda at him. "You can't buy this on the west coast. You have to make it last until you get home."

"It's an extra tube, but thanks again, big sister. I don't know how I made it through college without you watching over me," he said, putting the toothpaste into his bag.

"I don't either. If I hadn't gone to your graduation ceremony, I would have never believed you finished. Now, if you can make a living with an art degree, and not become a mooching, pesky, starving artist, little brother."

"You know me better than that. I'll be on my own in no time. I'll pump gas if I have to."

"That's beneath you. What would Dad say?" Sherrill picked up the handset and dialed their home number.

"Dad will have to get over the fact that I didn't—"

"Go into law like he did?"

"Yeah. Mom's okay with it. But Dad? Well, not everyone can be the perfect child like you, following Mom into teaching."

"Sure. Perfect in everything except my choice of men. Now shut up and talk to Mom. Here." Sherrill handed him the still ringing phone. "I'll get a couple of glasses of wine while you talk to her."

"Wine? You forgot I got the six-pack? Bring me a beer."

There was no answer after six rings, and he didn't leave a message. Jeffrey hung up the phone and sank into the couch. Sherrill handed him his bottle of beer and curled up on the other end of the couch. Jeffrey drank half his beer quickly then leaned back. Sherrill enjoyed the pause and sipped her new-found favorite wine, Mendocino Chardonnay.

"It sure feels good not to be driving," she said.

"Yeah," he said. "Coast to coast in two weeks! And I bet you've had enough of me."

"Almost." Sherrill laughed

"I'll head out tomorrow like I planned. Go up to Oregon then circle back around."

"Take it easy on the gas pedal. The prices have been going up with all these oil embargos and crises going on. President Carter said—"

"Okay, *Mother,* I'll be careful, but remember, I've got Dad's credit card so I'll be okay."

Sherrill glared at him for a moment then asked, "Will you stay here for a couple of days before you fly home?"

"Yep, tickets are set for next week." Jeffrey paused. "I'll go back to the Volunteer Center until I get a real job. It was fun, you know, with you, Paul, and me." He stopped, realizing he had brought him up again. "Too bad you stopped going there."

"Too bad Paul is still there. I couldn't go back, not after all that happened. I couldn't stand seeing him every day."

"He kept saying he was sorry."

"Saying and doing are different. He said 'sorry' a few thousand times too often, but that didn't change his behavior. He wanted everything except the responsibilities." Sherrill's hands twisted into fists. She pounded the arm of the sofa and added, "He thinks he can own someone and have his own personal social life on the side—a new flavor of the month, or week, with me, good old vanilla waiting for him at home." She took a gulp of her wine.

"Okay, okay, Sis. Sorry I mentioned it." Jeffrey added quietly, "You were doing great things there. Do you think you'll volunteer here, too? You've got to get right back on the horse—as long as there are no Pauls there."

"Not for a while. I got burned out. I've got a new job, a new life really, and I'm not ready to make a commitment of my time, or my emotions."

"Yeah," Jeffrey said, got up, and headed for the kitchen. "You did get pretty wound up with those charity cases, but you helped a lot of people. You'll go back to it, soon I'll bet." He opened the fridge and retrieved a fresh beer.

"I think the kids at the school will keep me plenty busy."

"And then you'll meet some new guy," Jeffrey said and plopped back onto the couch.

"I'm in no hurry," Sherrill said and took another sip. "Not like you were back there in Texas with that pretty girl at the Alamo."

"What girl?" he teased. "Oh, *that* girl! She was hot! And funny. I wish we'd had more time there. Forget the Alamo; remember the girl." He smiled. "She was a major highlight of our trip. I'll call her when I get back home. She gave me her number; I've got it somewhere," he said pointing to his cases and looking hard at the one with his journal safely inside.

"Try calling her tonight."

"It's too late."

"An hour earlier than at the folks."

"No. When I get home. Let's try Mom and Dad again," he said, picked up the telephone, and redialed the number.

Chapter 3

Same evening

Detective Russell Hurley, fourteen-year veteran of the Humboldt County Sheriff's Department, walked into his house and flipped on light switches as he closed and locked the front door. *I can't believe how late it is—time for bed—after getting some food!* he thought. He hung his coat on the doorknob of the coat closet. *I had to finish that damn report. Just a couple more minutes. Just one more look at that file*, he had told himself earlier. *At least it's a short drive home.*

He picked up the mail from the floor and tossed it on top of the pile of envelopes already on the table. He yawned. Russell stretched his arms wide, then ran a hand through his thick, red hair and scratched his head, trying to bring some blood back into his scalp and just maybe his brain. He kicked off his shoes and tossed them down the hall into his bedroom.

All he could think about was food, a cold one, some brainless time in front of the television, and sleep—especially sleep. He walked into the kitchen, opened the fridge, and stared inside. *What's for dinner? Same as last night! Leftover take-out.* He pulled the Eureka Pub and Kitchen's box out and started to open it. Then he paused and shoved the top back down. *Tasted like shit then; it'll taste like shit now.* He opened the cabinet door under the sink and slam-dunked the carton into the garbage can. Dishes from a breakfast too many hours ago were in the sink. Frustrated, Russell searched the fridge again.

The jangling telephone jolted him. As he slammed the fridge's door, he heard something fall over inside. *Damn! More to clean up ... later.*

Russell pushed aside the dishtowel, grabbed the receiver, and dropped it back into the cradle. A loud squeak of a hinge needing oil made him turn quickly.

"Shane. Good to see you, boy!" Russell said as the Keeshond-Shepherd mix bounded like a puppy through the doggie door and circled him three times. Russell could tell the dog wanted to jump up to lick him, but the training held. He rubbed Shane's head and scratched his ears, then kneeled and gave the dog a good rubdown. "How you doing, boy? Was it a good day?" He scooped the dog's pan into the bag of dry Senior Moments dog food and set it near the back door. Shane stretched then began to eat slowly. Russell filled the dog's water dish and returned to the refrigerator to forage for edibles.

The freezer finally gave up bread and sliced ham left from dinner at his brother's house last week. Russell was so hungry that the sandwich, a few slightly chewy carrot sticks, and a Bud almost tasted like a gourmet meal. The intrusive phone process occurred two more times before he simply turned off the ringer. *Let the answering machine get it!*

He added the plate and utensils to the pile in the sink, ran some water over them, then went into the living room and turned on the television. He sank into the sofa.

Routine. Same damn routine day after day. With Shane curled up at his feet, he tried to get comfortable, but the television could not distract him. *I've got to change the mundane routine, maybe change jobs! Or at least learn to leave it at work.*

Recent cases followed him like a vagrant begging for a handout: runaways, domestic abuse, missing dogs. *Everyone's got problems! I'm a detective. Missing persons? Most leave on their own. Same with dogs. Let someone else take care of it.*

Russell settled into his dark brown sofa and pulled the lever on the side for the recliner. He adjusted the homemade, green velveteen pillow under his neck and said, "Thanks, Mom," aloud as the ten o'clock news began.

He shifted restlessly, pulled the pillow out, and tossed it across the couch. Comfort eluded him. The voice of the newscaster faded, punctuating the visions still seen behind his closed eyes. Images of people from past cases floated through a mist.

She drifted by. *She* was a shadow rather than a recognizable person. He shifted his weight and tried to erase the vision. *She* came into focus and he knew her. *She* was running through a fog, looking over her shoulder, afraid that something terrifying was chasing her. Suddenly, *her* face was in front of him, only inches from his face, pleading for help, reaching out to him, screaming.

"No!" Russell shouted and sat straight up, his arms grasped at the image, the emptiness, the nothingness—the applause and laughter from Johnny Carson's punch line reached fever pitch. Shane sat up and stared at him, his tail wagging. His paw came up and rested on Russell's knee.

Russell looked at the graying muzzle of the dog and scratched him behind his ears. "At least you're still here, aren't you, boy? I can count on you." He stared across the room at nothing. *Ah, Christine, I miss you so much.* He took a deep breath and, allowing the tension to ebb, shook it off.

He clicked off the television and returned to the kitchen. "Out, Shane!" he said and shooed the dog out to take care of his business. He turned and finished his nightly ritual of setting up the coffee maker and shoving the dirty dishes into the dishwasher. He latched the doggie door behind the returning dog.

Russell shuddered when he thought of the dream again. *She's gone. She's been gone. Nothing more I can do. It's one more cold case. People die. People survive. Some simply disappear.* Not all cases would ever, or could ever, be solved. *What the hell.* "It's job security," he muttered and headed toward the bedroom with the dog plodding after him.

Chapter 4

Nearing midnight

"Ya-hoo!" Phillip Dunne yelled over the roar of the car's engine. *She ... what was her name? Oh, yeah, 'Bitch'! ... 'Wimpy Bitch'!* He downshifted to second to take the tight left turn ahead. He hit the brakes too late, fishtailed, and pitched dirt and gravel into the darkness. He grasped the steering wheel, fought for control, and tried to figure out whether to turn the wheel left or right. "Whoa! She was bitchin'! Better'n I expected," he yelled at the night. "Man, could she fuckin' cuss!" The car slid to a stop. "Didn't know she had it in her."

The headlights made contact with nothing. Only darkness in front of him, the front wheels had stopped sliding only inches from the edge of the road that dropped hundreds of feet to the Smith River below.

Dunne put the window down and looked out. He slowly backed up, and turned the car around on the narrow dirt road. He fought hard to keep himself calm. *What a rush! She wasn't great, but she was good! A bleeder, too! Another bleeding-heart liberal—easy prey.*

"Whooeee!" he yelled into the darkness. It was heard only by a night owl searching for its quarry.

The tires spit gravel behind the car as Dunne shifted, then threw gravel again when he jammed down on the gas pedal. The owl had stopped its hoots and listened for more from the intruder. The piercing screams only minutes earlier had shocked the forest into silence. Sounds of the forest's nightlife were returning when the engine roared and Dunne let out his primal cry.

Man, I need something more. A hit. I need a hit! He stopped the car again and reached into the back seat, pulling at anything he could grasp. The only bottle he found was empty. *Shit!* he started driving again then grinned.

He shifted into neutral, hit the brakes, spun the car in almost a full circle, and stopped with the rocky side of the mountain rising in front of him. He got out and opened the back door. He began tossing things over his shoulder: a sweater, tennis shoes, empty soda can, towel, everything. He was looking for beer, booze, a doogie, anything to sate his pervasive thirst.

"Fuck this!" he yelled and slammed the car door. There was nothing he wanted, just packed suitcases, boxes of household goods. No food, no liquid, no weed or tobacco or *good shit*.

Nothing! I don't believe her! Not a damn thing! I had to catch a ride with a fuckin' goodie-two-shoes!

The trees were closing in on him, their dark forms hiding everything, anything beyond their perimeter. The moon didn't cast enough light, and the beams of the headlights only shown straight ahead, over the gravel, to the edge of the one-lane road bordered by dense forest. The dome light gave little to see by; darkness enveloped the car.

Dunne began to sweat. His balls hurt where she had given one last, futile attempt to survive. He wiped his hands on his jeans, trying to dry his palms.

He tossed the shoes, sweater, all her junk back into the car. *Can't leave no evidence. As if I gotta' give a shit!* Clothes, towels, and books went into the back seat. He found her wallet and pulled out the cash—several twenties and a bunch of ones. No credit cards; just checks, useless since he could never pass for a Glenda.

He searched around the car again and again, afraid he had missed something. He got on his hands and knees and looked under the car. He walked to the side of the road and looked blankly over the edge. *Maybe something went off the road. Or under the car!* He searched once more around the car and twice more under it. The owl began its mournful hoot, the crickets their plaintive chirp. He was suddenly aware of another presence.

"Who's there?" he yelled at the emptiness. "Where are you?" The darkness was no longer vacant; it was filled with spectators, and every one of them knew who he was, where he was, what he had done. He searched the darkness, and found no one. He climbed back into the car, locked the doors, checked the mirrors, rolled up the window, and gunned the engine. Dunne wiped his hands on his pants to get the persistent sweat off.

The night was against him. Excitement and his cravings made him tremble. He shifted repeatedly between second and third, turned too sharply on the gravel road, braked too late on the turns, and spun out a third time. He constantly checked his mirrors to see who might be following him. His hands felt sticky on the knob and wheel.

Shit! I've gotta' do something about this! He rubbed his hands again and again on his jeans. *Water, something to get this off!* Sweat ran down his forehead; his whole body felt damp. He could not dry his hands no matter how often he rubbed them on his pants. He rolled the window down to listen for the river he knew was somewhere nearby. The cold, damp air engulfed him.

Five miles and thirty minutes from what had been Glenda, he spun the car again in the gravel on the next sharp turn to the left. *Shit!* The trees were close to the edge of the one-lane road, and there was nowhere to turn around. *At least I want to live through this. I'm too far into the woods— can't walk out.*

He spent the next three minutes maneuvering the car back and forth, got it turned around, and sped back down the old logging road. Forty minutes later he rounded a curve on the gravel road and saw headlights from cars on the two-lane paved highway about a quarter mile ahead. He turned off the car's lights and backed between trees and into a slight clearing. Behind him, the hill rose steeply. The other side of the gravel road dropped into a wooded ravine.

Afraid someone would see the car from the highway, he picked up fallen branches and draped them over the hood and top of the car. He climbed into the back seat to sleep off the physical and mental high. "Got to make it through the night without a hit," he muttered. *Almost better'n a drug rush ... almost,* he thought as he fell into a restless sleep, his sticky hands tucked under his armpits.

Chapter 5

Friday morning

The heater and the radio alarm both came on at 5:15–too early. *What's Elvis doing on this station?* Russell hit snooze once, dozed for the allotted nine minutes then threw the blankets off when music started again. He reached over and punched the off button.

He bent his knees, then his elbows and fingers and found no new aches. *Maybe I'll work out this morning.* He had put it off for the last couple of days. *Yeah, good jog'll do me good,* he thought as he stretched, bent over and tapped his toes ... *or maybe after work tonight.* He stuck his feet into his slippers, grabbed his frayed terrycloth bathrobe, and shuffled to the front door while scratching that itch that was ... *ahh, right there* ... every morning.

He opened the door, leaned down to pick up the ... *What? No paper? It's always here!* He reached behind him and turned on the porch light. Shane plodded up to him and sat down. "G'morning, mutt. I guess neither of us wants to go out. It's cold."

A faint siren pierced the otherwise silent morning. Russell bent over and patted the dog's head. "It's too early for this," he sighed as he stepped outside.

Concealed by the fog, he searched both sides of the steps and out to the sidewalk. He clutched his robe tightly and ran back empty handed into the warmth of the house. *There'd better be a good explanation for this! I pay a good tip every month to make sure it's here on time.* The siren sounded like it was getting closer then suddenly went silent.

Disgusted, he closed the door, trudged down the hall to the kitchen, and plugged in the coffee maker. He didn't dare trust the timer to leave it plugged in overnight. He'd seen too many cremated houses, to say nothing of their previous inhabitants.

"Okay, mutt, time to do your duty," Russell said, pulling on the back door. "Be patient, Shane. It's jammed again." He yanked on it twice before his brute strength managed to yank it open. He barely missed the dog's bushy tail when he pushed it closed. "So, you're moving slowly today, too. It's too early for both of us, isn't it?" He unlatched the doggie door, so the dog could come and go during the day.

The next stop was the bathroom to sit and read the paper ... *Damn! No paper. What happened?* Then he admitted to himself, *I've been spoiled.*

Showered, shaved, and standing before his closet, he stared blankly at his selection of shirts. Shane came back in and curled up on his cushion near the bed. "It was so much easier when I had only one option: navy shirt, navy slacks, polished shoes, badge, cap. Dog, you're lucky. You wear the same fur coat every day. Now, this!" he said swinging his arm in front of the clothes. Every morning he made the same pledge: I'm only buying white shirts from now on! Five ties are enough. Too many decisions this early are not good. He finally picked a blue and white striped shirt and dark blue tie, and he and Shane returned to the kitchen.

The dog barked then crouched to go outside through the swinging door and continued barking, fending off imagined threats in the back yard as he raced around the perimeter.

"Hush, it's too early. Come on in, boy. Come," Russell called through the door. "Thank goodness you don't have a picky appetite," he said and dropped a dog treat into Shane's bowl. A quick pat on his head was the end of the attention the dog received this morning—no different from every other morning. "Running late. Watch this place, Okay?"

He made one more attempt to find his paper, swore under his breath, unlocked his car, and pulled out of his driveway.

As he turned the corner at Park Street and headed toward Broadway, really Highway 101, Russell nearly rear-ended a black-and-white patrol car.

"What the—?" Officer Jim Carson yelled and jumped away from his cruiser. He stormed over to the car as Hurley put down the car's window.

"Hey, man, sorry. I didn't. ... Jimbo!" Russell called out. "What's up?"

"Well, besides nearly getting run over, I run into the super-sleuth Detective Hurley himself. How're you doing?" Officer Carson reached through the window and vigorously shook Russell's hand. "You live near here?"

"Yeah, not far." He didn't want anyone knowing exactly where he lived, not even another officer. Threats against their personal lives were getting too common—not paranoia, just caution. "What happened?"

"Another job justification—job security gone bad. Without criminals, we'd both be out of a job."

"That'd be okay with me. Need any help?"

"No, almost ready to wrap this up. Ambulance just left; tow truck just showed up. This guy was attacked for no apparent reason. He was beat up pretty bad but kept mumbling that he carried no cash, no drugs, nothing worth stealing. All he has is a car full of newspapers."

"What? Oh, shit! That was Smitty! That's lousy. Was he hurt bad?"

"Bruises, black eye, maybe a cracked rib or two. He'll be fine, eventually."

"Damn. Nice guy. Shouldn't have happened to him," Russell half mumbled to himself. "Well, good luck with the report." Hurley called out and cranked the window up. He shook his head and pulled away. "Sometimes the explanations suck!" He slammed his hand on the steering wheel and headed toward the Humboldt County Sheriff's Department.

Chapter 6

The next morning

"Hey, Jeff, try Mom again," Sherrill called out from the bathroom. "Mom and Dad must have been celebrating the empty nest."

Jeffrey was packed and ready. "Hey, Sis, you sure all your stuff's out of the car?"

"Yes. Déjà vu. You asked last night."

He and Sherrill hauled his suitcases, sleeping bag, and boxes to the car and secured them in the trunk. He tossed his shaving kit onto the passenger seat along with his brown leather jacket.

"Want to take the last couple of bottles of beer with you?" Sherrill called from inside the apartment.

"Naw. I'll finish'em off when I get back. Unless, of course you drink them first."

Sherrill came out with a blanket folded over her arm. "I won't drink your precious beer, I promise. Here, take this old quilt," she said holding it out to him. "I hear it gets cold up there."

"I don't need another mother, but in case you're right—," he said, pulled it from her arms, and shoved it into the trunk.

"Shouldn't have gotten a light-colored car," Sherrill said. "It shows dirt too easily. Next time I'll buy a cobalt blue instead of silver."

"You didn't buy this one. Dad did, remember? Graduation present?" He slammed the trunk lid shut and they turned back to the apartment door. "An Impala, and like their ad says, 'It's the car for the up-and-coming professional.' Is your mind quitting on you this young?"

"My mind? Quit? It's only getting started. Yours, on the other hand—" Sherrill giggled. Back inside, she picked up the phone. "Let's try home once more. Mom'll want to talk to you before you leave."

"It's awfully early. She's probably sleeping in after being out so late last night."

"You keep forgetting the time difference." Sherrill came out of the bathroom with one hand behind her back. "You are so absent minded. You're going to leave this here unless I pack it for you." She jammed the bright blue and red toothpaste tube into his front shirt pocket, grabbed the phone from him, and dialed the number again.

"Thanks again, big sister."

"Yeah, yeah." Sherrill made a face at him then said into the telephone, "Mom! Good morning. No, everything's fine. We're calling like we promised—every day or two. Jeffrey's still here, and we wanted to say 'hi.' He's leaving real soon, though." Sherrill grinned and whispered, "Not soon enough." She handed him the phone for one last good-bye before he would be hitting the road alone.

Chapter 7

Dunne woke with a jerk. He sat bolt upright and slammed his head on the car's roof. *Shit!* He looked around and rubbed the forming bump. His hands still felt sticky. *Where the fuck am I?* he wondered as he climbed out of the car. He was stiff and sore; his crotch hurt.

The sun gave a glow to the ground fog that had formed in the early morning cold. Dunne looked around. The car was surrounded by trees. A gravel road behind him dead-ended into a two-lane highway.

Oh, shit, yeah, he thought as he remembered last night and the kick. He smiled and rubbed his crotch. *Ooh, still sore.* He squirmed in the seat. *But it was worth it. Gotta' get moving.*

Phillip Dunne, aka Glen Short, shoved the branches off the car windshield and drove the car the few yards across the gravel road into thick brush and shut off the engine. He sat there for a full minute and stared into the distance. Looking over the hood, he could see bushes and the tops of trees. *Perfect. The car'll never be found.* He shifted into neutral then unscrewed the shift knob and stared at it. He turned it over a couple of times, examining it in the filtered morning light, then jammed it into his jacket pocket.

He used a sweater from the back seat to wipe the dash, door handles, steering wheel, anything he remembered touching. He took the keys out of the ignition and rubbed them on his pants leg then threw them as far as he could. He trudged to the rear of the car and, using his jacket to avoid leaving fingerprints pushed the car over the edge of the road. Dunne watched it roll through the brush and deep into the foliage. He could barely see it when it stopped, coming to rest against a trunk of an ancient redwood. *No one'll see that!* he thought, then kicked the rocks at the edge of the slope to cover the tire tracks.

It had been a restless night; his body was crying out for a hit, a drag, anything, even food. His mind was racing. *Gotta' get away from here. Somebody might've seen me.* He hiked to the end of the gravel logging road and paused at the edge of the highway. Once again, he stood waiting for a car to pass.

Voices from across the highway got his attention, and he could smell bacon frying. Dunne's stomach rumbled. He hadn't eaten much in the last couple of days. He crossed the highway and crept through the ferns and brush layered with fallen redwood needles. He could feel his heart pounding in his chest. He stopped and listened.

"Stop poking me! Daddy, he's poking me." Two young boys were chasing each other around a small trailer then started sword fighting with two short fishing poles.

"Put those fishing rods down, now!"

"Can we go now, Daddy? Can we?"

"Yeah, can we go fishing now?" the second child pleaded.

From behind a towering redwood, Dunne saw signs of only one family's campsite. *How many there? Two kids, a dad ... the mom? Maybe she's in the camper. Another broad within a few hours. Mmmmmm.* His stomach growled when he sat down on the damp foliage. *It'd be easy to get their shit. Hell, why wait?* He started to get up but heard the dad yell.

"You two kids ready yet? Come on, let's get going."

Dunne crouched down to wait for them to head for the river. His search for a woman took a few moments. Frustrated, he kicked the frying pan into the smoldering embers in the fire pit, and a swift punt sent the empty coffee pot into a nearby tree.

He found food in the ice chest in the trailer and ate well that morning. Not bothering to make a sandwich of the bread, cheese, and bologna, he shoved the slices into his mouth and washed everything down with a beer. He tossed the empty can into the shrubs at the edge of the campsite, opened another, then used the father's supplies to wash and shave at the campground's restrooms. Invigorated, he helped himself to their provisions stuffing crackers, a bag of cookies, and a couple of beers into his pack. He scattered the carrot sticks from the cooler in front of the trailer and twisted them into the dirt with his feet. *The kids will thank me for that.* He laughed out loud then stopped, fearing he might have been heard. He dropped to one knee and searched the surrounding trees for any signs of movement.

The family's car was parked on the far side of the camper trailer. He peered through the front window. *No keys, damn. ... Shit! An alarm.* He backed away quickly and took another look around. *Nothing worth anything here,* he said to himself. *No broad, no cash. No shit!*

He grabbed his pack and walked back to the highway as another car · approached. *The driver's alone. Good!* He stuck out his thumb, and the car pulled over and stopped. As he reached for the front door handle, a man sat up in the passenger seat and jerked his thumb toward the back seat.

"You headin' to—?" Dunne asked as he climbed in and pulled the door closed.

"Eureka," the driver interrupted as she drove on.

"The coast, huh?" *Shit! The wrong way!* "Uh, well, drop me in Arcata, okay? That'd be fine." *I'll head back north from there. This will at least give me a chance to rest,* Dunne thought as he resigned himself to returning to his hometown, at least where he'd lived for the six years before going to prison and now for the last few weeks since getting out. He pushed his pack to the floor and stretched across the seat, comfortably full, warm, and satisfied with himself. *I'll just catch another ride back this way later today.*

Dunne shifted in the seat. Something was bothering him. *What did I miss? Where the hell did I leave that car? Why did I leave it? Hell! I'll never find it again.* His eyes bore into the backs of the heads of the driver and her passenger. *No one else will, either.* He patted his jacket pocket with the gear shift knob and chuckled to himself.

Chapter 8

Friday a.m.

Russell Hurley parked in his usual spot across from the Humboldt County Courthouse. He paused at the curb and stared at the building. His stomach growled reminding him that he hadn't eaten breakfast, so he turned and headed for Elliot's Diner one block down the street.

He pulled out some change, paused in front of the newspaper stand, and dropped two quarters into the slot. He grabbed a copy, tucked it under his arm, and pushed on the restaurant's heavy glass door.

Carpenters, utility workers, and other working-class stiffs were sitting in small groups around the spotless diner. Its style was right out of the fifties—not remodeled, but well maintained.

"Well, good morning, Hon. You decided to join us again?" The red-haired waitress greeted him with a smile; her grey roots were beginning to show and the laugh lines around her eyes and mouth were visible under her makeup. Her black slacks and vest over her clean white blouse were spotless.

"You must live here," Russell said.

"Naw. The boss changed my hours back to mornings." Wanda picked up a menu and coffee pot. "You alone again this morning?"

He glanced at her and rolled his eyes.

"I know, I know. You'll be single forever." She laughed then added, "I'll meet you at your table." She paused to fill mugs at other tables.

He sat on the far side where he could watch the entrance, a cop-induced habit. He put the newspaper down next to him and turned the mug over as Wanda caught up with him.

"Coffee's fresh," she said and filled Russell's mug.

"That's what I like about this place. Fresh."

Wanda smiled and said, "Fresh—like me." She winked. "I'm still available." She handed him a menu.

"You keep reminding me."

Wanda pulled out her order pad then asked, "The usual? Sausage, bacon, ham, pancakes, and two eggs?"

Russell laughed. "I can't eat that!" He squirmed like he did when his mother was trying to make sure he ate all his vegetables before he could go out to play. "I'll have a small orange juice and a short stack."

"That's it?"

"Okay. Add a side of sausage—" His shoulders sagged, "and hash browns."

"That's more like it. Gotta keep our men in blue ready for action," Wanda said and headed back to the kitchen.

Hurley opened the newspaper and thought, *Must be a slow news day. Not much here. Good. Maybe I can catch up on my reports—lousy, routine reports.*

The door opened and three more customers entered. A young man rushed in, nearly bumping into an exiting couple, and strode up to Wanda. A few words were exchanged, and Wanda scowled. With a frown, she reached into her pocket, pulled out a few bills, and handed them to the man.

Within a few minutes, Wanda was at Russell's table with his food.

"Hey, how is Jake, anyway? I haven't seen much of your son lately."

"That's a good thing. *You* shouldn't see much of him."

"I take it he's been staying out of trouble?"

Wanda set the food on the table and sighed. As she poured his second cup of coffee, she said, "So I guess you recognized him, huh? Yeah, he's doing better and working steady. Can't say much about his girlfriend, though—you'll probably be seeing her more often than he will."

"A real winner, huh?"

"Yeah, pushing her limits and my patience. I wish my son wouldn't repeat my mistakes. You'd think your kids would learn and not mess up so much."

"Wish he'd learn by osmosis, right?"

"Oss– what?"

"Osmosis—that he'd pick it up because it flows from you to him."

"Yeah, you got it." Wanda returned to the kitchen and didn't come back until he was almost finished.

"Want another o.j.? It'll be on the house."

"Thanks, but no."

"Well, more coffee it is then," and she added a dribble to his mug.

"Thanks. Say where *is* Jake working now, anyway?" Russell knew that her son had been in and out of trouble since he was a teenager.

> *Nearly five years ago, a few gangs had cropped up in the area, and there had been word on the street that some skinheads were going to get it on with a group of Blacks near the mall.*
>
> *Russell and two other officers stopped the five white kids before they got to the parking lot. They'd put them into two different squad cars with Jake and some other smart-ass in the back of Russell's. Nothing had really happened that night and*

no one was arrested, but the two punks got an earful from Russell.

It took two more confrontations, three tattoos, and one arrest before Jake started to think about listening. He had been living on the verge of committing a serious crime; the arrest seemed to finally get part of the message through. Russell felt sorry for Wanda when she came to the station to check on her son but convinced her not to post his bail right away. "Let him get a real taste of what his future might be," he told her.

Jake was been spitting mad at both of them and cussed out his mother in front of officers and inmates the next day when she arrived to pick him up.

Russell heard him, spun around, grabbed the kid's shirt, and shoved him against the concrete block wall. "You apologize! Right now," he shouted inches from Jake's face. "That's your mother! Show some respect, you son of a—" He stopped suddenly and looked back at Wanda, who was standing two feet behind him, nearly crying and clearly in shock. "She loves you," he said. "I don't know why, except she's your mom and that's what moms do. Now earn her love. Show her some respect. Apologize."

Russell took a deep breath and let go of the kid. Jake's face went pale, but he thrust his jaw out and was ready to spit in Russell's face. Russell saw that and spun Jake against the wall again, grating his cheek on the concrete.

"What the hell! Police brutality! You fuckers saw that. He drew blood."

"Shut up, Jake," Wanda yelled. "Shut up or I'll leave you here for a week."

"What the hell? You can't do that. You've already posted—"

"She can do whatever she wants, Jake. I'd do what your mother says if I were you." Russell turned Jake around again and looked directly into his eyes. "Now apologize. She may not deserve you, but she deserves an apology."

The other officers did not move during the entire confrontation. A collective sigh was heard throughout the room when Jake finally muttered a barely audible, "Sorry."

"What?" Russell whispered. "I don't think she heard you."

"Sorry." Tears welled up in the teenager's eyes. Russell wasn't sure if it was true emotion or the pain from the scratched cheek.

"Again, with feeling."

"Hey, Mom, I'm sorry. I didn't mean this shit."

Russell rolled his eyes and glanced at Wanda.

She forced a weak smile and said, "Okay. That'll do. Let's go home." She looked at Russell then glanced at her son's arms, still handcuffed behind him. "If it's okay, Detective?"

Russell realized they were the center of attention and quickly removed the cuffs. He could not resist one more comment. "I'll be watching," he whispered into Jake's ear as he and Wanda headed for the front desk. Jake had given him a look that would have frozen molten lava.

"Detective? Russ? More coffee?"

"Uh, oh, sure. Sorry."

"Jake's laying concrete—learning about building houses and works at the docks when they call him. Works pretty steady and gets some overtime now and then. Trouble is his girlfriend drains him."

"That's why he was here?"

"Yeah, gas money. Seems he's always short."

"Have faith. He'll straighten out in time—he's got you on his side."

"As if time's what we've all got an endless supply of, right?" Wanda sopped up the coffee she'd spilled when she overfilled his mug then turned to tend to other customers.

Russell used to enjoy work. He had grown up here in Eureka, joined the Marines and served his time, even re-upped once to get more education benefits. He moved to Southern California for four years—two years too many. But Los Angeles gave him his police training and a college degree, and he paid it back with the required minimum years of service. He was so glad to move back to the solitude and quiet of the north coast.

The traffic, the smog, the anonymity, the continual brutal crimes got to him quickly. Crimes here were less frequent and were considerably less barbaric than in the big city, well, with one exception, that one, still unsolved crime from so many years ago. Her face flashed through his mind again.

Then there was the commute, the horrendously long commute down there. Here, it took only ten minutes to get to work—if he hit all red lights, seven minutes if he hit all green. That was about the only good thing about this job now. The rest was routine—monotonous, horrendous routine.

He liked taking the stairs to his office on the third floor of the Humboldt County Courthouse. It gave him a few extra minutes of exercise several times a day. There was talk about moving their offices to the first floor, which was more like a basement. With any luck, it was just talk. The few windows there were too high to allow any view, and he'd miss his workout.

If it wasn't foggy, from his desk he could see his car parked in the lot across the street. Beyond that, over the tops of other businesses and houses, the hills were visible in the distance. He liked the view and hoped it would take a lot more years to move the department downstairs.

In the winter, snow might stay on Kneeland for a few days, and it was an easy drive with his brother and nephews for a weekend romp with inner tubes. It was a different world from L.A., and he appreciated this part of his life. *This* was the *real* California.

"Hey, who brought in the donuts?" Hurley called out when he saw the pink box on the counter. "I thought we agreed to cut back on these things."

"Sam Johnson dropped them off after his shift," a uniformed officer said from across the room. "Said they were for improving our profile."

"Doesn't help a cop's image, either." No laughter, only a few smirks and snickers came from the other officers and detectives.

Russell's desk was nearly in the middle of the room, facing the windows. He liked being able to see outside while he did his paperwork. It gave him a sense of existence, of connection with the rest of the world.

He lined up his name plate even with the edge of his desk. "Det. R. Hurley" was etched into the plastic. "Not Russ, not Rusty," he would tell people who tried to give him a nickname, "and never Red," though someone tried that, and it stuck for the duration of his military service. His strong build convinced everyone else not to try to rename him a second time.

The in-box was emptied, most of the time. The out-box was picked up each evening and sent on its way. There was that one exception. One item was not obvious to anyone else. One smudged, dog-eared file folder was within easy reach, one piece of unfinished business kept close enough to touch, to remember. Securely planted under his desk lamp, he gave it a tap every morning as a reminder to himself that it was still there. It made it seem like *she* was still there.

He pulled out his chair, hung his jacket on the back, and sat down. *Another day of reports to get done, another day of satisfying the taxpayers' expectations of a safe community.* His phone started ringing before he unlocked his lap drawer. He jiggled the key to release the latch on the rest of the drawers then answered his phone. Another routine work day had started.

Chapter 9

Friday evening

Dunne's car ride back to the coast was tiresome. The couple in the front seat did nothing but bicker about the road, the weather, in-laws, and life in general. His relief of getting out of their car was palpable; he didn't think he could stand one more mile with them.

"Crescent City—this is fine. Let me out here," Dunne had finally said and climbed out of the car. He looked up and down the freeway—Arcata and Eureka to the south or back inland and head for Oregon again? *What the hell, might as well stick around Eureka for a while.*

He hitched a quiet ride to Eureka and headed for the Mad Cat Bar.

A few shafts of light filtered through the thick cigarette smoke. Dim neon lights from the juke box emanated a ghostly glow. A man wearing a stained apron was delivering a couple of beers for customers at another table.

Dunne tapped his finger on the table and shook his head. *Things were cleaner in the joint.* "Hey, Keno. What you lookin' at, shrimp?"

The scrawny man sitting across from Dunne said, "Nuthin'," and pushed his black-rimmed glasses higher on his nose. Long strands of graying brown hair were haphazardly draped across his scalp creating an unsightly attempt to cover his baldness.

"Hey, Keno, wanna' hear something funny?" Dunne took another long drag on his cigarette and gulped half his Bud. "I met a girl." His glazed eyes drilled through Keno and saw nothing.

"No shit." Keno twirled his bottle on the table. "And you just got out. Good move, man!" He picked up his bottle and sucked the last drop. Keno was out of beer and out of money.

The jukebox finished playing a mournful song of lost love. A customer, a redhead in her early forties wearing black slacks and vest with a coffee-stained white blouse, sat at the bar drinking a mug of beer; her shoes were off and lay on the floor. She was massaging her bare feet on the foot rail.

"Yeah, I met a girl." Dunne said, smashing his cigarette butt onto the table, missing the ashtray by two inches.

"No shit." Keno repeated while he checked his pockets. He found one quarter and a dime.

"Yeah. She was real good." Dunne finished off his last swallow and slammed his bottle on the table, the last of too many to count.

"No shit."

"Yeah."

"How'd you meet? You ain't been out but a couple of weeks."

"Hitchhiking. After spending so much time in that shit-hole they call a 'correctional' facility, I was heading up to Oregon to sign up for more unemployment." He smiled and patted his pocket with his California benefit check. "She picked me up, and we took off together. Really hit it off." He paused and looked out the window into the foggy darkness. "Yeah, her car was totally awesome. Got it up to 95 on 199."

"No shit? With those twists and turns and all?" Keno pushed his thin strands of hair away from his eyes and draped them over his scalp.

"Spun it out twice. A bitchin' red Mustang. Helluva car."

"No shit. Where's she now? How come she ain't with you?"

"Oh, hell, she's gone." Dunne paused and stared at Keno. He hadn't wanted to say anything about Glenda, but, hell, what a high! "Her car was bitchin'. She's gone. I did her. That adrenaline rush was the biggest kick I've had in years.

Keno's eyes widened trying to process the information. "What?"

Dunne stared at the woman sitting at the bar, but she was ignoring them, obviously tired from working another too-long day. She finished her drink and left.

"You 'did her'?" Keno took off his glasses and rubbed his eyes. "You mean you screwed her, right?" He tried to focus on the man across the table and searched for any kind of reassurance that his drinking buddy hadn't murdered someone.

Dunne, emotionless, stared at Keno and laughed at the little man's uneasiness.

"Naw. Let's just say she won't be back this way again—ever." He guffawed as Keno squirmed in his seat.

Dunne had spent all of Glenda's cash in one day—two hundred thirty-one dollars, gone. "She said she had enough of this nothing-happening, shit-hole place. Nobody dies of anything here but boredom."

Dunne watched for a change of expression from Keno.

"No shit," Keno said, shook his head trying to clear the idea that his friend might have done, and set his empty bottle hard on the table.

Dunne shrugged and said, "Let's go. We're through here."

With no cash left, Dunne and Keno stumbled out of the bar and into the dark, chilly gloom. Dunne went back inside for his jacket. A minute later, he realized he had left his backpack inside and pounded on the bar's locked door until the bartender peered through the window, the door opened, and the bartender shoved the pack outside.

Fog had settled on the coast for the winter, and streetlights emitted a string of eerie halos. There was a surreal aura to their world.

Keno's rusting hulk of a car was parked outside, but they passed it trying to walk like they were sober. A streetlight was out, making street signs hard to read. They turned left toward First.

"Why'd you come back here? I thought you was headin' north." Keno fumbled in his pocket for his keys so he could be ready for the lock when they found his apartment.

"Tried twice. Kept ending up back here. First the girl, then … then, uh, after I dumped her … uh, … the car, the first car coming by was heading back here. I was so tired, I didn't argue. Fuck! I just came back." He looked at Keno and saw no sign of comprehension. "I'll hang out a coupla' days then head back north. Another day or two before I sign up for unemployment won't matter." He looked around and didn't see any other options. "I'll crash at your place, okay?"

Keno groaned; that was the last thing he wanted. Another body, this body, anybody but him. Keno had known Dunne for fifteen years and every time they got together, Keno ended up in trouble.

"Can't you stay with your new friend?"

"I told you, she ain't able to have nobody over no more. She, uh, she's gone. Don't you listen?"

Keno hesitated. He looked at Dunne and tried to figure out what part of the story was the truth. He had never met anyone who had actually killed someone before, at least, not that he knew of.

"Well, you got a couch or something I can sleep on?"

Hell no! screamed in Keno's head, but said, "Sure, no problem."

After going around the block, they finally came to the two-story boarding house on Second Street. It once had been a stately home to a semi-prominent lumbering family, but now the white paint was peeling from the windowsills; the blue paint on the siding was fading, and the porch railing was loose. The interior had been gutted years ago and converted into apartments. Currently it was a boarding house for parolees, probationers, derelicts and addicts. All the lights were off.

The shorter man was being almost dragged by Dunne as they stumbled up the porch steps. Their bodies slammed into one of the carved roof supports, and they knocked over an aluminum lawn chair.

"Shhhhh. The old biddy don't like nobody coming in this late. Swears she'll kick me out."

"Aw, she wouldn't do that," Dunne said and staggered back down the steps to retrieve his backpack he had dropped.

"Naw, you're right. She needs the money too bad," Keno whispered.

The inside porch light cut through the night as the front door swung open. A short, white-haired woman stormed up to Keno.

"I'll see you in the morning," the landlady said, glaring at him. "Your Parole Officer was hanging out here this afternoon looking for you. Said you hadn't been to work."

"Shut up, bitch. P.O.s don't hang around nowhere. And you ain't my mother!" Keno said. Dunne pushed by both of them and stumbled into the hallway.

"Thank God for small favors!" she continued. "Make sure you see me in the morning. Your rent's two days late. I'm giving you notice if you don't pay tomorrow." She turned and slammed her apartment door behind her.

"Bitch!" Keno hissed, grabbed Dunne's arm, and headed for the stairs.

Dunne jerked his arm away, shoved Keno to the floor, stared at him for a moment, and broke into laughter. Keno joined him then they both stumbled up the staircase.

Keno dropped his keys three times. Dunne grabbed them and, after two tries, finally unlocked the door to apartment 2C. Dunne took one look at the couch directly in front of him, dropped the pack, fell across the sofa, belched, and began snoring loudly.

Keno stared at Dunne lying there. *Could he have done it?* he wondered then stumbled into the bathroom to relieve himself.

"Shit, you never 'buy' beer; you only rent it," he mumbled to himself. "It don't stay long enough to own it."

He wondered how Dunne would have killed the girl, if he really did it. Strangled her? Stabbed her? Broke her neck? *Naw, Dunne couldn't have done nothing like that. He couldn't have killed no one. No, he wouldn't have.*

Suddenly, his mouth felt different. Bitter saliva spread over his tongue. "Shit. Not again." His stomach twisted. He tasted it. His mouth filled with watery excretion. Keno zipped up his pants and leaned over and spit repeatedly into the toilet. Sweat beaded on his forehead as he spit again and again, unable to keep up with the flow. His glasses slid down his nose. The acidic bile began to burn his throat. A tightness grabbed him in the pit of his stomach and wretched its contents up and out. He heaved, and his glasses slid into the foul mixture of vomit and piss. He vomited two more times then grabbed a wad of toilet paper and wiped his face.

"Shit." Keno hesitated then reached into the toilet bowl, retrieved his glasses, and flushed. He rinsed his glasses, hands, and face then opened the toothpaste tube, licked the tip, and ran his tongue over his teeth. Keno stumbled into the bedroom and flopped across his unmade bed without even removing his shoes. He immediately fell into a deep sleep, erasing all conscious memory of the night's discussions.

Chapter 10

Keno's head was pounding when he woke the next morning. He stumbled to the bathroom. *What the hell did I do to deserve this shit?* he asked himself. "Oh, shit!" he said out loud when he remembered Dunne had come home with him.

As he zipped his pants, he peered into the living room. The couch was empty; the backpack was gone.

"Good riddance!" Kevin Norvil Luken, aka Keno, said and headed back to the bathroom to search for some aspirin. He looked at himself in the mirror and groaned. *Hell, I look fifty! And I've got ten years to go.* He pulled at his cheeks and made the skin taut and the wrinkles disappear. *I shouldn't be doin' this shit to myself! ... What the hell! I need a drink.* He headed into the kitchen for a liquid breakfast before heading to work.

Keno liked to drink. He liked to gamble. He loved the numbers in the Keno games in Reno and liked being called Keno. He liked to take chances with his money or with anyone else's that he could get his hands on. He was a big winner at Reno, but he was a bigger loser. He only won often because he gambled often. That had gotten him into trouble with relatives, three ex-wives, numerous ex-friends, ex-acquaintances, ex-neighbors, and made enemies of them all over the years.

The only people who associated with him these days were the ones who had not yet been drawn into his web of gambling or those who had enjoyed being on the winning side of his betting. Few people he knew had not yet been stiffed by "Lucky Keno" Luken.

Chapter 11

Four days later

Russell's phone rang three times before he answered it. "Detective Hurley here," he said then moved it away from his ear and paused to listen to an upset female. "Sorry, ma'am. That's Missing Persons. You've got to file a report." He paused patiently, then said, "Sorry. Let me transfer you to someone who will take your report."

He pushed the transfer key on the phone and dialed the four digits he knew so well.

Probably reporting someone who'll be back tomorrow anyway.

By noon the next day there were two messages from the same woman. About 4:30 she called again, sounding extremely stressed. "Maybe your missing person simply doesn't want to talk to anyone for a few days." Hurley transferred her again. *Poor guy, probably wanted to get away. From her, anyway.*

Early Friday morning there was another message, then another call. "You want Missing Persons, ma'am. I've given you their number." Det. Hurley hung up on her.

Friday evening finally arrived, and the phone had not rung for the last hour. The big bonus was there had been no more phone calls from that woman, whoever she was.

Quitting time came and went, and Russell Hurley was still at his desk composing the last few lines of the report about the dirt-bag who had messed up his lunch break. Sgt. Johnson was the only other person in the room and was there only because it was his shift.

Johnson was nearing retirement and asked for the night shift for the pay differential that would add to his retirement base. He'd rather have had a promotion, but that possibility was getting dim. The two men worked quietly at their desks, two islands of light in an otherwise darkened room. Johnson's phone rang, and he starting talking quietly. Hurley ignored him.

Other desks were cleared; confidential files and reports were locked away or delivered to the District Attorney's office down one flight of stairs in hopes there was sufficient evidence to file charges. A fluorescent light flickered across the room where a deputy forgot to turn it off. Even the captain's office was dark.

Russell was tired and hungry. He put a two-page burglary report with the attached list of stolen items into the proper folder, stuffed it into his top desk drawer for Monday's filing, locked it, and then saw the folder. He tipped the lamp, slid the folder out, opened it, and just stared at the first page. He could not bring himself to look any further. The pictures were already seared into his memory. *Someday I'll find the bastard who did this.*

He had not paid much attention to the file for the last week. The workload of cases seemed to follow the cycles of the moon, which sounded preposterous when said aloud. The statistics did not always support it, but this month it held true. There was a full moon last week and the number of cases doubled—three each of spousal and child abuse, one robbery in broad daylight, an arson at Washington Elementary, and unending calls and messages from someone named Sherrill Madison. He'd transferred her several times and had never gotten a return phone number. Then there was today's lunch-time mass of phone calls. Hurley was ready to leave the drab surroundings of the office, grab some dinner, and go home. He carefully tucked the aging file back under the lamp's base and started to get up. The phone rang.

"Hey, Johnson, could you get it?" he yelled as he grabbed his coat from the back of his chair and looked around. *Shit!* Johnson was at the other end of the room pouring himself a cup of coffee. Russell snatched the receiver and almost hung it back up. Instead, he snarled, "Detective Hurley. What?" His stomach rumbled so loudly he swore it echoed off the far wall.

Hurley heard, "Will you accept the charges ...?" before he interrupted with a loud "No!" He missed the phone base, and the receiver bounced once, slid off the desk, and dangled, twisting at the end of the cord. Hurley fumbled trying to catch it, missed, dropped his coat, swore again under his breath, and slammed the receiver back into the cradle.

As he stooped to pick up his coat, he heard the elevator door open. Staying low, he heard a female voice but could not make out what she said. She was talking to Johnson. *Good!*

"Yes, he's still here. His desk is right over ... well, he was here a second ago."

Hurley reluctantly stood up, draped his coat over his arm, and ignored them. He headed for the stairwell door but could see them out of the corner of his eye. The woman was nearly the same height as Johnson, good looking, dressed professionally in a dark pantsuit; her dark hair pulled high into a clip. This was a policeman's response: identify the major characteristics just in case you have to make an ID later. *I think I'll go straight to Elliott's Diner and get some take-out.* Food was the only thing on his mind.

"Oh, there he is. Detective Hurley," Johnson yelled across the room, "this young lady's here to see you."

Damn! Now what?

"You're Detective Hurley?"

I wish I wasn't. The voice sounded familiar. *Oh, no. No, it can't be and she's heading this way.* "Yes, I am. What— ?"

"So you're the guy who's too good to take my calls."

"My shift is done, and I'm hungry. Talk to Johnson. Goodnight." Hurley threw his jacket over his shoulder and again headed toward the stairwell.

"Listen, I need your help. I was told you are good. That you take care of business. You don't?"

Shit! Hurley kept walking through the maze of desks.

"I guess I was told wrong." The young woman kept up with him.

"All right. What is it? Your cat missing?"

"You talk to everyone like this?"

"No, only the ones who barge in here, late, and think they own the place. Look, Missus, Miss, Mizzz—"

"Miss Madison. Sherrill Madison. I've been trying to talk to you all week, but you've been too busy to take my calls."

"Madison? Nope. Don't recall."

"Twice a day, at least, I've tried."

"Oh, it *is* you!" Hurley sighed. Dinner seemed to be moving further away.

"Sorry. Missing Persons is a different department. Across the hall. Monday morning, eight a.m." Hurley opened the stairwell door. Sherrill Madison was close behind.

"I was told you'd look into this."

"Yeah, sure. First thing. There's still a dozen items before it, though, and right now getting out of here and finding food's top priority. Now, if you'll excuse me."

Sherrill was still right behind him when he reached the bottom of the stairs.

"I've heard you're a good cop."

"Who told you that, my mother?" he asked, the words echoing off the walls of the empty hallway.

"Very funny. No, the officer you kept referring me to." Sherrill did her best to get in front of him and make eye contact. "I filed that report with Missing Persons, but they seem to be ignoring me. Finally, a nice officer, Nona Simms gave me your number."

Damn! Nona! Take her out once and not call her again, and she finds a way to get even. A good reason not to date a co-worker. "I'll thank her later," Hurley said, opened the front door, and started down the wide concrete stairs.

"I drove four hours from Ukiah to talk to you in person."

"Ukiah? Why didn't you file the report there?"

"My brother Jeffrey was headed this way. He called the day after he left, talked about a five-hour drive, and mentioned the redwood trees and old Victorian houses. That means Eureka. He's been missing for nearly two weeks now."

"What makes you think he's missing?"

"He never called again. We talk nearly every day. Plus he took my car—promised he'd have it back to me before the school year stared. He simply disappeared. Vanished. He had a ticket to fly home—last week."

"You sure he didn't use it?"

"No, I checked with the airline."

"Maybe he just kept heading north. If he wanted to leave, you can't always get someone to come back"

"What's so hard about doing your job?" Sherrill asked.

Russell ignored her last question and decided to walk the two blocks to the diner, leaving his car in the parking lot. Maybe she'd take the hint and leave. His long, determined strides made her almost jog, but she kept up with him.

Chapter 12

Keno walked home from work, checked the fridge, and found one can of beer. It was open and flat. The bottle of cheap whiskey was empty amongst the dirty dishes in the sink. *Shit! Nuthin'.* Keno rummaged through drawers, checked pockets of dirty pants strewn across the bedroom floor, and checked the cushions on the sofa. He found a total of four dollars and twenty-seven cents. He left his apartment in a hurry with his booty.

Where the hell did I leave my car? Keno looked up and down First Street and saw only cars that he could only wish he owned. His was gone. *Who'd want that piece of crap? It looks like hell and runs … sometimes.* He had a hunch where to find it and walked back to the Mad Cat Bar. *Yep. It's here again. A week ago after Dunne left and now again.*

His '59 Plymouth Custom Suburban station wagon was parked a few feet from the bar's entrance. The old car had seen much better days. Its original cream-colored body had been dented almost everywhere possible and each scratch and chip in the paint had been sprayed with quick shots from a can of a metallic, rust colored primer. It now had more spots of orange than any other color. Keno didn't like to be seen in it but could not afford anything else. He glanced inside and saw nothing had been disturbed. His brown wool coat and probation papers were still on the back seat.

The light over the Mad Cat was lit even though it was daylight. He was thirsty again. *Good a place as any,* he thought, crushed his cigarette on the sidewalk, and went in. *Same place that shit with Dunne started ten years ago. And then again last week. Seems shit happens when I come here.*

Keno nodded to the bartender who did his best to ignore him. Even when he pushed a few dollar bills toward him, the bartender did not approach.

"Hey, a Bud!" finally brought some attention and a bottle. Keno picked up the beer and his change and headed for a booth in the back.

Keno sat mulling over what happened last week. He had hooked up with Dunne a bunch of years before. That era had ended up being the biggest losing bet in his life, a downer for everyone involved. Keno usually shied away from drugs, but only because he couldn't afford them. But Dunne had been a gold mine of opportunity. Dunne was a natural salesman; the money was good, the highs were fantastic. Yet, the lows were really low. Keno had spent a year in the local jail, *thanks to that son of a bitch.*

What had made it tolerable was that Dunne had gotten five years in prison and that had been extended almost another five for bad behavior. *But it sure was bitchin' fun before we got caught! Man, that was the life. But, shit! Glad I only got some jail time and probation; I don't want to go back to that hell hole. Stayed clean since then, too. Well, at least haven't gotten caught.*

Because Keno was short and scrawny, the other jail inmates had taunted him to eat, buff up, exercise, and grow another six inches so he could "be a man." *Jail ain't fun. Nuthin's worth going back there.* He had spent an occasional night or two back inside but nothing like that year. If he hadn't gotten into that bar fight a couple of months ago, his record would have been clean for the last four years.

The bartender was having a smoke behind the bar before the evening customers arrived. "Heard Dunne got out a few weeks back," he said as he picked up a dirty rag and approached Keno. "Thought that's who was in here with you a couple of weeks back."

Keno shrugged. "Ain't seen him since." He didn't want to get involved in a conversation. Something about that night with Dunne was bothering him, and he couldn't quite remember what it was.

"Another bad week in Reno?" the bartender prodded.

Keno shrugged again and tried to ignore him. Some cash. Gas money to get to Nevada. Another stake. That's what Keno needed. He wouldn't get paid for another two days, and he knew he had to pay his rent. His Probation Officer had told him to stay sober. Join AA. Stay away from trouble. He took a long drink of beer.

Chapter 13

Elliott's Diner was beginning to clear out when Russell entered the restaurant. Sherrill was right behind him and was surprised when Russell paused to hold the door for her. At nearly 7:45, most people were finishing their dinners and heading home or to a movie. Russell paused at the "Please Wait To Be Seated" sign then moved past it. Sherrill stayed right behind him.

"Hi ya, Hon. Two for dinner?" Wanda Corbin gave Russell a wink as she tucked a lock of red hair behind her ear.

"No. Just one. I'm alone."

"Well, you probably shouldn't tell that to the pretty lady tailing you. Come on. There's an empty booth back here. You're not eating alone tonight." Wanda grabbed two menus and started weaving her way between tables and booths.

After the second row, Hurley paused. Other diners continued with their conversations and their meals, ignoring the subtle conflict waging nearby.

"This will be fine, Wanda," Russell said and sat in a booth with his back to the wall.

Sherrill stopped and stared at him. Wanda plopped a menu in front of him and handed Sherrill the other one. Wanda smiled at her and pointed to the seat across from Russell.

"Do you mind? I'm off duty and trying to get some dinner here." Russell stared blankly at the menu.

"I haven't eaten either, thank you." Sherrill sat down.

"Can I get you two anything to drink? Anything from the bar?"

"A beer—the usual."

"A lemonade, please."

Wanda jotted on her notepad, then quickly said, "Be right back, Hon."

"Officer Hurley, I've been trying to talk to you because—"

"Listen, lady, and I use that term loosely, it's *Detective* Hurley. What are you doing? I'm off duty, hungry, and need to get home. Someone's waiting." *Shane's home alone too long, too often.*

"Sorry if I'm keeping you from your wife, but I need to talk to you and don't know how else to make you listen. If you have a plate of food in front of you, maybe you'll slow down long enough to hear what I've been trying to talk to you about."

"Doesn't seem I have much of a choice, does it?" Russell said and looked around the room at the other diners.

Wanda reappeared with a Heineken for Hurley and a pink lemonade for Sherrill. "Okay, Hon, what'll it be? Tonight's special is right there on the front page."

"What's good here?" Sherrill asked.

"Honey, it's all good here," Wanda replied. Even as she shifted from one sore foot to the other, she gave a reassuring smile.

"Okay, a chef's salad, please, thousand island on the side."

"And for you, Mr. *Suave Diplomat*? You need another minute? Or do you want the usual?"

"No, since the lady's treating," he said, his glare silencing Sherrill across the table, "I'll have the New York steak, medium."

"You want a baked potato?"

"No. Fries. And soup tonight, not the salad."

"Ooh, living on the wild side. Cholesterol climbing, bad moon rising. I'll bring your soup in a second." Wanda wrote the order and turned back to the kitchen. "Hey, Hank, a full bowl of greens and a New York slab, medium."

"Come here often, I see," Sherrill said with a smirk.

"Yeah, too often. I've got to stop making this place a habit."

Sherrill stared at Hurley then said, "Excuse me," and got up.

Wanda reappeared with a basket of bread and crackers, and said, "Business or pleasure?"

"Huh? Oh, her. Certainly not pleasure," Hurley answered curtly. "Maybe she finally left."

"Nope. She's headed for the ladies room."

"Hell," was his only response.

Wanda smiled and said, "Well, it's 'bout time, Russ."

"What?"

"A date. This should be a pleasure. How many years has it been? Who knows? It's the first time I've seen you with anyone besides a co-worker talking cop-and-robber stuff."

"It's not a date. Just a pesty bi—"

"You should treat her like a lady. And, well, maybe? Life's too short, and you're getting on in years. Of course, there's always someone right here for you," Wanda fluttered her eyelashes, turned a luring shoulder to him, "that is, if you ever feel the need," and laughed

"Stop it, Wanda."

"Yeah, whatever. It's been nearly a decade. A long time ago. Get over it; get past it at least."

Wanda left and returned with a bowl of clam chowder and the salad as Sherrill sat back down. "Get you anything more?" Wanda asked. She picked up the menus, looked at Sherrill then nodded toward Russell.

"No, thanks," came in unison.

Sherrill took a bite of tomato then said, "Detective Hurley, like I said, my brother is missing."

"Like I told you, 'File a missing-person's report.' I stopped handling those cases years ago." He opened a package of crackers and broke them into his soup. "Talk to Sgt. Simms again; she's nice. You'll like her. She'll listen." Hurley began to eat. It was hot, thick, rich, and seasoned just right.

"I talked to Simms. She transferred me to you—gave me your number. Didn't she say something to you?"

"Nope."

"Your boss didn't either?"

"I set my own schedule. And, no, he didn't say anything to me about your brother." He got Wanda's attention and said, "Could you make my order 'to-go,' please. I've got to get home and feed the dog."

Wanda jotted something on her order pad, tore out the page, and handed it to Hurley. She spun around and said, "Be right back."

Hurley took a quick look at the piece of paper, let out a "Huh," and stuffed it into his shirt pocket.

"Dog! That's a lame excuse. You couldn't own a dog. That takes a compassionate person."

Russell closed his eyes for a moment and drew in a deep breath. "It's late, and I'm really tired. You seem concerned, and I'm sorry, but you followed me here—in my private time. Monday someone will help you. For now eat your salad—follow me home, and I'll have you arrested for stalking." Hurley pulled a couple of twenties out of his wallet and dropped them on the table. "This ought to cover our meals. I can't let you pay. It might look like a payoff to someone watching this fiasco."

Hurley stood, turned, and nearly rammed into Wanda, snatched the take-out carton, whispered, "Stop playing matchmaker!"

"Well, why not?"

"You're all the same. You just want to change a guy. Change his clothes, change his activities, change his house," he whispered and stormed out of the diner.

"Damn him!" Sherrill said under her breath. "Civil servant, ha! He's barely human and certainly not *civil*!"

Wanda gave a slight shrug, picked up the soup bowl, and said, "Men! You gotta train 'em. Russell here is the *before* version."

Both women laughed.

Chapter 14

The first quaff of beer had tasted so good going down. Keno tried to make the beer last, but it was beginning to warm up. A few people came in, laughing, trying to get a start on the weekend. Keno ignored them, lost in his own anguish trying to think of a plan for the next big score. His job paid pennies over minimum wage, and he could not do anything more than barely survive on that. Money for gas and a quick run to Reno was what he needed.

"Hey, you look lonely."

The voice brought Keno back to the present, and he looked up into a silhouette against the lights from the bar.

"Yeah, it goes that way sometimes." He was not going to complain. "Just lucky, I guess."

"Want some quick dough?"

An easy opening line, and welcome too. Trying to contain his eagerness, Keno strained his neck to look up into the eyes of … *Oh, damn! It's Dunne!* "You still here?"

"Well, back again, yeah, and I'm flush," he said patting his shirt pocket. "What d'ya go for these days? Oh, hey, did you make that payment to your landlady?"

"Land*lady*'s a loose term. And, last week I did but not this week." Keno hesitated. There was something about their last meeting that haunted him. The conversation. The beers. The girl. *What did he say he did to her?* "What've you got in mind?"

"How much you need?"

"Like I said, 'What have you got in mind?'"

"An easy night job. There's a car I need to dump." Dunne sat down across the booth and stared hard at Keno. *I made a mistake with that bitch's car a month ago. I'm not messing around with this one.*

"So, how bad you need this done?"

"Bad enough I ain't telling you no more unless you're in, and you can keep your fucking mouth shut!"

Keno could see a glint in Dunne's eyes. The bared teeth, face twisting into a fearsome mask, and clenched fists made the hair stand up on Keno's neck. He looked around, but no one was paying any attention to them. He thought for an instant about getting up and walking out, but *cash*! The possibility of getting easy money was tempting. He had to hear the number. Keno could barely keep himself seated. The dollar bills, shit no, the tens, the hundreds were piling up in his mind.

"Not one word, I swear," Keno whispered. "Let me finish my beer. It's paid for."

"Order us both one, and you can finish two." Dunne laughed. "Like I said, it's a night job. We've got a couple of hours to kill."

An hour and five beers later, the last three rounds charged on some credit card Dunne had, the pair shuffled out of the bar like long-lost buddies. Night was settling in, and fog shrouded the streets. There would be no stars or moon visible tonight.

"Where's your car?" Keno managed to say.

"My car! I don't have a car."

"But you said you need to dump—"

"I never said it was MY car!" They both roared with laughter. People leaving behind them heard only the snorting and boisterous laughter and saw their stumbling walk. They hurried past.

"Fucking bleeding-heart liberals," Dunne yelled at their backs.

· "What d'ya mean 'bleeding-heart liberal'?" Keno asked.

"That's anyone who don't like me or who pisses me off or is ugly or ignores me or—" Dunne nearly tripped but caught himself with a telephone pole. He swung around and sat on the hood of a car.

"Hell, that sounds like you're pissed at the whole world."

"Shut up! The car's up north. Where's yours?"

"You're sittin' on it."

"This piece of shit? What's with all these spots? Looks like a fucking tiger"

"Naw. Don't you know nothing? It's a leopard. Tigers got stripes; leopards got spots." They roared with laughter again. "I ain't got the money for a paint job—yet," he added hopefully. "Or gas."

After filling up, Dunne drove Keno's rust-bucket for miles, north, east, then north again, into and out of national forest boundaries. Turns began looking the same, and Keno dozed off until discomfort nagged at him. He could take no more of it. He sat up.

"How much farther? I gotta piss."

"You sound like a kid."

"Shit. You said you wanted help to ditch a car, not drive across the state. Where'd you park this thing?" He squirmed in his seat. "It's so late, it's probably tomorrow already. I gotta piss," he repeated.

"We're close; and it's only midnight. You're used to staying drunk twenty-four-seven."

Trees, turns, passing lanes, narrow bridges, more trees, more turns, and they kept driving. Finally, Dunne slowed to let a car pass then turned left into a wide spot across the highway, a turn-out lane large enough for a big rig.

"This it?"

"Yep." But Dunne didn't stop.

Keno couldn't see a road, but several yards ahead, completely out of sight from the highway, sat a late model silver Impala.

"She-e-e-e—it! I've always wanted one."

"An Impala?"

"A real car. Look at this! Mags." Keno jumped out of his car and peered into the windows. "Leather tuck and roll, stereo, every knob and dial you can think of. Geez, it's got air conditioning. The car is ... hey, you didn't say nothin' about stealing no car! Where'd you get this bad boy?"

"None of your fuckin' business. You got your bucket of bolts over there. Shut up, and help me get some shit outta' the car."

Dunne pulled suitcases and a sleeping bag out of the trunk and a box from the back seat. He stuffed silver and gold jewelry into the pockets of his jeans and leather jacket.

"What d'ya need me for?" Keno asked over his shoulder as he relieved himself in a patch of ferns. He was awake now, but the air was cold, and his light jacket couldn't keep the dampness from penetrating to his skin. And, his skin was starting to crawl.

"Quit scratching yourself. It looks like you're coming down from a bad high."

"It's been too long since I had a hit for that. This place gives me the creeps. It feels like something died here."

"Not here."

"Huh? Someone died? Hey! I never signed up for no murder, not no accessory to no murder!"

"I never said nothin' about murder. Just someone died. People die every day. Now shut up and help me get this stuff out of the car. I don't want nothing to ID this thing."

Keno tried to put the things into some semblance of order. He wasn't sure why, but he felt like he should show some respect.

Keno tugged on a quilt hanging off the drooping limb of a tree. "Hey, how long this shit's been out here? This is pretty wet." He folded the blanket and carried it several feet away before placing it carefully on a fallen redwood tree.

"It don't take long for things to get wet out here. If it's not raining, it's foggy," Dunne said and threw stuff behind him, around him to his left, to his right. Suitcases popped open; the sleeping bag bunched up across ferns; boxes crushed small redwood trees and ferns. Dunne wiped every possible part of the car—mirrors, handles, doors, windows, dash.

"Here, you drive this one." Dunne tossed Keno the set of keys.

"You got the key?" Suddenly Keno felt a mix of thrill and fear, mostly fear. "Hey, man! I've been a druggie, a pimp, a boozer, but I ain't never had nothin' to do with killing!" His stomach wretched, but nothing came up.

"You didn't this time, neither. Now shut up and follow me back."

"Where're we heading?" Keno wanted to know how much longer he'd be hooked with this piece of scum. Until he got his money, of course.

"To the north bay. Arcata. By the old skating rink. I've got to dump this car so there won't be no prints and other shit for anyone to find."

"Why didn't you drive it back yourself?"

"Shut the fuck up. You're askin' too many questions."

"Where's my money?"

"Just get in and drive."

It was only fear that kept Keno from not leaving in the most 'rad' car he had ever driven. Fear and the need for money. The car drove easily and had great control and every dial and gizmo you could imagine. He scratched his arm a couple of times on the gear-shift lever since the knob was missing, leaving the rough metal exposed.

The car took the turns like they were banked high and wide. He figured he could get away from Dunne in that old heap of his, but Dunne always seemed to have a way of showing up. Keno did not want to cross him. No, he knew he would get crossed back, and he'd never have another breath to show for it. *And, I need the money!*

Chapter 15

The drive back seemed shorter. Keno felt at ease behind the wheel by the time they got to the coast. The car handled great, and he was sober enough now to keep the car on the road. He enjoyed every moment of the drive.

They arrived in Arcata before sunup. Keno knew where the old skating rink was, or at least where it had been.

The off ramp took him within two miles of the pier next to the old rink. Keno wondered how Dunne would be able to hide a car here so it'd never be found.

Dunne pulled up beside Keno and motioned for him to follow. Dunne drove past the old rink, past the parking lot, past old warehouses, past the last glint of light coming from the street. All the streetlights in this area had burned out long ago. No one came here any more.

Keno couldn't see much of anything through the fog. Suddenly Dunne was right in front of him, getting out of the car. The brakes held, but the gravel on the old frontage road made the car slide, nearly rear-ending his own piece of junk.

"Hell, man!" Dunne yelled and, barely holding his rage, jumped out of the way. "Watch what you're doing!"

"Sorry." Keno was almost sorry he hadn't hit him. At least this would be over before he was in any further.

"Drive it over there," Dunne pointed to the right side of Keno's car, "to the end of the wharf."

Keno pulled the car onto the edge of the pier and turned off the engine. He could hear the wood creak beneath the weight. Then he realized! *His* prints were all over this car, all over everything in the car.

"She-e-e-it! I've got to clean this up. They'll ID me for sure." He ripped off his shirt, popping off three buttons, and began to scrub every piece of plastic, metal, knob, leather, every place he could remember touching.

Dunne looked on, chuckled to himself, and whispered, "Hey, we've got to get moving! It'll be dawn soon, and I gotta' be miles from here."

Keno climbed out, pulled his shirt back on, and stared at the car. *Such a waste. Beautiful car.* Beads of sweat covered his brow, and his glasses were far down his nose.

"We gotta' take it out of gear," Dunne said. He pulled his jacket sleeve over his hand and reached in. He forced the gear-shift lever into neutral. "Help me push."

The car rolled easily onto the old dock, teetered on the edge, then slid off the end. It sank a few feet then paused for a moment before gliding beneath the cold, dark waters of Humboldt Bay with hardly a ripple. Bubbles rose from the car for several minutes then the waters were still.

Keno stood at the end of the pier and stared, amazed that nothing showed of the car. He gave a sigh of relief and felt the tension leave his arms. Unexpectedly, a chill ran down his back. He shook it off then turned to see Dunne staring at him; the chill returned.

"Good. We're done," Dunne said pulling at Keno's arm. "Let's go." They turned, climbed into Keno's old wreck, and headed back to Eureka. Keno felt like Dunne was watching him all the way back.

Chapter 16

The next afternoon

Elliott's Diner was nearly empty. Wanda took a deep breath and let out a long sigh. The breakfast rush was over and only one hour remained before her meal break. The tips had been good. One customer was at the counter, another sat at a table in back, and an elderly couple were finishing their meal in a booth near the back. All were relaxing with a newspaper or chatting quietly.

Wanda, dressed in her customary black polyester slacks, white blouse, and black vest, was finally able to take a break. Her feet were bothering her more lately, and the new, orthopedic shoes did not help. Her knees hurt too. Since she was working alone this afternoon, she slipped into the booth near the cash register, pulled her hair away from her face, closed her eyes, and sank her head onto her crossed arms on the table.

Seconds later, she sensed rather than heard the door open and groaned slightly. She lifted her head and started to rise.

"Don't bother getting up. I'll find a seat at the counter." Sherrill Madison, dressed in a silk, navy pantsuit with matching loafers, turned the swivel seat and began to sit.

"Nonsense. Here, take this booth," Wanda said and ushered Sherrill to the bench seat.

"Okay, but only if you'll stay where you are. I'm in no hurry to order, and if you're not busy—"

Wanda stretched out and grabbed a menu from the stack on the counter. "Here. Just in case you need something to read or my boss walks out and sees you with nothing."

Sherrill smiled and placed the closed menu on the table then slid onto the seat across from Wanda. "Tell me," she said leaning forward, "how long have you known Detective Hurley?"

"Russ? Gee, I don't know—twelve years or more, I suppose. You interested? You do know he's single."

"What? No. God, no! I'm in town looking for my brother, and this Hurley guy did his best to ignore me last night."

"That don't seem like Russ. Yesterday must've been real bad. He's a good cop. I'd trust him with my life."

"Well, how do I get in touch with him? I can't wait until Monday. I need to get back to work. It's a new job, and I don't have any time saved up."

"He's off 'til Monday. What do you do?"

"I'm a teacher. A reading specialist."

"You must be from someplace else. You don't sound like local folk."

"I teach in Ukiah."

"Ukiah? Naw, you don't sound like California. How long you been here? What part of the south are you from?"

"You can tell that easily? I'm from Georgia and studied linguistics. Thought I'd gotten rid of my accent."

"Part, not all. My mom was from the South. I pick up on it pretty easy. You've come a long ways. What brought you out here?" Wanda asked as she checked around the diner; no customers seemed to need any attention.

"It was time to leave. Get a new start."

"A man, huh?"

Sherrill smiled.

"I've been there. Wasn't quick enough in my own life. So you just up'd and left? That's brave."

"Yeah, plus, my folks were trying to run my life."

"They probably wanted to protect you."

"Maybe. But I didn't want protection. My brother saved the day. He found an ad for teachers out here and volunteered to drive out here with me. We had a blast for two weeks sightseeing."

"And now your brother's ... what? Left?"

"He stayed with me a couple of days in Ukiah then headed up this way. He should have been back more than a week ago. He was supposed to call me every day or two. I only heard from him once, the day after he left; it's been too long now." Sherrill sighed and shook her head. "He had a ticket to fly home last week."

"He wants some time to himself. He'll call you real soon." The customer from the counter left, and Wanda rose to clear his dishes and put the money into the register. She shook her head while she dropped the tip of three whole quarters into her pocket.

"I'm worried sick. He's always kept in touch. Not one word," Sherrill said after Wanda sat back down.

"Is he older, younger? What's he do?"

"Younger, almost two years. He's into jewelry ... gold and silver castings, earrings ... and a writer. He's nearly finished a great story. He's hoping to sell the book and get set up in a business where he can create. He was an artist." Sherrill gasped, "**Is** an artist. He's always been responsible and kept in touch. Mom and Dad haven't heard anything either." She pulled a napkin from the holder and dabbed her eyes and nose trying not to lose control. She had not had a chance to talk to anyone for a long time, and when she called her parents, everyone got upset.

"Don't you worry. He'll turn up. Just a kid feeling his oats. Probably like my son Jake, wanting his freedom and all." Wanda heard footsteps and looked over her shoulder at the couple across the room. "Be right with you," she said to the man approaching the register. Wanda rose and took care of his ticket then patted Sherrill's hand before she turned to take fresh coffee to the couple.

Moments later, Wanda slipped in beside Sherrill who was now sobbing quietly into a handful of napkins.

"No one's paying attention." Sherrill took a deep breath. "Jeffrey's been gone too long. He always calls. Me. Mom and Dad. He'd never ignore us. Never. Unless ... unless something hap ... happened!" The tears came easily. Wanda put her arm across Sherrill's shoulder and patted her back. "He would never simply disappear. He has to be, has to be all right!" Sherrill sputtered.

Wanda glanced around the restaurant. The man in back was now engrossed in a crossword puzzle, and the cooks were taking a break in back. The next rush wouldn't start for a while.

Wanda'd had two children and had wanted more, but the men she met never stuck around. She always wanted to be a good mother. After losing her baby girl in her first year, she doted on her son Jake, who had been a problem since his sister died when he was three. He had been in and out of trouble and quit high school in his junior year. Wanda had the capacity to listen to anyone who needed help and nearly adopted Russell Hurley after his tragic loss nearly a decade ago. It was her way of feeling needed. If she couldn't succeed with her own child, maybe she could help someone else now and then.

"Hey, I bet he ran out of change. He'll be calling soon. Is there anyone at your place to answer the phone? Someone you can call?"

"I checked my answering machine last night and again this morning," Sherrill said wiping her nose. "Nothing. I know something terrible has happened. I can't even talk to Mom and Dad without them getting hysterical, especially Mom. Poor Mom. Jeffrey's her baby." Sherrill took a deep breath.

Wanda reached around her and pulled the napkin holder within easy reach. She pulled a bundle out and handed them to Sherrill.

"Thanks. I'm so sorry. I didn't mean to dump on you. I don't know what to do." Sherrill looked at Wanda. "I can't get anyone to listen. There's no one at work I can really talk to. No one cares. No one who could help, anyway."

"Well, we'll see about that. This situation's lasted long enough. I'll be right back, Hon." Wanda brusquely got up and headed toward the alcove in back.

Sherrill dabbed her eyes, blew her nose as quietly as she could, and headed toward the restroom to wash up. When she passed Wanda, she heard the waitress say, "I don't give a shit if it *is* your day off. You're a goddamned public servant, and you've got a public down here that needs serving. Get your ass down here, now!"

When Sherrill returned, Wanda had wiped and set the table. A fresh glass of ice water was waiting for her. The older couple had finished and were heading toward the register. They glanced at Sherrill, whose cheeks were flush and eyes bloodshot. The gray-haired woman said quietly, "It'll be all right, dear. Whatever it is will turn out all right," and touched her gently on her arm. The elderly man with her smiled warmly in agreement.

Sherrill nodded at the couple and tried to say, "Thanks," but only came up with something garbled, pleasantly surprised at the small-town friendliness of strangers.

"You go back there and sit down." Wanda nodded toward the booth. "I'll bring you a salad and bread while you decide what else you want to eat." Wanda gave up the idea of her own meal break and nibbled croutons and lettuce pieces behind the counter.

Sherrill was finishing her fruit salad when the door opened with a bang. She looked up and recognized Det. Hurley as he headed for Wanda.

"What's going on? This place being robbed? This had better be serious!"

"Believe me, Russ, it's serious. Now get over there and talk to that young woman. Better yet, don't talk. Listen." Wanda, the only person he let get away with calling him Russ, gave him a gentle shove toward Sherrill's booth. "She's scared, and I think she might have reason to be."

Russell Hurley stood firm and scowled at Wanda. "You brought me down here for this? Wasn't I clear enough yesterday?"

"Hush. You got my note. I meant what I wrote."

"You still trying to set me up?"

"No, the damsel is in distress and needs a knight. Get off your high horse, and get your sorry butt over there," she said, giving him another push. Slightly off balance, Hurley headed toward the booth.

Sherrill smiled to herself. She had just met Wanda and here she was taking care of her. *Friends show up sometimes when they are really needed. If the cops were any good, I might actually start to like this town.*

Det. Hurley, dressed in a 49ers sweatshirt, well-worn jeans, and paint-splattered tennis shoes, sat down across the table and finally listened to Sherrill's story.

Chapter 17

Friday evening, two weeks later

"Hurley here." It was getting close to quitting time, and he reluctantly answered the phone. "Yes, I saw the article. ... No, the young man is still missing. ... Yes, his sister just moved from the east coast. ... No, I think you covered it." He listened for a bit more, then said, "No, the sister returned to her job in Mendocino County. She didn't stay here long. She calls daily and comes back up here every weekend." He took a deep breath during the reporter's next question. "I can't say, but you did a good job writing the story. ... Of course, we've put out a bulletin and description of the car he was driving and the plates. ... Yes, a follow up might be a good idea, go ahead. ... You should talk to Sgt. Simms; she's in Missing Persons. Yes, I'll transfer you."

He hung up and sat at his desk. *Too bad it's a small department ... no money for an information officer.* He had listened to Sherrill and assured her that everything would work out though he knew it was probably a lie. He reviewed his notes of Sherrill's description of Jeffrey, the car, and the route he had planned to take. He had written "Madison, Jeffrey" on a new file folder and kept his notes and a photo of Jeffrey inside. Today, he slipped a piece of paper into it with the reporter's name and time information, and slid the folder into his drawer. "Everything will be fine," he had told Sherrill. Now, if he could just believe it himself.

He pulled the old file from under the lamp and opened it. A piece of paper covered the graphic pictures of the victim and the car; he did not like to see them unless he was in the mood to search again for clues hidden in the photographs. The words were easier to take, though he seldom read them anymore. *Of all the unsolved crimes, why you?* He shook his head, closed the folder. *Just like you, this kid has disappeared.* He slid it back under the lamp's base.

Almost five. Time to shut down. He reached up and turned off the lamp.

The phone rang again. *Damn!* "Yes. ... Yes, I'm Hurley. ... You found what? ... Where? ... Why call *me*? ... It matches what? ... I'll be right there." *Double damn!*

Hurley got into his own car and turned on the radio. He punched the button for the local news station which made the announcement almost immediately: "Car Found in Bay." The rest of the news report went on to say that two kids had skipped school and saw something shiny in the murky water. One boy had shoved the other off the old pier. The boy floundered for a moment, then realized he could stand on something solid. Kicking at it, he realized it was the top of a car. They had run home and told their parents who called the police.

The license plates had been removed, the VIN number on the dash had been scratched out, and the owner's identity was unknown. Divers were searching the muddy waters, and so far a driver had not been found. There were no signs of foul play nor any reason for an accident that would have put the car there.

Chapter 18

Keno heard the radio report on the five o'clock news while he was stocking shelves at the 6th and L Street Market. "A silver Impala was found in the north bay. A local search and rescue team is making repeated dives searching for the driver and any indication of why the car might be there. There are no signs of an accident, and the car appears to have been in the water for some time. It will be pulled out tomorrow when the proper equipment can be brought to the site."

Sweat ran down his temples pulling strands of hair into his eyes, and his glasses slipped down his nose. He tried to put the boxes of sugar cubes neatly on the shelf, but they would not line up. His hands wouldn't stop shaking, and another box fell on the floor.

Just then, the store manager walked by. "Got the shakes again? Isn't it about time you cleaned up your act?"

"No. I ain't had a drink in days. Can't afford to with this job."

"Finish this shelf and get out of here. I don't want the customers seeing you like this."

"Thanks. I'll make up the time tomorrow. I promise." *Yeah, like I'm comin' back here.*

"Sure, sure." The manager returned to the office area to work on his paperwork while Keno shoved the last five boxes onto the shelf, crushed the cardboard carton, and removed his apron on his way out the back door. *What the hell!* The carton and the apron both went into the garbage bin.

His hands continued to tremble, and his head was pounding. No amount of liquor would take away this fear. *They're going to get me for sure. My prints are all over that car. Hell, Dunne said they'd never find it.* Never *didn't last very long. I gotta get out of town. Where? How?*

Find Dunne. It's his fault this happened! He got me into this shit! Where the hell is he? The Mad Cat?

Keno had twenty-two dollars in his pocket. He didn't dare go back to his apartment. *They'll be waiting for me!* The Mad Cat seemed like the best place to go and the most likely place he'd find Dunne.

Keno bought a beer and took it to the back booth. The lighting was not good there, so no one would notice him, yet he could see everyone coming and going. His glasses kept slipping and needed to be pushed back. Two hours. Three. He bought more beer, picked up a bowl of pretzels off the bar, and returned to his burrow. Once in a while, someone would play a tune on the jukebox. He even dropped in a couple of quarters to help pass the time. When "Stayin' Alive" and "Hotel California" were through, he played them again.

The red-hair woman returned. She had on the same black pants and vest over the white blouse. Keno stared at her as she climbed onto the bar stool and kicked off her shoes before ordering. She rubbed one knee.

"Which choice tonight?" the bartender asked.

"Beer. Any will do."

Wanda was tired every night when she got off her shift. This Friday was no different. The walk home took her past the Mad Cat Bar, and she frequently stopped in to spend some of her tip money. A beer or a Scotch on the rocks. It didn't matter. A drink took the edge off her aching feet and knees. She had not owned a car since her twenty-year-old VW Bug blew its engine, and her son told her he could no longer keep it running.

"Your car isn't worth shit, Mom," Jake had told her. "Don't you think you should buy something else?" She ended up having it towed away— $35 to get rid of it.

"Why do I need a car anyway? Everywhere I go is close by. Besides, I can't afford anything decent." Jake gave her rides now and then, but he was often too busy working two jobs to chauffeur her around. So, she walked to and from work five days a week, to the grocery store when she was hungry, and to the Mad Cat when she was thirsty or lonely. Wanda frequently got thirsty and lonely on the way home.

She recognized most of the customers; she was there often enough to know who was a regular. The short, skinny man in the back booth had been there many times and smiled at her often. Wanda wasn't in any permanent-male-search mode, but once in a while a little attention from a man made her feel young again. Some nights she wasn't too picky.

Keno, tired of waiting for Dunne to appear, watched Wanda sitting there, sucked in a deep breath, ran his fingers through his thin hair, pushed his glasses back again, and walked over.

"Hi. You must've just got off work. You look tired. Pretty, though."

"Yeah? Sure. I am tired."

"I think I seen you here before. Where do you work?" Keno was already beginning to think he might get some action tonight. That might include a different place to stay besides his apartment where the cops were probably already staked out.

"Waitress at Elliott's," Wanda answered as the bartender placed the mug of draft in front of her.

"Waitress, huh? I'll bet you're damned good. How long you been doing that?"

"More than twenty years." Wanda wondered why he was hanging around then figured there was only one thing on his mind. *Not tonight! I'm pooped. Besides, he looks creepy—and his glasses are ugly.*

Keno sat on the stool next to her for a few minutes, turning his empty beer bottle like he was reading the label over and over. "I'm Keno, er Kevin."

"Wanda," she said.

He finally tired of his glasses, took them off, and shoved them into his shirt pocket. When a slow song started playing, Keno-er-Kevin slid off the bar stool, pulled himself as straight as he could and asked, "Wanna dance, *Wanda*?" Keno grinned at his private joke.

Wanda shrugged. "Sure, why not?" Her feet, without shoes, were beginning to feel better, and she didn't want to sit the night away, alone.

It was nearly eleven when Dunne entered the bar. The dim light played off his features, making the creases in his face seem even more severe. Keno flinched when he saw him over Wanda's shoulder.

Wanda felt the tension and stepped back. She saw Dunne and immediately headed for the barstool. Keno sat next to her, and Dunne sat next to him.

Dunne saw Keno's empty bottles and said to the bartender, "Two beers, Budweiser Lagers. And one for the lady."

"Where the hell you been? Did you hear the news? They found the—" Keno whispered.

"Yeah. So what? They ain't gonna' find nothing. It's been in the water too long. Besides, we cleaned it up good."

The low talk made Wanda listen even harder, though she had no idea what they were talking about.

"Forget about it," she heard the taller man say.

Dunne's confidence made Keno relax a bit. "You really think so? We did wipe it down, didn't we?"

"You're panicked!" Dunne stared at Keno. "What've you been saying? Hey, you been talking to her? What'd you tell her?" Dunne jerked his head toward Wanda.

"Nothin'," he whispered. "I didn't say nothin'."

"I seen how close you two was dancing. What's she know?"

"Nothin'. I swear." Keno didn't like Dunne's insinuations. He had seen his paranoia before. It usually meant he had been shooting up or snorting and was either still high from the coke or coming down from it. Keno fidgeted with the napkin. "I never said nuthin' about what you—"

"Shut up!" Phillip Dunne walked around Keno and sat on the other side of Wanda.

"You been hearing anything new?" Dunne looked straight into her eyes. "You two been talking about anything interesting?"

"No." Wanda squirmed. The man's domineering attitude made her uncomfortable.

"What'd he tell you?" he demanded and leaned closer.

"Like what? We talked about work and danced some. Nothing more." Wanda looked up at his scowling face and cringed

Dunne looked around the bar and wondered who else could have overheard the conversation. He was sure Keno had talked to her.

"I told you, I ain't told her nothing," Keno whispered from behind. He saw his chance of staying at her place disappear.

"The night's young; let's dance. You're lonely; I'm lonely. Let's make some time together," Dunne said and pulled Wanda by the arm into the middle of the room. He held her tight and started to move in time with the music. "Did he tell you about me? What'd he say? Anything good, or was it all bad? I ain't as bad as he says."

"Like I said, he didn't say anything about you at all. I've got to get home; I have a long day tomorrow." She turned slightly.

Dunne gripped her arm tighter and pulled her closer. "We can make it a long night tonight, if you'd like."

"No, I'm leaving," she said, pulled away, and returned to the bar. She slipped her feet into her shoes.

"Hey, don't leave," Keno said. "We have more time before they close."

"No, I've got to get home." Wanda took a last drink of the beer and bent over for her purse. Keno watched every move she made and stared at her retreating rear.

"I need to see more of her," he said.

"Sure you do. How much you tell her?" Dunne persisted.

"I told you, nothin'." Keno cowered like a whipped dog.

"Right. I gotta piss. You follow her. Find out where she lives. Don't let no one see you." Dunne gave Keno a shove toward the door.

Keno left and Dunne headed for the restroom.

Chapter 19

Wanda was sorry she didn't have a car tonight. Her feet were killing her, and her back was aching. It felt like a bruise was forming where that jerk had grabbed her arm. She shivered and pulled her sweater tightly around her shoulders. She looked around. *Another block to go.*

A party was breaking up in a house across the street. She paused and listened to the music still blaring. People were laughing and hugging as they left. She felt the chill and hugged her sweater closer then climbed the steps to the second floor of her apartment building, and put her key into the lock. The door pushed open; it was not latched.

She reached inside and flicked the light switch on. *Jake,* she sighed to herself. Her son was there, sprawled on the couch, asleep. A cigarette dangled from his fingers, still smoldering.

"Jake! Wake up! What the hell you doing? You're going to burn this place down." She took off her sweater and tossed it over the back of the sofa.

"What the—" Jake sat up, looked at his hand with a glazed eyes and stubbed the cigarette out into a plate of cold spaghetti lying on the floor. "Oh, hi, Mom," he mumbled.

"Don't 'Oh, hi, Mom' me! What're you doing here? You're supposed to be at work."

"Uh, I ... well, I kinda got ... uh, they laid off ... uh ... some of us. They don't have enough business to keep ... uh ... us busy."

"Not again! When are you going to grow up?"

"Mom, lay off," Jake said. He picked up the plate and headed for the kitchen.

"You've got to get a job and keep it. You using again? You just got out of rehab."

"No, Mom. I promise. I'm clean. They laid me off, for real. They didn't fire me. They promised they'd take me back in a week or two when business picks up again."

"Look at you. You're a mess. What've you been doing?" She started picking up glasses and other dishes and carried them to the kitchen. "Are you still in school?"

"Quit nagging. The semester don't start for another month or two. I'm signed up for a class right after Christmas. I'll keep going this time, I swear," he said as she returned to the living room.

"That's what you said last—," Wanda said. "Oh, never mind. You're a big boy now. It's up to you."

"I said I'm clean and I am! What the hell do you want from me? I can't live your life for you. And you can't live mine." Jake grabbed his jacket off the arm of the couch.

"Where are you going this time of night?"

"Out. Maybe I'll be back tonight. Maybe not." He slammed the door behind him.

Wanda kicked off her shoes and bolted the door. She pulled the shades, turned on the television, and sat down on her Thrift Store sofa. She switched channels until she found a re-run of Geraldo Rivera interviewing an actor she didn't recognize. She pushed Jake's dirty clothes off a chair and put her feet up. An hour later, Wanda turned off the television and stood up. As she stretched, she heard a knock on the door. *Jake must be back,* she thought. "Forgot your key again? I'll let you in," she said and grasped the deadbolt knob.

Chapter 20

Exhausted and cold, Dunne crept into Keno's apartment. When he flushed the toilet, Keno rolled over and asked, "Where the hell you been?"

"Checking on something." Dunne fell across the brown corduroy sofa and began snoring almost immediately. He had not been able to carry out his plan because some dumb, punk kid had interrupted him.

Keno pulled his pillow over his head trying to blot out the pungent odor of marijuana smoke that had permeated Dunne's clothes.

A few short hours later, he swore at himself, *Hell, the sun's up. I forgot to pull the damn shade again!* He got up and shook his head when he saw Dunne on the floor next to the couch. Keno went to the kitchen and started a pot of coffee. "A quick shower and I'll feel like a million bucks," he mumbled to himself as he trudged into the bathroom.

Ten minutes later, feeling like a worn out dollar bill, Keno finished dressing and went for the coffee. Dunne had already poured himself a cup and was searching the fridge for food.

"You got no milk?" Dunne was shoving cans and bottles around, knocking some over.

"This restaurant's out. You could always buy some—help get some food, you know."

"Fuck that. I bought you enough beer last night to cover any shit I eat." Dunne sipped coffee from the chipped mug and winced at the bitterness. "This tastes like piss water." He slammed the mug down, spilling half the dark fluid, and headed into the bathroom. Keno poured himself a cup, added three scoops of sugar, a taste he acquired in jail, and drank it quickly. He poured himself another cup, emptying the pot.

Dunne stormed out of the bathroom and straight for the door.

"Where you going?"

"You my mother? I've got some business to finish," Dunne yelled and slammed the door behind him.

Keno shrugged, opened the cupboard and snickered. The non-dairy creamer was right in front.

Chapter 21

Sherrill drove north on Highway 101 Friday night just as she had done for the last several weeks. Like the other Saturdays, she went to the Elliot's Diner for breakfast and usually for lunch too.

Wanda was a good listener and fun to talk to. Though they were totally different, Sherrill liked Wanda, especially since she had convinced Detective Hurley to take her seriously. Besides, there had not been time to make other friends, and Wanda's smiling face was always good to see.

Sherrill decided to sit at the counter. "Where's Wanda?" she asked the young man setting out paper napkins and silverware.

He placed a mug in front of her and filled it with coffee. "She's late," he said handing her a menu.

Sherrill looked at it and decided to have the fruit bowl and a side of hash browns, just for extravagance.

As the waiter put a glass of water in front of her, he asked, "You know Wanda?"

"Only from here. She's been friendly. Why?"

"I'm wondering if you might know why she didn't show. If she called in, nobody told me about it."

"Sorry. I can't help you. Something must have come up."

The door opened and Sherrill heard, "I thought you might be here."

She recognized the voice and turned to see Det. Hurley approaching. "Well, good morning, *Officer* Hurley. How are you?"

"Fine, and it's still *detective* to you, ma'am," he said with a smirk and sat on the stool next to her.

"I'm fine, thanks," she said, then quickly added, "Any word? Any new information?" She took a drink of water and picked up the napkin to catch the drops that fell onto her lap.

"I take it you didn't listen to the radio on the way up here last night."

"No. Listened to my music. Why?"

"There's something I want you to look at. It's twenty minutes from here; if you're ready, we can go now."

Sherrill looked at him. This was not the same man she had argued with a few weeks ago and the brusk *detective* she had talked to on the phone nearly every day since. He was dressed neatly in a sport shirt, slacks, and a jacket. He was actually being polite, even if a little curt. This was out of character. She was worried.

"What's happened? What's going on?"

"You'll see soon enough."

Sherrill stuffed the napkin into her pocket, slid off the stool, and immediately forgot about the food she had ordered. She followed Hurley to his county-issued car. *Surprise, it's clean! Must be someone else's,* she thought and climbed in. "Is something wrong? Have you found something?"

Hurley frowned and looked at her, nodding slowly. "We'll talk on the way."

He drove north on the highway for about fifteen minutes, exiting into Arcata. Det. Hurley wound through side streets then pulled past an old building and headed toward the bay.

A group of about twenty on-lookers had gathered, curiosity seekers who had heard the news on the radio.

Members of the fire department were there with one truck. Sheriff Deputies, plain clothed and in uniform, were milling around near the end of a pier. A tow truck was inching back onto the pier, the back-up alarm piercing the morning mist. Every face was somber; muffled comments could be heard as Sherrill and Russell walked toward the gathered deputies.

"Hi, ya, Detective," Sgt. Johnson said. Sherrill noticed his solemn expression and tone of voice. He stood still and took a quick, embarrassed glance at Sherrill. Sgt. Johnson was in uniform, his cap on straight; after all, the news cameras were there. His jacket was zipped up against the cold, and his countenance and attitude gave Sherrill a chill.

"You're sure it's the Madison's car?" Russell asked.

"Looks that way. Right color. Impala," Sgt. Johnson said.

Sherrill grabbed Russ's arm and said, "This is where my car was found? Where is it?"

Russell remained quiet and pointed toward the water. Sherrill's eyes widened as she looked at the choppy water. She shivered and wished she had retrieved her jacket from her rented car.

The beeping back-up alarm stopped, and the tow-truck driver emerged from the cab, yelling, "You guys set yet? I don't want to spend too much time on this pile of rotting timbers."

"A few more minutes," came the answer from Johnson. "I'll check." He walked to the end of the pier and looked over the end into the brown, gloomy waters of Humboldt Bay, searching for signals from the scuba divers. He pulled his radio from his hip, punched a button and spoke into it. Static came back in response. "Hang on," he called over his shoulder to the truck driver.

Sherrill walked toward the dock while Russell talked to two officers. As soon as he noticed that she had kept walking, he rushed to her.

"No! Don't," he said and stepped in front of her. "Don't go any farther."

"Why? What's going on? What's it doing here? Did you find...?" She was afraid to consider the obvious. She asked the questions but really did not want to hear the answers.

"Let's go over here," he said, gently guiding her off the pier and away from the spectators. He stood a few moments and looked over Sherrill's shoulder into the distant clouds hanging over the ocean. He always had trouble talking to families of victims, even women made of ice. Russell looked into her eyes. Her concern was hard to bear. He took a deep breath. He had been through more difficult times. *It's harder when it involves children or someone I know, but it's never easy.*

He glanced over her shoulder once more before saying, "Yes, we found your car. At least we think so."

Sherrill trembled. Nervous apprehension overrode her hunger pangs.

"What is it? Is it ..." She couldn't finish. She knew. She fought the urge to cry, but tears filled her eyes. A silent scream welled inside and stayed in her throat; a low groan escaped.

"We found an Impala that looks like the one you described." He paused and looked to the skies for reassurance that something was up there, something more than this place where they stood. "We think ..." He stopped. He knew he had said enough. "Let's go back to the car. You can sit there and wait until it's out."

Sherrill pulled the napkin from her pocket and wiped her eyes as she walked back to the car with unsure steps. She sat quietly and watched the activity increase as the divers took the two truck's chains and hook and attached them to the vehicle. *No, it can't be. They've made a mistake.*

Russell pulled a blanket from the trunk and handed it to her then returned to the pier. He knew the two divers who were trying to hook the car up. The water was murky; silt stirred up every time they made a move.

The divers' face masks were so fogged up even with the special goop smeared on the glass it difficult to maneuver. One was treading water near the pier. "Too far, bring it up," the diver called out to Sgt. Johnson standing above him. Johnson held his hand to his ear and yelled for him to repeat what he'd said then made hand motions to the tow-truck operator to reverse the direction of the hook. The diver put his his regulator back into his mouth and disappeared into the water. A moment later he reappeared and yelled. "Hold it there!"

Johnson signaled OK to the tow-truck driver.

More movements, more silt, more swearing, and finally the chains attached. "Okay! Pull!" was bellowed.

The winch turned; the chain grew taut. Two heads popped above the waves and moved backwards, away from the rising car. Suddenly a sickening sound came from under the pier. The two in the water began swimming away as hard as they could. Sgt. Johnson felt it the same time he heard it. The dock trembled under his feet and began to teeter. The wood was slick from the fog, and Johnson's shoes refused to grip. He barely had time to yell, "Stop! Stop! Drop it back down!" before he lost his balance, fell onto his backside, and slid off the pier into the muddy waters.

The truck driver, standing at the rear of his tow truck, could not hear over the noise of the winch and continued the hook's pull on the car.

Another officer ran to the truck, slapped the front fender, and yelled, "Stop! Turn it off. Drop the chain. The dock's giving away!"

The driver paused to comprehend what was happening then turned off the winch. He looked over his shoulder and saw the sergeant struggling in the water. The car fell faster than he would have expected then realized that the pier itself was giving away.

"Oh, my gaw ...!" he muttered and jumped into the cab and started the engine.

The officer ran off the dock, and the truck jerked forward. The pier collapsed, and the tow truck hung precariously off the edge, its back wheels spinning. Only the axel prevented it from sliding off the last few broken timbers that were still attached to the one remaining pillar jutting at an angle toward the shore.

One of the divers saw the sergeant fall into the water and swam to his side. Blood oozed from his forehead, and his jacket was torn. His hat was floating nearby and moving away with the waves.

Russell and several other officers ran to the tow truck and held onto the front bumper until they realized that it was stable. The driver climbed out, slammed the door, and raced for the shore. The loss of weight in the cab changed the balance. The truck shuddered a moment before it slowly slid into the brackish water.

"Shit!" came in unison from the driver, Russell, and the others nearby. Gasps and whoops followed from the bystanders who were moving closer. Officers waved them back out of the way as the truck came to rest with the cab and hood protruding from the bay.

What had started as an hour-or-two project had suddenly turned into an all-day undertaking. An immediate call brought an ambulance for Sgt. Johnson. His clothing and jacket were in much worse shape than he was. A few dabs of antibiotic, a bandage, a warm blanket, and a few good laughs from his fellow officers put him into a surly mood.

The news crews were quick to respond and had focused their lenses on everything as it happened. Sgt. Johnson being pulled out of the bay by the scuba divers would be as big a lead story as recovering the car.

A larger tow truck arrived within an hour. With much noise, cursing, complaining, and cooperation among the two drivers and the officers, the first truck was pulled from the rickety pier and moved out of the way.

The car was a lot more trouble. The divers, after being in the bay so long, were starting to develop hypothermia and had to get out.

Officer Carson arrived with some McDonald's burgers, sodas, and fresh coffee. After handing the food out, he approached Russell and nudged him with his elbow. "Hey, remember that newspaper guy who got beaten up a couple months back? Smitty?"

"Yeah, what's up?" Russell looked past Carson and saw another diver arriving with his gear.

"Well, we found out yesterday that poor Smitty was roughed up because some bastard on his route thought he was having an affair with his wife. Smitty swore that it wasn't true, but his ribs were still broken. The jerk's going to spend some jail time. In the meantime, the idiot's wife filed for divorce."

"Glad to hear it. Glad one case is solved." He forced a smile, shook Carson's hand, and added, "Thanks for letting me know."

By two in the afternoon, divers were suited up and ready to try to reattach the Impala to the larger truck's chain, hook, and winch.

The sun was beginning to share some warmth, so Sherrill followed Russell to the edge of the water and watched them wade in knee deep before putting their masks and fins on. A chill came over her when they disappeared under the choppy waves.

It seemed like forever, but within minutes, two heads bobbed up and relayed signals that the car was ready to be hauled out. This time, it went smoother. The tow truck guided the car around the end of the fallen pier and dragged it through the mud and over the broken shells of the bay.

Sherrill gasped as soon as she saw the silver color. "No, oh, please, no!"

Chapter 22

The Mad Cat was dimly lit. Keno sat quietly at a back table. *Maybe Dunne won't show up, but I gotta talk to him, the son of a bitch. A mooch too. Eats everything in the fridge. Never buys nothing.*

As if he had been called up by the negative thinking, Dunne sat opposite Keno.

"They pulled it out. They got it. They'll—"

"Shut up. They'll find nothing," Dunne whispered.

"You're not the one who drove it the last hundred miles. You're not the one they'll—"

"I said shut the fuck up! Someone'll hear you. You want someone to testify against you?"

"Testify? I didn't do nothing but drive the car. You, you must've—" Keno didn't want to say what he thought Dunne had done, but he was pretty sure that Dunne had killed somebody to get a car like that. "I'm leaving town."

"You want to leave? Good. Go grab a small bag. Don't get much besides your toothbrush." Dunne smiled at Keno. "We're leaving the state. We're flyin'. Hey, grab my stuff that's at your place, too."

"Flying? How? I ain't got no dough."

"I'm treating," Dunne said and patted his shirt pocket.

"Where we going?" Keno looked at his watch; it was nearing noon.

Dunne stared across the dimly lit bar at two posters on the far wall. One showed the Rockies, snow covered and brilliant. The other had scenes of sandy beaches, palm trees, and hula skirts. "I've been thinking about Hawaii. This place is too damn cold. No one's friendly here."

"Hawaii? Damn, you mean leaving the state for real, don't you? Hey, they ain't got fog there, do they?"

"Hell, no."

"When do we leave?"

"In a couple of hours. We'll go to San Francisco and fly outta' there. Go get our stuff, and I'll meet you back at your place. Be ready."

"How we paying for it? I got no money."

"You're asking too many questions. Just go. See you in an hour." Dunne pulled out a ten dollar bill from his wallet. A credit card fell to the floor.

Keno bent over to pick it up. "Hey, man, this ain't yours."

"Shut up," Dunne hissed. Then confidently added, "Yes, it is. Look." Dunne pulled out a driver's license. The edges were frayed like the plastic had been pulled apart. The picture under the clear cover was Dunne's, but the name was not.

"Who's this?"

Dunne snatched the license away, stood up, and shoved his chair a bit too hard under the table. The noise got the bartender's attention.

"Need another round?"

"Naw, we're leavin'," Dunne said and threw another bill on the table. "This place is all yours." Dunne put his hand over his shirt pocket where the credit cards were. He'd had them for a while now and wanted to get more use out of them before reports were filed and the cards were cancelled. He had already pawned some jewelry, fenced the luggage, and ditched the car. He was ready to move. Oregon wasn't far enough away. "I'm ready to blow this town."

Chapter 23

"Mom, have you seen my green flannel shirt?" Jake yelled while tossing clean clothes from the basket Wanda had brought up from the basement laundry room.

"Where you going?"

"I got my job back."

"You what?" Wanda sat down and put her head in her hands.

"Yeah. My Probation Officer talked to my boss. He and I went there this morning while you were asleep and worked it out. Got my same hours—swing shift. Hey, you don't look so good."

"Yeah, I'm not feeling so good. Upset stomach. I'll be okay."

"What about your job? You get sick leave?"

"No. I called the diner and told the boss I'll make up my hours next week." Wanda smiled to herself. She and Jake argued a lot, but he was a good kid. Maybe he'd turn out all right after all. "Your shirt's in the closet. Pack a lunch if you need it."

Jake Corbin laughed. "Good golly, Mrs. Cleaver, you sound like my mom." He pulled off his dirty undershirt and dropped it on the couch. Spots of gray mud were hardened on the front and sleeve. As he pulled a clean one from the basket and headed to the closet, he heard his mom chuckle. "It's good to hear you happy again, Mom. It's been too long. And thanks for putting me up last night."

"Yeah, last night, the night before, twice last week, and for most of nineteen years of nights before that. Why aren't you at your own place?" she said, needling her son and glad he seemed ready to talk. So many times he wouldn't. Last night he had been in a sour mood. He had stormed back into her apartment, said he needed to sleep there, and crashed on the couch.

"Maggie's mad as hell again. Threw me out. Wanted me to make a score for her."

Wanda's good mood changed in a heartbeat. She sat upright and screamed, "No! You didn't! You said you're not using any more!"

Jake shook his head, "No. Not me."

"You can't." Wanda continued, ignoring his protests. Her face flushed, tears welled in her eyes. "Don't break probation. You gotta test every week." she said. Crying softly, she added, "It messed up your dad's life, killed him. Nearly wrecked mine. Not you, too."

"Don't worry, Mom," Jake said, taking her arm. "I'm not ending up like him. Sit down. You don't look so good." He helped her ease onto the couch. "I quit. Won't never start again, I promise."

Wanda took a deep breath and reached up to draw Jake close. She had always wanted to protect him, but he had grown up so fast.

Jake stepped back. "Don't overreact so much. Lay off me."

"You've got to get away from her. She's no good for you."

"She needs me."

"She'll drag you down."

"That won't happen." Jake stepped away and added, "I gotta go."

"Move back in with me for a while. It'll get you away from that tramp. It'll help us both out, and you can save something."

"Don't get on my case! I'm doing the best I can." He stood up and added, "And that girl, the tramp you call her, is going to make you a grandma soon."

"Oh, God, no! A drug baby? And you, you're too young!"

"I'm almost twenty. I can take care of myself and her and the kid. She'll change. She'll clean up."

"Like hell she will! She'll change when they find her cold body in some alley with a needle in her arm. You'll be stuck with a baby, a baby born to an addict. You just lay concrete when work's available or on call at the docks. Neither job pays enough to raise a family. You'll be stuck in a hell-hole like this the rest of your life." Wanda waved her arms around as she looked at the dingy apartment then wiped tears off her cheeks with the back of her hand.

"Lay off, Mom," Jake yelled. "I'll do all right." He grabbed the sandwich he had made, shoved it into a plastic, drug-store bag then into his jacket pocket, turned, and slammed the door behind him.

Wanda slowly looked around her one-bedroom apartment; her entire life was in that small space. Deep, heaving sobs dropped her to her knees. She picked up Jake's dirty tee shirt and wiped her face on it. The cement scratched her cheek, and she used the shirt to dab at the blood.

"Damn kid! Why won't he listen?" she said to the mirror by the door. She headed to the bathroom to wash up then stopped suddenly when she heard the door open an inch. *Thank God! He came back.* Wanda sniffed big, wiped her face again with the shirt, and reached for the door. "Jake, I'm sorry. ... Who are—?"

Chapter 24

Russell and Sherrill drove back to Eureka in silence. He knew it was time to stay quiet, that nothing he could say would make her feel any better. He knew she was feeling the same emptiness he had felt so long ago. "A hole in your heart as large as your fist—it's a hole that can never be healed," someone had told him back then. "Time passes," others told him, "so get over it." *Get over it! Hell, no. You can't. You shouldn't. If you loved someone, you should never get over it.*

"You'll get *through* this somehow," Russell finally whispered, half to himself, half to Sherrill. He put his hand on hers and pressed ever so slightly.

"How? Who? Why?" was all she could say.

"We don't know. Yet. You have to know that everything will be done to find the answers." He felt awkward. He had said things like this to dozens of other families over the years but never got used to it. Almost ten years ago someone had broken the news to him. He remembered the officer's eyes while he told him his fiancée's car had been found in northern Del Norte County. Traces of blood matching hers were on the front and back seats. He knew immediately he'd never see her again. He always thought of that other officer when he had to talk to someone about the most terrible loss that life throws at you. He felt sorry for that officer; he felt sorry for himself, and he felt sorry for the victims and for the families. "I understand," he said softly to Sherrill.

"You? You understand?" She let the tears fall freely but tried in vain to stop her nose from running. She had a wad of wet tissues in her hand. "You can't understand. You deal with this, this *shit* every day. You get used to it."

"You never get used to it. At least *I* don't. And, yes, I do understand." Russell pulled his hand away, suddenly feeling self-conscious

"The car. How did it get like that? How did it get there? Where's my brother?"

"You really want to talk about this now?"

"Yes! I want to know! I want the bastard caught. I'd like to shoot him myself."

"This probably isn't the right time to talk about—"

"When the hell is the right time?"

"I mean here in the car. Want to go to Elliott's and get some coffee? Dinner?"

"No." She wiped her cheeks and looked at the front of her blue silk blouse. Tears had left streaks. "I can't face anyone else right now. I want to go to—"

"Your hotel?"

"No. Yes. No. I don't know. I should call Mom and Dad." She took a deep breath. "What do I tell them? We still don't know anything."

"Just tell them what you *do* know." He paused for a moment. Eucalyptus trees bordering the bay flashed by. "You shouldn't be alone right now. Do you have a friend in town?"

"No. I don't know anyone here but you and Wanda, and I don't know her well enough to impose. Just take me back to the hotel; I'll be all right."

Russell stared at the road ahead then glanced at Sherrill. "Why not come to my place for a bit? It's not far."

"*Your* place?" The hesitation sat heavily in the air. Then her voice softened. "Not far?"

"Nothing's far in this town. I'll fix a pot of coffee and make sandwiches. You must be hungry. It'll all be on the up and up."

She gave a faint smile, but only for a second.

"I'm not leaving you alone for now." He passed her hotel and, pushing the speed limit, cut across two traffic lanes, and headed for home.

The house was dark. He usually left a light on if he knew he was getting home late. But when he had left this morning, he thought he'd be gone only a couple of hours. He fumbled for his key in the dark and finally turned the dead bolt. Opening the door, he felt something brush his leg. *No, not tonight!*

"Shane, get back here!" He knew there'd be another chase of the dog who liked to make a break for the street whenever he could. But tonight, the dog had other plans. Shane had found a different scent and immediately put his nose to befriending this new person.

"Shane, off!"

"No, it's all right." Sherrill wiped her cheek with her sleeve and squatted down to pet the fluffy, dark fur. "What a beautiful dog. What kind is … is HE?"

"Yes, a *he*, well *it* really. He's a Keeshound-Shepherd mix. They're very protective, well, at least *usually* protective. Off, Shane," he called as the dog tried to put his paw on her knees. "I'm sorry. I haven't trained him well. Now that he's getting old, there probably isn't much use."

"That's okay," Sherrill said and rubbed the dog's fur. His ears tickled her cheek when she put her face near his. She stood and followed Russell into the house; the dog stayed close to her. "Shane. That's a great name for a dog. Is that Shane as in *danke schön*, or as in *chein* for French dogs, or as in 'Come back, Shane'?"

"A bit of all of them. Someone else named him. She was a bit of a romantic."

"She?"

"Uh, yes. My fiancée." Russell paused for a moment, then added, "That's another story; it's why I understand what you're going through."

Sherrill looked at him quizzically then realized he was talking about something, or someone, lost in the past. "She's … she … oh, I'm sorry," she said softly.

He led her into the living room and moved old newspapers and magazines from the couch. "Here, have a seat. I'll fix some coffee."

"Not coffee. Do you have anything else?" Sherrill said.

"Coke? 7-Up? Water? Beer? Really, making a pot is no trouble."

"7-Up, please. No caffeine tonight."

He brought a glass of ice and the cold can. She glanced around then pulled a magazine over to use for a coaster. Russell chuckled.

"What's so funny?"

"I've never bothered taking care of the furniture in here. Didn't think it deserved it." He sat at the other end of the couch then immediately got up and left the room. He returned a moment later with a box of Kleenex. "Here, just in case."

"Thanks."

"Music?" Russell didn't know what to say or do. Sherrill shrugged, so he turned on some light jazz then sat in the recliner across from her.

"Hey, I probably shouldn't be here. I shouldn't put you through my personal problems." Sherrill glanced at the dog who had curled up on her feet. "Is he always this much of a guard dog?"

"I'm surprised. He doesn't usually take to strangers."

The phone rang and Russell left to answer it. He listened for a moment and said, "Yes, I know her." He pulled his hand over his face, and shook his head. "What? You sure? Sure it was her? … How the hell? … Neighbors found her—?" He mumbled a "thanks" to the caller and slammed the receiver down. *Damn, this is shit.* He picked up the entire telephone and paused; he thought for a moment about throwing it across the kitchen but stood for a full minute not moving. *Damn, damn, damn* kept repeating in his head. He firmly put the phone back on the counter, unplugged the cord from the wall, and shoved it against the backsplash. He wiped a tear from his cheek.

Taking a deep breath, he headed toward the living room but paused when he saw Shane comfortably settled. Russell said then glanced at his watch. *It's late. Dog's gotta be hungry.* He returned to the kitchen, filled the dog's food dish, and put fresh water in the other bowl.

Shane raised his head at the sounds but laid his head back on Sherrill's feet. She leaned over and tickled the dog's left ear.

"Is everything okay, Detective?" she asked.

"Yeah, be back in a second," Russell said and headed for the bathroom where he closed the door and turned on the hot water. He looked at himself in the mirror and grimaced. *Can't tell her now, not today. She's been through too much.* He wrung out a steaming washcloth and wiped his face then threw it into the tub as hard as he could. He shook some of the tension from his hands and arms, then splashed cold water on his face. The towel he used to dry with followed the washcloth into the tub. He glanced back into the mirror and saw a sullen face staring back at him. *Maybe she won't notice. Sure, right!*

"Looks like you've made a friend for life," Russell said sitting back down and trying to avoid eye contact. "Nothing ever came between him and food before. I've never seen him like this," *at least not in the last decade.* He remembered Shane as a puppy; he had been *her* dog. He would follow *her* around the house everywhere. She would go out; Shane would go out. She would jog; Shane trotted beside her. When she ate, Shane ate. When she sat down, Shane would curl up and place his head on her feet. Russell shook his head, bringing himself back to the present.

"I hate to talk business, but there are some things that need to be taken care of, soon. Come into the office tomorrow—"

"Tomorrow? It's Sunday."

"Oh, right. On Monday come in and give us a list of everything you remember that your brother had. Even the littlest things. Try to remember details, brand names, whatever."

"How will that help?"

"Yes, well, we'll check local pawn shops to see if anything of his has been sold—if someone's trying to raise some cash. We'll check around town, up and down the coast, and try to find any leads we can. I've made calls already, but had no specifics; time to make more calls. Someone out there knows something. We just have to find the right someone."

"How long does something like that take?" Sherrill asked. Shane was now resting his chin on her lap, and she was gently petting him.

"Hours, weeks, forever. Who knows?" Russell stopped breathing for a moment as he watched her eyes darken.

"Forever? I couldn't live if I never find out what happened."

Russell looked down at his dog and muttered, "You find a way to live without knowing." There was no reaction from Sherrill. *Maybe she didn't hear me.*

Chapter 25

Keno and Dunne left for San Francisco hours later than they had planned. They took turns driving Keno's old station wagon since neither could stay awake. They stopped frequently to trade places and take turns driving places and to relieve themselves in the bushes beside U.S. 101. They took a two-hour nap in a turnout near Laytonville. Dunne figured they were half-way and didn't want to chance falling asleep behind the wheel.

Light tapping on the window woke them both, and a bright beam of light blinded them.

A voice from behind the light said, "Open your window, please, sir."

"What? Who…" Dunne mumbled then pulled the lever to bring the seat back up and rolled the window down half way. All he could see was the light and khaki clothes.

"CHP. You okay?"

"Uh, yeah. Just getting some sleep. Been driving too long."

Keno was waking up and began sweating when he heard, "CHP."

"You haven't been drinking, have you?"

"No. Not since, uh, since two days ago." Dunne held his breath in case some boozy smell might be lingering.

"Have any drugs in your car?"

Dunne chuckled. *Why? Do you want some?* He bit his tongue and shook his head. "No, sir! Nothing."

"Okay. But it's not safe here. You should move farther back from the edge of the road. Get plenty of rest so you don't fall asleep driving," the officer advised.

"Of course, Officer," Keno said.

The officer returned to his cruiser, and Dunne put the window back up, releasing a long sigh.

"We gotta get outta here," Keno said. "Move it."

"No. We'll let the cop get a good lead. I don't want to chance running into him again." Dunne reclined the seat, crossed his arms, and closed his eyes.

Keno stared into the darkness surrounding the car. He couldn't stop the twitch in his legs.

Chapter 26

Russell took his mind off the phone call by switching through the TV channels. The teaser for the Channel 3 Late News started with, "A woman's body was found this afternoon, and a car, reportedly belonging to Jeffrey Madison, missing for more than two months, was recovered from Humboldt Bay. Details at—" He clicked off the television.

"Can I get you something to eat?" he asked.

"No. No, thanks. I don't know what I want right now. Just answers. I've got so many questions, I can't think straight."

"Questions like: where is your brother?"

"No, I know I'll never see him again, at least not alive." Sherrill took a deep breath. "My questions are more like: How could someone do this? How can I call our ... my parents and tell them?"

"I'm glad you didn't call them tonight," he said quietly. "It's late, much later on the east coast. Let them get one more night's sleep."

"Yes, yes. Of course," she said, relieved to hear a logical excuse not to call. She wiped her eyes again and took a drink of the soda. "Which way to the bathroom?"

"Down the hall, first door to the left." Shane pulled himself up and followed her. He sat by the door with his ears searching for sounds.

While she was gone, Russell picked up the empty cans and went to the kitchen. He pluged the phone back in and called dispatch. "The report is accurate? ...Yes, that one. ... Damn! Any idea of who might've ... Who? Any suspect? ... What? No. You sure? ... Thanks." He hung up, grabbed a can of vegetable beef soup from the cupboard and the can opener from the drawer. He rattled pans around until he found a small one and started heating the can's contents on the gas range. He found some French bread in the freezer. He had finished buttering it and putting it into the microwave when Sherrill came around the corner. She looked slightly better.

"Jeffrey and I spent most of our last night together in the kitchen," she said. She looked around at the pine cabinets and blue-tile counter top. "Yours is cozier. Mine is sterile, modern."

"This old place needs some serious remodeling. Been planning on doing it for quite a while."

"No, don't touch it. It's warm, friendly."

Russell looked at her. *No changes? No suggestions?* She looked tired. "Hungry?" He poured soup into two bowls and retrieved the warm bread. He saw that Shane was finally eating his dinner.

Sherrill ate half of her soup and nibbled at the bread. "I'm sorry. I can't eat. No appetite." She got up from the table and walked to the sofa with Shane only a step or two behind.

Russell rinsed the pan and bowls, put them into the dishwasher, and set up the coffee maker before returning to the living room. Sherrill had picked up the pillow his mom had made, tucked it under her neck, and leaned back on the couch. Her eyes were beginning to close. She sat up suddenly when Russell entered the room. "Oh! I'm sorry."

"No, that's all right. Please. Just relax. You deserve it. I'll take you back to your hotel any time you want."

"In a few minutes. It feels so good to sit, nothing to do—" her words trailed off; her eyes fluttered, then closed.

Russell sat across from her. Black hair fell gently across her shoulders, her face finally relaxing. He went to wake her up but stopped. He looked at her, shook his head, and quietly went to the hall closet. He pulled out a quilt from the top shelf. She barely moved as he nudged Shane out of the way and covered her with the blanket.

He straightened up and looked at her. For the moment she was no longer just a victim's sister, an irate citizen angry at the system, mad at God and humanity for the loss of her brother. He saw a beautiful young woman, a loving sister, a worried daughter.

"Come on, Shane," he whispered. "Shane. Shane!" He gave the dog a nudge. "You've got to go out."

The dog pulled himself up, stretched, followed Russell into the kitchen, and went out the doggie door. He returned a moment later.

Russell locked up then and gave Shane a good rubbing on his neck and back. "You like her, don't you, boy? Come on, let's go to bed." Russell headed for his bedroom, but the dog went straight for the sofa, gave Sherrill a quick sniff, and curled up on the floor beside her.

Exactly like ten years ago—Shane's always preferred women. Russell took one last look at the dog and shook his head. *I've been replaced,* he thought and headed down the hall, turning off the lights as he went.

Not only that, I'm stupid. What the hell am I doing letting her stay here? He glanced back at the couch. He shrugged then yawned. *Too late to take her to her hotel now,* he decided. Besides, the bedroom was only steps away.

Chapter 27

Sunday morning

The rising sun was barely breaking through the coastal fog when Dunne and Keno pulled into the parking garage at San Francisco International Airport. Dunne parked far from the entrance.

"Why you sweating so much?" Keno asked while they were standing in line to buy the airline tickets.

"Shaddup," he responded. "Keep her attention on *your* license, not mine," he said as he jerked his head toward the clerk behind the Pan Am Airline's counter.

Dunne handed over a credit card but hung onto his driver's license. Keno kept her busy with his, talking about his picture that still showed him with more hair and with less gray.

The clerk turned toward Dunne and asked, "Excuse me, sir. Are you feeling all right? You look pale."

"Yeah. Flying scares the shit outta' me. Get sick sometimes too."

"Well, our airline is safe. Accident free. You'll be fine," she said then added, "Your ID please."

Dunne held it out, covering most of the height, weight, and hair color details with his thumb, while the clerk noted that the name matched the credit card information.

"Thank you, sir," she said as she jotted numbers on the tickets and handed them to him. "Have a nice flight."

Chapter 28

Russell woke to the smell of coffee and the sound of dishes clinking in the kitchen. His mind slipped back ten years. *She* was in the doorway, holding a tray with a cup of coffee, glass of orange juice, and pancakes. With his eyes still closed, he could imagine *her* coming closer, smiling. He wanted *her*, reached for *her*, but *she* wasn't there. He opened his eyes and still smelled the coffee then remembered yesterday and last night. *Sherrill. It must be Sherrill in the kitchen.* He climbed into his sweatpants, grabbed a sweatshirt off the end of the bed, and headed to the kitchen.

"Good morning!" he called out as a warning that he was approaching.

"I let Shane out. Hope that's okay," Sherrill said. "I found your coffee maker ready and thought I'd start the day off. By the way, your back door sticks." Sherrill caught the look of amazement on Russ's face. "You forgot I was here?"

"No, uh, no. It's just that ... I'm not used to someone ... anyone—" He ran his hand through his hair, trying to smooth it. "Not that I mind," he added.

Shane nosed open the doggie door and came back into the kitchen. Sherrill knelt down, greeted him face to face, and scratched him behind his ears.

"You're feeling better?" Russell asked. "Are you doing all right?"

"Yes ... No!" Sherrill answered, surprised by the sincerity in his voice. "I'm trying not to feel anything right now. I hope you don't mind, but I used your phone and called my parents."

"How'd they take the news about the car?"

"Like you'd expect. Dad's mad as hell and Mom's a basket case."

"Well, at least you got through that all right. Right?"

"Almost." Sherrill took a deep breath and exhaled slowly. "Sorry about crashing on your sofa," she said. "Want a cup?" she asked picking up the pot. She poured the black morning-starter into a hand-decorated mug. "Why's this say 'World's Greatest Uncle'?"

"My nephews. We goof around once in a while."

"Hmmm. You're an uncle, huh? Listen, about last night. I'm really sorry I fell asleep out there. I didn't mean to be a bother."

"No problem. I mean it. I'm sorry I didn't get you back to your hotel. I ... uh—"

"Hey, it's okay. Your reputation is safe with me," Sherrill said then smiled. "I won't tell anyone."

"Thanks," Russell said while heading toward the front door.

He found the Sunday paper on the porch, just as it should be. *I guess Smitty's back. Thank God. Bastards are everywhere, doing each other in.* Russell paused on the porch and looked down the block. The neat houses of the neighborhood covered the truth that he saw every day: *Nothing but crime everywhere. Damn shame.*

The sun was up, the air was crisp. There was a bit of frost on the windshield of his car since the clouds that had brought so much gray and desolation over the last few days were gone. A few wisps of white clouds touched the sky. *If it weren't for crime, I'd be out of a job. But, hey, that might be all right.*

Russell heard the laughter of his neighbor's children as they clamored into their mini-van for a Sunday trip. He waved to them as they closed the car doors and started backing down the driveway. The kids made faces at each other, then at him. He returned his ugliest grimace he could muster this early.

He stretched, tugged at the rubber band on the newspaper, and went back inside. He noticed that Sherrill had folded the blanket. The sounds from the kitchen were new but familiar and comfortable at the same time. He smiled to himself even though he knew the feeling was superficial. The reality of the day was going to hit as soon as he walked into the kitchen. Sherrill would have to deal with her personal loss, the car, her parents, and still not knowing for sure what had actually happened to her brother.

Russell opened the newspaper, and a picture of Wanda stared back at him. He immediately refolded it and tossed it on the table, far from Sherrill. He took a deep breath and said, "Hey, let's go get something to eat, my treat."

"I don't know. I haven't showered, and I feel kinda' grubby."

"You look great. Better'n I do, by a long shot."

"Where? Elliott's?"

Russell paused.

"No, let's try someplace different. There's a new restaurant on Broadway." He pulled his jacket and her coat out of the closet, checked for his keys and wallet, and said, "Let's go."

Chapter 29

Dunne was relieved. Getting the airline tickets had worked out. The ticket agent had held onto the credit card long enough to make him nervous, but his lies covered her questions. "Pre-flight apprehension" or some other shitty remark from the clerk made him snicker. Dunne paid for both tickets with the kid's credit card and did his best to disguise his signature, but the clerk didn't pay much attention to it.

The flight was uneventful and, except for the occasional use of the cramped toilets and cursing at his inability to turn around, Dunne slept most of the way to Hawaii.

The plane landed at the Honolulu Airport in bright sunlight. Dunne and Keno ignored the ads for Don Ho playing at Duke's that were posted on the walls. The humidity was heavy, and a few clouds lay on the horizon. Dunne and Keno had gained three hours so it was still morning. A crowded bus ride through heavy freeway traffic took them to the center of Honolulu where they walked from hotel to hotel trying to find a room. The Hilton, the Sheraton, and other beach-front hotels were booked.

"Shit. Now what?" said Keno, walking fast to keep up with the taller Dunne.

"What's your problem? We've only tried five. There'll be a room. And not so many stupid tourists."

They walked past glitzy stores filled with luxury items and tourist shops with T-shirt racks on the sidewalk. Traffic bustled by as the two turned up Lanai Street.

Keno shrugged. "We could always camp out."

"Hell, no. This is a vacation."

They passed open-air restaurants, some with thatched roofs and pillars covered with palm branches. Rattan chairs and bamboo tables were scattered under the patio covers.

"I'm starving. Let's eat." Keno turned into the next opening that offered an empty table. Dunne grumbled but followed him. Within moments, a tall, striking blonde arrived at their table with menus and water.

"Hi, I'm Rose. I'll be back in a second for your orders," she said between chews of her gum. Her Hawaiian print blouse hung loosely over her large breasts.

She ain't wearin' a bra, Dunne realized. A bright piece of green, leaf-print fabric was tied around her waist for a skirt. It hung opened and swayed when she walked, exposing her legs nearly to her hips. Dunne stared, watching the gentle movement of her body. He elbowed Keno and whispered, "Look at her. She's hot."

Chapter 30

Two men entered the dingy apartment building on F Street. One was dressed in a Eureka City Police Department uniform, the other in street clothes. A third officer, in uniform, was at the back door in case the suspect bolted. Half the lights in the hallway were burned out. At least one of the fixtures was completely missing on the second floor, and wires dangled from the wall. The unmistakable smell of urine hung in the air. Burger and taco wrappers littered the hall; spider or dust webs hung from the ceiling. An empty beer bottle was in the corner.

"301. This is it. Ready?" the casually dressed man asked the officer behind him.

"Yes, sir."

"Good. Stand back." The plain-clothed officer tapped lightly on the door and stood aside. No response.

The officer paused then knocked again, harder. From inside, they could hear something stirring.

Jake vaguely heard something and rolled over, still tired from working all night. The docks had been cold, and his muscles ached from moving so many cases around the wharf.

"You expecting anyone?" he asked the sleeping female beside him. She mumbled something. He hauled himself out of the bed, tripped over his boots, stumbled to the door, and opened it an inch.

"Jake Corbin?"

"Yeah."

"Were you at your mother's place last night?"

"Maybe. So? Who wants to know?"

The officers identified themselves then asked, "Can we come in?"

"What the hell for?"

"To talk. We need to talk."

"What about? I'm clean." Jake knew his place could be searched any time while he was on probation but didn't want to make it too easy for them.

"About why you did it."

"Did what?" Jake gripped the doorknob and braced his bare foot at the bottom.

"Your mom's neighbors heard you two arguing yesterday. Day before, too. They called 9-1-1 after your fight last night."

"Yeah? So? We always argue. Never for long, though. What's goin' on?"

"We're coming in." The officer shoved the door hard.

Jake yelled as his foot was pinched between the floor and the door edge. He fell to the floor and rolled out of the way.

"You're under arrest for the murder of Wanda Corbin," the second officer said as the two pushed their way into the room and pulled Jake to his feet. He stood on one foot; his left foot ached too much to put weight on it.

"For what? Mom? Dead?" he said. "What? No!"

The officer took advantage of Jake's loss of balance and turned him around, cuffing one wrist quickly, then the other.

The second officer had entered the room behind the first, gun drawn.

"Bet you've heard this before," the first officer said while he turned Jake back around. "'You have the right to remain silent. Anything you say can *and will* be used against you in a court of law. You have the right to talk to an attorney and have him present with you while you are being questioned—'"

"No! It can't be. She was okay when I left. I swear! Maggie!" he called over his shoulder, "Wake up! Get me an attorney. Maggie!"

After finishing the Miranda Warning, the officer spoke into his radio.

The third officer had heard the commotion upstairs and intently watched the rear, second-story window until he was sure no one was going to climb out and try to escape.

The radio came to life and the "all clear; suspect in custody" came over the air. He shrugged and went around to the front of the building.

Jake had been allowed to dress in sweats and to shove his feet into shoes before being led down the stairs. He tried to wipe a tear away with his shoulder but couldn't quite get it. "You're wrong. She can't be ... I didn't—," he protested as the third officer opened the back door of the patrol car and pushed him inside.

Chapter 31

Sherrill and Russell finished their breakfast of a hot and tasty selection of sausages, pancakes, and juice. As the waiter added fresh coffee to their cups, Russell squirmed in his chair. He knew he had to tell Sherrill about Wanda but wanted time. *Time. It could end in an instant, at any second. For any of us.*

"Excuse me," Russell said and stood up.

"Sure," Sherrill said while tearing open a packet of Sweet 'n Low and pouring it into her coffee.

Russell left the table but paused before he got to the restroom door and dropped coins into the slots of the telephone. The desk sergeant answered quickly and confirmed the report from yesterday. "In fact," the sergeant told him, "Corbin's son, Jake, was brought in this morning."

Russell ran his free hand through his hair. "Hey, is Captain Reardon working this weekend?"

"Yep, just came in."

"How's his mood today?"

"What do you think? Weekend ruined. Still trying to quit smoking. Foul."

Russell sighed. "Transfer me anyway, please." A moment later, Russell jumped right to the point. "I want the Wanda Corbin case."

"You know her, right?"

"Yeah."

"You know her son, too, correct?"

"Yes. I want to make sure this gets handled right."

"You're too personally involved, too close. Can't let you do it."

"But—"

"No buts. You're not getting this case. You've got your hands full with the Madison situation. Let me know Monday how that's going—first thing."

"I know her habits; I'd be the—" Russell realized he was talking to a dial tone. He shook his head, hung up, and returned to the table.

Russell sat down and asked, "What are your plans for today?" He realized it was a stupid question as soon as he asked it.

"No plans. I don't know what to do besides go back to Ukiah and get back to work. I'm glad I already called Mom and Dad. I was afraid they'd hear something on the news first."

"They're three thousand miles away. It won't hit the national news from here," he said and helped her with her chair when she began to stand up.

"Let me know what I owe you for the phone call."

"Don't worry about it. I'll cover it."

"Why are you doing this? Do you show this much attention to ... to every victim's family?"

"I don't know exactly." Then Russell smiled. "It was something Shane told me."

Sherrill looked at him. "Your dog talks?"

"Never mind." Russell looked away before saying, "We've got to talk. Something's happened." He pulled out his car keys, unlocked the passenger door, and opened it for her.

"Something more? Like what?" She slid into the seat.

"Yes. Well. Um. It's ... uh. It's Wanda. She's dead."

"Wanda?" Sherrill stood back up and stared at Russell.

"Yes, Wanda Corbin, the waitress. Um, her son is ... well, it looks like her son killed her."

"No!" Sherrill's voice went an octave higher. "No, not Wanda!" She took a deep breath and let it out slowly. After nearly a minute, she continued, "And not her son."

"Well, that's what it looks like. Her neighbor heard a fight and saw him storm out the night she ... she, uh, she was killed."

"What's going on in this town? What is causing this, this rash of—?" Sherrill pulled her coat more tightly around her.

"Killings? Crime in general? We usually only have a handful of murders every year. Two so close together?" Russell paused. "In the last decade or two, drugs have taken hold of so many people. It drives them to do things they wouldn't usually do. Desperation. Addiction. Stupid thinking. Bad decisions. Bad people. Previously good people doing dumb, bad things."

Sherrill looked down and wrapped her arms around herself. "She was nice. I really liked her. And you knew her pretty well, didn't you?" She slid back into the passenger seat and closed the door.

Russell walked around the car and climbed into the car. "I've known her for more than ten years. She worked at Elliott's since, well forever. She seemed to take me on as her charity case—" He slammed the car door closed. "—thought I needed a mother, I guess, and we became friends." He took a deep breath. "So you met Jake, too?" He pulled out of the restaurant's parking lot and turned onto Broadway, heading toward her hotel.

"Once," Sherrill said. "He came into Elliott's when I was there, plus she talked about him—a lot. She said he'd been a handful, in and out of trouble. I think he took the GED. He seemed pretty settled when I met him."

"What did you think of him?" Russell tried not to sound like a detective interrogating a witness so he paused before he asked, "Did Wanda say anything about problems?"

"No. He was nice, polite. She did say that he registered at the junior college for classes next semester."

"That's an improvement. I heard some of his stories."

"He didn't seem like someone who would do anything to her, not hurt his mother." Sherrill took a breath. "Have you talked to him yet?"

"No, it's not my case. I probably won't have anything to do with him."

"We should go see him; you've known him for a long time. We could probably tell if he's telling the truth."

"We?" Russell asked.

Sherrill shrugged, "I'm pretty good at reading people."

"I thought you needed to drive back to Ukiah, get back to work."

"Yes, well, I do need to get started." She looked out the window, focusing on nothing in particular. "Maybe I shouldn't push it right now. I'll go back and talk to the principal tomorrow and come back up Tuesday." Sherrill was talking softly, almost to herself. Russell could barely hear her. "I'll sign up to substitute up here and get an apartment," she mumbled.

"Are you sure you're all right?"

"Uh. Oh, yes. Sorry. My mind. It's—" She continued to stare out the window.

"It's trying to comprehend the incomprehensible."

"Yes. It's the pits. Too much. I guess I really should be going. It's a three-hour drive, and I'll be doing it twice in the next few days."

"You're coming right back?"

"Yes," she said, still a bit distracted. "I've got to see what I can do up here. This seems to be the last place my brother was. There must be some answers here." Almost to the hotel, Sherrill said, "My car's not at my hotel. I left it at Elliott's. Remember?"

"Oh, right." The drive back to Elliott's Diner's parking lot took them past the courthouse.

"That's where he is?" Sherrill asked, pointing at the top floor of the building.

"Who?"

"Jake. Wanda's son. That's the jail, right? I can't get him out of my mind. I remember Wanda said something about his girlfriend being a loser, a junkie, I think." She looked out the window at the five-story structure, probably the tallest building in town. "Let's stop. An extra hour won't make that much of a difference. Besides, it'll take my mind off … off—"

"Off all the shit that's happened?"

"Not the word I'd select, but that's the idea."

"You sure you want to go into a jail? Have you ever been in one—ever?" Russell let his car idle in the diner's parking lot while they talked.

"No. It's not a place where I'd want to spend much time, but I think I'm right about him."

"I don't think you want to—" Russell realized what he said and added, "I mean, I don't think it's a good idea."

"Are you trying to tell me what I want to do, or are you trying to protect me?" Sherrill looked at him. "I don't need protection, and I want to get my mind on someone else for a while. If I can be a little help, then I'll do it. Besides, if anyone can help, it's you."

"So now you're telling me what *I* can do?"

"Well, yes." Sherrill laughed and relaxed a little when Russell chuckled too. "You can get in there, and me, too—just for a minute," Sherrill added.

"It'll be more than a minute," he said. "Trust me, nothing in the courthouse takes 'just a minute.' You'll see." He shifted into drive and headed back toward the courthouse's parking area.

Chapter 32

Dunne watched the waitress walk away, her hips swaying and her long blonde hair moving with each step. Keno, pushing his glasses back up his nose, watched Dunne. The best response Keno could manage at this stage of exhaustion was a yawn, "Yeah, sure. Sure she's hot," he said and slowly nodded his head.

Rose, the waitress, returned minutes later. "Hi, what'll it be, Sweetie?" She smiled and winked at Dunne. "I recommend something with teriyaki—a burger or steak. How about it?" She smiled and flipped her head sending her hair behind her shoulder.

Keno rolled his eyes.

The service was good, the teriyaki burgers delicious, the beer cold, and Rose enticing. Dunne watched her every move. Keno could not distract him and ordered another beer.

"Say, Rose, do you know any place that will have a room available at short notice?" Dunne asked when she brought them their tab.

"You came without a place to stay? That's gutsy ... or stupid. You've tried the hotels around here?"

"Yeah, but they're full. I'm, we're looking for a place to crash," he added to keep Keno from mentioning camping again.

"There's a small hotel about a mile up Beretania Street and right on Punchbowl—the Wailea. It's nothing fancy, but it's affordable. And, it's got showers," she added with another wink.

The directions sounded easy to follow, so the two picked up their backpack and duffle bag and headed up the street.

"How come you didn't rent a car? It's hot here." Keno paused and pushed his glasses back up the bridge of his nose. "And the humidity is heavy. Can't you afford a car?"

"Shaddup. You're whining. Didn't want no record of getting a car. The walk'll do you good."

The light breeze was warm, and the sweet-scented air gently swayed the palm trees. Keno and Dunne stopped at a tourist shop and each bought shorts, T-shirts, sandals, and a couple of six-packs of Budweiser. Dunne smirked when the clerk glanced at the credit card signature and the phony ID but didn't question either one.

The two men were able to get a room with twin beds at the Wailea. *So far, so good on these credit cards,* Dunne thought as he signed the register J. Madison. The tired clerk didn't mention identification. The two tourists tossed their purchases into the dresser drawers while downing a couple of beers. The moment they hit their pillows they were asleep. The showers would wait.

Chapter 33

Russell locked Sherrill's brown leather purse in the trunk then reopened it when he remembered she would have to have her driver's license to get in, and out, of the jail. He led her to the third floor where they had met all those weeks ago. He opened the bottom drawer of his desk and secured his hand-gun.

On the elevator, Sherrill noticed that there was no button or number for the fourth floor; the numbers skipped from three to five.

The doors opened on the fifth floor, dim with only one small, narrow window, maybe six inches by two feet. A deputy was silhouetted behind a small desk.

"Hi, Detective." The young officer smiled broadly at the two visitors. "What are you doing here?"

"We came to see the Corbin kid. Which section is he in?"

"B. 211."

"Get him out for me, will you?"

"Sure. IDs first, though."

The uniformed officer checked their IDs and had them sign the visitors' log book. He asked about weapons and pagers while he made a few notes of the time and whom they were visiting. After filling out an orange index card, he reached across his desk and pushed the intercom button. "First door," he said and handed the card to Sherrill.

Almost immediately the heavy metal door across the room slid open, directed by someone unseen. They walked into an area about the size of an elevator and the first door slid closed. It felt like an airlock, separating the good air from the bad so no pollutants would escape.

Another officer was on the other side of a thick glass window. "Passes?" he said into his intercom.

"Hold your driver's license up with your visitor's pass," Russell said quietly and held out his badge.

Sherrill held both items up to the window. The officer nodded, pushed a button, and the second door opened into a sterile concrete and steel room. They stepped onto a solid concrete platform high above the floor of the jail. Gray concrete block walls, concrete floors, and high concrete ceiling surrounded them. Eight stainless steel tables were scattered around the floor one flight of stairs below. Each shiny table was octagonal; four round stainless steel seats protruded from the base. Two men in orange jumpsuits sat at a far table playing dominoes. A television set was attached to a large, secure bracket high on the wall far from anyone's reach. A college football game was on and the sound was turned too low to hear. Two cameras, in opposite upper corners of the room, were aimed across the vast area.

A steel stairway was directly in front of them. Immediately to her right, Sherrill saw a wall made almost entirely of thick glass. Through it, she could see a green glow of two flickering television monitors.

Sherrill whispered, "This is pretty elaborate for a county jail."

"Well, we're the only human-storage-facility for a couple hundred miles. They've been renovating this old building for a few years; they started here in the jail section." *And they start on our offices in a few months*, he thought to himself and shuddered. "It's designed like the newer prisons. Some of these guys stay here for a year—prisons keep 'em longer than that. Those cameras," he added, pointing at them, "record everything that goes on in here," Russell said quietly.

An officer approached a table in the glass-walled room, punched one of the many buttons, and called out, "Corbin, 211. You have visitors." He pushed another button, and the cell's door began to clatter open, then stopped with a clang when it was opened six inches.

Sherrill looked at Russell and asked, "Why'd they open it so little?"

"Safety. Just in case it's the wrong door. Controls the movement in here."

"Oh, okay," Sherrill said slowly. She stepped toward the stairs then suddenly pulled back and grabbed the rail. She looked through the grillwork to the floor far below. "The stairs. They're mesh!"

"Yes. They don't want anyone hiding anywhere in here. Everything is as open as possible—visibility. Don't worry. They're safe. Steel. They'll support a couple hundred pounds." He smiled. "At least."

She cautiously took the first step, glad she had not worn a skirt or heels today, then continued down. Russell was right behind her, the metallic sounds of each step echoing in their ears. The waxed concrete floor was shiny, adding to the sterile setting. Across from them was a row of doors only a few feet apart. Another set of stairs of the same type of grill work rose to a second tier with another row of more cell doors. Sherrill quickly did the math; two tiers of cells, and two men per cell—potentially a hundred men, all criminals, or at least suspected criminals, crammed into the space of a high school gymnasium. She shuddered.

Chapter 34

Keno sat on the edge of the bed and tried to stop his leg from twitching. He stared for a full minute at the picture over the headboard of the peaceful sunset over the white sandy beach. Then he grabbed the pillow and wiped his shaking hands dry. He and Dunne had slept late then talked for several minutes after they had woken up. Dunne was in the bathroom.

What Dunne told him didn't surprise Keno. *I should'a known what he's been doing—didn't want to believe it. Now I'm in the middle of it. Shit! How many did he say he's killed? Why'd I ask? Why'd I come with him? He killed Wanda, and I kinda' liked her. And what'd he mean, it was either Wanda or me? I told him I told her nothin'. How long before it is me?* Keno glanced at the bathroom door. *Thank God he's ignoring me,* he thought then buried his face in the pillow and wiped the sweat from his forehead. That conversation had been revealing, too revealing.

"Where d'ya think that car came from?" Dunne had asked him. "Where do you think I got the money and the credit cards? I sold this kid's jewelry, pawned his shit. And you? You're an accessory. You're in this as deep as I am. Aiding and abetting and all that shit." Dunne had laughed as he combed his hair just so and straightened his collar.

The toilet flushed and the bathroom door open. Keno sat quietly and didn't move—except his hands were shaking, and his foot wouldn't stop tapping. His glasses slipped down his nose. Dunne stepped back into the bedroom.

"You mean you—," Keno mumbled and pushed his glasses back into place.

"Don't sweat it. They'll never find the bodies. At least not the two up north."

"*Two* up north? *Plus* Wanda's? What'd you do with hers?"

"Nothing. She won't even be missed until next week when she don't show up for work. I didn't leave no clues. And we're long gone."

When Keno heard "we," his left eye developed a tic. "What about this Rose here? You got plans for her, too?" He took his glasses off and stuck them into his shirt pocket and drained the last of the warm beer in his can.

"Plans? I never plan. If she's as good as she looks, I'll hang with her a while. Hawaii's cool. I've always liked it here."

"You been here before."

"Yeah, as a kid. Lived here with my mom for a while."

Keno stared at the floor and shook his head then got up, went into the bathroom, and splashed cold water on his face. The sweat was gone, but his hands were still shaking. He couldn't believe Dunne had told him. He had been with Dunne on and off for a couple of months now and knew him years ago—*I never had a clue*.

"Did this just start? And what'd you mean, 'the *two* up north'?" Keno asked from the bathroom door. "Were there others before?"

"Before when?" Dunne asked and let out a hearty laugh.

Chapter 35

Sherrill looked up to the bold 211 on the door and saw a young black man stick his head out. He looked directly across the room at the officer standing behind a glass wall.

"What's up?" the inmate yelled.

"You Corbin?" the officer asked.

The man shook his head and disappeared back inside the cell, quickly replaced by Jake Corbin.

"I'm Corbin. What the hell's up?"

Russell called up to him, "Good day to you, too! Come on down; let's talk."

"Do I know you?" Jake said as the cell door slid open then closed quickly behind him.

"We've met; come on down."

Jake hesitated, then mumbled, "What the hell," and started down the stairs. He had on the same color of jumpsuit as the other men in the cellblock. The thin flip-flops made a slapping sound with each step.

"They don't let them have shoes, belts, or much of anything for a few days in here. No shoelaces, either," Russell said quietly to Sherrill.

"Why not—?" then paused when she realized that it was to prevent suicides. "Oh. This can get depressing, can't it?"

"And violent," Russell added.

"Hey, I *do* know you," Jake said to Det. Hurley. "You know, uh, knew my mom. And you?" he said looking closely at Sherrill. "You were at Elliott's."

Sherrill studied the young man. His shoulders were hunched, his dark hair, the same reddish color as Wanda's, was mussed. He looked completely drained, defeated, and scared—unlike the two men sitting at the far table. They continued to play dominoes, slamming their tiles on the table.

Russell motioned for Jake to sit at the table at the opposite end of the room from the men. Sherrill sat across from him and Russell remained standing. He paced back and forth behind Sherrill and kept his hands out of his pockets.

"So, you remember me," Sherrill said. "I'm glad. Your mom was nice to me. She talked about you at the restaurant, shared your recent accomplishments."

"So?" Jake replied. "So why the hell are you here? You bringing her back or something?"

"Drop the attitude," Russell snapped. "This woman might be the only one who thinks you didn't kill her, didn't have anything to do with … with your mom's death."

Jake looked down and grunted.

"Did you do it?" Sherrill asked.

"No. And hell, no!" Jake said and looked at Russell. He straightened his shoulders and sat taller. "Probably shouldn't talk to you without an attorney here."

"You want one here?" Russell asked.

"Only need one if I'm guilty, and I'm not. So no." He ran his fingers through his hair and wiped his face with both hands. "Just want my mom back."

Sherrill and Russell asked about his relationship with his mother, where he was the night she died, what he had done, where he had gone. They discussed what his plans were, how he had been living the last couple of years, about his girlfriend's addiction problem, the fact that he was approaching fatherhood, his previous drug use, how Wanda had felt about all that, how she had helped. Jake started to relax. More information came freely, and he talked lovingly of his mother. He had not been the perfect child; she wasn't always the perfect parent, but both obviously cared for each other.

"What happens next?" Jake asked.

Chapter 36

"You know, before-before," Keno said to Dunne. "Years ago when we hung out together, before you were sent up to Folsom. Were you killing people then, too?"

"You know I was," Dunne said. "You were with me when I picked up that girl after the fair."

"You didn't pick her up. She ran out of gas, and you almost hauled her into your car. Said you was giving her a ride to the gas station where I used the bathroom. You was gone when I came out. Had to walk home." Keno shook his head. *This is too much. I thought I knew this shithead!*

"Yeah, that's right. I remember. You chickened out. As soon as you headed for the john, I filled up the gas can, and we took off. Left my car and got into hers. She kept saying her boyfriend was expecting her. Fuck him. Fuck her. She didn't like my game."

Keno stood at the bathroom door and stared at Dunne.

"I got you by the balls, don't I?" Dunne laughed again. "You've been part of my fun from the beginning ... and you didn't even know it. What a dumb shit." He flopped onto the bed and kept laughing.

Sweat rolled down Keno's forehead. *I should take him out. Yeah, that's what I should do. Whack him. I'll get a gun and—use a knife and get him while he's sleepin'. No, he'd get me first. I'd be dead for sure. Why'd I come with him?* He clasped his hands first behind his back, then decided he didn't like to feel defenseless and swung his arms to the front. *I gotta get outta here.* He looked at Dunne still laughing on the bed. *Has he really killed, what? three people already? I'm probably next! I ain't worth shit right now. I gotta go.*

In a few steps, Keno was at the door. "Have your fun with Rose." Keno fought to keep his voice calm. He didn't want to give Dunne the opportunity to tell him any more. *There might be others, and I don't want to know.* "See you later," he said and grabbed the doorknob.

Chapter 37

Russell cleared his throat and said, "Well, Jake, you'll be visited by a Public Defender. I assume you can't afford an attorney. He ... or she will explain what's going to happen."

"This is shit!" Jake interrupted.

"I recommend that you cooperate. If you really didn't do it, you need to get everything out and convince them to keep looking for someone else."

Jake grunted, "Sure. You bet."

"Sarcasm won't get it." Russell was through; he tapped Sherrill on the shoulder and motioned with his head that it was time to leave.

Sherrill stood and held out her hand. Russell reached for her elbow but pulled back. Jake took her hand and shook it firmly.

"You need to listen to him," Sherrill said. She glanced at Russell and noticed the perturbed look on his face. "What?"

Russell glanced at her hand then back at her. She let her arm drop to her side. Jake headed back up the stairs as his cell door slid open.

As Sherrill and Russell headed toward the exit, Sherrill asked, "What?"

"You should not have touched him. He could have—"

"What? Taken me hostage? He ... uh ... oh."

"Yes, he could have."

Chapter 38

Keno heard Dunne laughing at him and the phone was ringing as he closed the door behind him. *Bet it's Rose—tracked him down. Probably Dunne's next victim ... just as long as it ain't me.*

Keno only had what was in his pockets: a few dollars, some coins, a comb, and the room key. He wandered aimlessly around the tropical paradise, slowly realizing he had left without his return airplane ticket. He turned and took two steps back in the direction of the motel then stopped cold. He knew he'd have to face Dunne again but wasn't ready.

Keno walked through downtown Honolulu, bought a couple of cans of Coors and sat on the beach drinking them. Back at the motel, he walked around the block dozens of times and kept looking at the room he shared with Dunne. *Wonder if he's there. What's he going to do if I go back in?* He stubbed out his latest cigarette and lit another. When he saw a tall man approaching, he moved behind a shrub with white blossoms. The plumeria flowers emitted a sweet smell that reminded Keno of his first ex-wife's bath bubbles.

It was getting dark, but Keno could tell it was Dunne returning to the room. His size and stride gave him away. *Damn! I coulda' gone in.* Dunne's broad shoulders and disheveled hair were easy to recognize. Dunne was alone. *Rose must be working her shift at the restaurant.*

Keno watched from behind his bush while Dunne unlocked the door and disappeared inside. The tender, white flowers exuded a syrupy odor. Keno stifled a sneeze.

I really want to know what he's up to before I go anywhere. Keno stood straighter and threw his shoulders back. *Time to face him. I've gotta' get my ticket.*

He approached the door but saw the desk clerk coming. *He's onto us.* Keno walked past the room, ducked behind the noisy ice machine, and peeked around the corner. He heard him knock on the door. *He's gonna' kick us out. I've gotta get out of here.* Keno looked again and realized the clerk was not at their room but had stopped one door short.

"Here are your towels, ma'am," the clerk said glancing over his shoulder and slipping quietly into the room.

Shit, everyone's doin' it here! Everyone but me.

As Keno approached the door to his room, it opened. He and Dunne nearly collided.

"What the ...?" Dunne said, looking down into Keno's fearful face. "What the fuck you doing back here?"

"I gotta get something, the, uh, the ticket."

"You ain't got that? Forget it. Let's go eat. Maybe a show. How about one of those touristy things on the beach? You know, them hula girls and all that shaking."

"Uh, sure." Keno tried to look around Dunne, but he blocked the doorway. "Why the hell not?" *Guess there's nothing wrong with a free meal.*

Dunne slammed the door behind him, eliminating the chance Keno had for getting the ticket off the dresser.

I'll get it tonight when we get back.

Chapter 39

A quiet, "Oh, a hostage," Sherrill said and wiped her hands together. She looked back over her shoulder into the jail with men secured behind the steel doors. She and Russell hadn't spoken as they climbed the stairs. "That would be scary."

"And maybe fatal. We have a 'no-hostage' policy; we won't negotiate with inmates to save someone."

An even quieter "Oh" was all she said.

She looked again at the cell block. Besides the gray walls, ceiling, floor, and the shiny steel tables, she noticed the hand rails and cell doors were painted a dark forest green and the cell numbers added above each door matched the color. She had not realized there were any other colors besides gray concrete and the orange jumpsuits. She chuckled at her own obvious nervousness.

"Nice décor," she said.

"I knew you'd like it," Russell responded.

"Why are there two men … inmates? Is crime this low?"

Russell clenched his teeth to prevent a laugh from escaping. "There are more, but they only let them out for a few hours a day. Those two are the tier tenders, the janitors. They get a bit of extra time outside the cells. The job's got perks, plus maybe a few cents an hour."

They didn't say anything more while they showed their IDs again to the officer behind the glass wall. He wouldn't open the door until he saw them, though they had been the only two visitors in the room and the only two leaving.

They showed them again as the first door closed and before the second door opened. The officer they had first met once again checked their IDs, took Sherrill's visitor's pass, and had them note their exit time in the sign-in log. The lock on the elevator was released.

They remained silent until the doors slid open at the third floor.

"Impressive, isn't it?" Russell stepped out first and put his hand on the elevator's lever so the door would stay open while Sherrill exited.

"Pardon?" Sherrill asked, clearing her throat.

"The security. It's pretty impressive?"

"I would hope so." Sherrill paused a moment then said, "How often do you do this?"

"As seldom as possible. I don't unless I have to."

"A part of your job that is—?"

"Is just too real," Russell finished. They walked between the desks with darkened lamps. No one else was in the office this afternoon. The few officers on duty were on patrol.

He retrieved his pistol, relocked the desk, and headed back to the stairwell.

Sherrill gave a little gasp when she looked at the clock. "My God! That took a long time."

"Like I said, nothing in here takes 'just a minute,' more like hours. I'll get you back to your car so you can be on your way."

She glanced at her watch, glanced at the ceiling for inspiration, then looked at Russell. "Let's go get coffee first," she said. "We need to talk."

Chapter 40

Keno patted his stomach, and Dunne guzzled another beer. Dinner was great; the teriyaki steak was delicious. The restaurant's lanai opened onto the beach, and they could watch all the sexy girls walk by. Keno decided to try a Mai Tai cocktail but scrunched his nose at the sweet, fruity taste. He finished it then had a couple of cold beers. When the bill came, Dunne pulled out the credit card and placed it on the tray.

The waiter picked it up and returned a few minutes later. "Excuse me, sir," the young man said, "could I see some ID, please?"

"Is there a problem?" Dunne had learned early that the best defense was a great offense. Challenge anyone, especially a younger and smaller person like this kid; they usually backed down.

"We need to see some ID before we can take your card, sir."

"Sorry, my license is in my room. I didn't bring it with me."

"Then, I'm sorry, too, sir. We need ID. Without it, we cannot accept the card."

"Why the hell not? This is good!" Dunne raised his voice. Intimidation and embarrassment of the young man were going to be easy. "My credit's good back home; it should be good here!" Dunne looked around, pleased that he had gotten the attention of several other patrons.

The waiter flushed and stammered, "We, uh, please, sir."

"Let me see the manager!" Dunne demanded. "We'll get this settled. Where the hell is someone in charge? Who runs this crappy place, anyway?"

The waiter looked around nervously, fumbled, and dropped his pen. He stooped to pick it up then dropped the card and charge slip. As he stood up, he said, "Just sign here, please, then leave."

"Oh, so now my card is good enough for you?" Dunne was beginning to enjoy the waiter's awkwardness. He loudly added, "You want me sign where? Oh, here?" He roared with laughter.

Keno stood up and moved behind a couple of other tables and tried to leave quietly.

Meeting up at the exit, Dunne said, "You were sure quiet in there. I didn't embarrass you did I?" and burst out laughing again.

"Hell no. Didn't want to get punched," he said. *Punched ... or worse.*

The other patrons watched them leave, shook their heads, and returned to their meals.

Dunne and Keno walked to the International Market Place a few blocks away. The shops were opened late every night, and the commotion and abundance of tourists were a great distraction. Keno had to hustle to keep up with Dunne and bumped into him when Dunne stopped at a booth.

"You like this? Think Rose would like it?" Dunne held up a string bikini in bright blues and pinks.

"Rose? Uh, yeah, sure. Why not?" Keno looked around at all the shoppers and shuffled his feet.

"I'll take this, and that beach towel, and … a pair of those sandals. Size 11, men's. Yes, those are for me. … Shit, no, the bikini's not for me." Dunne scowled, and the clerk cowered though he was still chuckling to himself.

Once again, Dunne pulled out the credit card. Once again, this sales clerk asked for ID.

"What the hell? My driver license is back in the room. It's in the safe. The Hilton right there on the beach. Would you like to call them and check my credit?"

"No, sir," the clerk said confidently. "I need to see some ID. If you'd like me to hold these items for you, we're open until ten. You could come back with your license or cash and make your purchase then." He stood as tall as he could but was still inches shorter than his customer.

"Hell, no. If my card's no good for you now, I won't give you my money later. Fuck you." Dunne picked up the card and stuffed it into his shirt pocket. He stormed off toward another booth farther inside the Marketplace.

Keno noticed the clerk was smiling. *They must go through this every day,* he thought. He let Dunne get a bit ahead of him and watched him stop at another counter that displayed sterling silver jewelry, wood roses, and pottery made by island locals.

"How much for that necklace with the dolphins?" Dunne asked the pretty young woman behind the counter.

"Nineteen ninety-five, plus tax." She smiled at the rugged man.

Keno watched from several feet away. *Oh, shit. Here we go again. Why do these women fall all over him?* He examined the mugs with sea shell patterns stamped into the sides and handles made like an elongated conch shell.

"I'll take that one and the matching earrings," Dunne said pulling out a traveler's check. "You take Travelers Checks?"

"Of course, sir. Make it out to Island Originals and sign it. No problem."

Dunne made every effort to sign Jeffrey's name on it, taking care to make it look like the signature already on the check.

"Thank you, sir. May I see your ID please?"

Keno rolled his eyes. *Here we go,* he thought turning and taking several steps toward the street.

"Where the hell you think you're going? Get back here," Dunne hissed then caught himself and turned to the clerk. "Shit," he said under his breath. "Sorry, I left my wallet in my room at the Hyatt. That's me, all right."

"I'm sorry, sir, but I can't take this. I'll have to call my manager."

"Forget it," Dunne said, grabbed the check, and stormed away pulling Keno with him.

"You have traveler's checks? Where'd you get those?"

There was no response from Dunne. They both maneuvered around the tourists with packages, baby strollers, and children in tow. Dunne glanced several times back over his shoulder and glowered at Keno.

"Ain't none of your fucking business," he snarled.

Several sets of parents looked at him with disgust and scooted their children away.

"Let's get out of here," he said and pulled on Keno's arm.

When they got back to the motel room, Dunne stormed into the bathroom and slammed the door. Keno sat on the edge of the bed then realized that this was his chance to get his airline ticket.

It's not here! Where the hell is it? He started opening drawers as quietly as he could, glancing over his shoulder and listening for the door to open. He didn't see his ticket anywhere. *Where the hell did it go? Did he hide it? Where would it be?* Keno went to the nightstand beside Dunne's bed. Nothing but a <u>Bible</u>. He opened the drawer of the second nightstand—nothing. He glanced at the bathroom door then opened the dresser drawer that had Dunne's clothes. *There it is,* Keno thought and began to reach into the drawer.

The bathroom doorknob turned. He quickly shut the drawer, stepped toward the television, and hit the power button. "Wonder what's on?" he said and turned the knob.

"I don't give a rat's ass." Dunne flopped across the bed. "We've got to get out of here. You got any money on you?"

"Only a couple of bucks."

"I'll get some," Dunne said, got up, and opened the door.

"Where? How?"

"Ain't none of your fuckin' business." Dunne slammed the door behind him.

Keno sat on the bed for several minutes and stared at the television screen. A movie was starting, some buddy-cops thing. *The same old bullshit—cops always catching the bad guy—yeah, right!* Keno got a warm beer out of the water-filled Styrofoam ice chest. Dunne had finally remembered to get something to keep the beers cold, but the ice had melted long ago. Keno opened the can, took a long drink, and sat on the bed, pillows behind his back. He wanted to wait and be sure Dunne wasn't coming right back.

Keno rolled over, saw the clock, and realized he had fallen asleep. *Three hours! Shit!* He went into the bathroom and splashed cold water on his face. The late news was almost over. During the next commercial, he opened Dunne's dresser drawer again, carefully pulled out his ticket, and slipped it under his pillow. He made sure Dunne's ticket was still there and the envelope looked unopened.

Keno opened the door and looked outside. It was dark, and a breeze helped with his sweat problem. He closed the door, locked it, and threw the security latch over the bolt. He saw the air conditioner and went over to turn it on. Nothing. He pushed a button. Still nothing. He pushed, prodded, turned levers and knobs several more times then gave it a kick. No change.

He opened the window an inch or two for some fresh air; Keno had not yet gotten used to the humidity. It felt stuffy. *I'll stay here one more night. Then I'm gone!* He clicked off the television set just as the latest suspect was being escorted into the local courthouse. He kicked off his shoes and curled up on the bed.

Pounding at the door jolted Keno out of his sleep.

"What? Who? Who's there?"

"Open up, you mother fucker!" The pounding continued. "Open the door."

"I'm coming," Keno called out. He stumbled and fell over his shoes.

"Damn it! Open the door! Why'd you lock it?" Dunne yelled.

Keno released the latch and deadbolt and opened the door.

Dunne pushed his way in, shoving Keno against the wall. "Why the hell did you lock the door? You know the fuckin' key don't work when you lock everything!"

"Sorry."

"Sorry don't cut it!"

They both looked at the ceiling. Someone was stomping in the room above and began yelling, "Shut up! Go to sleep."

Dunne roared with laughter then yelled, "Shut up yourself, you mother fucker!"

Keno moved to the far wall, putting two beds between them. He didn't say a word except "Sorry" again.

"Shut the fuck up, twerp!" Dunne yelled. He threw a plastic bag down on the bed and stormed into the bathroom.

Keno heard the shower start and figured Dunne would be in there several minutes, so he moved to Dunne's bed, lifted the edge of the bag, and peeked inside. *Three wallets, one of 'em's fat! Shit!* He looked again at the clock. *2:30—can't go anywhere now. But I'm out of here tomorrow for sure!*

The running water ended and the sound of crashing glass and a loud slam of the toilet lid startled him. The bathroom door opened, and Keno looked up to see Dunne standing there, staring at him. Keno saw a red mark on his cheek. *Looks like he was in a fight. If he got that scrape, I'd hate to see the other guy.* Keno shivered though the night was quite warm.

"What're you looking at?" Dunne yelled. "You lookin' at something?"

"No. Nothing."

They both turned toward the back wall when they heard someone's fist pounding on the other side. "Shut up!" came from a male voice on the other side of the wall. It was followed by more pounding.

"Go fu ..." Dunne started.

Keno waved at him and said in a loud whisper, "It ain't worth it. We'll get kicked out. Let's get some sleep." He tried his best at a smile hoping it would calm Dunne down.

"What the hell," Dunne said and pushed the plastic bag to the floor. He pulled the spread off the bed and fell onto the sheets. He was snoring loudly within a minute.

Keno waited to make sure Dunne was sound asleep and walked cautiously over to the side of the bed. Dunne's snoring was loud and rhythmic. The white, plastic, grocery bag had fallen between the bed and the dresser. Keno approached silently and poked at the edge with his left hand. With his right, he quietly reached inside, felt for the thickest wallet and pulled it out. He tiptoed into the bathroom and pushed the door closed before turning the light on.

He cautiously opened the wallet. *Shit! What a wad!* Keno pulled at the stack of bills and several cascaded to the floor. *Shit! They're all hundreds!* He counted. *Eight, nine, ten, more! Fifteen, sixteen, seventeen! Shee-it!*

Keno's hands shook. He needed a drink. He knew before he glanced around the small bathroom that nothing was there. Water would not quench this thirst.

Dunne'll never miss one ... or two. There were also a couple of twenties, tens, and smaller bills. He looked around and noticed that the mirror was broken, the cracks feathering out from what looked like a fist hitting it nearly in the middle. He glanced at the door and listened to

Dunne's loud snoring. Keno pulled out several of each of the bills and stuffed them into the pocket of his shorts. He turned off the light before opening the door. He slipped the wallet quietly back into the plastic bag then moved the bills from his pocket into the same envelope that held his ticket. He shoved his new riches and the ticket back under his pillow.

Keno shook his head then quietly removed his Bermuda shorts and climbed into his own bed. *This is too much! I won't last much longer with this guy. I gotta find someplace else to go. But where? I don't know no one on this island.* He, too, was soon asleep, but tossed and turned most of the night. Visions of someone running raced through his mind. The scene was clear behind his closed eyes. He was the one running; Dunne was doing the chasing.

Chapter 41

As soon as Sherrill woke up Monday morning, she knew she had made the right decision the night before. That confidence had not made sleep any easier. She climbed out of bed and peeked through the heavy, tapestry curtains of her hotel room and saw the light fog. She rummaged through her suitcase and pulled out her notepad. She dialed the number for the school office more than two hundred miles south in Ukiah.

"Is the principal there?" she asked the secretary. "No? Do you know what time he'll be in? … Okay. I need to tell you I won't be in today," she said. "No, I'm not really sick. Well, yes, I am. I'm too sick to be there. I'll call the principal back and explain, thanks." The white lie was easier than going into a long explanation to someone who didn't know her and didn't really care whether or not she was in her classroom. She bit her lower lip and hung up.

She had never let anyone down: not her parents, her teachers, or her brother; but she knew she was letting the school down. She would call the principal in a couple of hours, tell him what had happened, and ask for a couple of days off, unpaid if necessary.

She and Russell had talked for another two hours last night over dinner. He did not agree with her decision.

"There's not much you can do here," he had told her. "You might as well go back to work."

"I might in a few days," she had replied. "Whatever I can do to help here is more than I can do from so far away."

He'd given up when he realized she was not going to change her mind.

She sat on the edge of the hotel's bed and mentally listed the things that had happened in the last few months. *I can't believe it's been so long, so long ago since Jeffrey left.* She pulled her legs up to her chest and sat wrapped in herself for several minutes, then she rolled over into the fetal position. She buried her face in her pillow and screamed, ridding her body of some of the tension from the weekend's emotional incidents.

She lay there for another minute. Her face was dry, her throat, a bit scratchy, but tears would not come. She sat up straight and stared across the room then let her eyes wander. Her reflection in the mirror was dim in the morning light. *My God! Is that me? I look so … so tired!*

She put her feet flat on the floor, squared her shoulders, and pulled out the band that had controlled her hair all night. She shook her head to let her hair out of its binding, took in another deep breath, held it a few seconds, then blew it out.

She pulled on a sweatshirt over her nighttime T-shirt and decided no one would know the shorts she was jogging in were the ones she had slept in. *A quick run will do me good,* she thought, grabbed her room key, and headed into the chilly Humboldt County air.

Her thoughts were jumbled, but she knew they would clear. Calling her parents had been the most difficult task she had ever performed. The new task lay before her: find her brother, even it was just to find his body, and take him home. Justice, she hoped, would follow quickly.

Sherrill ran west, toward the bay and the docks lined with fishing boats. The streets of the old area of Eureka were bordered by buildings in various stages of dilapidation or renovation. Gingerbread fronts of a few old storefronts had been transformed into stores displaying antiques, used books, or professional fishing gear. One old building displayed local artists' paintings, ceramics, and jewelry.

Her pace started briskly but soon slowed to a steady walk. *I'm more out of shape than I thought,* she said to herself then turned to retrace her steps. Her breathing was heavy and deep. *Tomorrow I'll add a couple of blocks and stretch before I leave.*

She walked a block inland and turned north on Third Street toward her hotel. Up the slight incline and in the distance, she could see the stately Ingomar Mansion. The well-kept Victorian pride of the city held court over the other nearby houses from the same era, all now anachronisms, each a silent tribute to the timber barons who opened the north coast's resources, coveted the world over. Redwood trees, prized for their durability and beauty, and the bounty of the sea had brought fortunes to the secluded territory. Over-fishing, lumbering that outpaced the trees' re-growth rate, and government intervention and over-regulation brought the economy to a crawl and nearly devastated the area. However, these economic hardships did not lessen the old-time beauty of the Pink Lady, her larger brother the Ingomar Mansion, and the other beautiful Victorian houses built in the area's heyday.

Sherrill was glad she'd decided to stay in Eureka for a while and was even happier she had left the room. Until today, she had not noticed the beauty of the waterfront nor had she taken in the ambiance of the historical surroundings. Every weekend since Jeffrey disappeared, she drove here from Ukiah, grabbed quick meals at Elliott's, then spent hours asking anyone she met if they had seen her brother. She had talked to the Times-Standard newspaper reporter and given him a picture of Jeffrey. The next day an article had been published and sporadic requests for information followed on the local television news.

She put hundreds of miles on her rental car going to nearby towns and campsites. Some people remembered being asked by a detective; most just shook their heads and said they were sorry. The picture of him that she carried was worn; she would now keep it in a secure spot in her wallet.

She walked around the old mansion and examined the craftsmanship of the builders. Even the landscaping was maintained in the original style as a tribute to the era of the building's beginnings.

Her hotel was not far. She took several deep breaths and picked up the pace, her thoughts clearing. *If I'm getting involved, I'm getting in all the way!* She unlocked her door and headed straight for the bathroom. Her image stared back at her from the mirror. Her hair was disheveled and her cheeks rosy with a healthier blush than when she had left. *I've got to see this to the end, whatever that might be.* She showered, dressed then grabbed the phone to call her principal to submit her resignation. The school teacher had left her hotel room, and now, an hour later, her determination was set. She was the newest member of the investigation team.

Chapter 42

Russell got to the office early Monday morning. He pulled Jeffrey Madison's file from his desk drawer and reviewed the record of the myriad phone calls he had made over the last several weeks. After the television reports and the newspaper published information of Jeffrey's disappearance, he received dozens of phone calls, but none led to solid clues.

He had called all the nicer hotels and motels in the larger cities more than two hundred miles from Ukiah. Nothing. Then he had called the smaller motels—still nothing. He had shown pictures of the make, model, and color of the car to many clerks, spending so much time on the Madison case that he had not done much writing lately and some reports were late. Up to this point, it had seemed a lot like a missing person's case, but Sherrill's persistence, and now the car, convinced him it was much more.

Pages of phone calls—dates—times—numbers—persons he talked to—their responses to questions he asked were tucked in the file folder. One call verified that Jeffrey had traveled north on Highway 101. The clerk at the Fortuna Motor Inn verified that he had spent one night there— the same night he left Ukiah. He had checked in about four in the afternoon and had checked out about eight-thirty the next morning. So far, there was nothing suspicious, just a tourist heading north into redwood country. Further phone calls and interviews showed nothing. No one at restaurants, campgrounds, or even gas stations remembered seeing him.

This week would be filled with more phone calls to motels and campgrounds north and northeast of Eureka. *Kinda don't expect to find anything. I'm now willing to bet he never spent another night anywhere— alive, anyway.*

Before he could start making more calls, Captain Reardon called Russell into his office "Close the door," his boss told him.

Russell stood there for a moment. *His in-box is always full. Does he ever do anything besides paperwork? That's not for me; maybe another promotion isn't what I want.*

Reardon cleared his throat and shoved a piece of sugarless gum into his mouth. "All your attention can't be spent on one case. We're here to protect everyone—the ones still alive, too."

Russell shifted his weight a couple of times and explained his reasoning on spending so much time on the Madison case. "If there's someone out there willing to kill a young man, a kid, then no one's safe. We've got to get this guy."

"You're right, but wrong at the same time. Keep up with the cases coming in. Get Devlin to help you. You don't have to do this alone." Reardon picked up his pen, bit it, and started chewing on the end. Shuffling the few pages of a report, he nodded his dismissal.

"Yes, sir," Russell said, turned, and walked back to his desk. He knew there wasn't any use in arguing with Reardon, and Inspector Devlin was good at his job.

Reports. Routine doldrums. Work in a rut. Follow the path, the well-worn path. That's the part of police work every officer hates, well, except for Sgt. Johnson, Hurley thought. The interviews, the investigations, the solving of the crimes, even ticketing a speeder now and then, were tolerable. They helped keep people safe, to say nothing about keeping the adrenaline pumping. It was the aftermath, though, the required documentation of what had happened that drove too many good officers out the door to other professions or an early retirement.

Besides Jeffrey Madison's and Wanda Corbin's cases demanding attention, there were two more spousal abuse complaints and a neighborhood squabble that had escalated into a fist fight. And that last one was just a block from his house. If he hadn't been driving past, the two men could've really hurt each other. As it was, the smaller man's front tooth was broken and the other received a pretty good shiner. *Reports! Damn routine reports.*

A couple of hours later, he was nearing the bottom of the pile when the phone rang. He took a deep breath and let it out before answering. "Yes. ... I see. ... Spousal abuse that went too far? ... You have someone there? ... Yes, I'll be there in twenty minuets. ... 'K. ... No, thank you." He hung up and let out a sigh.

Chapter 43

Keno jerked awake. He had fallen asleep facing Dunne's bed and didn't change his position all night. He stretched and peered at the still sleeping Dunne. Keno's head was pounding. *Didn't sleep much last night. Shoulda' bought aspirin.* He pulled a Bud from the warm water in the ice chest and popped it open. Bubbles flowed out of the top and oozed over his hand. He frantically slurped at it, trying not to miss a drop. It was warm but it had what he needed—alcohol. Then he rushed to the toilet.

As he came out of the bathroom, he heard Dunne talking softly into the phone.

"Where 'bouts do you live? Okay. I'll meet you in an hour," he said and hung up.

"Who you got lined up already?"

"Rose. She slipped me her phone number," Dunne said and headed to the bathroom.

"I don't believe this shit. I come all this way with you, and you take off with some broad already."

"You jealous? You and me, we ain't a couple. Take a walk. Go to the beach. Find a broad of your own. Go camp in a park." Dunne flushed the toilet and reached for the shaving cream.

"What's that supposed to mean? You coming back here with Rose?" Keno scratched his own three-day beard but decided not to shave.

"Maybe."

"Shit. I might as well stay on the beach. You don't need no third party interrupting your games." Keno pulled on his shorts and surfer T-shirt. He looked at himself in the dresser mirror and felt like an islander. "How long you planning on staying here?" he asked.

"Don't know. Maybe a week."

"Shit, man. I gotta report to my Probation Officer day after tomorrow. I forgot all about that."

"Ticket's in the dresser. Take yours and leave anytime you want. I ain't holding you here. Go on home."

"Maybe." *Good, he didn't notice I'd been in his shit.* "I kinda need to get back. I might pick up with that waitress, Wanda wasn't it? The one we met back at the Mad Cat."

"Can't." Dunne came out of the bathroom wiping his face with a towel. "You don't remember shit, do you?"

Keno paused for a moment. "Shit. That's right. You did her, too."

"Told you. I took care of business." Dunne threw the towel back in the bathroom. "You talk too much, about the bitch up north, the kid, and his car. I know you told her about the car." Dunne chuckled while he watched Keno pacing around the room. "You're fun to watch. Women ain't worth shit."

"You get out of prison and two months later you've left a trail of blood, a lot of bodies? Shit!" Keno started sweating; his heart was pounding. "You telling me—"

"I ain't telling you nothing you don't already know."

The loud knock on the door startled both of them.

Dunne scowled and yelled, "Who the fuck is there?" The pounding on the door became intense. He threw his pillow at the door then grabbed the alarm clock and hurled it. The loud crash was immediately followed by pieces of plastic hitting the dresser and ricocheting over the bedspreads of the twin beds. The pounding stopped.

"Open the door! This is the manager." The pounding resumed. "I'll call the police if you don't open this door."

"God, what a hell hole!" Dunne said. He headed toward the door and reached for the knob. "Shit!" he hissed as he stepped on pieces of sharp plastic. He opened the door and yelled, "What the hell do you want!"

"We had complaints last night. From the rooms above and on both sides. You two made too much noise. You gotta get out of here. Today! Now!"

"Fuck you!" He slammed the door closed in the manager's face.

"I'm calling the police if you're not out in half an hour," the manager yelled through the door.

"Come on," Dunne yelled at Keno. He hurled a pillow at Keno's head.

Keno deflected the pillow with his left arm. "Shit." He got up, pushed his feet into his shoes, and shoved his belongings into his duffle bag.

"Where you planning on going?" Dunne asked.

"Don't know. How 'bout you?"

"Anywhere but here!" Dunne said and grabbed his backpack.

I've heard him say that before. How long before he runs out of 'anywhere but here' places to go? Keno went into the bathroom, pissed again, then threw his toothbrush in with his clothes—clean and dirty.

"I'll probably head north," Dunne added. "Waimea Bay. Great waves and some caves great for camping. I'll crash there until I get enough of a bank roll to get a nice place." Dunne sat on the edge of the bed and picked up the telephone.

"Who the hell you calling?"

"Rose."

"Again?"

"Yeah. Now beat it." Dunne threw another pillow at Keno.

Keno picked up his bag and headed for the door. He stopped short. *Do I dare?* He shoved his glasses back on. *I have to.* He retraced his steps and retrieved the envelope from under his pillow. He was careful to not let Dunne see what was in it besides the airline ticket.

"Can't forget the ticket home," Keno said through a forced smile.

Dunne grunted as he pulled the phone cord from the wall. "Where'd the bitch go?" he yelled at the phone.

Keno left the room, paused after few steps. *I gotta change my ticket dates. Probably can't get a seat today. Need a place to stay.* He turned toward the motel lobby.

"Where's the Salvation Army Center here?" he asked the manager.

"Don't know. Here's the phone book. Look it up yourself." The phone book landed on Keno's hand. "You two cost me. Two rooms emptied this morning and the third is still yelling at me. Get the address and get out. Your friend gone yet?"

"He'll be out in a minute. I'm goin' a different direction." Keno turned page after page looking for the address. With the number and directions safely written on his ticket envelope and tucked into his pocket, Keno left the motel. He saw Dunne slam the room door and did his best to ignore him. Again trying to be invisible, Keno watched Dunne head toward the beach and the busy streets of downtown Honolulu.

Keno pulled the envelope from his pocket, read the directions once again, and headed toward his safe haven.

It took him more than an hour to find the Salvation Army Center. The gray-haired man behind the counter grinned broadly when Keno entered. His broken front teeth were stained from years of heavy smoking and coffee. The snake tattoo on his upper arm circled twice around his left bicep; its head was baring two fangs dripping venom. A single tear drop tattoo at the corner of his left eye was beginning to look smudged. His shirt collar was turned up to almost cover the lightening bolt inscribed on his neck.

Took a few years doing hard time to earn those tats, Keno said to himself. *Glad I still have my skin in one piece and no broken teeth, yet.*

"Got a room?"

"Sure. Been here before?"

"Not here. But been in others like it."

"You know the rules then. No smoking inside. Doors close at 9:30—lights out at 10—up for service at 7—breakfast at 7:30."

"Yeah, yeah. I know."

"Sign here. First two nights are free. After that, they want a donation. Of course, you have to—"

"I know. I'll help in the kitchen. Mop floors. Whatever I have to. I know the routine. I need a place for only a night or two ... until I get a plane ticket changed."

Keno made up a phone number for emergency contact and put some digits and some street name on the register. He didn't care and couldn't remember what he wrote one minute later.

"All right, uh, Mr. Smith. I'll show you where you can stow your things." The older man stepped around the front desk and led Keno to a dorm room with a half dozen beds. "This is your bunk here," the man told him and pulled a sheet, blanket, and pillow from a cupboard. He tossed them on the second cot from the door.

"Thanks," Keno said and dropped his bag into the middle of the bed. *Leave my things in here for a minute, and I'll never see them again* he thought as he made sure his ticket and the envelope were still tucked tightly in his pocket.

The bathroom was relatively clean. The shower felt good. He lay on his bunk for an hour before the guy from the front desk approached him again.

"Thirsty?"

"Hell, yes!"

"They serve juice in the cafeteria. Let's go."

"Juice? Hell, no! I didn't come here to dry out."

"Then why?"

"Just a bunk. I'm leaving. Wanna' beer?"

"I ... I ... sure. Yeah!"

"What do they call you, anyway? Snake?"

"No, why?"

Keno laughed to himself. "No reason. Mind if I call you that?"

The man paused for a moment, looked at his arm, then said, "Sure, Snake. I kinda' like that."

The two men headed down the street to the nearest bar. It was dark and cool inside. A quick memory of Wanda flashed through Keno's thoughts but the first beer erased it. The third beer opened Keno's mouth and kept it moving. By the fifth beer, Keno had told Snake the entire story. Snake just listened.

When Keno went into the bathroom, he saw himself in the mirror. His hair looked thinner. He stuck his glasses into his shirt pocket then pulled at his cheeks and looked into his bloodshot eyes. *At least I'm still alive.*

As he washed his hands, he realized they were shaking again. *What the hell am I doin'? I've just told the whole damn story to this 'Snake' guy.* He rinsed his face and decided *Snake'll forget about it. He's probably drunker'n I am.*

Keno was wrong. As soon as he sat on the barstool, Snake grinned at him. Keno shuddered at the grizzled face with the reddened nose from too many years of alcohol. The broken teeth and the sparse hair made Snake look antique. Dunne's face flashed in Keno's head.

"What you grinning about?" Keno asked.

"I was thinking. You ain't got much money, right? I ain't got none. I bet you could pull off a deal with all this information you got." Snake grinned. "Interested?"

"In what?" Keno wasn't too drunk to turn away from something that might make money.

"We could use the phone at the desk and call this guy's family. You know, tell 'em we got word on where their kid is. See? We string them along until they send us some dough then we tell 'em what happened."

"I don't know where he is. I only—"

"That don't matter. You can call the po-leece, make them think you do. Until they send something. I'll even do the talking."

"Let me think about it." Keno had one more beer then counted the money he had left in his wallet. There was plenty, way more than enough to drive back home. *Maybe I'll buy a six-pack at the store on the way back to the Center … Shit, no booze allowed in there! Did Dunne really leave?* His head spun as various scenarios crept in. *Did he follow me? Where the hell is he? I'm dead. I gotta' know. That beach he talked about can't be too far. It's a friggin' island.*

"Hey, man," Keno said. He slid off the barstool and slapped Snake on the back. "Good talking to you. I'm heading out. Watch my stuff if I don't get back in time tonight."

"Where you going? You just signed in today."

"I gotta' check on something," Keno said then straightened up and stretched.

Snake got up from the barstool and tripped over the rung. He caught himself before falling to the floor. "That's how I broke my teeth," Snake said and bellowed with laughter. "Hey, before you go, let's make that call," he added and grabbed Keno's arm.

Chapter 44

Sgt. Johnson saw Russell's expression darken. "What was that about? Are you okay?"

Russell shook his head, reached for the file folder under the lamp, and pulled it out.

Johnson's jaw dropped. He knew the case in that file and knew Russell never looked at it when others were around. He and everyone else in the office respected the unspoken hands-off policy, and Johnson watched in silence as Russell opened the folder and flipped through the pages to the pictures near the back of the pile.

"Hey, man, did something come up? Is there something new?"

Silence. Russell stared at the first photo of the car then started to flip to the next one.

"Who called? Is it this case?" Johnson asked and nodded his head at the folder.

Russell shook his head and closed the file and pushed it back under the lamp.

"What'd they find?" Johnson said.

Russell stood up and looked eye-to-eye at Johnson. "Nothing. Nothing's been found, not about this case, anyway." He slapped his hand on the edge of the file to emphasize the point.

"C'mon," Johnson persisted. "Something happened. What is it?"

Russell headed for the coffee pot where another box of donuts was sitting. He grabbed a glazed one and shoved half of it in his mouth. A big gulp of bitter coffee washed it down. "Mmmph," he mumbled, letting out a few crumbs. He swallowed hard and said, "That was the sheriff up north. They found a car down an embankment along a logging road near the Smith River."

"Oh, I fish up there every year. Great spots for salmon along the river."

"Well, they found a car but no body."

"Kinda' like what happened to Christine, your—?" Johnson glanced at the folder.

"Yeah. Kinda' exactly." Russell took another bite of the donut.

"Ooh. Wow. And no body?"

"Nope. Nothing."

"Wow." Johnson repeated and reached for a chocolate-covered cake donut. He downed it in two bites. "Man, these donuts are the best."

Russell finished his coffee, tossed his Styrofoam cup into the trash, and pushed past Johnson. He plopped back into his chair and pulled out the next file needing a report.

"C'mon. Details, man," Johnson persisted. "What'd they find? What was, or wasn't there?"

"Look, Sergeant, there's nothing more to tell. They've checked for fingerprints and found nothing. Whoever did it left nothing. Again. They're sending photos—should be here in a few days." He shook his head and stared at the blank report form in front of him.

Sgt. Johnson shoved the paper aside, grasped Russell's arm and said, "Let's go get some real food. You've been here all day. Time to get away for a few minutes." Without resistance, he led Russell to the elevator and punched the lobby button. "You haven't even eaten lunch yet, have you? Donuts don't count. Time for nourishment."

Chapter 45

"Call now? Sure. Won't hurt nothin'," Keno answered.

Snake and Keno made it back to the Center. Another man was at the front desk.

"Hey, man, I'll take over again. My break's over," Snake said as best he could.

"Break? You been gone two hours! You owe me, man." The door swung shut behind the man as he headed outside for a smoke.

"Who do we call?" Snake asked.

"Call? Shit. The kid's name was—" Keno wracked his brain with no results. "It was something like Madden, Matson— Hell, I don't even know where he's from. Can't call the family."

"Who the hell, then?"

Keno dropped into a chair and covered his face with both hands. "There's a cop back home." He pushed his glasses back up his nose and ran his fingers through his thin hair. "What's his name?" Keno paced in front of the desk. "This cop ran me in a couple of times. Gave me a break once. What the hell was his name?" Keno leaned against the wall then sank to the floor with his hands covering his face. *Name? Who? H ... something. Hur? Hurry? Shit! I've got his address back home. What was— ?* "Hurley! That's it! Hurley at the Sheriff's Department."

"Okay. I'll make the call." Snake dialed "O" on the phone and asked for a collect call, person to person. However, the desk officer refused to accept the charges, and besides, she said loudly into the receiver so Snake could hear over the voice of the operator, "He's not in right now. He's out working."

"Yer loss. I got information about the car in the bay and a missing kid. I'll try tomorrow," Snake slurred and hung up the phone. He looked down at Keno still on the floor. "Hey, man. You don't look so good."

Keno had started sweating and shaking. *Not again!* His stomach was churning so much foul swill that he thought he was going to throw up. *I haven't done that in a couple of weeks. And, I didn't have that much to drink.* He held his hands out in front of him. He had to clasp them together to stop the shaking.

"You gonna' be okay?" Snake actually sounded concerned.

"Yeah. I gotta see some guy." Keno could only think it was more than the beer. *It's not knowing what Dunne's doing.* "Gotta make sure this dude's not stayin' anywhere near here. Then I gotta get the hell off this island," he said, took off his glasses, and wiped his face with both hands.

Keno got up, put his glasses back on and headed out the door. *I've gotta make sure Dunne ain't going back, ain't going back to Eureka. At least not soon. That phone scam sounds okay. Maybe I'll get enough of a stake to pay off my Probation Officer, or whatever fine the judge throws at me. Oh, hell—the rent's due again.*

Keno hurled the contents of his stomach into the shrubbery in front of the Center, wiped his mouth with his shirttail then headed toward the highway onramp. He held his thumb out and hoped someone would pick him up.

Chapter 46

Within minutes of leaving the motel, Dunne had hitched a ride from a car full of kids heading north. Surfboards were secured to the roof, and the corner of a beach towel hung from the trunk. Three teenage boys seemed happy to find someone to share the cost of gasoline on their way to catch some waves. The ride was long; the kid drove like his grandmother. The car slowed as it entered the parking lot at Waimea Bay, and the driver held his hand out towards Dunne who shook his head.

"What? That's a bitch. You don't have any money?" the boy said.

"Not for you idiots," Dunne said, jumped out, and slammed the car door behind him. He jogged a few yards through the lot then stopped to look around. The white sands sloped into the crashing, foam-topped waves of the Pacific. *It ain't changed*, he thought. *How long's it been since I was here with my mom? Fifteen years? More? Still looks great.*

He turned and looked across the highway at the banyon trees and undergrowth hiding the old, dirt road that went far into the shrubs. He could see cliffs rising above the treetops. He shrugged his backpack higher onto his shoulder, paused at the edge of the highway for a couple of cars to pass, then walked across.

The tracks of the dirt road were right where he remembered. For several yards, he followed the parallel ruts, now almost covered by weeds and brush. *Ah, there's the path. Right where it was back then. Looks like hardly anyone comes here. Good.* He inhaled the humid air and ducked under the low-hanging branches. Pushing aside the bushes and tree limbs, he trudged into the foliage.

A few dozen yards farther, he stood near the long, tuberous roots of a banyon tree and looked at the base of the cliff. *No shit. The footholds are still here. Unreal. It's like hardly a day has passed.*

He let his backpack slide off his shoulder, caught it with his left hand, then flung the pack over his head. It disappeared into the void of a hollow in the cliff. *I still have the aim.*

Lava had flowed for millennia, leaving layers of hard rock over the softer dirt. Years of erosion cleared out voids between the layers of lava, some large enough for human habitation.

Dunne had located the caves long ago after moving to the islands with his mother and her husband. As a teenager, he had roamed the island, searching for its treasures and places to hide instead of going to school. The caves had proven to be the perfect spot.

Betcha kids use these for screwing around, he thought as he climbed the dirt wall and hoisted himself into the opening six feet above the level ground. *Ahh, this will be perfect. Well, shitty really, but it'll work until I* pick up *enough cash.*

He walked through the parking lot and along the beach looking for opportunities. Before noon, he had acquired a cooler and hefted it up to his private cave. By mid-afternoon, he had a sleeping bag, Coleman lantern, a couple of wallets with too little cash and well-used credit cards, and two beach towels. He lifted a couple of six-packs from another cooler and found a forgotten bag of ice next to a parked car. After stashing his latest haul in the cave, he drank a beer and stretched out on the sleeping bag. His growling stomach woke him an hour later. He stretched and climbed down the side of the cliff in search of items to add to his hoard.

Chapter 47

Russell and Johnson were back from their lunch in less than thirty minutes, and the food settled much better than the donut had. As Russell pulled on the stairwell door handle, the officer called out, "Hey, Detective. Wait a sec. There's a note here for you." He started rummaging through the paper on his desk. "Oh, here it is." The officer held up the pink message slip. "Somebody called about the Madison case."

"What? Who? What'd they say?" Russell returned to the desk and snatched the paper. "Did you take this message?" he asked squinting at the message.

"Um, no, not me. Bennett was here. Her writing is always gibberish. The officer ran his finger down the schedule. "Sarah Bennett. She'll be back tomorrow morning."

"Thanks," Russell said, shoved the message into his pocket, and turned toward the stairwell. Back at his desk, Russell draped his jacket on the back of his chair and pulled the note from his pocket. He stared at it then flattened it on the top of his desk. He reached into the back of his lap drawer, shoved papers aside, and pulled out a crumpled sheet—his own phone number list of the people he worked with. He added numbers to the list as he was given, or overheard, them. *Ahh, 'Bennett.' Found it,* he said to himself and dialed the number scrawled in the lower corner of the page.

Chapter 48

Snake stood at the counter at the Center and drummed his fingers. He fidgeted and squirmed. *Keno left. We really should get this thing started. Hell, I could use some cash.* He looked around the room and checked outside the front door. No one else was around.

How long's Keno going to be gone? Where the hell'd he go? It's getting late. He pulled out the piece of paper with the detective's name scrawled on it. "Hurley. Humboldt County," he read. *I'll try to get this shit started.* He went back behind the counter and stared at the telephone.

Gotta do this. Snake took a deep breath and picked up the telephone receiver and dialed "O." When the operator came on, he gave her the information, paused then said, "Yeah, I said 'Hurley at the Humboldt County Sheriff's Department.' He's a cop. Call him." He forgot to ask the operator to make it a collect call and was surprised when the officer said, "Please hold." Snake's hands began to sweat.

Chapter 49

Russell held the phone to his ear and finished dialing Bennett's number. He scratched the back of his neck, expecting her answering machine to pick up, and counted the rings, two … three …, before Officer Bennett finally answered.

"Hello, Bennett? … Yes. It's Hurley. Sorry about calling you at home, but about this phone message you took a bit ago. … Yeah, the one who tried to call collect. What do you remember about it?" He listened for a moment then added, "Okay. That's all then? Nothing more? … The car in the bay? … Any names? … No? " With a grunt and a "Thanks," Russell hung up.

Russell jotted a note on the back of the pink message slip. He stared out the window for a moment then picked up the phone again and dialed "O."

"Operator. Can I help you?"

He identified himself then said, "We received a call, a collect call, and I need information about the source." He told her the telephone number and the time written on the message slip.

"It'll take a few minutes to get that for you. I'm operator number 19 and will call you back at this number within a half hour."

"Thanks," Russell said then spent the next twenty-five minutes writing reports. When the operator called back, she only had information that the call had come from a phone in Honolulu. She gave him the number and the address of the call's source. Russell wrote all the information on a sheet of yellow tablet paper and thanked Operator 19 for her help.

After he hung up, he dialed the number and listed to an unfamiliar voice say, "Salvation Army, may I help you?"

"Uh, yes. I got a call from a man there an hour and a half ago. Is there any way of finding out who used the phone to make a long distance call?"

The voice gasped and said, "Long distance? Let me transfer you to our manager. No one supposed to use the phone, especially not long distance."

The manager was angry but polite. Unfortunately he had no idea of who used the phone. The person usually assigned to cover the front desk and phone, he insisted, was trustworthy and would not abuse the access. However, that man was out on a job interview and others had traded shifts, so he wasn't sure who had been there at the time of the call.

Russell resisted the temptation to slam the receiver down. The paper with only the phone number to the Honolulu Salvation Army was now wadded in his hand. He straightened it and shoved it into Jeffrey

Madison's file folder. He stared out the bank of windows to the hills beyond.

What's someone doing in Hawaii ... and after killing here in Northern California? What's the connection? What could someone know way over there?

He pulled the message slip back out and called the Honolulu Police Department. Russell kept talking to the officer who answered until he was transferred to a detective who promised to swing by the Salvation Army Center later that afternoon. Russell added the detective's name and the time of the call in the "message" section of the pink paper, slipped it back into the folder, and put it into the desk drawer with the other active files.

He slammed his open palm on the desk, got up, and started across the room. He tried to avoid Sgt. Johnson's desk. One meal a week, one a month, really, was more than enough time to spend with him.

"Any progress on that case yet, Detective?" Johnson asked.

"Not enough. Nothing. Nowhere to start."

"Where you heading?"

"Out," Hurley said. He heard the sound of a phone ringing in the distance as he pulled the stairwell door closed behind him. Halfway down, he heard the door open above.

Johnson yelled, "Hurley! Phone. You'll want to take this one."

Chapter 50

Keno got out of the car, said, "Thanks for the ride," and pushed the door closed. His stomach rumbled, and Keno burped. *Glad I didn't barf,* he thought, swallowed hard, and patted his stomach. The two-lane bridge at Waimea Bay was just ahead, and the parking lot and beach were across the road.

Keno checked for cars, jogged across the highway, and onto the sand. He paused and looked up and down the beach. *I know this is where he said he'd be. Where the hell is he?* He clenched his fists and held his arms straight at his sides.

Checking around, he saw the river, a creek really, that came between two steep mountains covered with green. Banyon trees, with their huge trunks, grew and spread their roots giving protection to ferns and smaller trees. The damp soil gave birth to hundreds of plants. Unique species of vegetation made it a beautiful paradise, an easy place to hide, an easy place to disappear.

With his hand shadowing his eyes, Keno looked across the blue Pacific. Clouds hung motionless in the sky, caressing the horizon. Waves broke too close to shore for people to do real surfing, and families with small children played at the water's edge.

He said he'd be in a cave on the beach. I don't see no caves. Keno walked along the sand, ignoring the squealing and scampering brats. Some groups were beginning to pick up their towels and picnic baskets and heading back to their cars.

He closed his eyes, crossed his arms, and rubbed the tight muscles below both shoulders then the nape of his neck. He raised his chin and swiveled his head, trying to release the tension. When he opened his eyes again, he only saw the ocean.

This is probably the only time I'll ever be here, Keno thought. He sat and wiggled his butt into the sand and took off his shoes then twisted his feet, letting the sand filter between his toes. *The sand almost feels soft ... and warm. Wow.*

He walked along the beach; the warmth of the sun relaxed his stiff muscles. He turned back then waded into the water, first ankle deep, then to his knees, and finally sat, letting the waves lift his body then settle it back down. *Back home you can't go in more than ankle deep; you'll either freeze or the undertow will pull you out. This is so cool.* He closed his eyes, stretched his arms into the water, and let the water buoy them.

Keno spent nearly half an hour in the water. Even the yells of the children were silenced by the crashing breakers. Freedom. Warm water, surf, waves. No cares, no fears. The world around him ceased to exist. *No wonder they call this 'Paradise.'*

"Keno? What the hell you doin' here?"

Keno's stomach twisted as he jumped up, spun around, and splashed salt water into his face. "What?" he said, spitting out the brine. *Shit! He snuck up. Didn't see him first.* He scrambled out of the water, grabbed his shoes, and stared at Dunne.

Dunne was carrying a bag of food. "I thought you was leaving."

"Yeah, well, it takes a coupla' days to change tickets. You stayin' here long?"

"Until I get more cash then I'll find a real place to stay."

Keno relaxed. *That's what I came to hear.*

"Come on," Dunne said and jerked his head toward the mountains. "I'll show you my digs."

"I thought you said you was in a cave. I don't see none," Keno, still sopping wet, said while digging his feet into the warm sand. He smacked his socks across his gritty feet, knocking most of the sand off, then shoved his feet back into his shoes and stuffed his socks into a pocket.

"Cave? Oh, yeah, you're thinking like a mainlander. It's over there," Dunne said pointing across the road. Mountains climbed high on either side of the wide, green valley filled with trees and thick shrubs. "Those overhangs there on the left are lava levels, and there's caves under 'em. Been there for hundreds of years, thousands, probably. I've even found some cool shit."

"No shit?" he said. *Who friggin' cares?* Keno was still feeling nauseous following the drinking binge with Snake. He jogged to catch up with Dunne and crossed the highway.

Dunne followed a dirt road that Keno could hardly tell was there. The path was overgrown with tree limbs, weeds, and brush. Plants kept slapping him in the face, and he tried to duck or push them out of the way. In front of him, Dunne was chuckling while he let go of branches as the two trudged through the valley.

Keno followed a few feet behind, then stopped. *What the shit is his foot doing in my face?* He looked up. *A cave in the air?* Keno took a deep breath and followed Dunne up the ragged rocks. The foot holes were almost too far apart, and he grabbed at roots and plants to pull himself up the cliff. He climbed into the sheltered area behind Dunne.

"So, this is your cave, huh?" Keno said looking around. *Looks like he's settling in. Good.* A cooler was shoved to one side and two rocks had been placed, or at least leveled, for seats. *Maybe he's really here for the long haul.*

Wonder where he got this stuff? Hell, he stole it. Then Keno shivered. He had forgotten that he had helped himself to cash from one of the wallets. He shook it off. *Guess he didn't notice,* and he exhaled with a long sigh.

"This is where you live?" Keno asked.

"For now," Dunne said. He shuffled, hunched over, across the sandy floor toward the cooler.

"How'd you find this place?"

"Stayed here a few times years ago. Before the, well, before I went over to California and got sent up. Grew some good weed back in there," Dunne said and pointed farther up the canyon. "Made pretty good money."

"Any left? Uh, weed, not money."

"Checkin' it out tomorrow. Spent the day picking up a few items I need to set up housekeeping." Dunne snickered

Well, I guess that answers where he got the cooler and other shit.

Dunne continued, "You planning on staying long? You know, uh, well, Rose is—"

"Staying? Hell, no! You and Rose can do whatever you want. I got a place to crash tonight, but I'm outta' here tomorrow––for sure."

"Well, there's another cave about a hundred yards that way," Dunne said, pointing back toward the beach. He pulled two Coors out of the cooler and tossed one to Keno.

Keno caught it then stood up, his head easily clearing the roof of the cave. He began shifting his weight from foot to foot and looked at Dunne. *This guy's never worked a day in his life. How come he never seems to worry about nothin'? Whatever Dunne wants, he gets. No work. No bills. Nothing. Not even a conscience.*

"What makes you so ... so—? Keno set the beer down, unopened.

"Bad?" Dunne laughed and grimaced at Keno.

"Well, yeah. So stinkin', shitty bad? What do you get out of it?" *Why the hell'd I say that?* "You sure ain't got much ... living in this cave." Keno could feel a bead of sweat crawl down his spine.

Dunne took a long drink of his beer and let out a snarl. *Sure like seeing this bastard squirm.* Dunne chuckled. "It's what I need, and that ain't much. Naw, I get a rush. 'Adrenaline high' they called it at Folsom. The prison shrink said I had a high tolerance for pain and a high need for pleasure." Dunne took another swallow of his beer, then said, "Hey! What's up? Drink. It didn't cost you nothing."

"I ... I've had too much today. My stomach—"

"Yeah, I've seen your stomach in action, remember?" Dunne finished off the first beer and pulled another from the cooler and popped it open.

"What do you get out of all this?" Keno said as he looked around the cave. There was barely enough headroom for him, and he'd watched the much taller Dunne have a hard time moving around. *How could he be comfortable in here?*

"This is different. A challenge. I figure there's some weed still up the hill. Beer's here. Booze and weed—they help break the boredom." He took another gulp of Coors. "Want something stronger? I got better shit." He nodded his head toward his backpack.

"Uh, no." *Can't get into that shit. It kills people.*

Dunne set the can between his legs, and stared out the cave opening. Doin' shit gives me a high like doin' *it*, almost as good any way. Especially when *they* don't want to do it." Dunne laughed again.

Keno cringed. *I've been here too long.* He edged closer to the opening. The guttural rumble coming from deep inside Dunne made him shiver. He looked back over his shoulder and saw the drop to the ground was not as bad as he thought. *Why the hell'd I come here? Gotta' go. I can probably jump this and be okay,* he thought and shifted his weight back and forth.

"Yeah, there are times when the high comes easy." Dunne leaned forward and glared at Keno.

"Easy? You find it easy to—?" Keno didn't want to think about what Dunne had done at least three times recently, much less say it out loud. He took another step toward the mouth of the cave.

"Easy to off people? Kill 'em?" Dunne took another long drink. "Take their shit? What d'ya want me to say? 'I'm sorry?' Cry myself to sleep?" He gulped again. "Maybe blame it on my mom? Hell, no! She done her best by me. It's easy. And the rush. What a fuckin' rush! Nothing's better'n watchin' someone beg." Dunne laughed again and threw the empty can across the dim cavern and stood up. "My adrenaline starts pumping; the sheer joy, the sheer—" Dunne's body shook, starting at his shoulders and moving out and down to his arms and legs.

"Power? And control?" Keno asked almost in a whimper, remembering something a counselor said. "How many times? More'n the three recently?" Keno sensed it would be more than Wanda, some woman up north, and then the kid with the car.

"Oh hell, yeah." Dunne looked up at the solid lava ceiling. "The one broad you met before I got sent to Folsom ... the gas thing, remember? Naw, you already forgot, you friggin' ... ."

Keno shivered; he hadn't realized Dunne had killed her, and that was so long ago. "Four, huh?"

"Hell no. At least two more. There were a couple of bitches camping together in a trailer, probably homos." He spat on the ground. "Fuckin' homo bitches. I showed 'em what it's really all about." His laugh was almost a growl.

Keno began pacing near the cave opening. "Six, huh? Shee-it! Why?"

"Like you said, yeah, the power. The sheer power. When I see it in their eyes—when I know they know I got control, and they know there ain't nothin' they can do to stop it. Whoa!" He grinned and his whole body vibrated.

Keno thought he saw Dunne's hair quiver then watched his smile turn to a sneer. Dunne's eyes danced. Keno looked into the face of this man he had known, or thought he had known, for years and stood still. He didn't recognize him—the contorted face, the shaking body.

It was silent in the cave. The afternoon sunlight filtered through the overhanging branches and vines. In the distance, waves crashed onto the white sands of the beach, and passing cars could be heard on the highway.

"You really ain't drinking?" Dunne asked. He popped the top from another can and pulled his pack of Camels from his shirt pocket. Opening it, he pushed aside the cigarettes and pulled out a reefer. "Hey, buddy," Dunne said lighting up, taking a long drag, holding it, and exhaling slowly. He noticed that Keno was hovering near the cave opening. "You ain't got no worry. You're safe here. Chill, man."

"Naw. Not right now." Keno looked around the cave. He was aware of how alone he was with this maniac and saw nothing he could use for defense. The rocks were either too large for him to pick up or too small to be any good. He looked again at the drop to the ground.

"You get pleasure when there ain't nothin' they can do?" Keno muttered. He shuddered and turned back to Dunne. "How many ... uh, how many times have you gotten this, this rush?" *Why the hell did I ask that?* Keno said to himself. *There ain't nothing I can do now.*

Dunne took another drag and let the smoke out in a steady stream. He tossed the third empty can at the other two and looked squarely at Keno. "How many times? Not enough. Not never enough." The smirk returned, and Dunne gazed past Keno to the outside world. All was quiet. Dunne looked out but saw nothing worthwhile.

"You need help."

"Not from you or nobody else. You turning into a shrink or someth'n?" Dunne said leering at Keno.

"No, hell no. But you know, counseling might—"

"That shit? Already did—back when I was a kid. My mom got school people to talk to me. Their do-gooder crap just kept com'n up with *their* reasons why I did things."

Keno inched backwards a bit more. "*Their* reasons?"

"Yeah. Shit like, 'Bad behavior is a bad response to a bad situation,' or 'My parents were to blame,' or 'Negative attention's better'n no attention.' There was one who even said that I wasn't so bad; I just didn't know *how* to be good ... I was a 'broken child.' Whatever the hell that's supposed to mean."

"Yeah, that does sound like shit."

Dunne reached in the cooler and pulled out a bottle of Bud. He tugged on the cap several times before he realized it wouldn't screw off. "Shit!" He threw the bottle against the rocks, shattering it, sending a shower of foam and shards of glass in all directions.

"My mom was okay. Step-dad, too, I guess. They treated me fair, but I didn't want what they wanted." Dunne glared at Keno then glanced at the broken glass scattered across the floor of the cave. "You ain't gotta' worry. Sit down. Here, have a drag," he said and offered Keno his joint. "This weed here's the best in the world, except, of course, what Humboldt's got."

"Uh, maybe," Keno said as he searched Dunne's face for any sign of humanity, any hint of emotion besides hate or rage. He leaned toward Dunne, and started to reach for the joint. Keno looked at the gnarled face but was keenly aware of Dunne's hands. He paused a moment then pulled his own hand back. "Naw. Never mind. Where I'm stayin' won't like me commin' in smelling like a pot house."

Dunne took another long drag and leaned back, digging his heels into the floor of the cave.

Keno figured Dunne couldn't get up quickly from that position and looked closely at his eyes. Seeing no signs of movement, Keno checked the pack for a filter and pulled out a cigarette. *Gotta keep my brain clear. Shit, I've never passed up a joint before—or beer.* He fumbled for his matches, dropped them, and while picking them up from the sandy floor of the cave, moved to the cave's opening.

Dunne was studying the roof of the cave when Keno turned, jumped to the ground, and began running as fast as he could. Then, "Oomph, what th—?" Keno mumbled. He had collided with someone, and the two tumbled to the ground. "Shit. What're you doing here?" he said looking into Rose's face. They struggled to untangle.

"That's the thanks I get?" Rose said brushing leaves off her blouse then pulled at a grocery bag. The sun silhouetted her, revealing her body through her sheer gauze skirt.

Keno looked up. The legs, the peasant blouse that hung loosely over her shoulders exposing bare breasts—everything was visible.

Dunne poked his head outside the cave and yelled, "Up here," from his perch. "You should be able to climb it easy. He did." He pointed to Keno and laughed.

Keno scrambled to his feet and turned away. "Last I'll ever see of her, I bet," he mumbled and headed toward the highway.

Chapter 51

Russell raced back to his desk, grabbed the phone, and said, "Detective Hurley here." He was panting. "Who's calling?"

"This here is, is—well it don't matter who I am. I got a buddy here in Hawaii, Keno Smith, who says he got some info on a car there in California and about some dead kid from somewhere on the east coast."

"Hawaii? Keno *Smith*?" Russell wracked his brain. Something about the name sounded familiar, but he couldn't place it.

"Yeah. That's what he said. So, do you want the info or not? It'll cost you."

Russell wasn't surprised. Calls like this came in from people trying to extort money for information they didn't have. *But if this call's really from Hawaii; they don't usually come from that distance.* "Of course we want information. Tell me what you know, and I'll see if there's something in a fund somewhere."

"Hey, you find out where that fund is, and my friend and I'll call you back tomorrow. Have five grand ready."

The line went dead, and Russell listened to the dial tone for a couple of seconds before he hung up.

"Was there anything to it?" Johnson asked, standing behind Russell.

"No, not yet," Russell said slowly. "But might be. Something's different about this call. Not like the standard garbage when there's nothing to tell."

"Why? What?"

"He mentioned a name. 'Keno. Keno Smith.' That mean anything to you?" Russell turned to Johnson.

"Yeah. Sounds familiar. Well, the 'Keno' part does anyway. Hmmmm. I'll think on it and get back to you."

Russell pulled out his list of open cases and scanned it, but nothing stood out to connect 'Keno' to anything. He dialed. "Records? ... Good." He briefly explained the case, then continued, "Yes, could you look up a name for me? Keno. ... Last name? Well, he said 'Smith,' but I don't think so. ... I'll get back to you if anything changes. ... Yes, yes, thanks. Call me back if you find anything."

He hung up, jotted the date and time on the record page in the file, paused for a minute, then picked up his coat and headed down the stairs and outside to his car. When he got to the hotel, Sherrill wasn't there so returned to his car to wait.

Twenty minutes later, Russell saw Sherrill close her car door and head toward the hotel's entrance. She was dressed professionally in a brown pants suit, and her dark hair was clipped up. He gave her a few minutes to get to her room before he entered the lobby.

"Could you call Sherrill Madison's room, please."

The clerk nodded, dialed the room number, and handed Russell the receiver.

"Good afternoon! ... Ten minutes—lobby. ... Please."

Chapter 52

Rose handed the grocery bag up to Dunne then climbed into the cave.
"Where's he going?" she asked.

"Who?" Dunne said, digging through the bag's contents.

"Your little friend. He knocked me over trying to get the hell out of here and ran off toward the beach. Looked like he'd seen a ghost."

"Don't know. Don't care."

"Okay," Rose paused and looked back toward the highway. Through the trees she caught sight of Keno waving his arms wildly in the air attempting to get a car, any car to stop. She laughed. "I thought I'd see how you were doing at setting up house. Brought you some housewarming gifts."

"Really?" Dunne inhaled deeply on his doogie, held it in, then blew the smoke out slowly. "You ain't one of those bleeding-heart, liberal bitches bringing food to the homeless, are you?"

"No."

"No what? Not a liberal or not a bitch?" Dunne let out a raucous laugh and looked at the tiny stub pinched between his fingers. He took his last drag of this piece of Maui Wowie.

Rose rolled her eyes. "Take your pick. I'm not into politics. So liberal or conservative, it don't matter to me."

Rose reached over to Dunne and pulled the pack of cigarettes from his pocket. She flipped open the pack, took out a reefer, and lit it. Pulling in the smoke, she held it, then sat down and rolled over onto Dunne, kissed him full on the mouth, her tongue intertwining with his. She blew her smoke into his mouth.

He felt her body relax on his as he turned his head and blew out her smoke. He wrapped his arms around her and felt her tenderness.

She let the joint fall onto the sandy floor of the cave and pulled her blouse down. "Kiss me here," Rose said, her large, tanned breasts fully exposed. He obliged, kissing her first on the neck and working his way down. He kissed her right breast then the left. He sucked longingly on each while she writhed sensually to his touches. She caressed him, and he rolled her over and lay on top of her. It was wonderful.

Then Dunne reached out, grabbed her wrists, and held them tight over her head, pushing them into the grit. Everything changed.

He pinned her arms to the ground with his left hand while he unzipped his pants with his right. She twisted her torso as his touches, his groping, turned harsher and more forceful.

"You're hurting me," she whimpered.

"Shut up, bitch!" Dunne hissed, then caught himself. "Shh. Quiet," he said and continued to hold her and kiss her. He forced his tongue into her mouth so hard she gagged, and his knee jerked hard into her groin.

She tried to pull her hands free and twist away, but he was too strong and too heavy. She turned her head, but he followed her movements. Her cries for help and her pleas for him to slow down and be gentler were muffled, then she couldn't make a sound. There was nothing she could do to stop him from entering her, pushing, forcing his way. She gasped for air; the longing to touch and explore his body was gone. She wanted to breathe, to get away, but she couldn't move. She felt it. She felt him. She felt little else. All her energy was taken in trying to catch her breath.

Exhausted, Dunne relaxed his full body weight on her, and Rose could not squirm out from under him. She realized he still held her arms over her head, and she could hardly inhale.

"Get off," she barely whispered. "I can't breathe."

Dunne didn't move. He inhaled deeply and held his breath while he lay there, pinning her to the ground.

Rose felt dirty. The floor of the cave was gritty and something sharp was cutting into her butt. She could feel fluids ooze from her, yet she did not feel the longing she had the first time they had been together. Something was different; he was different. This time she had not been allowed to share in the intimacy, the touching. Nothing had happened for her the way it had before. Every muscle hurt. This time, he was rough and she was sore—inside and out.

He relaxed his grip on her wrists, and she pulled her arms free.

"Get off!" she snarled, put her hands on his chest and shoved. He rolled off of her onto his side and began snoring.

"Well, I hope it was good for you," she whispered and rolled away.

Chapter 53

Sherrill had taken time to change. Her new jeans and sweater were more appropriate for the cooler temperatures of the north coast instead of working in a special ed classroom in a warmer climate. "What's up?" she asked.

Russell thought he knew what he was going to tell her. But now, with her there and her brown eyes still looking distressed, he wasn't sure. "How's that list coming? The one of your brother's things. You have that done yet?"

"Almost. I'll bring it in tomorrow. I got our photos printed and I'm going through them to help me remember." She looked at him and added, "So, what else?"

"Um, well, we got a phone call." *Why'd I say that?*

Sherrill walked over to the sofa near the lobby windows and sat down. "From whom?"

Leave it to a teacher to use correct grammar, even at a time like this, he thought. "Not sure, really," he said.

"What was it about?"

"Well, not sure about that either."

"Then why are you here?" Sherrill looked at him. "It's got to be more than a list of Jeffrey's belongings."

"Okay, a phone call came in. Some guy in Hawaii—"

"Hawaii?"

"Yes. He says he knows something about your brother's car. Didn't say more than that. He's going to call back tomorrow."

"Nothing more?"

"Not yet."

They sat in silence for several moments, the awkwardness increasing. "Um, we also found a couple of receipts in your brother's car. We're trying to work with them to read the stores' names and the dates."

"Huh?"

"Well, they were in the water so long, they're pretty washed out. We got some techs working on them. They're good, and we'll get some information." More silence. *Why'd I come here, anyway? What did I think I was going to tell her?* He took a breath. "How about dinner?" he asked.

"Are you asking me on a date?"

"Well, technically, no. I can't have dates with a member of a victim's family. We can simply call this 'dinner' instead."

"Well, then, it looks like I'm being kidnapped. Know a good cop I can call?"

"Nope," he said, glad she had lightened the mood. He opened the lobby door for her and pointed to his car across the parking lot.

Chapter 54

It was dark when Keno got back to the Center. At the front of the building, he could see shadows moving behind the closed glass doors. He tugged on the knob. *Damn. It's locked.* He walked around the building and peered into each window. When he made it to the kitchen window, he saw Snake washing dishes.

Keno wiggled through the shrubbery next to the building and tapped on the window. "Hey, Snake! Let me in."

Snake glanced around. Seeing no one behind him, he returned to washing a greasy pot.

Keno tapped again. Louder this time. "Snake! Snake, out here. Open the door. I gotta get in."

Snake finally looked out the window. "Keno? What the hell you doin' out there? It's past curfew. You can't come in."

"Just push on the door. Open it."

"Can't. Alarms."

"Then open the friggin' window!" Keno yelled.

A look of resignation came across Snake's face; he stretched over the sink, threw the latch, and shoved the window open. Keno clamored inside and fell into the sink full of pans, hot water, and suds. Soaked and cursing, he climbed out and grabbed a damp dish towel off the counter.

"Hell of a way to come home," Keno said.

Snake was laughing so hard that he dropped the pan he had been washing. The clanging reverberated throughout the room.

Within seconds, the night supervisor yelled, "What the hell's going on in there?" as he came around the corner.

"Nothing," Snake yelled back and pushed a pan and another towel toward Keno. "Here, dry," he whispered.

"I thought you were alone in here. Who's this guy?" the supervisor asked.

"Keno. Keno Smith. I told you, he came in this morning. He's been helping me clean up."

"How'd he get so wet?"

"This pan slipped," Snake answered while he picked up the sudsy pot. "Sent water flying everywhere. Never seen nothing so funny in my life. Really drenched ol' Keno here."

Keno shifted his weight and tried to laugh.

The supervisor looked at them, shook his head, and returned to his nightly ritual of supervising the site from in front of the television. He had already missed too much of the football game and didn't want those two fuck-ups to interrupt him again.

"Thanks," Keno said and used the dishtowel to dry himself off.

"Hey, I gotta' protect my investment."

"Investment?" Keno had forgotten about the scam to get money out of Hurley and maybe the dead kid's family. "Oh, yeah, that shit. Yeah. Tomorrow morning. We done here yet?"

"Close enough." Snake drained the sink and hung up his apron.

Keno put the last dish in the cupboard and draped the towel over a hook. He followed Snake to the dorm. Sleep didn't come easily, and when it did, it was interrupted by more visions of running, tripping, and never being able to outpace Dunne.

Chapter 55

Sherrill didn't wait for Russell to call her about the phone call from Hawaii. She entered the Sheriff's Department office area fifteen minutes after he arrived at work.

"What are you doing here? The call hasn't come in yet."

"Good."

"Maybe it'll never happen. It could have been a prank call. Besides, it's too early. There's a three-hour difference and people there aren't even awake yet."

"Then I haven't missed anything. I'll sit over there," she pointed to a couple of chairs by the counter, "and stay out of your way."

"You bet you will. I'll be right here catching up on paperwork." He glanced at the folder under his lamp but, for the first time in years, didn't pick it up as soon as he sat down. "Over there though," he said cocking his head toward some chairs near the coffee pot at the back of the room.

She walked over and sat down. A copy of the Humboldt Times-Standard newspaper lay on the seat of the next chair. She picked it up but watched Russell concentrating on the paperwork in front of him, pausing once in a while to make or answer a phone call.

An officer stopped next to his desk and asked a question. She strained to hear it but didn't hear her brother's name mentioned. The officer seemed satisfied with the answer and walked away.

A man sitting in the glass-enclosed office at the end of the room appeared to be in charge of the people. *Does that make him a lieutenant? A captain? Is there anything higher in a police department. A general?* The thought almost caused her to laugh out loud. *Can't trust the TV shows for reality.* The man's name and title on the door were too far away to read, and she didn't want to wander around the room. *That would invite trouble.*

With Russell busy and ignoring her, busy with obviously unrelated business and phone calls, Sherrill read the newspaper's headlines and scanned a couple of the more interesting articles. Then she turned to the page of puzzles and pulled a pen from her purse.

Chapter 56

The island morning air seemed fresher, not as humid as yesterday when Keno and Snake went out the front doors to smoke. Keno was glad to be leaving soon. He called the airline to confirm he could change the reservation, but found out he had to give up the better seat he and Dunne had enjoyed on the trip to Hawaii. He stomped out the cigarette butt and kicked it into the gravel by the sidewalk, then checked his watch. "Let's call. Let's get it over with."

Snake dialed "O" once more and asked for a person-to-person, collect call for Det. Hurley. When he was put on hold, Snake said to Keno, "We can still try for some money from the kid's family. Remember his full name?"

"John, no, Jeff, something. A president, I think."

"Ford? Uh, Nixon?"

"Not recent. One of the first. Started with an M."

"Washington? ... Oh," Snake was talking into the phone. "Detective Hurley? You in charge of homicides? ... Good. We got some information, but we need some money." He grinned at Keno. "Look. You want it or not? I ain't foolin'. We know ... uh, yeah, we. This guy and me." Snake shuffled his feet and moved the phone to his other ear. "How the fuck should I know? Yeah, the kid's name was Jeff M something." He looked at Keno and waved his free hand in circles for him to say something, hoping he'd remember the last name.

Keno whispered, "Madison. That's it! Madison."

"Madison," Snake repeated into the phone. "No, I ain't talking to nobody. You want the info or not? ... Then you gotta' come up with some cash. ... Yeah, right." He looked at Keno then said, "Five grand. Five thousand dollars." He shrugged at Keno and puffed out his chest. "Yeah, five for me and five for my buddy Keno here."

Keno frowned. "What!" he whispered. "You said my name, you idiot. They know me."

Snake shrugged at Keno and yelled, "First the dough then the info." Snake listened for a moment then yelled, "Yeah? Well, find the money then we'll talk. Maybe his family'll give us something," and slammed down the phone. "Fuck!" he said to Keno. "Those jerks don't know nothing. They've got a chance to learn sumthin' and they don't know what to do with it. They say they're lookin' to see if anything's available to pay.

They ain't got nothin' so they ain't getting' nothin'." Snake fumed for a minute then said, "We'll try back in an hour. You hungry?"

"We already ate."

Snake ignored him and headed to the kitchen. "That's what's great about helping out here. You got free run of the place. Food whenever. Here." He tossed Keno a banana.

Keno nearly dropped it, then held it up to look at it. It was smaller than the bananas back home.

"It's edible," Snake reassured him. "Peel it. They're pretty good."

Keno dropped the peel into the garbage bag under the sink and bit off half the fruit. The flavor was fuller, richer than any other banana he'd ever eaten. He smiled and let out an "mmmmmm."

"Island grown fresh," Snake said. "No shipping to get 'em here. They buy these and the other fruits down the way, from a farmers' market."

Keno was too wrapped up with eating fruit that actually had flavor to pay attention to Snake, who was now rummaging through the fridge looking for something more substantial. Keno was amazed as he watched Snake slather the bread with a blob of mayonnaise, slices of onion, tomato, cheese, sliced ham, and two leaves of lettuce. Two thick slices of dill pickle topped it off before he smashed the whole stack together with a second slice of bread and began eating as if he hadn't eaten in a week.

"Too bad we ain't got no beer to wash it down," Snake said between mouthfuls. Keno only nodded and decided it was time to get a ride to the airport.

Chapter 57

Sherrill's head bobbed a couple of times, but she fought dozing off. She removed her jacket and hung it on the back of her chair and sat back down to work on the crossword puzzle.

"Psst."

She turned toward Russell.

"Psst," Russell waved his hand to let her know to come to his desk. He punched the button for the speaker phone and adjusted the volume.

She sat and listened to the conversation, biting her lower lip.

"How dare he?" she spat out at the first mention of money.

Russell put his finger to his lips and shook his head. His scowl silenced her.

As soon as he hung up, Sherrill stood up and shouted, "Who the hell does he think he is to take advantage of this. I'll—"

"You'll what?" Russell nodded to her and then at the chair next to his desk. He looked at her and said, "What you want to do is nothing worse than what I'd like to do. We've been through this kind of scenario before. Thank goodness there aren't many people who would call to extort money." He watched her stand. "Stop pacing; sit down, please." He drew a deep breath. "Unfortunately, there isn't much any of us can do about it. Not yet, anyway. I'm willing to bet this guy doesn't know anything. If he did, he would've given up more to convince us."

"You should have promised him something. My dad would've—"

"Would've been out five grand, maybe ten, and have no more information than we have now. If this jerk does know something, this won't be the last time we hear from him. He'll want something we can really give him."

"Like what?"

"Like, assuming he's involved, a trade for a lighter sentence. The name 'Keno' sounds familiar to a couple of us here, but Records couldn't find anything without a last name. They searched documents going back a couple of years and found zilch. Someone'll remember this idiot. Guys like this have been around a while. He'll stew on it then fear will drive him to make a better offer."

"He won't hold out for more money?"

"What good's money when you're sitting in prison? If this guy really knows something, he'll contact us again."

"Hell of a way to start a day."

"You're telling me?" Hurley looked at his "IN" box and picked up the stack of files still left from the weekend. Holding up the paperwork, he glanced at the file under his lamp. Then he turned to Sherrill and said, "All this, on top of your brother's case."

"On top?" Sherrill had noticed a look of sadness when he had stared at the lone file stuck under the lamp.

"Figure of speech. Your brother's is taking priority, but we haven't had a whole lot to go on. This may lead to something more." He glanced again at the stack of files then looked at Sherrill.

"What've you got? Nothing so far?"

"We're making progress."

"That sounds like something to say to get people off your back. What've you been doing? Sitting around here? Eating donuts?" Sherrill was shaking, and her face was flushed.

Russell scowled at her and stiffened but said nothing. Jeffrey's file was on top his desk with his notes, lists of phone calls, interviews with his family back east, answers to questions asked. He wrote notes from the phone call, shoved them into the file, closed it then looked at Sherrill. "We've had little to go on, but that doesn't mean we aren't doing anything." He gripped the file folder and waited for her to settle down and his own temper to ease. "There's been no information coming in from any of my phone calls, trips, or interviews around the entire area." He sighed then said, "What are your plans now that you're unemployed?"

Sherrill glared at him then glanced at her brother's file. "Okay, I got the hint. I'll back off—for now." She looked back at Russell. "I'm driving back to Ukiah to collect my things—be back tomorrow. Can't say I'll miss that drive very much." She took a breath and continued. "I'm seeing this through, not leaving until it's finished. I still have a teaching credential, and I signed up to substitute yesterday ... should start getting calls in the next few days. I'll find a studio apartment or something else cheap."

"You might find a waitress job open," Russell joked, then realized it wasn't at all funny. "Uh, sorry. You'll find the rents are easier to handle here; but, of course, the pay is a bit lower too. It's kinda' like living in the past." He looked out the windows at the surrounding buildings, none more than two stories tall. "It takes a good ten years for new trends to catch up to the life style here. You may find you don't like it."

"A slower pace? I don't think it'll be a problem." She picked up her purse and stood. "I see you have a lot to do ... I'll be on my way," she said and took her jacket off the back of the chair.

"Do you need a ride back?"

"I'll walk, thank you."

Chapter 58

Rose awoke with a start. Dunne was sitting on top of the ice chest and smoking.

"You son of a bitch." She got up and pulled a paper towel from the roll she had brought and dabbed at her rear. In the dim light, she could see the blood. "You hurt me."

"Thought you'd like it rough."

"Not much." On the ground, she saw shards of brown glass protruding from the sand. "How about one for me?"

"Smoke or brew?"

"How about both?"

When Dunne got off the ice chest for her to get a beer, she pulled out one of the last ice cubes. She popped the top, sat down next to Dunne, and rubbed her wrists with the ice.

Within minutes, the two were rolling on the floor of the cave with Rose gasping with pain, pain mixed with pleasure, fear mingled with delight, subsiding to excruciating joy, wrapped in the fruitfulness of being alive. Two members of the human race were caught in the timeless, classless rapture of taking each other. Hands feeling each other's bodies, touching every part of the other's being … her softness, roundness and his power, determination to stay in charge – through shared sweat, the heavy breathing, panting, the hardness, the elation.

More beer, more weed, more of each other for hours until they both fell asleep still intertwined like braided strands of human limbs sleeping the sleep of complete satisfaction with themselves and with each other.

Chapter 59

"I'm outta' here," Keno said and put his change back into his pocket then counted the bills he had left in his wallet.

"What?" Snake turned and watched Keno head into the dorm room to retrieve his duffle bag. "You can't go. What about our deal? We'll get some dough out of this. I need some—"

"I need to get off this island. I'm dead if I stay any longer. If—" Keno shuddered.

"I need some money, man. We had a—"

"Shit. We had shit. I'm leavin' and ain't never comin' back. I'm gonna' talk to this cop and—"

"What? You're walking into the Po-leeese Deee-part-ment?" Snake hissed. "You're gonna' get the money for yourself—cuttin' me out."

"I ain't doing that. I don't give a shit about the money any more, just scared they'll get me for murder ... or helping that dumb-ass out." Keno inhaled deeply, then added, "And I ain't going to the police department. I followed this cop home once a coupl'a years ago. Happened to come up behind him at a stop light—lives by some ancient gas station thingy, some little building. Figured knowin' where he lived might come in handy some day. I'm goin' to his house and talk to him there."

"You're droppin' a dime!" Snake raised his right arm and pulled back. "Turnin' into a SNEE–itch!" He swung wide. "You ain't worth SHEE–it!" he yelled.

Keno easily ducked, and Snake nearly fell over.

"Hey," Keno said, "you ain't no worse off. I'm leavin'," and shoved Snake to the floor. Keno turned and pushed past the supervisor who was coming to tell them to shut up.

Back in the dorm room, Keno pulled his cash out of his pocket and counted. *There's enough for the bus to the airport and gas to drive back to Eureka. Even have enough left to stock up on some beer ... and maybe a trip to Reno. Yeah, Reno. Gotta get back there ... change my luck.*

Keno stuffed his few things into his duffle bag and left the shelter. His skin itched, and it wasn't just his arms. His nose, cheeks, and tops of his ears were bright red. Even his scalp was sore; there was no protection from his thinning hair. Yesterday he played like a two-year old in the surf. The sand was white; the sky was blue; the ocean's waves thundered to the shore and were topped with frothy, white foam. He had jumped into the incoming waves, thrown himself into the breakers attempting to body surf, and sand-burned his chest at least three times. Even the pieces of coral that cut his feet and stung in the salt water were bearable yesterday. He had never been as happy as he was ... yesterday.

Today, his sunburn was driving him nuts and his feet hurt. Yesterday, he didn't have a care in the world. "You're only as old as your feet feel," his grandmother had told him years ago. Today, he felt over a hundred.

Today, he knew what fear felt like—fear of pain, of death, of someone he once spent a lot of time with. Last night, Dunne's story and his new girlfriend brought reality to Keno's world.

I'm alone in a foreign country. Well, Hawaii seems foreign anyway. Sure, everyone speaks English, but this is a friggin' island. I can't hot-wire a car and go home. Sweat collected on his forehead, and he felt the droplets behind his ears; his glasses slipped down his nose. There was no ointment in the world that would take care of how his skin felt today.

Keno had made some tough decisions over the last few hours. This day, today, right now was the first day of his new life. He was not going back to Dunne again. He had his return ticket in his pocket, and he was leaving.

He climbed aboard the bus and said to the driver, "Let me know when we're at the airport." He took a window seat and leaned his head against the smudged glass. Images of possibilities raced through his mind as his surroundings faded, his eyes closed, and his imagination took over.

> *"Here, have another beer," Dunne called out to Keno as he tossed another can across the bonfire into the darkness where Keno sat.*
> *"Thanks."*
> *"Now take a walk," Dunne had shot him a look that told Keno to disappear for a while.*
> *"Sure. See ya'." Keno stood, turned and tumbled over the log he had been sitting on. Dunne and Rose laughed so hard that they rolled off the stump they had been sitting on and fell onto the white sand and into each others' arms. Dunne held Rose close, tight. His hands began fondling her body, each hand taking a turn while the other held her. Rose smothered him with kisses, oblivious of the grip he held her in, reveling in the clutches of blissful ignorance.*
> *Keno shook his head in disgust and turned away. As he headed down the beach into the darkness, he brushed sand off the beer can and popped it open. He sucked the foam that formed on the top. Keno looked at the black sky speckled with glistening dots of light, the sand lit only by the moon and*

*glimmering phosphorescence of the waves atop the blackened
sea.*

*He could hear their laughter and enthusiasm for longer than
he wanted. He sat on the damp sand as the tide receded,
waiting. When it had been quiet for a few minutes, he decided to
head back.* The grinding of the bus gears being shifted
interrupted his dream briefly.

*Dunne and Rose were wrapped in each others arms and
talking softly. Rose let out a giggle. I know. I'll give them a
shock. They'll think it's funny! The sand silenced Keno's
footsteps as he sneaked up behind them, intending to scare the
living shit out of them. He was careful so they would not hear
him. He didn't want to ruin the surprise.*

*The words were becoming clearer, but Keno could barely
make out the words. "Tomorrow ... rent a car ... just the two of
us ... fun ... alone together."*

"Alone, just you two? What about me?" Keno mumbled and
jerked. His eyelids fluttered. The person sitting next to him on the
bus shifted uncomfortably. Keno's eyes closed again.

*Rose asked, "What about your little shadow, what's his
name? Aren't you two Siamese twins or something?"*

*"Shit, no. That little bastard won't leave me alone. Haven't
been able to shake him since we got here ... not yet anyway. I'll
find a way to dump him."*

Keno knew.

His sunburned skin, stinging and blazing hot a second ago, turned
to an icy chill.

Keno knew what "dump him" meant to Dunne.

*Keno looked around. Those two don't know I'm here! He
started taking steps backwards, being careful so he wouldn't
stumble. When he figured he was far enough away, he turned
and ran. He figured wrong.*

*Dunne and Rose heard his feet pounding on the sand. Dunne
looked over his shoulder, stood up, and yelled, "Keno! What the
fuck you doing? Where you going, ... Buddy?"*

*But Keno kept running. He didn't care where; he just ran as
fast as he could. Suddenly, somehow Dunne was right in front
of him—his scowling face inches from Keno's. Rose stood
behind him, her face colorless. Blood was dripping from her
stomach. Then Dunne's hands reached out, and Keno could feel*

the fingers on his neck and hear a sinister laugh coming from deep inside Dunne.

Keno jerked awake in a sweat, bolted straight up, and yelled, "He's here!" His eyes opened wide. "He'll kill me. He already killed—" He looked around at the other bus riders. *A dream. A shitty dream.* He wiped his face with his hands, leaned back, and let out a long sigh.

The man who had been sitting next to him was gone.

Chapter 60

Keno was still sticky with sweat when he got onto the airplane. He ignored everyone and quickly turned toward the window as soon as he sat down.

The plane ride put Keno into California later than he had figured; it was pitch black in San Francisco and few people were in the airport. He found his car, reached in through the window they had forgotten to close, unlocked the back door, and crawled in. Back on the mainland, no nightmares disrupted his sleep.

The sun shining through the windshield woke him. He checked his pockets for the cash. *Enough still there. Thank God!* He climbed over the seat and sat behind the steering wheel. *Keys. Keys? Where'd I put them?* A sinking feeling came over him as he checked his pockets. *Shit! They must be back at the shelter! In Hawaii!*

He climbed out of the car and searched under the seats, between the cushions, in the glove box. *A screwdriver. Aha!* Keno crawled back into the car and searched under the dash. Pulling at the wires, he twisted a couple of them together and then punched the screwdriver into the ignition keyhole. *What a bunch of crap! Hot-wiring my own car!* With a sharp twist, the car rumbled into life. *Here's one reason to buy an old junker. No security system!* He said to himself and smiled then shifted into gear and drove toward the exit.

He hit the brakes. *What the—! I gotta pay for parking?* "How much?" *Shit.* He handed three twenties to the attendant and got only a few ones in return. *There goes the stash of beer and the trip to Reno.* Finally, he pulled out of the parking lot and headed north on U.S. Highway 101.

Keno stopped in Santa Rosa where he gassed up and picked up a soda and burger. He tried to call Det. Hurley again but only talked to an officer. He had given up on getting any cash from the deal; now he was concerned with staying alive and out of jail. He kept checking his rear-view mirror.

Five miles past Willits, the car's idiot light came on indicating the engine was overheating. Keno pulled over into a wide spot on 101 and cursed all the way to the front of the car. He popped the latch and lifted the hood. He grabbed the radiator cap. *Shit! That's hot!* and jerked his hand away. He pulled away so fast he hit his knuckles on the support rod. Blood. He licked his wounded knuckles. *Shit! Dirty rotten—*

Keno scrutinized every car that passed. The drivers—a blonde female, a black male, a dark-haired girl, a Hispanic, and a lot of other people, young and old. If there were passengers, they, too, got a close inspection. So far, he didn't recognize anyone. No Dunne.

Keno climbed back into his car and pulled a chunk of ice from his soda cup and wiped his burned fingers and bloody hand. He dropped the rest of the ice into the radiator. *This is why I shouldn't leave home—and won't never again—well, unless I'm going to Reno.* He wrapped a soiled rag around his knuckles, let the car cool then drove back to Willits.

Keno fruitlessly tried to call Det. Hurley again from a phone booth at the Shell Station. *Always some story: He's at the lab; he's checking some evidence; he's out at a crime scene; he's at lunch.*

Keno put water into the radiator and bought a gallon of coolant, just in case. The old car didn't have much left to give. The gas gauge was now forever stuck on full, and he figured he could go a couple hundred miles, probably Garberville, before refueling—but not quite all the way back to Eureka.

At Garberville, he fueled up again and added more coolant and water. *Seems more like a strainer than a radiator. Don't see no leaks, no steam.*

He tried to call Det. Hurley again but still had no luck. *I shoulda' become a cop. Seems like they're never in the office.* His stomach growled. The odors of a nearby taco stand caught his attention, and he slammed the car door. He gave the car the hardest kick he could. His toe left a dent a half inch deep in the door. He limped to the order window and spent half the money left in his pocket.

An hour and a half later, Keno pulled up to his apartment building. *A parking space right in front! Wow! At last something's going right!* He sat in the car for several minutes. *Maybe I'll dump this heap in the bay like the other one.* He pulled his jacket out of the duffle bag and put it on. *Gotta' figure out what to do. Gotta' have a plan. I gotta' talk to Hurley.*

He pulled on the door handle then paused. My *Probation Officer. I gotta' call him quick.* He hit the steering wheel with the heel of his hand, still wrapped in the dirty rag, and the horn started blaring. *Damn!* He pounded on the steering wheel, but the blaring continued. He ran to the front of the car, popped the hood once more, and jerked on wires until it stopped.

Keno returned to the driver's door and pushed the lock button down, then laughed. *Why protect this heap?* He shut the door and wiped his hands on his pants. *Shit! I don't have my apartment keys, either!*

"What the hell are you doing out here?"

Keno spun around to see his landlady at the top of the porch stairs, hands on her hips.

"Don't you know you're supposed to be quiet at this hour?"

"Late? It's only six!"

"Six, my ass. It's nearly nine-thirty. Time for bed."

Keno looked at his watch and said, "No, it's six ..." *Shit, I lost three hours flying back. Forgot to reset my watch.*

"Can't get no sleep." The woman was at the top of the stairs, leering at Keno. "I gave you notice. Slid it under your door last week. You have until tomorrow to get out."

"You can't—"

"Can. Going to. Did." She didn't move a muscle. "I've had it trying to find you to get the rent, your Parole Agent—"

"Probation Officer, I ain't on parole."

"Whatever," she said and glared at Keno. "He's been knocking on my door every other day, and then there's your drunk friend hanging out around here."

"Friend? Dunne's here?" Keno looked around, his eyes darted from bush to tree to cars in the street. "He's back?"

"He ain't here now. I mean when he was staying with you. After you had went to work, he even hit on me. Couldn't hardly believe it." She let out a strange laugh. Then looked straight at Keno and said, "You gotta' go. You got to tomorrow."

Keno looked around again, expecting to see Dunne, or maybe his Probation Officer, coming up the sidewalk. "I gotta' have a place to live."

"Yeah, but not here," she said, turned, and slammed the door.

Keno paused for a few seconds then bounded up the steps and pounded on her door.

"What the hell?" The landlady came out with a baseball bat over her shoulder.

"Keys. I lost my keys. Could you open—?"

"Keys'll come outta' your deposit," she said and climbed the stairs to his landing. "Doubt you'll get any of *that* back."

Once inside, Keno ran his fingers over his scalp. *P.O. Gotta call him. Number. Where's his number?* He dug through his drawers, tossed papers on the floor, knocked over wastebaskets. *It's gotta' be here somewhere!* He couldn't find the number anywhere, though he did find an extra set of keys he had stashed away in the back of the junk drawer in the kitchen. He picked up an official-looking but crumpled business card. *Hurley's. Too late to call him at work.* He shoved the card into his pocket and scratched his head. *To hell with it,* he said to himself and opened the fridge. It was almost empty, but he looked anyway.

He found a cold beer in the back of the veggie drawer. *Did I put that there? Maybe I hid it from Dunne so I'd have one left.* He popped the top. Walking toward the bedroom, he glanced at the sofa cushions one more time. *No Dunne.* His hands were shaking so badly, the beer spilled on his hand. He licked the sweet nectar and hardly missed a drop. Then he tossed the empty can at a wastebasket, missed, and shrugged.

He sat on the edge of his bed and wrapped his arms around his head. His shoulders drooped. He shuddered and heaved a huge sigh. *Where? What? Gotta' contact somebody.* Keno picked up the telephone. *I'll ask information for Hurley's home number.* After he dialed the first number, he realized something was wrong. He tapped the telephone's switchhook button over and over again. *No dial tone? What the—? Shit! They've cut me off. Gotta' talk to somebody.*

He pulled Hurley's card out and stared at it then turned the card over. Hurley's address was on the back. *Oh, that's right—I must've wrote it down.* He smiled. He knew what to do.

Keno tiptoed down the stairs, cracked open the front door an inch, and peered outside, looking for anyone, anything that didn't belong. The few streetlights illuminated enough for him to feel secure to step onto the porch and check around the shrubs. Keno climbed into his car but no amount of coaxing or twisting the wires would get the engine to start. *Oh, yeah, I pulled the wires out. Horn was blasting. Maybe I grabbed too many.* He got out, looked around again, saw nothing unexpected, and headed toward Fourth Street, his thumb ready to catch a ride.

Chapter 61

His house was dark when Russell pulled into the driveway. *I thought I left the porch light on. I knew I'd be late.* He locked the car and checked the front windows and door. *No signs of entry. Perhaps the bulb burned out.*

Someday I'll clean out that garage enough to actually use it for a car. He looked down the dark driveway to the back of the house and saw nothing unusual, so he headed toward the steps. He glanced into the cloudy night's sky. *Maybe we'll see stars and the moon again ... someday.* He sorted the house key from the others, the car, trunk, office, desk, garage door, and an unknown key he'd had on the ring for what seemed like forever.

Russell swung the door open and flicked the switch for the floor lamp. Nothing. He clicked the switch for the porch light and it came on. *Power's not out. Must've forgotten.* He walked to the sofa and turned the knob on the table lamp. *This one's out too? Two light bulbs at once? What're the odds?* He looked behind him, down the hall to his office. A light was on. *I know I didn't leave that one on.*

Russell tugged on the strap on his holster twice before the snap opened. For the first time in his life, he pulled out his service pistol and released the safety inside his own home. He heard a whimper then sensed, rather than saw, movement. *Someone's in the kitchen.*

"Shane? That you?" he half whispered, half spoke.

More movement, but this time he could tell it was too high to be the dog. Russell quietly pushed the front door open all the way. *Nothing behind the door.* Grasping the gun tightly in his right hand, he tip-toed to the only other lamp in the living room. He felt for the table lamp with his left and turned the switch. Nothing. *Shit!*

"Who's there? Shane, you okay, boy?" he called out. "I'm a police officer. I've got a gun. Either get out now or—?" He did not want to shoot, especially in his own house. Not just the mess, but the paperwork. *Shit!*

A crash from the kitchen and a loud yowl happened at once. Then screaming.

"Fuck you, mutt. Shee-it. Get the hell off me!" came from inside the house.

Russell didn't recognize the voice but was glad to hear Shane's growling. The sound of another crash, breaking glass, and barking then the back door being thrown open were followed by more glass breaking. Then silence.

Russell, staying low beside the back of the sofa, headed through the dark living room, the dining room, and into the kitchen. None of the light switches worked. Crunching glass and stickiness greeted him as he stepped on the linoleum floor.

His left foot hit something round and hard, and his shoe lost its grip. He grabbed into the air and caught the refrigerator handle with his left hand. As the door swung open, the dim light from inside the fridge filled the room, and he sank to the floor, seat first.

Then he heard a heart-rending sound—a whimper.

"Shane? Where are you, boy? Stay. Stay, Shane. I'll find you." Russell searched the shadows in the kitchen. Another whimper. Russell saw the dark shape of his dog under the kitchen table and put his left hand to the floor to stand up; a shard of glass cut into his palm. Jerking it out, he tossed it onto the floor and sat again into the stickiness. He realized he was sitting on more pieces of glass.

Carefully pulling himself up, Russell could see shards of glass strewn across the floor. The back door was hanging by one hinge, and its window was broken out. *A pen. I slipped on a pen!* A Bic was rolling across the room and stopped when it reached a rag near the door.

Russell clambered up and scrambled outside. *Nothing!* He checked the yard and down the driveway. The light from the streetlights barely helped. *Damn it! He's gone.*

He headed for Shane. A toppled chair lay across the dog's back. Another whimper.

"Stay, boy, stay still; I'm coming." Russell holstered his gun and carefully pulled the chair away. Whoever had been in his house was long gone and unimportant at this point.

"Okay, boy. I've got you." Russell moved the table and knelt beside the dog. He petted his head and looked for wounds. Shane only responded with another soulful moan. Russell could see some blood coming from his mouth.

"My God, who did this to you?" Russell pulled a light bulb from the cupboard, and replaced the broken bulb in the kitchen fixture. Then he searched the magnets on the side of the fridge and found the one shaped like a dog. He grabbed the phone and dialed the veterinarian's emergency number.

Russell quickly explained the situation and the answering service transferred him to the vet. He repeated the info and finished the call with an emphatic, "Meet me at your office! Now!" then added, "Please," before he slammed the phone back onto the cradle.

Chapter 62

It took Keno more than an hour to walk home. The fog was thick, but the cool air felt good after Hawaii's heat and humidity. *What the hell'd I do? Why'd I go inside? Could'a waited on his porch, but no! I had to check around back.* Keno kept walking, holding his arm. *Same damn arm as my hurt hand—didn't know he had a damn dog.*

It was too easy—doggy door just askin' me to come in. Too easy. Then that dumb dog woke up and started smellin' me. Shit!

Keno was cold and damp when he climbed the stairs to his apartment. The first thing he did was take a warm shower and wrapped his bleeding arm in a washcloth.

He turned on his television and turned to a station with news. *Thank goodness they didn't shut off the power ... yet.* He sat on the couch with the towel wrapped around his waist and massaged his sore arm. *They're not saying nothin' about the Madison guy.* He sighed, leaned back into the cushions, and pulled the towel tighter. The newscaster reported again on the murder of Wanda Corbin, waitress from Elliott's Diner. *They still think her kid killed her? Dumb shits.*

His looked at his reddened knuckles. *They'll heal.* He lifted the washcloth. *Damn dog.* He went back into the bathroom, found a roll of gauze, and wrapped the open wound. *Well, I hear that a dog's mouth is cleaner than a human's.*

Chapter 63

Russ's drive to the vet's seemed to take forever though it was less than five miles down the hill and a couple of miles up Broadway. Whimpering continued from the injured dog lying on the back seat of his car. A bit of blood stained the upholstery.

The lights inside the veterinary office were already on; Sam Reed, DVM, had arrived moments before. He held the door open for Russell to hurry in with Shane.

Sam spent precious minutes hovering over the injured animal, checking his vital signs, lifting paws, poking ribs, and checking legs. He pulled a thermometer from a drawer and turned to the dog.

"The paw is cut," Sam said, "but not badly. Nothing seems to be broken."

"What about the blood on his mouth?"

"It doesn't seem to be his," Sam replied. He patted the now quiet dog.

"No?" Russell sighed with relief. "Good! That means he might have done some damage to that, that—"

"Are *you* okay?" Sam asked. "Let me see your hand."

"I'm fine."

"What happened?" Sam wrapped Russell's hand in gauze and taped it.

"I'm not sure. Why is Shane so, so lethargic?"

"It looks like the wind was knocked out of him. Like he was thrown, or kicked, hard. No broken ribs, though." Dr. Reed removed the thermometer and rubbed Shane's head with a vigorous motion and nuzzled him—nose to nose. "Your temp's normal, boy," the doctor said to Shane. "You took quite a blow tonight, didn't you? But, you're going to be fine, aren't you?" He straightened up and looked Russell in the eye.

"What *did* happen tonight, Russell?"

Russell had known Sam for nearly eleven years—ever since Russell and his fiancé had brought Shane to Sam for puppy shots. Russell had kept taking Shane to Sam's office for routine shots, neutering, and general care, and the two had become friends, attending "Humboldt Crabs" baseball games in Arcata together.

Russell knew that Sam trusted him with the dog, and Sam knew Russell would never do anything to hurt an animal. Shoot a bad guy, yes. Feed him properly? Yes. Not give him enough attention? Probably. But hurt him? Never!

"Sam, I don't know what happened besides someone broke into my house. Shane's the only witness, and he's not talking." Russell sighed. "If you want, you can read the report, but it won't say much more."

Sam filled a syringe. Approaching Shane's hind end, Sam said, "Just a sedative. It'll keep him quiet and make sure he gets a good night's sleep." Shane hardly moved.

"Shane sure didn't like some stranger being there. I guess he tried to convince him to leave."

"Anything missing?"

Russell paused for a moment, stroked Shane's head, and continued. "Didn't take time to check. Anyway, can we save some of whatever was in his mouth? Maybe it'll give us a blood-type match, at least something to work with."

"Way ahead of you, Copper," Sam said with a smile. He turned toward the counter and picked up a prescription bottle. "Your wish is my command. Do with this as you please," he said and dramatically handed it to Russell. "It might be a bit contaminated with dog saliva, but any good forensic scientist should be able to tell dog from human."

"At least we can try. I'll stick it in my fridge at home. The lab can handle it from there." Russell stuffed the bottle into his jacket pocket. "If I ever catch that bastard, whoever has a chunk of skin missing, I'll get him for breaking and entering at least."

"Don't forget animal cruelty." Sam gently patted Shane's head. "Want me to keep him overnight?"

"No. NO! Shane might've saved my life tonight. I'm not letting him sleep here."

"Good. Glad to hear it. But, I wasn't going to make him sleep here, either. If you weren't taking him home, I was. This dog deserves better."

"Better'n what? Me?"

"No. Just *more* of you. More attention. More loving. More walking. More exercise. More of the good life. You're never home. How can this dog feel loved?"

"He knows I love him."

"Yeah, yeah, yeah. Your feelings ooze from your pores. At least I know he gets food and water. I'll give you a call tomorrow and see how he did overnight."

"Okay. Hey, Doc, thanks. I owe you one."

"You owe me more than *one*! Wait 'til you see my bill. It'll be quite a few ones!"

They laughed, and Russell carried the sleeping dog back to the car while Sam turned off the lights and locked up behind them.

His house was still dark, and Russell decided to check it out before carrying Shane back inside. Drawing his gun once more, he reached for the doorknob. Without thinking, he turned it. Then he froze. *Unlocked? I forgot to lock the front door?* He quietly and quickly moved to the hallway and found the light switch. It worked. *Great, the one switch within reach that works, and I didn't try it.*

He pulled two light bulbs out of the cupboard. As he started to unscrew the old bulb, it flickered. *What the—? They're just unscrewed? A* frugal *burglar?* The rest of the lamps were unplugged. The house glowed after he checked all the rooms.

"A dog's life," Russell whispered to the dog sleeping in his arms and lowered him on the cushion next to his bed. He turned on his night-stand lamp, sat next to Shane, and gently petted the sleeping dog's head.

Guess I know what my next project is, Russell figured and went back to the kitchen to survey the mess. *Locking up wouldn't have made any difference with the back door hanging loose like that.* Glass crunched under his feet. *Gotta' clean this mess up,* he thought and grabbed a broom.

He swept a path across the floor to the back door and tugged on it, propping it against the kitchen counter. It wobbled from one hinge. He made his way through the door and went to the garage. *Boards. Nails. Where's the damn hammer? Okay, got it.* He hauled the materials back inside and made fast work of securing the door and covering the broken window. *That'll hold tonight.*

He found a dirty rag and dumped it and the dustpan full of glass into the trash bag under the sink.

One more check of Shane—it was well past midnight and Russell headed to the den to jot down a bit of what happened for his report. *Report! I didn't call this in!* Then he realized he had cleaned up. *Damn! I've destroyed evidence. Some* professional *police officer I am.*

The rag! Russell retrieved a clean plastic bag, and stuck his hand inside. Wearing it like a saggy glove, he carefully pulled the rag out of the garbage and saw the blood on it. *More evidence if we need it, if they investigate thoroughly.* He pulled the plastic bag over his hand to envelop the rag, twisted it closed and stuffed it into the refrigerator. Then he remembered the prescription bottle in his pocket and also put that into the fridge.

Russell headed into the living room with a pad and pencil to jot down what happened. *Nearly fifteen years on the force and I tainted my own crime scene. Hell of a detective I am. I'll never hear the end of this one.*

Chapter 64

Close to 2 a.m. and exhausted from the long, cold walk home and the dog fight, Keno dropped onto his own bed. He tossed and turned for a few minutes. *This has been the worst night of my life, well, not counting time spent with Dunne.* His thin sheets were rumpled and the blankets fell to the floor twice. He opened then closed the window around five a.m. and went back to bed. He didn't fully wake up until eleven.

In the shower the soaked gauze fell off his arm and swirled to the drain. He picked it up and tossed it into the toilet. After he dried off, he tied a dish towel around his wound. Dressed in almost clean clothes, he went into the kitchen and automatically looked in the fridge for a beer. *None!* His hands were shaking as he picked up the telephone to call Det. Hurley. *Damn! Forgot. No dial tone. Can't call. Gotta' get outta' this mess.*

Keno dug through his drawers, shoving around his briefs, socks, bits of paper, receipts, addresses, a forgotten crumpled five-dollar bill, miscellaneous phone numbers, undershirts, and found nothing. *Wait! Cash!* He dug through again and pulled out the wadded bill, flattened it on the counter, carefully folded it in half, and stuffed it into his hip pocket, adding it to the money left over from his trip home.

He checked his windows twice and, half way down the stairs, he went back up and checked the lock on his door. *Man, he's after me.*

He walked three blocks to the 6th and L Street Market and checked the pay phone near the store. There was no change in the slot, but he did hear the buzz, letting him know the phone worked. He hung it back up, stood, and stared at it while his stomach twisted into a knot. He shoved his hands into his pocket and felt the bills still there. He took a deep breath and entered the store.

"A bottle of Jack," he told the clerk.

"Jack Daniels?"

"Jack *shit*; I don't care! Just gimme something! Anything strong!" He jabbed his pointer finger past the clerk's left shoulder at the bottles on the shelf. "That. Gimme that one."

Keno dug the money out of his pocket, slammed it on the counter then grabbed his change. The clerk put the bottle in a small, brown paper bag. Keno had the bottle cap twisted off before he got to the door. Outside, he leaned against the brick wall and took a swig. The cool liquor seeped down his throat. He felt a warm sensation, his muscles relaxed, and his hands stopped shaking. *Who said this ain't good for you?* he thought and took another swig. Now thinking more clearly and his gut reaction to get out of town diminished, he headed for the telephone booth at the side of the store.

Keno *dropped his dime*, made his call. Of course, *dropping a dime* cost Keno a quarter. The roar of a passing logging truck caused him not to hear anyone answer the phone.

"Hello? Hello?" came a voice. "Who is this?"

"Sorry, I was tryin' to get the Sheriff's Department."

"This is it, fella. How can I help you?" the officer said.

"Yeah, right. Who's in charge of the murder?"

"Murder? Are you reporting a murder?"

"Naw. Er, yeah, it's a murder, but it happened a while ago. Who's in charge? Hurley?"

"Depends on which murder. We've had a couple recently. Got a name?"

"Lukin, Keno Lukin."

"When was *he* killed? I don't remember a Lukin victim."

"Shit, man, that's me. I thought you wanted *my* name." Keno waved the receiver away from his ear and almost hung up.

"No, what's the victim's name? I can't connect you to the right detective unless I get a victim's name."

"Oh, okay. It's Marshall, like the president."

"President ... or victim?. You sure?"

Keno's took another drink. "Sure I'm sure. It was a president's name. M ... M something."

"Could it have been Madison?"

"Yeah, that's it! Madison." Keno was proud of himself and rewarded himself with another sip.

"I'll connect you to Detective Hurley."

About time! Hurley. That's who I was hopin' for. Keno took another drink. *Maybe I shouldn't do this—should just run.* He tried to hang up the phone but missed the cradle. Then he heard a voice, "Hello? This is Hurley. Who's this?"

Keno fumbled the phone, hitting his sore knuckles and his swollen arm on the shelf inside the booth trying to grab it.

"Shit! Damn it!" was all Det. Russell Hurley heard in his receiver.

Grasping the phone upside down, Keno slammed it into the cradle with the cord on top. His hands were shaking so badly that some of his precious liquid spilled down his shirt and pants.

He grabbed the bottle, still in the bag, and stood it on the shelf under the phone. The crumpled paper under the bottle made it teeter then tip.

Keno caught it before it hit the ground. Holding it with both hands, he filled his mouth with the burning elixir and swallowed another gulp.

Keno saw the courthouse across the street and down a couple of blocks. He sank to the ground and sat staring at nothing, wondering what to do. *Hurley. Why'd I go into his house last night? He probably knows it was me. I'll be doin' time again. Can't do no more time. Shee-it.*

He took another sip then wiped his hands on his pants. *Call again? Leave? Can't—car's busted.* He was sweating even in the cool air. The sun, starting its afternoon descent, could be seen through the bank of gray fog. *I'm dead. No matter what I do, I ain't worth shit. Dunne? The cops? What the hell, ain't got nothin' to lose—'cept my life.*

Keno stood up, dropped another quarter into the telephone, and dialed the number again.

"Humboldt County Sheriff's Department. May I help you?"

"Yeah, it's me again. Gimme Hurley."

"Just a moment. I'll connect you."

Chapter 65

The sun had risen, but Phillip Dunne ignored the beginnings of the warm, new day. He slept on top of the sleeping bag; the food Rose had brought was gone, but Dunne had been able to keep his cooler full. *Got plenty of money ... again, after that friggin' Keno took some.* The cash Dunne stole covered the food bills when the credit cards were questioned.

He walked. He exercised. Last night he had jogged along the beach for two miles before returning, walking along the side of the road. He had been out of breath but nothing like last week after his first run. Now up to two miles each way, Dunne figured he would make it to four miles each direction within the week. Getting back in shape was one thing he intended to do.

While in prison, he had run the track every chance he got. He had won every unofficial race with any idiot on the yard who took his challenge. His stash of cigarettes and ramen noodles was kept well supplied within days of his being locked up. Every other inmate thought he could beat Dunne, but every one of them lost the bet. The consequences suffered by one Hispanic cholo who had not paid immediately sent a lesson to everyone else: pay your debts as soon as they're due or don't be stupid enough to challenge him. Dunne had learned how to pound someone's gut to avoid broken bones and visible bruises, but the delinquent inmate couldn't stand straight for three days. Others took note; everyone from every ethnic group paid quickly. It didn't take long before the only ones willing to take him on were the "fish," the new inmates moving into the cell block.

He had felt good while in prison because he had kept himself in shape. Since getting out, he had lived the easy life—getting unemployment and welfare benefits from two states, hitchhiking, bumming off Keno, taking what he needed, enjoying what he wanted no matter how he got it. But he had not kept up any exercise regimen—until now.

The damp weather of the north coast of California, where he and his mother had lived after moving back to the mainland with her third husband, did not entice him to do outdoor activities. *This is where* real *men were meant to be. Why'd Mom move away after only four years? I loved it here ... got away with a lot of shit back then, too. Life was good.*

Dunne stretched, pulled out a joint and lit it, drawing in as much as his lungs could hold. He climbed out of his personal cave and headed toward the road that ran between his shelter and the beach. The warm days, the moonlit nights with the cool ocean breeze kept the tourists coming and provided him with more than he needed. *This is almost too easy*, Dunne thought. He looked up and down the highway and headed toward the white sands of the beach at Waimea Bay. *Good and easy*. He took another drag on his joint, held it for a moment, then blew it out slowly, deliberately. As soon as the traffic cleared, he jogged across the lanes and through the parking lot.

He stopped and shifted his weight back and forth, forcing his bare feet into the sand. The laces of his tennis shoes were tied together, and the shoes were draped over his shoulder. The breeze played its fingers in his now sun-bleached hair. Waves rolled in, heaving white foam onto the sand.

Shells were scattered at the shoreline, some as small and pink as a baby's fingertip and were coveted by island souvenir shops and jewelry stores; tourists competed with local beachcombers for these tiny treasures. Larger shells washed ashore with each surge and were eventually tumbled smooth by the abrasive sand unless they were collected by children playing in the surf.

Dunne's stomach rumbled. It was too early for picnic baskets and coolers filled with beer to be left open while their owners splashed in the surf and hovered over their children. Always craving more money and new credit cards, he looked around but saw no one who might have left wallets under beach blankets. No cars were left unattended with the windows down an inch to prevent overheating the interior and the owner's valuables not so securely stashed under the front seat. Only one car was in the parking lot, and its occupant sat behind the wheel, asleep. *Someone will pull in soon and spend the day on the beach, and I'll get what I need.*

He tilted his face to absorb the full rays of the sun then turned toward the highway. The beach sloped steeply to the ocean, and he had moved closer to the bank with each turn. His left foot felt for the sand, but it wasn't there; he lost his balance and flailed then rolled down the bank into the pounding surf.

Dunne's eyes, ears, and mouth filled with brine as he floundered in the waves. Gaining a foothold, he took a step up the bank; another wave pelted him from behind. Again, he rolled and thrashed at the bubbles surrounding him. This time when he stood up, he was nearly waist deep. *What the hell? Getting in deeper?* He turned and looked back at the ocean and another wave caught him square in the face.

Coughing and sputtering, Dunne turned toward the beach. Fighting to get his feet secure in the sand, he scrambled up the shore. *Damn! Fuck this!* Dripping wet, coughing, still cursing the stinging salt water in his eyes and throat, he ran up the beach before he turned to face the ocean.

He searched for his tennis shoes. *Not there, not there? Where?* Then he saw the specks of white beyond the first rolling wave. *What the hell? How'd ...* The decision whether to get them or not was mulled for only a moment. He needed those shoes. He had worked hard for them. The kid's credit card had not been accepted at the first two stores he had gone to, and it took some talking to convince the clerk at the third store that the signatures really did match. Yes, he wanted those shoes back.

Dunne pulled out his pack of cigarettes and matches and realized they were soaked. "Damn," he hissed. He threw them to the ground then headed toward the pounding waves.

Waist deep, Dunne leaned forward and dove through the next approaching wave. Coming up on the other side, he searched the next crest for his shoes. Several strokes later, he saw them rising on the incoming surge. He easily swam to them and wrapped the laces around his left wrist. He turned onto his back and floated there for several minutes, enjoying the throbbing of the vast ocean and the buoyancy of the salt water.

He rolled onto his stomach and looked back at the green island rising from the surf and realized he was farther out than expected. He transferred his shoelaces to his teeth and reached arm over arm, feet kicking hard at the swelling waves. Several strokes later, he paused again and looked at the beach and wondered if he was making any progress through the receding tide.

Chapter 66

Russell hung up the phone and laughed. "Kevin Lukin. Who would have thought?" The other officers in the room looked at him then shrugged and returned to their own reports or phone calls. Russell cleared his desk of the county's latest spousal abuse report. He fingered through the files in his bottom drawer until he found the "J-K-L" folder. Several pages in, he found "Lukin" and pulled the papers out.

Yep. I remember him. That's the "Keno" character who called from Hawaii. The information roused a memory—a sleazy memory. *Keno, that's right. He was in a store when it got robbed a few years back. He was a suspect because he was drunk on the job but got cleared a few days later.* Russell put his file back in the drawer and walked to the windows that overlooked the street below. He saw a small man dressed in poorly fitting clothes and a denim jacket warily checking for the traffic in both directions though it was a one-way street.

He watched the man cross in the middle of the block. *Could get you for jay-walking. And this is the idiot who says he knows something about Madison? Well, I'll listen. Haven't found any real leads so far.*

Russell looked beyond the buildings' rooftops. The foothills were visible through the light mist. *Too much has been going on here lately in addition to the usual, normal crimes. Madison. Wanda. A Humboldt State graduate heading north went missing up north. Major crimes are usually few and far between here. What's going on?*

Russell pulled Jeffrey Madison's file out of his drawer and reviewed the items inside: pictures of the car in the bay taken from every angle, photos of what was found in the front and back seats and the trunk: redwood needles, a white button, a couple of faded receipts that Forensics was still working on, and notes from the phone calls. He had talked with Eric Devlin, the investigator also working on the case, but he hadn't learned anything new either. Russell had extended the search into Del Norte County to the north, Mendocino County to the south, and Trinity county to the east and expected more reports to be coming in, but Russell was getting impatient and frustrated. He had spent hours looking for anything that would be a clue. Fingerprints were impossible to retrieve; bay water had eliminated all chances of recovering any.

There wasn't much else inside the car. The signatures on the receipts had been verified as being Jeffrey Madison's; Sherrill had identified them two days ago, and Forensics confirmed it. So far, there wasn't one solid thing to go on, nothing, just so damn many non-productive phone calls and interviews. If there were other charges to Jeffry Madison's credit card, they were not in the system yet, and the card companies had no more to report. *It's like he disappeared, vanished into thin air, just like Christine.*

Russell looked up when he heard the elevator doors open, but no one got off. The doors began to close, and he saw a hand reach out and push back the safety bar before the doors met. The doors opened again, and a head with thinning disheveled hair and black-rimmed glasses peered around the edge.

Russell watched the scenario unfold and smiled. *Not much to laugh at in this business,* he thought, closed the file, and slipped it back into his drawer. *Find humor where you can.*

Keno stepped off the elevator and headed toward him.

"You're Lukin, right?" Hurley asked when Keno neared his desk. "You look familiar. Have you been here—?"

"Yeah, a while back. Hey, man," Keno said looking at the floor. "I need help. My ass is ... someone's gonna' kill me. You got me outta' a tight spot a few years ago and, well—"

Hurley turned away and took a deep breath of fresh air. "You've been drinking already today?"

"Naw. Hell no." Keno covered his mouth and coughed.

"Your hand. Where'd you get those scratches?"

"Got mad and punched a wall."

"Which got more damage? You or the wall?"

"Me." Keno didn't like cops, and this one's interest was unnerving. He took off his jacket and shoved it onto the back of the chair, but it fell to the floor. Reaching to retrieve it, his shirt sleeve pulled up, revealing his bandaged arm.

"How's your arm?"

"What? Oh, it's fine."

"What happened?" *Bet he was in my kitchen last night.* "Why'd you do it?"

"Uh, do what?" *Maybe he don't know it was me. Maybe—.*

"Why'd you break into my house last night? Why'd you hurt my dog?" Russell pulled out his handcuffs and laid them on his desk in front of Keno.

Keno gasped. "Sheee-it! I didn't break in. I don't do no breakin' to enter." Keno looked past Russell at the other officers in the room then twisted in the chair to check behind himself. He looked Hurley in the eye and said, "I didn't do nothin' to your dog until he came at me!"

"Yeah. He would've licked you to death."

"What? Hey, man, I didn't know. Dogs ain't never liked me. Got bit twice when I was a kid."

"Probably deserved it," Russell whispered. "My door is barely hanging on," he said. "Should make you fix it."

"Sure, sure. Anything you say. I'm okay with a hammer." Keno reeked. The spilled liquor on his shirt and pants had dried, but the odor surrounded him.

I wouldn't trust this guy with a pillow; forget handing him a tool. "I'll decide later how you'll repay society for your improprieties." *Should arrest him now, but I'll wait to hear what he says.*

"Impro ... pro—?"

"Crimes!" Russell said and shook his head. He paused to give Keno some time to think about it and opened his drawer. He pulled out a pen and tablet. "Now, tell me what you know. Who did this? Who killed Jeffrey Madison? You?"

"No," Keno said glancing around the room.

"Were you the one calling from Hawaii?" Hurley asked.

"Yes. Uh, no. It wasn't my idea. Some old con named Snake's idea."

"Snake? Snake who?"

"Ain't got no idea. Met him at some center. Salvation Army."

"Come on, Lukin. You must know something. What about Madison?"

"Well, yeah, but I need something in trade."

Russell glared at Keno. "Trade? How about five to ten for breaking and entering?"

"I don't do no breakin' and entering. I just went through your doggie door."

Russell's eyes widened as he inhaled then leaned toward Keno and said, "How about life in prison for murder? How's that for a trade? Come on. Confess."

"What? No!" Keno sputtered. "I didn't kill nobody. I just know something about some shit."

"No promises until I know what you have." Russell tapped the pen on the tablet.

"The Madison guy. I know about his car. The bay. Where it was dumped."

"Uh-huh. You could've read that in the paper. Everybody knows that. When did you kill him?"

"I told you, I didn't." Keno pushed his glasses back up his nose. "I know where the car came from. Where the guy's shit is."

Russell stopped doodling and looked at Keno. "You know? Then tell me, who did it?"

"I ain't sayin' nothing more until I know there's a deal comin'.."

"How would you know about this if you didn't do it?"

"I ain't no murderer. Like I said, I never killed nobody. What can I trade?"

"We can talk about it." Russell shifted in his chair, crossed then uncrossed his legs. "Who did it?"

"Not sayin' yet. Let's deal."

"Then you do know, huh? What've you got in mind to trade?"

"The guy's going to kill me." Keno was wringing his hands in his lap. He looked down at them. "My Probation Officer's after me. Probably lost my job. Landlady's kicking me out. Nothin's goin' right. Shit, everything's goin' *wrong. Real wrong.*" Keno squirmed and looked around the room again; he checked over both shoulders. "You can at least talk to my P.O. for me."

"Sure, I can do that. No other guarantees yet, though."

"Can you at least try about the job? And that old biddy, er, landlandy?"

"I'll see what I can do." Russell sighed. Promises were easy, some impossible to keep.

Keno exhaled noisily, and Russell leaned back as far as he could with falling out of his chair.

"What've you been drinking?" Russell waved his tablet to dispel the odor.

"Some shit. My nerves ain't too good."

"Maybe you should get something to eat."

"If I leave, I ain't comin' back. I'll be dead."

"Who's going to kill you?" Russell asked. *The booze will probably kill him first.*

"Not until I know I'll be safe," Keno insisted.

"So, it's the same guy – the one who killed Madison and the one who's going to kill you, right?" Russell made a note on the tablet. "Okay. Tell you what. I'll write up the breaking and entering report and hold on to it. If I need to use it, I will." He paused to make sure Keno heard him. "For now, I'll get you some food and find a place for you to stay a couple of nights." *The jail provides security housing,* Russell chuckled to himself. "If it all works out, I just might lose that report. Until then, we'll hold you here."

Keno nodded. "I'll be safe in here … and don't have to pay no rent."

Russell shook his head then dialed the jail's kitchen. The officer told him the meals for the day had already been prepared and the cook had left, so he called Elliott's Diner. "Hi. This is Hurley at the department. A burger and fries, oh, and a soft drink."

"Coke," Keno said.

"Make that two of each. Two Cokes, two burgers and fries. ... Yes, please deliver them to the third floor like usual. Thanks."

"Room service. Not bad bein' a cop."

"Not a perk. I'll pay. You owe me for two things now." Russell wrote a couple of words on his tablet. "Tell me what you know about the car," he asked knowing he wouldn't get a name until Keno had some food. "Where'd you first see it?"

"Up north."

"Uh-huh."

"It was in a bunch of redwoods."

"Okay." *Right. Maybe, just maybe, this guy knows something. The redwood needles weren't in the news reports. I've got to get over and see the inside of the car for myself again. Time ... not even enough time to look or write the damn reports.* "Interesting."

He could have read about the car's location being up north but probably not the pieces of redwood inside. "Anything more?" Something nagged at Hurley. He stared at Keno's face. *Not even a hint of guilt.*

Chapter 67

The midday sun beat down on Dunne as he sprawled exhausted on the beach. He was sticky from the salt water, and sand was under every piece of clothing. His whole body itched, but he was alive.

Fuckin' island. Ain't nothin' but water everywhere. Dunne opened his eyes and two pairs of wide, brown eyes stared down at him. *Kids. Damn kids.*

"You okay, mister?" the boy asked.

"Mommy thought you were dead," the girl said. Her black hair blew gently in the breeze. "Mommy called the beach patrol. She told them you were—"

Beach patrol! Shit! Dunne struggled to his feet and said, "I'm fine. Go tell your *mommy* to mind her own fuckin' business," he said and brushed sand off his arms.

Both kids' eyes went wide, and they craned their necks to watch the towering man rise in front of them.

He glared down at them and snarled. They immediately turned and ran. "Mommy, Mommy. He's not dead!" Both children lunged at their mother and clutched her tightly.

Dunne jerked his hand up, stepped toward her, and growled. The mother's expression made him laugh. She grabbed her kids, turned, and ran. He smiled, pleased he could still send shivers through others.

His expression changed. *I've got to get the hell out of here.* He grabbed his soggy shoes, turned and ran back to the road, glanced quickly in both directions and headed for his cave. A few feet into the underbrush, he stopped and put his shoes back on. They were wet, gritty, and smelly. He stood up and thought, *Maybe I shouldn't head back there, not give myself away.* He returned to the side of the road and stuck out his thumb. *Back in town I can get what I need. Money. Better shoes. Food. I'll look Rose up again. Ain't seen her for a coupla' days. Wonder if she's avoiding me?* A lunch wagon had pulled into the parking lot, and the smell of the fresh malasadas, the sweet island dessert, filled the air even across the road. His hunger pangs grew stronger.

Several cars passed before one stopped and picked him up. He and the driver shared few introductory words then spent the rest of the drive back to Honolulu in silence.

Within a half hour of walking along Waikiki Beach, Dunne found a pair of dry shoes that fit well enough and were sand free. Tourists were always leaving them to wade barefoot in the same Pacific Ocean that beat on the shores of the west coast of the mainland. There were socks inside his wet shoes, but he threw them into the nearest trash barrel. A picnic basket was open a few of yards away, and Dunne helped himself to a bag of chips and a chunk of cheese.

Looking toward the tall hotels that lined the beach, he spotted a set of outdoor, public showers. He stripped off his shirt and draped it over his shoulder then leisurely walked over to them. He pulled off his new shoes, setting them behind the shower then pulled the lever.

Clear, cool water rushed out, rinsing off the sticky salt water and sand. The water refreshed him. He pulled his Bermudas and briefs open to rid them of the grating sand inside and then rinsed out his shirt.

He opened his mouth and stood under the shower head with the cool water flowing over his face. He opened his eyes. He focused on a sign attached to the pipe. It read, "Not Potable; Do Not Drink." *What the hell!* He spat immediately. *Fuckin' hotels. Too cheap to get decent water out here.*

The water spigot turned off automatically and Dunne pulled the lever once more. It was the first shower he'd had in at least three days. When the water turned off the second time, he grabbed the shoes and walked toward the ocean and sat in the sun, yards away from the pounding waves. The sun was almost directly overhead and the warmth dried him quickly. He grinned as he heard a commotion to his left. *Some sucker just discovered his shoes are gone or their lunch was raided.* He continued to laugh and lay back on the sand. The waves boomed onto the beach, grinding the pebbles and shells into more sand to deposit at the edge of the ocean.

Chapter 68

"What's this guy's name?" Russell looked squarely at Keno. "No promises, no deals until you tell me."

"You've got to get me somethin' before I say too much."

Russell sighed. *I'm getting nowhere.* "Okay. Where was the car? Which road did you take?"

"I don't remember," Keno said and slurped on his Coke.

"What's the guy's name?"

"I ain't that stupid. Not until you put somethin' in writing."

"The car then. Which way did you head out of town?"

"North. No, east. Um, yes … no. I'm not sure."

"You're telling me you don't remember? Where was the car? Come on, Keno, it's getting late," Russell begged. A map of Northern California was unfolded on his desk, and they were both staring at it. "There are only three roads heading north out of here—101, 299 east to I-5, and farther north there's 199. Which one?" Hurley threw his pencil across his desk; his chair squeaked as he leaned back.

"Sh-rrf-y." Keno swallowed hard then sucked on the straw to wash down the last bite of his burger. "Sorry. Can't remember which one. I wasn't doin' so good that night. Slept most of the way there. Drove back." He squeezed a packet of ketchup over his fries and shoved five into his mouth. "Oh, I popped some buttons off my shirt too."

Russell added "buttons" to his notes and underlined it three times. *That button was certainly not mentioned to the press.* He smiled to himself.

"Give me a minute," Russell said. "Maybe there's a way." He went to Captain Reardon's office, tapped on the door, and hesitated at the entrance. "Hey, Cap," he said. "Didn't you say you were using someone to help you quit smoking? A hypnotist?"

"Yeah. So?" Captain Reardon continued working on his latest budget revision. He didn't look up. "You got a desire to be under someone's suggestive powers?"

"Not me. I've got this, well, this suspect, accomplice probably, out here who knows something about the Madison kid's car."

"Most of the county knows about it, whole state, hell, probably the country." He punched a few numbers into his calculator, pushed the "add" then "total" buttons then grunted. He jotted some figures into the margin of the first draft of his report. "What's he got nobody else has?"

"Says he was with the suspect and helped him ditch the car—*after* the kid was dead, of course. Claims he had nothing to do with the murder."

"Murder? He's sure the kid's dead?" The captain stuck his pencil between his teeth and glanced up.

"Says the guy told him more than once that he 'offed' him."

Reardon slowly put his pencil down and looked directly at Russell. "You believe him?" and nodded toward Keno Lukin sitting at Hurley's desk.

"Yeah. He had some information that wasn't in the papers."

"So, you want to what? Hypnotize him? What do you think *that* will tell you?"

"Which road they took to get to the car. How far it was. Where the car was hidden for a while. He claims they dumped Madison's belongings before they drove back here and pushed it into the bay. Maybe the kid's body's up there."

"So you really think he's dead, huh?"

"I hate to say it out loud, but he would have made contact with his family by now. So, yeah, he probably is."

Captain Reardon opened his card file and shuffled through. He pulled out the business card for 'Serena Devine – Spiritual Connections and Hypnotic Assistance' and handed it to Russell. He added, "Good luck." Looking squarely at Russell, he added, "Do you need to talk to me about fraternizing with victims or their families?"

Russell stared at his Captain, shook his head, and said, "No. Why?"

Reardon looked him up and down, and said, "See me when you do need to," and picked up his pencil, started chewing on it, and returned to his task.

Russell let out a long sigh, turned, and went to the first empty desk. Her business card was shades of lavender and covered with stars and what looked like fairy dust. He dialed Serena Divine's number. *What the hell is this world coming to?* he wondered while he listened to the phone ringing in his ear.

Chapter 69

The day was drifting away and Phillip Dunne's hunger was rising. The nap on the beach had felt good, and he had been on the island long enough to have a tan, so he did not burn. He stood and shook the sand from his clothes. The shoes were a bit snug, and, without socks, they rubbed his heels. He knew he would have to find something that fit better, and soon.

Folding chairs, umbrellas, and blankets covered the beach. Dunne started wandering among them, looking for untended belongings. He noticed a blonde in a string bikini stand and start yelling at a young boy toddling toward the surf. She took off at a full run, racing to get to him before he got too close to the waves.

Her purse is right there. Thank goodness for brats. He strolled over to the woman's chair and sat down. Confident that no one was paying any attention, he leaned back, pulled her purse toward his left arm, reached in with his right hand, and pulled out her fat wallet. *Stupid bitch.*

As he was tucking the wallet into the front of his shorts, he stood up.

"Hey, what the hell are you doing?" The voice was deep and loud, certainly not the mom's.

"Just checking my wife's things, she's over—" he started to point toward the ocean and looked at the approaching man. *What the hell? What is he, a body builder?*

"That's *my* wife's stuff. Put it back." The man grabbed for Dunne's arm but grasped air.

Dunne had pulled his right arm back and swung, but missed the man's face. However, to avoid the punch, the man stumbled and tripped over the chair behind him.

Other sunbathers clamored to gather their children and move a safe distance from the ensuing fight but were suddenly pleased when Dunne turned and ran. He heard a female voice call out, "What happened, honey? Is everything okay?"

No, bitch. I got your shit. Now start crying on your hubby's shoulder.

Dunne turned away from the ocean and glanced around to get his bearings. He raced for the pathway between the swanky hotels and headed for the busy street ahead. He slowed to match the pace of the tourists and blended with the hordes of tourists browsing the shops.

Wandering through the area without anyone pointing assured him that no one had followed from the beach. He found a quiet corner behind a rack of jeans and pulled the cash and credit cards out of the red and orange stripped wallet. *What an ugly piece of shit.* He counted the small handful of bills, left the coins, and kept two of the credit cards. He shoved his booty into his front pockets and slipped the wallet into a trash can near the door on his way out.

Rose must be on duty by now. Maybe she's missed me as much as I've missed her. He scratched at his groin and felt a familiar rise in his body. *Yeah, I've missed her.*

Chapter 70

The next morning, Serena Divine, Hypnotist Extraordinaire, arrived at nine and efficiently did what her business card promised. Russell had given her notes on what they were looking for but knew he couldn't know all possibilities that might come up.

Keno, nearly twenty-four hours in protective custody, was dried out and sober, and Serena quickly had him under her influence. Russell wasn't sure if it was because of Serena Divine's skill or Keno's mental capacity. Whichever, Keno started talking about the drive to get the car.

"We headed north, went way north. I thought we was in Oregon, but he said no we wasn't." His eyes were open and he kept moving his hands as if steering a car. "We pulled onto a side road."

"Which way did you turn?" Russell asked.

"Shhhh!" Serena admonished.

"But we need to know—"

"Hush. Let him tell it in his own way," she whispered.

Keno was unfazed. "We drove into the trees."

Russell turned away and smiled, wanting to respond to that comment but didn't dare.

"There was another car, a really cool car, there with all kinds of shit in it. Sleeping bag, suitcase, blanket, pillow, some pictures and some rings and jewelry."

"Ask him about a journal."

"Quiet!" Serena hissed, "Or get out."

"I dunno what other shit was there." Keno was moving his hands now as if he were tossing things over his shoulder. "We cleaned it outta' the car and drove it back. It took all night. It was one cool car." Keno blinked several times then closed his eyes. His chin dropped to his chest.

"I think he's through," Serena said.

"Through? We don't know where this is yet. We need more details."

"He can't give them to you sitting in a police station." Serena looked around at the desks, windows, partitions, and shook her head. "You need to get him out on the road."

"What? Drive? Take him?"

"Yes. While he's under suggestion."

"You'd have to go too?" Hurley's shoulders drooped.

Chapter 71

Sherrill had driven the round trip to Ukiah one last time—her belongings crammed into the trunk and back seat of her rental car. Even the passenger side was filled with books and boxes of linens. She unlocked the motel room door and she heard the phone ringing. She dove across the bed and answered it.

"How about fraternizing with the enemy tonight?" said a familiar voice.

"What? Fraternizing? Enemy?"

"Just a figure of speech. Never mind. I've got some news," Russell said. "Seven okay?"

They had their second dinner-not-a-date since the car was found. They sat across from each other in a nice restaurant near the bay.

"Nice choice," Sherrill told him. "Any suggestions?"

Russell ordered wine then offered a couple of choices; they ended up ordering the same item. After talking about her drive, the insurance company's stalling tactics for replacing her car, the potential for substitute teaching jobs, and how her boss in Ukiah had reacted to her resignation after less than three months into the school year, Russell said, "We have a lead,"

"A lead?" *Finally. It's about time,* she thought, but said, "Where Jeffrey is? Or—"

"Where the car was cleaned out."

"Car? What do you mean—cleaned out?"

"There wasn't much in it when we pulled it from the bay. Our source says—"

"Source?"

"The same guy calling from Hawaii. He gave up on the extortion idea and decided survival was more important." He watched her concentrate on the croutons, shoving them into a pile on her salad plate. "He and this other guy headed north where the car was and tossed a lot of things out, things you had on your list of Jeffrey's possessions. Then he drove the car back here. I don't know what we'll find, wherever that place is."

Sherrill stared across the room then took another sip of her wine. "What's next?" she asked then looked back at him.

"Well, we're driving to the site tomorrow—early." He paused, jabbed at his salad, and watched her expression change to deep contemplation.

She was looking past him, or maybe through him. "What?" he said. "What are you thinking? You're working tomorrow, right?"

She didn't respond for a moment then said, "Scheduled to."

He sighed in relief and quickly asked, "Which school?" trying to change the subject.

Dinner arrived and the conversation continued about teaching, food, redwoods, tides.

Russell left for work the next morning before the newspaper was delivered, and the fog was still thick when he arrived at the courthouse. *Maybe it won't be too bad of a drive,* he hoped as he took the steps two at a time to the front door. He entered the office area and noticed Sgt. Johnson sitting at his desk. Beside him, Serena had already started Keno on relaxation exercises.

Several minutes later, Russell whispered, "Everyone set?"

"Yep," Johnson replied, and Ms. Divine, with her finger to her lips, nodded.

The walk to the squad car was brief. A young officer was leaning against the trunk waiting for them. Ms. Divine opened the front passenger door for Keno. Calm and looking a bit dazed, he talked about his old car with leopard spots while climbing into the front seat and pulling the door closed. Ms. Divine got into the back behind him, and Sgt. Johnson joined her. Russell sat in the driver's seat. A second car with Investigator Devlin and another officer followed.

With Ms. Divine whispering prompts from behind, Keno began talking about the turns, trees along the highway, and dots in the middle of the road flashing their reflected light into his eyes as he relived the night drive he had made a month earlier.

About two hours of driving north on Hwy 101, Keno directed them to turn onto Hwy 199. Miles later the "Six-Rivers National Forest" welcome sign greeted them. Russell swiveled his head several times, stretching his neck. *Can I remember all six rivers? Let's see, Smith, Klamath, Trinity ... three more. Gotta stay awake.* Russell clenched then relaxed one hand at a time on the steering wheel. *Eel River, ... oh, yeah, the Mad River, one more. Never can remember all six.*

At least another half hour later, Keno blurted, "Here. Turn right here!" He was bouncing like a child on the seat. "Turn right here," he repeated and pointed straight ahead.

Russell couldn't see any space to the right that would accommodate a car but put the blinker on.

"Not right. Left," Keno moved his hand and almost stuck his finger into Russell's face. He was pointing across the road into a clearing.

"You said right."

"Yeah, turn left right here. Left."

Russell growled to himself, flipped the blinker for a left turn, paused to let an approaching car pass then turned into the wide spot across the road. Tire tracks were nearly obscured by fallen tree branches and redwood needles then disappeared completely a couple of yards into the forest. Driving carefully, he pulled around a few trees and curved through the towering redwoods.

"Yeah. This is it. This is where we got the car," Keno said excitedly.

Russell looked around. *I don't see where the car could've been.* Farther ahead, he saw the stately redwoods standing sentinel over a small clearing, preventing even a beam of morning sunlight from entering. Russell pulled to the left and parked his car near the opening. The other car pulled up and stopped behind Russell.

Everyone got out of the cars. Damp ferns and fallen redwood needles silenced their steps. They walked toward the area with hushed reverence; it was eerily peaceful.

Giant trees surrounded them, guarding the serenity while the officer strung yellow police tape, securing the scene, as if it would make a difference.

Keno walked up to Russell and pointed across the clearing. "The car was over there. Stuff was hanging out of the trunk, and some shit was already on the ground. A blanket was wet; I folded it and put it there." He pointed at the blanket partially obscured by foliage.

"Okay, thanks," Russell said. "Please get back into the car now, and don't go anywhere."

"Where'd I go, anyway? Ain't nothin' around here," Keno said and climbed into the back of the car.

Serena Divine sat on the front passenger seat and watched the activity. She let her sandaled feet dangle out the door.

Any signs of a car having been in the clearing were now hard to see; the ferns had grown back and more redwood needles had fallen. There were no obvious signs of a crime.

There may be no victim here, but Russell felt something. *It feels like someone is still here,* he thought, and the hair on the nape of his neck and arms stood up. *There's no sign of someone fighting for his life, but there's a chill.* He felt something against his shoe as he took a step and pushed the ferns aside with his foot. *A shaving kit. Damn. Keno wasn't lying.* He signaled one of the deputies to come over and hang more yellow tape, enlarging the search area.

Russell looked up at the magnificent trees towering over them before searching further and listened. Silence was only interrupted by the hushed sounds of distant traffic and the quiet conversation of the officer with Keno and Serena. *In another life, I could stay here and listen to this nothingness.* He stood still then realized, *Hey, I can hear my own heart beating. This could be heaven on Earth—it's like feeling the pulse of the world here.* He paused a moment and took one more look around then pulled out his notebook and pencil. He jotted a note about the item he'd found but didn't pick it up, leaving it for the officer with the camera.

Devlin walked up behind Russell and cleared his throat. "Did you notice where we are?"

"Well, besides in the far reaches of Northern California, where?"

"Not too far from the California-Oregon border. It's less than a mile up the road, maybe a lot less."

"That close?" Russell asked. "You're certain we're still in California?"

"Well, maybe we went north after turning off the main road."

"Um, check it out, would you? If we're in Oregon, we have a problem with jurisdiction. A defense attorney will tear our case apart."

"Sure," Devlin said, pulled a compass and measuring tape out of the trunk of the squad car, and walked into the forest.

An officer spoke up. "Found two open and empty Samsonite suitcases here." They were at the edge of the clearing, along with three teak jewelry display boxes, their black velvet-lined drawers flung aside and empty.

"Make sure to get pictures before moving anything," Sgt. Johnson reminded everyone. "And mark where it is on a diagram. You've all got bags and tags, right?"

Russell nodded in agreement. *What's that?* He looked toward the highway. *A car coming? What the hell? Who? How could anyone else be here? And why?* "Hey, Johnson, check that out. No one else should be here," he said and turned back to the scene. *A blanket, the same color Sherrill described.* He opened his notebook and jotted more notes.

Voices. Johnson's and a female's. Something familiar. Oh no! She didn't. She couldn't have.

Sherrill walked toward the clearing; redwood needles clung to her pants. She noticed two people sitting in one of the squad cars with the doors open and watching the activity in the clearing. One was a scraggly looking guy with thin hair and thick glasses and the other was a young woman dressed in flowing purple scarves, a colorful skirt, and sandals.

"Is he the one who—" Sherrill asked.

"What the hell are you doing here?" Russell yelled, breaking the silence and glaring at her.

"I told you I was going to participate whenever and wherever I can. So, here I am," Sherrill answered.

"How the hell'd you find us?" Russell clenched his teeth.

Sgt. Johnson frowned at Russell then walked away.

"It was easy," Sherrill said looking around. "I kept back a bit from the second squad car. Almost too far back to see you turn in here. Almost."

"You're going to contaminate the scene." Russell stood between Sherrill and the clearing, his hands on his hips. "You've got to go. You'll ruin our case."

"Case?" Her pitch rose a full octave. "You have a case? Who?"

"No. No one yet. At least not for sure. We ... I told you last night." Russell sighed. "Don't change the subject. You need to leave. Now."

Sgt. Johnson, Keno, Serena, and the officer were staring at them.

"Then put me to work," she said, staring him in the eye.

"No."

"Yes. What could I do to help? Give me something to do."

"No!" Russell threw his hands in the air. "You're hopeless." He turned and stomped to the edge of the clearing, staying outside the perimeter. "Stay there. Don't move," he yelled over his shoulder.

"Hey! Yes, you," Russell yelled at the officer. "How did you let someone follow you? Are you an idiot? Didn't you see someone behind you?"

The deputy muttered, "Yes, sir. Uh, no, sir. I saw a car behind me but didn't think anything of it."

"Well, you thought wrong. We've got a serious problem here. You get the honor of escorting this ... this *lady* back to her car."

"Uh. Yes, sir."

Sherrill cleared her throat and said, "I'm not leaving. I've got a vested interest in this. I can help identify my brother's things."

The officer walked up to her, and Russell nearly yelled. "You are *not* helping. I'm not losing this case because of outside interference. If you stay, all evidence collected here will be compromised. You *are* leaving."

"No." Sherrill folded her arms across her chest.

Russell turned to the officer. "Escort her to her car and make sure she leaves."

"Yes, sir," answered the officer. He turned and lightly grasped Sherrill's arm.

"Arrest her if she doesn't cooperate. 'Resisting.'"

"Yes, sir."

Sherrill pulled her arm away and scowled at Russell.

Russell looked at her and shrugged. "No choice, ma'am," he said. "Either leave or he'll arrest you." He turned and walked away; he could feel the blood pounding through the veins in his head. He paused, put his hands to his face, and pushed them through his hair.

A minute later, Russell heard a car engine start. The sound faded as it headed toward the highway. *Thank you, God,* he said looking through the trees to the sky above and exhaled a long sigh. He checked the squad car. Keno was still there, sound asleep. *At least he's not interfering.* He quietly closed the car door. *Oh, the Van Duzen River! I can never remember that sixth river. Why now?* He shrugged and called out, "Okay, people, show's over. Let's get to work."

Sherrill, on the verge of tears, climbed into her car, started the engine, and backed toward the highway. She frowned at the deputy who was watching her, then grinned broadly, showed her teeth and growled to herself, tempted to stick her tongue out. She boldly waved and pulled into the traffic lane heading back to the coast.

A quarter mile away, she could no longer see the turnoff where the officers were searching for her brother's belongings. Just ahead, she saw another turnout, pulled in, shifted into park, and set the brake. She glared ahead at the nearly empty freeway, clenched her fists, and pounded on the steering wheel. *Damn him. Damn him and his damn rules.* She let the car idle for a few minutes to allow the warmth to build inside before she turned the key, stopping the engine, then sat there glaring at the road ahead.

Two and a half hours later, plastic bags and cardboard boxes were lined up next to the patrol cars. Clothes, a toothpaste tube, jewelry cases, a journal, and many other personal items had been photographed, tagged, and carefully placed into bags or boxes. The area was trampled, and the yellow tape removed.

"Something's missing," Russell said.

Devlin looked at him and asked, "What?"

"I'd hope we'd find Madison's body."

"Hoped?"

"Well, I'd rather find him alive, but we know he's not. This case has been hanging there for too many months now—no body, no primary crime scene, all these things piling up, but nothing to show he's dead for sure."

"Doesn't give you much to build a case on, does it?" Devlin reached down and picked up two plastic bags with tagged items in them.

"Circumstantial evidence leaves a weaker case," Russell said and looked around at the scene, now cleared of Jeffrey Madison's possessions.

"But convictions are still possible." Devlin said and turned toward the squad cars.

"Possible but not certain. I like certain," Russell said and followed Devlin. "We're done here, folks. Let's pack up and head back," he called out. *The serenity is certainly gone.* "We're all accounted for, right?" he said and checked on Keno who was sitting sideways on the edge of the back seat of the patrol car.

"Yep," Johnson said while tossing the bags into the trunks. When he had finished, he slammed the trunk lid closed. Keno jerked at the sound.

Russell noticed that Sgt. Johnson was the only one who still looked fresh. *How on Earth can he do that?* Russell wondered. *And, there aren't even any newscasters here so he can show off.* He shook his head in dismay.

Russell tapped Devlin on the shoulder. "Hey, what'd you find about our location?" he asked.

"That we're still in California."

Russell smiled. "Good. Thanks. Probably should get a survey team up here to verify, though."

"I agree," Devlin said and made a note on his pad.

They climbed back into the cars, slowly backed out, and turned onto the highway. Russell let the other squad car pull ahead. Russell's muscles relaxed as he pulled into the traffic lane. His hands squeezed the steering wheel tightly when his radio crackled to life.

"Sir, that woman's car is just ahead. Thought you'd like to know."

"Thanks," Russell said. *Damn.* He frowned, hit the siren, and pulled in behind Sherrill's car. He climbed out and walked up to her window.

Sherrill jumped when she heard the siren and rubbed the sleep from her eyes. She rolled her window down then grasped the steering wheel. Grinning broadly but gritting her teeth, she asked, "Can I help you, officer? I wasn't speeding, was I?"

Didn't expect that! Russell thought and smiled to himself.

"Well, at least you left the scene. Thank you for that. It was the right thing to do."

"I realized that—about ten minutes ago. Didn't like it, but I understand." She took a breath and asked, "What did you find? Are you sure it was Jeffrey's stuff."

He nodded slowly then realized the thought of sitting in a car for two hours with Johnson, Keno, or any other officer all the way back to Eureka sounded repulsive. "We could talk about it on the way back if you'd like," he said. He hesitated for a second then looked at Sherrill and asked, "Would you mind if I rode with you?"

Sherrill's arm hairs rose with goose-bumps. She gripped the steering wheel harder and tried not to flinch. "You ... you don't have to escort the prisoner ... and the psychic?"

"Psychic?"

"Judging from the way she was dressed, she's *has* to be a psychic."

"No, she's a ... oh, never mind. Let Johnson and the officer take care of *them*—one of the perks of *not* being an officer."

Sherrill let her hands fall into her lap then nervously clasped them together.

"You're offering to drive?" She paused then added, "Sure beats driving alone."

He walked to the squad car, looked at Sgt. Johnson, and said, "I'm going back with Ms. Madison." He nodded to Keno and said, "I'll talk to your P.O. first thing tomorrow then meet with you. Maybe you'll give us more information?" He didn't wait for an answer, straightened up, smiled, and headed back to Sherrill's car.

Russell wanted to avoid details of what was found amongst the trees. He knew they were Jeffrey's belongings since Sherrill had given him that list of his things. He decided he was not going to tell her about the few surprises they had picked up: receipts from a store, a diner, and a gas station—more things to keep him busy over the next few days and perhaps help tighten the noose on Keno's cohort, whoever that was.

Sherrill broke the silence. "I knew his stuff was there. I could feel it when I walked into the clearing," she said. "You found his journal, didn't you?"

"Um, yes."

"His toothpaste too? You know he couldn't find the Crystal White in stores here on the west coast."

Russell gulped. "Yes, it was there." He glanced at Sherrill and noticed a single tear running down her cheek.

An hour and a half later, the radio newscaster was finishing up the *News of the Hour* and said, "The acre of marijuana was found fifteen miles east of Eureka."

"Ah, more home-grown found. More job security."

Sherrill laughed then patted her stomach when it growled.

"What's so funny? My stomach's making more noise than yours," Russell said.

"No, I'm really not very hungry. I laughed at the 'home-grown' you mentioned," she said pointing to the radio. "How much is grown here anyway?"

"The area's pot reputation circles the globe. Some of the best, I've been told."

"Told? So, you never smoked it."

Russell laughed. "Couldn't be a cop if I had."

"Same with being a teacher." She looked out the window at the passing houses in Arcata then asked, "You've really never smoked pot?"

He ignored her question and said, "In fact, the tag line that radio station uses is 'Home-grown radio.' They repeat it at least once an hour, twenty-four-seven. They advertise that they don't use nationally syndicated radio deejays. Besides, this is Humboldt County where 'the grass is greener' and it really *is* home grown."

"Oooh. Job security. Right?"

"Well, I don't like to look at it that way. It's a menace. It's—"

"Better than Maui Wowie?"

"According to rumors."

"So, you have *never* tried it? Really?"

"Well," his grin was obvious. "It's not in my personnel file. Back in the days when I was a new hire, you couldn't 'fess up to using anything stronger than coffee, except an occasional beer, of course."

"But you did try it?"

"Once in high school and again in the military. But now that I've told you, you're sworn to secrecy," Russell said with a broad grin. "Ate a bunch of junk food. Kinda' liked it but not enough that I wanted to keep using it. Don't miss it. Besides, beer is legal. Beer is good."

"Be glad you didn't go for a teaching credential. Laws are strict enough that if you get caught, you never get into a classroom."

"Was it hard not to give in?"

"People like to make it sound hard, but if you don't try it, you never miss it."

"If more people thought like you, I'd be out of a job."

"So it *is* job security, huh? No drugs, less crime, less abuse, fewer cops." Both laughed.

A bit farther down the highway, Sherrill's eyes grew heavy and closed. Her head rested against the window pane and her breathing became steady.

Russell looked at her then at his watch. *Oh, no. It's later than I thought.* He checked ahead for oncoming traffic and turned off the highway onto a two-lane road.

Chapter 72

Serena Divine rode back with the officer in the first car. Sgt. Johnson and Inspector Devlin were in the front seat of the second squad car, and Keno was in the back seat; a mesh screen separated the front from the back. Keno, after sleeping most of the morning and early afternoon, was animated on the way back.

"Keep your seat belt on, Lukin," Devlin said over the seat back. "We'll cuff you if you can't keep it on," he added.

"Say, Keno, what can you tell us about the car?" Devlin wanted to get Keno to relax and work up to the big question.

Keno gave some information about driving Madison's car but stopped a minute later. "That's all until I get a deal."

"Come on, Keno. Who did this? Tell us. Even Ms. Divine said to tell us what you know."

Keno, settling into the long drive back to Eureka, shuddered. *Dunne's gonna' know I'm doin' this. Don't know how, but he'll know.*

"Who was it, Lukin?" Sgt. Johnson asked. "What's this scum-bag's name?"

Keno froze, his muscles tightened, and he stared out the side window. He swallowed hard.

"Come on, Lukin. Hurley's talking to your P.O. tomorrow. He'll help you out. You might as well tell us. We'll pass it on to Hurley how you cooperated."

Keno wiped his hands across his face then ran his fingers through his thin hair. Without telling them Dunne's name, he told how he had met Dunne years ago, that Dunne had been to prison, but didn't divulge any information about the trip to Hawaii. Keno took a deep breath.

Devlin and Johnson interrupted and prodded for details. Devlin wrote everything down but was frustrated by the limited information. Every comment Keno made elicited more questions. Devlin finished writing and looked at Keno. "Did this guy say *why* he killed Madison?"

"Yeah. Said he wouldn't buy him a meal. I'll tell Detective Hurley more after he talks to my P.O."

Devlin rolled his eyes. "Okay. Is there anything you *will* tell us?"

"Well, this guy's killed before. A couple of times. Killed some waitress too, just before we left town."

Devlin and Johnson looked at each other then Devlin turned and looked at Keno. "What? Do you know any of their names?"

"No. Some redhead from Elliott's. Don't know nothin' about the others."

"Your friend killed Wanda Corbin?"

"He ain't my friend." Keno squirmed in the seat. "And, yeah, he done it. He told me."

"Can you prove that?" Devlin and Johnson asked at the same time.

"Don't know how. Wasn't there," Keno responded. "I'm done talkin'."

Devlin looked at Johnson; Johnson glanced at Devlin, their mouths open, and there was silence for several seconds.

"Wow! Hurley's going to want to hear this," Johnson said.

Devlin nodded and said, "This changes things."

Chapter 73

Sherrill woke up when Russell had slowed and made a sharp left turn.

"Where are you going?" she asked. "Is this the scenic tour? Why'd you turn here?" She sat upright and looked around. Arcata and Humboldt Bay were behind them, and they were driving across flat pastureland heading toward hills covered with redwood trees.

Russell glanced at Sherrill. Her hair was a mess, and her clothes were rumpled, but she looked more relaxed than he had ever seen her since they met.

"I'm drained," Sherrill said and yawned before asking, "Where are we going?"

"I forgot. I have an appointment."

"Now? It's getting late."

"Well, it's not really an appointment. It's dinner."

"Out here? Is there some old, quaint restaurant out here?" Sherrill squirmed in the seat and wiped her hands on her pants. She looked at Russell and waited for an answer. "Is this another case of needing a detective to solve the problem of a missing school teacher and a cop?"

"Nope. Wrong. No restaurants, and there'll be no one missing on this trek." Russell smiled. "I hope you don't mind. I nearly forgot that my sister-in-law invited me over tonight, and I can't disappoint my nephews," he said and turned onto a narrow two-lane road that twisted and turned around the contours of the hills rising on the left. Redwoods lined the edge of the road and filled the hillside.

"This is beautiful." The scenery sped past showing off its deep, verdant forest on one side and the pastures on the other.

"All that," Russell said sweeping his arm towards the flat pasture, "is reclaimed bay. Years ago all this was covered with water until dykes were built over there," he waved toward the bay, "and decades ago some woman donated all those eucalyptus trees that are planted along the shore as a wind-break."

"A historical review now. Hmmm." Sherrill lowered the window. The cool air rushed in and blew strands of her dark hair into her face. She brushed them away as she inhaled the salty air and exhaled slowly. She tugged at the seat belt. Everything felt close. Tight. "I'll be imposing. You should take me back first."

Russell glanced at her and tried not to show his concern. *A change of scenery'll do her good. And, who knows, a little family drama might take her mind off her situation.* "One more person won't be a problem. They have two growing boys to feed. My sister-in-law always cooks a big meal. Besides, I'm already late." He felt the cold air hit his face and added, "It's really cold out there. You might want to keep the window up."

"*You* might be cold," she said and took in another deep breath. The trees seemed so close, so large, so tall. "Where are we going, anyway?"

"Out into the country."

"Eureka's not country enough?"

Russell chuckled. "Hey, they're nice people, but I could take you back if you *really* want me to."

She took a breath before answering, "No, maybe being with other people might—"

Silence lay heavy for a couple of miles. A right turn took them past more open fields, fences framing horse pastures, barns set back from the road, and houses set back even farther.

A small, green marker named the location: "Freshwater." Older houses now lined the road, some in disrepair, others being renovated.

"Quaint."

"We're almost there," he said.

He made a right turn up a steep, narrow and twisting dirt road, a paved driveway, then a large, two-story house appeared ahead. A wide staircase led to a redwood deck and a double-door entry. Two cars, one a mini-van, were parked in a carport under the right side of the house.

"'MYREKA'? What kind of license plate is that?" Sherrill asked when Russell pulled in behind the mini-van.

"I'll explain later," Russell said, climbed out, stretched, and turned to take in the view. He could see a bit of the flatland through the trees and ferns. Green was everywhere, and crickets chirped.

The front door burst open and four arms flailed over two heads of bright red hair. Two young boys bounded across the deck and down the stairs. "Uncle Russ! Uncle Russ!" seemed to echo.

Sherrill stared as the arms wrapped around Russell's waist. *Kids. Children. Boys. Someone's family. What* am *I doing here? And with* him? *And his family?* She noticed Russell had left the key in the ignition, and an idea flashed, *I could scoot over and get out of here.* Her mind was racing. *Leave. Turn the key and drive away.*

The snap of her car door opening startled her, and her purse tumbled to the ground. Sherrill looked up and saw Russell standing there, offering his hand. She glanced back at her hand and pulled the key from the ignition and held it out to him. "Bad habit. Shouldn't leave keys in the car, *officer.*"

Chapter 74

Sherrill stood by the car and watched a taller, slightly older replica of Russell step onto the deck. "Hey! Welcome."

"Can you handle this?" Russell whispered to Sherrill. "We *could* go if you need to." The concern in his eyes surprised her.

"I, um, I guess I'll be okay." Sherrill looked at the two redheads bounding back up the stairs to their father. "I guess a change of pace would be good." She tucked her purse under her arm and headed for the stairs.

The house was comfortable, decorated in warm, cozy hues of peach and cream. Family pictures hung in the entry and down the hall. Grandparents, kids, parents with kids, and one that Sherrill paused in front of. An older couple, obviously the grandparents, was in the picture along with Russell's brother, a very pregnant woman, and a younger Russell with a pretty woman.

"Hi, and welcome."

Sherrill jumped slightly at the voice behind her and turned to see a friendly smile and a hand reaching out to her. It was attached to the woman who was pregnant in the photo.

"I'm so glad Russell brought someone with him. I'm Joanie—brother's wife—kids' mom. The driver of the big car down there."

"Oh, the one with the interesting license plate, 'MYREKA.' What's that—"

The two redheads rushed by, arms extended, ending her quest for an answer. "Vroom. Vroom. Uncle Russell says we're like jet planes. I want to fly when I grow up. Like Superman."

"Me, too," the older brother yelled. "But fly real jets."

Joanie laughed, "Yes, flying low … always moving and at incredible speed … and noisy. Come out to the kitchen with me, and we'll chat. Richard and Russell can watch the boys." Sherrill smiled at the ease Russell blended with the young boy's activities.

After plates of spaghetti, salad, French bread, broccoli, and a bottle of really good Napa Valley Merlot, Sherrill and Russell walked into the living room while the two boys were being put to bed.

"You're so lucky; you have a great family," she said and sank into an overstuffed chair.

"Thanks, but they were on good behavior tonight. Wait until you see the *real* clan and the whole bunch in action."

"The whole bunch? There's more?"

"Yep," Russell said and picked up a pillow as he sat on the sofa. "Our folks are on an extended vacation. They retired last year and are driving to the East Coast to see long-lost relatives and won't be back until after the New Year."

Sherrill wriggled in the chair enjoying the comfort. The second glass of wine at dinner was helping her relax, and she looked around the room. Her gaze paused at the entry, and she remembered. She cleared her throat, and asked, "There's a picture of you with your family and a woman. Can I ask if you're involved with someone?"

"Nope."

"'Nope, can't ask' or 'nope, not involved?'"

Russell paused, and his face went blank. "Just 'nope' for now."

"That picture then. That's ... *she's* the reason you understand what happening?"

"Yep." Russell twisted on the sofa cushion.

"I'm sorry; I didn't mean to ... ," she started then saw Joanie and Richard returning.

"Kids are in bed, reading to each other," Joanie said and sat down near Sherrill.

The conversation changed to the remodeling done to the house, local schools, and hiking, and it remained casual and friendly. Sherrill was beginning to feel at ease, and the few questions about why she was on the West Coast received straight-forward answers.

"More wine?" Joanie asked. She and Sherrill walked back into the kitchen and continued chatting while Joanie pulled a new bottle from the wine rack. Then, suddenly, they stopped talking and listened to the voices from the other room.

"I said, 'Leave me alone!'" Russell's voice had a sharp tone. "It's none of your damn business."

Sherrill's eyes widened and she looked at Joanie, who simply shrugged. "Sibling rivalry. Those two haven't grown up yet." They stood silently in the kitchen while the men continued.

"Hey, man," Richard's voice answered, "I'm just asking ... looking out for my kid brother. You've got to get back into life. Stop screwing around and—"

"I've got a life. Let me live it ... me! *You* ... butt out!"

"Hey, I'm sorry. It's been ten years—"

"Nine years, eight months, three weeks, but who's counting?"

Russell stood up and looked down the hallway where the family pictures hung.

"See? That's what I mean. You've got to move on."

"I'll move on when I'm ready to move on."

"Well, what about her?" Richard nodded toward the kitchen.

"Who?"

"Your date? That's what I was trying to ask about."

"She's not a date. She's, uh, she's helping with the case. That's all." Russell glanced toward the kitchen. "So, leave me alone." Russell stood and added, "It's time to go." He looked over his shoulder as his sister-in-law and Sherrill stepped out of the kitchen. "Thanks, Joanie," he said. "Dinner was great."

Sherrill mumbled something but was finally able to say aloud, "I'm in total agreement. Dinner was great, your boys are fun, and it was a nice evening." She hesitated then added, "You know, however, I never heard what 'MYREKA' means on your car."

Joanie smiled. "It has to do with 'Eureka' becoming '*Your*-reka' which then became 'My-Reka' and 'Arcata' becoming 'Are-' or '*Our*-Cata.' Our kids made up the words, and we got the license plate."

Sherrill tilted her head and scrunched her nose. "Huh? ... Oh!" she said and laughed.

They headed toward the front door. Russell was silent, and Richard stayed in the living room.

On the drive back to town, Sherrill kept the conversation light, avoiding the comments she had overheard. She told Russell about a studio apartment she found, how long she had to wait to move in, her recent furniture searches, and the classrooms she substituted in.

Russell pulled into the hotel parking lot and stopped at the entrance. After a pause, he looked at her and asked, "Why are you laughing?"

"Well, first, I had a wonderful evening. The day up north was lousy, but your nephews are cute and your sister-in-law is nice, and a great cook. However—" she stopped and waited.

Russell looked at her and said, "Is it about what you heard Richard and me fighting about? It's that he won't—"

"No, not that. I know how families can be. But, this is *my* car," she said and laughed again. "I'll have to drive you home ... or back to the courthouse. Where'd you park *your* car?"

Chapter 75

Wonder what day it is? Oh, who gives a shit? Dunne was spending his time jogging, sleeping, collecting wallets, eating, and trying to talk Rose into spending more time with him.

"Rose, let's go to my space. It's private there," he said as they walked along the beach. He was looking for the excitement he had felt when they first met. *Something's missing. She's not the same.*

"No," she answered, "it's more romantic here." *And more public.* "I like it better in the sand than on the floor of your cave."

"We could go to your place. It'd be even better on your bed."

Something about the look on his face, the twitch in the corner of his mouth, made her uneasy. Yet, the excitement was electrifying. *I've never felt such a thrill before,* she told herself. *Besides, he'd never hurt me bad. I think he loves me.* "When it gets dark and we think everyone's gone, it's fun," she told him. "It's like we're cheating or hiding. Maybe someone could catch us."

"Yeah, catch us," Dunne whispered.

The sunset was brilliant; dusk settled around them. They walked along the beach away from the families. Dunne scratched himself, paused, and grabbed her arm. He spun Rose around and kissed her hard. His hands roamed over her body, searching for that feeling he used to have with her.

She rose on her tiptoes and reached her arms around his neck, lifting herself off the sand and kissing him back, tongues intertwining, raising emotions. He felt inside her, and she tensed then dissolved in his arms. They fell to the sand and rolled over each other in the dim light of the new moon.

I could live like this for a long time, forever, he thought. *Well, maybe for another hour at least.*

"I've got to get back," Rose said later as she stood and rubbed her sore arms. *He was mean again tonight.* "I need to get some sleep and clean up. Early schedule tomorrow."

Dunne grunted, stood, and looked around. *Damn. People. Witnesses.* Another couple was walking hand in hand and wading at the water's edge. He looked at Rose and back at the couple, gritted his teeth, and wiped his hands on his pants. He turned and headed toward his cave.

"You're leaving me here?" Rose yelled.

"Walk alone," he called over his shoulder and jogged across the road. "You'll be safe on the beach."

"You're kidding—I don't believe it. You're leaving me here?" she yelled. "Come back! It's a long ways back to my car." She realized she was shouting at emptiness. *Bastard. If this is love, it sucks.*

Dunne had disappeared into the bushes across the road. The couple ignored her, laughing at their own conversation, and continued walking up the beach.

Dunne entered the shrubbery and turned around a few feet in. He saw Rose trudging through the sand toward the parking lot. *She'll get home. What the hell.* He turned back toward the cave then heard a twig snap. *What was that? Who's there?* He spun around and tried to see who was behind him. *No one. Just like in town this afternoon ... and yesterday. I know someone was behind me, watching me.*

He may have *thought* he knew it, yet whenever he checked behind him or looked at reflections in windows, no one was there. His paranoia was strong. He was alone, but he *knew* someone was there. Yet no one was paying any attention to him, again ... still.

I'll get Rose to look, too. Tomorrow. Maybe she'll see who's there. He turned and looked around again before heading toward his cave.

Chapter 76

First thing Monday morning, Russell left the office to check on a few cases held over the weekend. One family was at home, but the other two were not. Finding them at their jobs took a couple of hours. When he had done all he could, he returned to the office and headed toward Investigator Devlin's office.

Sgt. Johnson intercepted him. "Any word yet on that Mustang they found in the trees up north?" Sgt. Johnson asked.

Russell kept walking and answered, "No, nothing. Pictures should've been here already."

"Why are we looking into it, anyway? It wasn't in our county, not in our jurisdiction," Johnson asked keeping pace.

"Owner went to college here; they're following up, looking for leads."

"Let me know when you get the pictures, okay?"

"Sure, no problem," Russell said.

"Say, did you read the report on your desk, the one about what Keno said on the way back? About Wanda's—?"

"Just read the first couple of lines … didn't have time to finish it yet," Russell said as he neared Inspector Devlin's office.

"Well, he said—"

But Russell heard nothing more; he opened Devlin's door.

Devlin, the phone to his ear, waved him into the room. "Okay. ... Good. ... All right. … Okay, we'll be in touch." He motioned to Russell to sit in the chair near the desk. "Give me a call if anything comes up. Thanks," Devlin said and hung up the phone.

As soon as the phone was down, Russell asked, "Any progress in Hawaii?"

"Perfect timing. That was Det. Ha in Honolulu."

"Ha? You're kidding, right?"

"No, and don't say anything to his face. You'll regret it." Devlin shook his head and pointed his pencil at Russell. "They'll put a couple of officers in the area where Keno said the guy's been staying and will call back this evening. Says there's a bit of trouble reported about somebody fitting Dunne's description. Petty stuff so far."

"Well, Dunne's done plenty here to make up for it," Russell said. "Ha's pretty sure they'll have him in custody by the time someone gets there, right?"

"Patience, *my son,* patience."

Russell shifted in the chair. "Not my strong point," he muttered.

"No kidding," Devlin said.

"Make sure you tell Ha about this guy's size. Keno Lukin says he's been working out, getting in shape. He may be a lot to handle. He might be with a girl, too."

"A girl? You're not serious."

"You doubting Keno's word?" Russell laughed out loud.

"I'll let him know," Devlin said and wrote a few notes on his pad. "Where does the paperwork stand? Is it ready?"

"I'm picking it up later today," Devlin said. "Detective Ha wanted to make sure everything was done legally, so there'd be no problems with the extradition later."

"Can't blame him. Will you be the one to go over to get him?" Russell stood but didn't move toward the door.

"Want to, but can't. Wedding—my niece. Since my brother died, I get the honors of giving the bride away. I'll go next time."

"Right. Sure. Next time we have a murder suspect to pick up in Hawaii?" Russell reached for the door knob. "Sure thing ... maybe next month," Russell laughed.

"So, you're the next in line to go. Tickets have been requested. Detective Ha said some of his men have spotted him and know where to look. They're confident they'll have him in custody by tonight. Ever been to Hawaii, Russell?" Devlin asked

"Um, no. Had plans a few years back, but they didn't work out." *One honeymoon that didn't happen.* Russell added, "Haven't thought about going since. Who'll going with me?"

Devlin laughed. "The budget won't pay for more than one on a trip like this. You're in it alone."

Two hours later, Devlin's phone rang again. He mostly listened then said, "Be careful. You might want an extra person with you when you pick him up. ... Yep, he's a big guy. A girl might be with him too." He drew a line through the words "strong" and "+ one" on his list, then added. "Thanks, our detective will be there tomorrow afternoon. Gives you plenty of time to find him. I'll fax the details to you as soon as I have them." He laughed then asked, "You do have one of those new fandangled fax machines, don't you?" He nodded and added, "Great," and hung up.

Devlin made another quick call then stood and yelled out his door, "Russell, get in here." As Russell came through the door, Devlin added, "You leave tomorrow, oh-dark-thirty. Your ticket will be ready to pick up within the hour."

Chapter 77

Sherrill yawned and stretched. The wine from Friday's dinner and then another glass last night had their desired effect: she had slept soundly over the weekend, finally. The phone had not rung this morning, so she wouldn't be working today, though one day without substitute teaching meant one more day without income.

At least I'll have some alone time. She showered, dressed quickly, and went directly to Elliott's Diner.

"A fruit cup, please," she told the waiter. "And coffee." After a brief conversation about how much Wanda was missed, the waiter described where Wanda had lived. Before she left the restaurant, Sherrill told the waiter, "I can't believe her son did it. I talked to him, and he didn't seem angry enough. He looked genuinely sad but not guilty."

The waiter nodded.

Sherrill left her car in the parking lot and walked to Wanda's apartment building. No one answered the door next to Wanda's, and yellow police tape was still stretched tightly across the front; the seal still intact. She turned and knocked on the door across the hall.

After knocking a second time, the door opened a crack and a gruff voice said, "What the hell you want?"

Sherrill stepped back. "I, uh, I'd like to ask you a few questions about what happened here a while ago."

"You a cop?"

"No." Sherrill paused a heartbeat. "No, but I'm working with them. Kind of a special assignment."

"Uh-huh." The door started closing.

"Please. I want to ask a couple of questions. No strings. No hassle."

The door stopped moving. She could see the chain was still attached.

"I don't talk to cops."

"I'm not a cop. Honest. I'm a friend of Wanda's, *well*, was a friend. I want to fill in some holes. Those cops don't tell me anything." She gave as non-committal smile as she could.

"Show me your badge."

"I don't have one. I'm really not a cop." Sherrill shrugged, trying to look unofficial. "Did you hear anything the night she, uh, she died?"

"I told the cops I didn't hear a thing."

"Okay. You *told* them you heard nothing, but what did you *really* hear?"

The door slammed, and Sherrill stood stunned. *People don't do that, at least not where I'm from.* Then she heard the chain rattle on the other side of the door, and it opened wide. The gruff voice belonged to a balding, heavyset, sixty-ish man wearing a dirty T-shirt and stained jeans.

"You don't believe that I told 'em the truth?" He chuckled. "I like that in a woman. Com'on in."

"Thanks. So, what *did* you hear?" Sherrill stepped inside but kept the door opened behind her. She relaxed a little when she realized the man was holding a paint brush, and the odor of fresh paint hung in the air. The wall across the room glistened with wet paint, an eggshell-white.

"It's more what I didn't hear. Them cops don't ask the right questions."

"Okay. What didn't you hear?"

"Well, I heard her kid leave. I even heard his car door slam and him drive away. Never heard that car of his come back. Can hear the racket a block away."

"So, you know he left?"

"Hell, yes. He took off like a bat out of hell. Like I said, I could hear his car leaving." The man dipped his brush into the paint can and started slathering it on the wall.

"Then what?"

"A minute or two later I heard knockin' on her door, and she said, 'Jake, you back?' or something like that. Then her door opened, and I heard nothing."

"Nothing?"

"Nothin' but an 'Oh' and thud. Nothin' more." He shrugged and started painting carefully around the edge of the window trim.

"Ew."

"Yeah. Ew."

"You're sure it wasn't her son?"

"Naw. I don't think it was her kid who done it."

"Oh, and why not?"

"Kid didn't have time to get back. He took off so fast, he was doin' sixty within a block." A blob of paint fell onto the window sill, and he pulled a rag from his back pocket and sopped it up. "That guy was here within a half minute or so of the tires screechin' away."

"Guy?"

"Yeah. I peeked out when he went back down the hall."

"What did he look like? Hair color? Height? Can you describe him?"

"You're soundin' like a cop."

"I'm not, just want to find out what happened."

"Well, I saw him from the back, that's all. It was some big guy, bigger'n her son. But I couldn't see his face, not even his hair color."

"What was he wearing?"

"All I can say is a white T-shirt and jeans."

Sherrill's shoulders drooped. "You didn't check on Wanda? You weren't worried about her? You didn't call the police?"

"Hell, no. I don't go messin' with other people's business. It was quiet again and not interruptin' television."

"Do you remember what time it was?"

"Not exactly. But *Columbo* was on, had been for a while—love that Peter Falk. Oh, and Jake was wearin' a plaid shirt. The other guy wasn't. Pretty cold for just a T-shirt"

"You didn't tell the police about this?"

The man shook his head. "Nope. Told you, I don't like cops. Don't ever tell 'em *nothin'*."

Sherrill looked around the room. Furniture had been moved away from the walls, but otherwise it was neat and clean. *Seems like a pretty reliable guy.*

"Hey, lady, that's it. I gotta' get back to work before my paint brush dries out."

"Oh, sure. Thanks. By the way, what's your name?"

"Bob. That's all you're getting. Don't want more cops coming around. Don't like talkin' to cops."

Sherrill left shaking her head. *How do I tell Russell I went behind his back? There's no reason to doubt Bob, but how do I give Russell this information?*

Sherrill ate a quick lunch at a little place not far from the courthouse. Marcelli's served the best ravioli she had ever eaten. *I could get used to the food here,* she thought. She thanked the waitress, left a decent tip, and headed to the courthouse.

She took the stairs and looked around for Russell, then saw Sgt. Johnson across the room.

"Have you seen Russell, uh, Detective Hurley? I've got to talk to him."

"He's avoiding everyone today. Good luck. He left to go home and pack for Hawaii right after talking to the Inspector."

"Oh, uh, Inspector … was he up north where Jeffrey Madison's stuff was found?"

"Yeah, except when he was traipsing through the woods."

Oh, that's why I didn't see him. "Where's his office?"

"Right over there," Johnson said, pointing behind her.

Sherrill stuck her head into Inspector Devlin's office. *Good, I didn't see him up in north.* "When's Detective Hurley leaving for Hawaii?"

Devlin looked up and smiled. "You're Officer ... uh—?"

"I'm new here," she said, stifling a snicker. "I need to talk to Detective Hurley and hear he's heading for Hawaii."

"Yep. Leaves tomorrow 5 a.m."

"Know where he'll be staying? I've got some info on the Madison murder."

"Want to share it with me?" Devlin looked at her with his pencil ready to write.

"It's ... just background information."

"Well, you can call him tomorrow afternoon in Honolulu ... Waikiki Motel 6," Devlin said with a snicker.

"Okay, thanks," Sherrill said and headed home to pack.

Chapter 78

The shadows from the towering palm trees were nearly gone; the sun was nearing its zenith. The temperature was rising inside the forest-green sedan. The humidity was high, and two of the three men inside scanned the surroundings.

Traffic was picking up as people left work for lunch. Tourists heading for shopping centers or nearby beaches were not interested in cars parked along the street, even unmarked police cars on a stakeout.

The older man behind the wheel pulled his graying hair into a ponytail then shifted his weight. Det. Ha checked the rear-view mirror and side mirrors for the umpteenth time. "Nothing's happening," he muttered and settled again into the wait-and-watch mode.

The middle-aged man in the back sank lower into the seat, trying to be invisible and seriously wishing he could disappear. Officer Carnahan had been on too many stakeouts and felt out of place in shorts, sandals, and tourist shirt. Unlike the other two officers, his hair was cut short, military style.

"Any coffee left?" the young man in the front passenger seat asked and opened the glove box. Nothing to read but the car manual," Officer Rhodes said and slammed it shut. "Anything else to eat?" He rummaged through the rumpled napkins and wrappings on the front seat between him and Det. Ha. He began to slap his bare knees in a rapid hip-hop rhythm and shake his head, tossing his long, dark hair in beat with some imagined music.

Detective Ha rolled his eyes and Officer Carnahan yawned, and didn't bother covering his gaping mouth.

"Hey, where's that picture of our guy?" Ha began rummaging through the trash and newly added newspaper then looked up. "Look. Is that him?" He pulled the picture from the pile and nodded in the direction of a tall, blond man approaching. He discreetly passed the photo to Carnahan, checked his weapon, put it into a holster in the small of his back, and shifted his weight to pull his shirt tail over it.

Carnahan took a look, "Hair's lighter. The rest fits the description." He glanced up and nodded. "Shit, he's not alone. This idiot *does* have a girlfriend. Unreal."

Rhodes opened his door.

"No! Stay!" Ha said and grabbed Rhodes' arm. "Not yet. Let him get to the beach. We don't want a confrontation on the street. Too confined. Too many tourists."

The two-minute wait seemed longer to the two experienced men; it seemed more like an hour to Rhodes.

"All right, let's go," Ha finally said. "Hey, Rhodes, act casual. This is not to end up in a chase scene from the movies."

"Okay, okay." Rhodes looked sullen.

The three officers walked to the beach, taking turns looking around so each could subtly take stock of their suspect. The three men looked like tourists with their animated talk, jokes, and their true appreciation of the splendid view.

Dunne was wearing a pair of cut-offs, a loose fitting Raiders T-shirt, and was barefoot. He was carrying a grocery bag.

The girl with him looked about twenty-ish, five foot five, 120 pounds. She wore a long, flowing, lavender, sheer skirt, a tank top, a great tan, and apparently nothing else. She and Dunne were laughing at an unheard joke as the three men approached the couple.

"Hey, dude, dudette! What's hangin'?" Ha called out to Dunne. All three cops waved half-heartedly while they took in the area one more time. Ha stopped and nudged Rhodes. Carnahan kept walking.

Dunne paused and said, "Not much." He stared at Ha then started walking again.

"You know of any good places to eat?" Ha asked.

"Yeah," Dunne stopped again and glanced at Rose. "There's a restaurant not far. They give real good service," he said, then laughed.

"Which way? What's the name?" Ha asked stalling until Carnahan, a couple yards away, had turned back towards them. Ha knew for sure that this was the scum they were looking for.

"Back that way," Dunne motioned over his shoulder.

Dunne turned at the same time that Ha pulled his revolver and police ID out. Rhodes held handcuffs in his right hand.

"Honolulu P.D. You're under arrest for—"

Dunne gave a smirk and stepped back. "What took you mother fuckers so long?" he said with a shrug.

Rose, mouth and eyes open wide, nudged him with her elbow.

"Uh … what the fuck for?" Dunne added.

"Murder, first."

Rose seemed to ignore the guns, took a step in front of Dunne, and faced the officers. "Who? Where? Who'd the hell he supposedly kill?"

Dunne, however, knew an opportunity when he saw it.

In a split second, and in one single movement, Dunne squatted and threw sand forward and over his shoulder into the officers' faces, pushed

Rose towards the two in front, and bolted across the sand toward the street.

Arms flailing, hair flying, Rose fell, cursing, into Ha. Rhodes, to the right of Ha and slightly behind him, jumped aside and let Ha and the woman tumble to the ground.

The woman struggled with Ha, and it took him longer than he expected to subdue her.

Carnahan turned and moved quickly, but the sand Dunne threw hit him in his face. Spitting and brushing sand from his eyes, Carnahan could only hear Officer Rhodes yell, "Stop!" and the sounds of Ha and the woman swearing at each other. Suddenly he heard a gunshot, and he fought to see clearly … then a second shot and more yelling. Carnahan yelled, "Don't shoot!"

Ignoring Rhodes' command to stop, Dunne ran like hell to the street and turned left but wasn't sure where to go. He checked nearby cars for a vulnerable driver. The thunk of the bullet imbedding itself into a power pole, followed immediately by a sharp report from a gun, startling him. A second bullet slashed his shirt and ripped through his upper left arm. "Shit!" he hissed and grabbed at the pain. Blood spread through his fingers.

"Damn, don't shoot! Too many people," Det. Ha barked at Rhodes.

Rhodes was running hard to catch up with Dunne.

Det. Ha grabbed Rose and snapped a pair of handcuffs around her wrists.

"Fuck you!" She spun around and spat in his face before he could stop her.

"Back at you," he said and pushed her toward Carnahan. "Here, watch her. Be right back," he said, turned, and took off after the two runners.

In the distance Det. Ha could see the suspect yards ahead of Rhodes. Everyone else seemed to be moving in slow motion. He raced toward the two men.

"Where's Dunne? Where the hell'd he go?" Ha asked Rhodes when he caught up with him. Rhodes was doubled over panting.

"Dunno. He went that way," Rhodes gasped or air and nodded. "Caught a ride in a blue Beemer. Can you believe anyone would give a ride to that shithead?"

"You call it in?"

"Uh, no. Not yet." Rhodes was still panting.

"License?"

"Shit, no."

Ha scowled at Rhodes, pulled out his radio, and reported what he knew, which was nothing more than the color and make of the car and the direction it was heading. He clipped his radio back into its holder. "Did you see the blood back there?" he asked.

"No. Did I hit him?"

"I think so. There's blood on the sidewalk and some wood splinters from a power pole."

"That explains why he was holding his shoulder when he dove into the car."

"Well, might slow him down a bit. Now to figure out where he's going."

Ha and Rhodes rejoined Carnahan and the woman and made sure she was securely cuffed. Ha figured they could hold her without charges for a day or so. Angry with Rhodes for being too anxious to shoot and with himself for telling Devlin they'd have Dunne in custody this afternoon, Det. Ha helped the woman into the back seat and slammed the door. He hoped she would confirm where Dunne might be heading—perhaps the beach up north.

Chapter 79

Russell, standing at the counter in the Motel 6 lobby, saw the shadows flicker off the marred vinyl chairs and worn linoleum floor. He turned and saw someone familiar pass the palm tree and approach the hotel entrance. *No, not again.*

"Nice seeing you here, Detective Hurley. Isn't the weather great? A lot warmer than Eureka. And *clear* skies. Don't you love Hawaii? Especially this time of year." Sherrill, pulling her suitcase behind her, walked up to him.

Well, she got the title correct, at least. "Didn't you hear me? I told you to stay out of this. You need to go back, now."

"I heard you and chose to ignore you." She stopped in front of him, let go of her bag handle, and crossed her arms. "Say, who's watching your dog, anyway?"

"My brother. And don't change the subject. I mean it. You shou—" He heard his voice rise in pitch and took a deep breath. "You shouldn't be here," he said in a calmer voice, took her suitcase and led her to a couple of blue chairs by the front window. "How'd you get here? I would've seen you on the plane."

"Missed the last flight out of Eureka, so I drove to San Francisco last night. My folks bought the ticket." She grinned at Russell expecting a lecture.

"Should've known," Russell muttered. "You've got to leave. There's nothing you can do here. And it might be—"

"I don't care. I've got to stay close to this," she said and pulled her arm from his grasp. "It gives me something to hang onto," she said, leaning against the chair back.

Russell saw her expression change and the tone of her voice grow serious. "Sorry I yelled at you, but you need to go."

"I'll hang back, promise. Won't compromise the situation, whatever happens. I need to feel like I'm part of the search for the monster who ... who did it."

Russell scowled at her and said, "You're leaving." He walked back to the registration desk. "Can you get a ticket to San Francisco, any airline, leaving tonight?"

"We don't do that, sir."

Russell pulled out a twenty and slid it toward the young man behind the counter. "Does this help?"

"Sure, a bit," the clerk said.

Russell sighed and plunked another twenty down. The clerk picked up the telephone.

"I'm not leaving," Sherrill insisted from behind him.

"If I have to arrest you for obstruction of justice, I'll do it."

"I know you won't do that."

"You can board the plane in handcuffs. I don't care." *She's nuts, crazy in an intriguing way,* he thought and smiled to himself. *But she's putting herself in danger.*

A few moments later, they heard the clerk hang up and say, "Excuse me, sir. Everything's booked through tomorrow night. Would you like—?"

"Check again."

"I have, sir. A couple of conventions are ending, and the flights are full."

Sherrill cocked her head, crossed her arms again, and started to stick her tongue out at him but immediately pulled it back in. "See! I'm staying," she said.

"Not for long," Russell muttered.

"You have my reservation?" she said to the clerk as she stood and approached the counter. I'm Sherrill Madison … booked it yesterday." After she signed the registration card, she snatched the handle of her suitcase and wheeled it toward the exit, heading toward Room 233.

Russell watched her leave then turned to the clerk. After he finished his registration chore, he said, "Keep trying to get a flight … tonight or tomorrow morning, early. Let me know as soon as you find something … anything," and slipped a ten across the counter.

"Sure. No problem," the clerk said picking up the bill. He folded it with the others and tucked them into his shirt pocket.

Russell threw his bag onto the bed and pulled out the slip of paper with Det. Ha's phone number on it. After a half dozen rings and three transfers, he reached him. Their exchange of pleasantries was brief, then Russell's questions got serious. Hearing the answers, Russell sank onto the bed and asked, "What? You don't have him yet?" *What the hell am I doing here then?* he thought. *Captain's going to kill me.*

"We had a glitch," Ha told him. "Thought we had him … almost had him, but he bolted. Someone got in the way. We got his location but don't want to confront him there this late in the day. Too many tourists. Too dangerous." Russell could hear Det. Ha tapping his pencil on his desk and let out a long sigh. "We've got his girlfriend—"

"A girlfriend? So, it's verified?"

"Yep."

"Didn't want to believe that … not with a guy like this."

"Well, anyway," Ha continued, "she finally told us exactly where he's been living and that all his stuff's still there. She's pretty sure he'll go back before he finds another place to crash. She claims he doesn't know where she lives but have someone posted at her house anyway. Meet me tomorrow morning at seven, and we'll go get him."

Russell wrote the police station's address and directions on the tablet on the nightstand and said, "Okay. Thanks. See you tomorrow. Seven sharp."

As soon as he hung up, he called the front desk. "Any luck?"

"With what, sir?"

"The plane ticket. Did you find anything?"

"I'm sorry, sir. I just came on duty. Can you tell me what you're talking about?"

Russell rolled his eyes. "Never mind," he said and slammed the phone down. He covered his face and ran his fingers through his hair.

Chapter 80

Sherrill was glad Russell hadn't called her with information about a flight leaving the island. She didn't want another face-off with him and a possible escort to the airport. *Maybe he gave up, resigned himself to my being here.*

For breakfast, she ate one of the oatmeal bars she had packed. *Oh, hell. I forgot to tell him about Wanda's neighbor, Bob. Today for sure.* She pushed the last bite into her mouth. *I'll pick up some fruit later*, she thought as she washed the dry bar down with a gulp of water and stuffed two more bars into her purse. *Okay, time to go.*

The sun was cracking the horizon when she climbed into her rental car. *Clear view of parking lot,* she thought and opened the local newspaper, the first of several things she had to read.

Nearly half an hour later, Sherrill jumped when she heard a car door close. *Damn. I dozed off.* She craned her neck over the steering wheel and caught sight of Russell checking his mirrors, start his engine, and begin to back out of the parking place. She waited until he had pulled onto the street before starting her engine. *Keep way back. Don't lose him. Okay, he turned right. Slow down, girl. I can't get too close.*

Ten minutes later, she watched him pull into a parking lot in front of a large, official-looking building then climb out of his car. *Did he just turn and wave? At me?* Stunned, she rolled to a stop then parked across the street from the only exit from the Honolulu Police Department. She settled in once again with her paper and magazines. "Man, stakeouts must suck," she mumbled and pulled out a pen to work on the crossword puzzle.

Half an hour later, Sherrill noticed four men in civilian clothes leave the building. Russell was chatting with a good looking Hawaiian with long, dark hair streaked with grey. They both turned and talked to the two men behind them, one about Russell's age and the other much younger. A couple of uniformed officers followed them; everyone looked serious.

She tossed the magazine and pen onto the passenger seat, turned the key, and let the engine idle while she watched the men climb into two unmarked cars. An hour and a thirty-mile drive later, Sherrill saw the lead car with Russell inside pull into a nearly empty parking lot next to a bridge.

The second car drove across the bridge, pulled into a wide spot, and stopped. She drove past the officers' vehicle and followed the road until she was out of sight. Checking carefully, she made a U-turn and headed back toward the parking lot. *Probably only fooling myself. He knows I followed him. At least the officers didn't notice me.* She saw that Russell and the other three had started walking away. *Good. They won't see me,* she thought, turned, and let the car roll into an empty spot straight ahead. She shut off the engine and looked down the beach. *Ah, there he is.* She climbed out of her car and stood by the door.

She watched Russell walking across the white sand. His khaki shorts and blue T-shirt looked out of character, yet she knew she couldn't expect him to live in slacks, button-down shirts and ties.

She noticed how confidently he walked toward the unknown but also how natural he looked among the families on the beach. She had seen a break in his armor once or twice, but here he was waving and talking to people. A Frisbee nearly hit him in the stomach, but he caught it and flung it back to the boys a few yards away. *First with his nephews and now this. Maybe he does have a human side after all.*

There had been a couple of times when he was tired, and she could see a far-away look in his eyes. She thought at the time that it was more than frustration with the job. There was more … a hurt hiding inside. Just yesterday, he got that look that said, maybe, for an instant, he regretted something, something from another life, another part of him that was now missing. He had said that he understood her pain when she realized her brother was really gone. Then there was that picture at his brother's house—a woman with him, one he never mentions.

This person, *this* Russell, walking on the beach wasn't dressed like a cop, but he still held onto the respect and the profession. *I can see why people say they can spot a cop a mile away. They seem to have that aura about them.*

Sherrill chuckled to herself as she watched him walk along the crest of the sand dune that dipped toward the ocean. She watched until he and the other men were far away, but she still felt the safety he emanated. She wondered what it was, that world he disappeared into once in a while.

She climbed back into the car and leaned back against the seat. To her right, the highway continued in a curve across a creek then turned and disappeared beyond the tree-covered hills that dropped to the sea. The sun gave a warm glow, and the sweet scent of the white plumeria filled the air. Her eyes began to close.

Images of her brother played before her.

She and Jeffrey were both laughing. They were young again, playing in the sandy beaches of the Atlantic. Their mom and dad were nearby, watching, protecting. Suddenly Jeffrey kicked her sand castle, and she screamed at him. Then they were older, plotting together, teens trying to coerce their parents into agreeing with their scheme to get permission to go to a party. The next instant she and Jeffrey were working at the Volunteer Senior Center. She could see him, hear him, even smell his aftershave. He was fulfilling the community service portion of his senior year high school requirement. She was nearing college graduation, and almost finished with her teaching credential.

Behind closed eyes, she saw her ex-boyfriend walk into the Center, and he and Jeffrey exchanged their customary high-five. Paul was approaching Sherrill to give her a hug, but she smelled someone else's perfume, not her Chanel, and pulled away.

The air in the car suddenly chilled, and Sherrill sat upright. She felt the tear rolling down her cheek and wiped it away. Was it for Jeffrey or because of Paul's cheating ways?

She squirmed in the warm car. *I'm glad he hasn't called. I'd slam down the phone in his ear anyway.*

Who cares about him? Jerk. Another tear stopped at her lips, and she tasted the salt. *Why am I crying? Jeffrey's gone; I'm sure of it, and Paul's not worth it, asshole.* She sat up and wiped her damp cheek.

"This is beautiful!" Russell said, turning a full circle and nearly bumping into Det. Ha. He soaked in the views of the beach, the ocean, and the trees that filled the small valley between the two cliffs rising on either side of the creek. "You must wake every morning thanking your lucky stars you live in this paradise."

Det. Ha looked at him, grinned, and said, "If it's all you know, you somehow learn to live with it."

Russell laughed and said, "You look like a native ... a hippie native with that long hair of yours."

"I *am* a native. And, my long hair is part of me. Helps me blend with the others here." Ha laughed. "You look like a haole."

"A what? A howl-ee?"

"Close. A haole is someone with pale skin, short hair, dressed in a silly flower shirt. You know, an obvious tourist, a mainlander—and a bit derogatory. And you'll be burned to a crisp before the day's half over."

"Okay, okay. Enough harassment of the tourist. What's happening? Where to next?" Russell asked Ha and looked around again. There were a few families several yards away, and the children were all preschoolers.

The ocean was a cerulean blue; the sky the deepest azure; a few wisps of clouds hung over the horizon. In the other direction, the highway cut a line between the beach and the trees growing between two towering cliffs.

The creek that flowed through the trees ran under the bridge, spread silently over the sand, and flowed into the sea. The morning air was cool and refreshing.

And to think there's a cold-blooded killer holed up in those trees. A contradiction in life. A contradiction of humanity. Russell shook his head. *A damn shame.*

"Well, we're about set," Det. Ha said. "Don't forget, he'll be desperate and may be armed. Be careful." Ha continued, "His girlfriend told us he's in a cave right over there." Ha handed a pair of binoculars to Russell and pointed at the second overhang from the road. "The first two officers will be across the road on the left, two others down that way." He pointed to the right. "We—you and I—go in straight on." He paused and added, "Ready?"

Chapter 81

Dunne was kicking things around in the cave. In the dim morning light, he was furiously shoving his pants, sandals, and other belongings into the backpack. Empty beer bottles and cans were strewn across the floor of the cave. His pack of cigarettes had no more joints left. His eyes were bloodshot, his veins were throbbing on his forehead and his arm was aching. The bandages he'd stolen from the pharmacy pulled the skin together, and the iodine stung when he changed the dressing.

"Where's my wallet? Where the hell's my bag of weed?" He kicked the ice chest, and the Coleman lantern crashed against a rock, shattering the glass. "Shit," he muttered.

He picked up the backpack, threw it over his shoulder, and started climbing down. Looking to the right toward the road, through the trees, Dunne saw two men by the road. *That's odd. What're they doing?* He hefted himself up a little higher and looked more carefully. *What the hell? Cops? Fuckin' broad. Shoulda' offed her when I had the chance.*

Then he looked back up the canyon but knew there was no way out in that direction. *Gotta go out that way,* he thought, jumped to the ground, and headed into the undergrowth.

Chapter 82

Sherrill wiggled to get comfortable in the car then remembered where she was. She opened her eyes and looked around. *Wonder if I slept?* She glanced at the clock on the dash and shrugged. *Not more than a few minutes.*

Three officers in uniform—didn't see them before. No, there's more ... another group behind them. They were all headed back toward the parking lot. Russell was between two other men, and all were dressed in casual clothes. *Oh, no. They're coming this way. Too late to leave.* She scrunched lower trying to hide herself behind the steering wheel, wishing she could disappear. She searched for a way to get out of her car and walk away.

Suddenly there was rapping on the passenger-side window.

"Yes?" she said trying to sound innocent. "Yes, *officer?* What is it?" She reached across and rolled down the window then noticed that the other officers continued and crossed the road. She didn't see the Hawaiian officer.

"Why'd you follow us here?"

Sherrill looked at him but didn't answer.

"You've got to leave now!"

"Gee, officer, I'll stay out of the way. I won't start any trouble, sir." Sherrill sat motionless. *Wonder what handcuffs feel like?* She felt sweat form under her arms and on her forehead.

"There could be trouble. You could get hurt." Russell frowned. "I'd hate to have to call your parents and give them bad news about another child of theirs."

Sherrill winced and looked down. "You won't have to. I just want to see this scumbag get caught," she said but thought, *Get himself killed ... I wish.*

"Don't. Go back to the motel and sit tight." Russell sighed then added, "I don't want you to get hurt." He looked over the top of the car at Det. Ha and shook his head.

"Who's she?" Det. Ha asked.

"Victim's sister."

"You brought her with you?" It was Det. Ha's turn to glare.

Russell swore under his breath and said, "She followed me ... us here." He glanced back at Sherril. "Last night I ordered her to go home, but obviously she didn't."

"You should take her back."

"I'm not leaving. I'm going to get this bastard."

"If she—" Det. Ha started.

"She won't," Russell said, then looked at Sherrill and added, "If you interfere, I *will* arrest you. Obstruction. And anything else I can think of. What's this—my third time to threaten you with this?" He reached for his handcuffs. *Keep her in the car,* he thought.

Det. Ha's radio crackled. "He's on the move," came over the speaker.

"Gotta go," Ha snapped.

Russell pushed the cuffs back into his waistband and said, "Go back to the motel, now!" He shot another harsh look at Sherrill, straightened up, and followed Ha across the road. *Please, don't get hurt.*

Chapter 83

Dunne was stooping as low as he could and was heading toward the far side of the wide valley. His eyes darted back and forth, searching for any movement in the brush. *Someone's behind me. No, they're over there.* The creek was ahead, and the rising cliff beyond that. He was sweating. Rocks and fallen branches grabbed at his legs, and he tripped several times. The trees and undergrowth slowed him, and his wounded arm burned.

Two more over there, by the creek. Shit. Maybe I can get a car. He hesitated, looked around again, and wiped sweat from his forehead. *Where are the cops? Where'd they go? Shit. Can't see 'em.* He took several steps and checked around, listening carefully for any sounds that might indicate someone was approaching or following him. His eyes darted from side to side; sweat was dripping from his forehead, burning his eyes.

A bird chirped overhead and Dunne jumped. He took a deep breath. *I gotta get out of here. This is shit.* He started creeping toward the highway. *Car. A ride. I gotta—*

A cracking sound! Dunne dropped to the ground. He stayed perfectly still, completely silent.

Det. Ha clicked on his radio and whispered, "Can you see him?" His radio crackled loudly, and Ha twitched. He put his hand over the speaker trying to quiet it.

"No, sir," the officer responded. "He was heading through heavy brush toward the creek; he took off running then headed back toward the caves."

Ha and Russell looked at each other and dropped their shoulders in unison. They stood at the edge of the road and stared into the brush. The overgrown trail was barely visible, but Ha made out the tracks leading into the shrubs. He could see bent grass, broken twigs, and a footprint in the soft soil every yard or two. Ha nudged Russell, pointed, and headed straight ahead. Russell followed, immediately ducking under overhanging limbs and pushing branches out of the way.

A few yards in, Ha stopped and signaled to Russell to come closer. "I heard something," Ha whispered and pointed ahead toward the wall of the mountain ahead of them and slightly to his left.

Russell held his breath and listened, then he nodded. He held up his right hand and indicated with a thumb's up that he was ready to go farther. *Damn, he's heading back to the parking lot ... where Sherrill is.* His heart was pounding and sweat was rolling down his back as he and Ha ran to catch up with Dunne.

Dunne heard people approaching and, still crouching, moved ahead. He pulled his backpack higher on his shoulder because it kept catching on shrub limbs. *Gotta get to the road. This is shit.* He moved off the trail and fought the brush heading toward the road.

Movement. Two guys to my left. Too close! Dunne stopped and held his breath then moved ahead slowly. *The road's nearby—almost there. To hell with trying to get across the creek,* he thought and broke into a run, dodging limbs and breaking through branches and shrubs.

Russell and Ha heard the noise at the same instant they saw movement. *What the—?* Russell was nearly knocked over by the large man who bolted past them. He and Ha spun and ran after him.

Ha yelled into his radio, "We're on him! Heading toward the road." Then louder, "Stop! Police," he called out and stumbled over a fallen log. Regaining his footing, he took off. Russell was trying hard to catch up with Dunne who had made it to the highway.

Dunne took a quick look in both directions, hoping to force a vehicle to stop. *Damn. No cars.* Dunne ran across the road into the parking lot at the far end, away from the exit. He frantically looked around for a car that wasn't locked. He could hear footsteps behind him crossing the road when he heard an engine start two yards to his right. *Two broads.* He ran to the car, opened the blue and white Chevy's back door, and jumped in. "Move it!" he yelled.

The two teenagers gasped and started to open their doors to escape when he grabbed their hair and yanked hard. Their heads were forced against the seat back. He let go of the driver's hair and wrapped his left arm around the passenger's neck. "Move it, I said," Dunne said to the girl at the wheel.

Chapter 84

Sherrill was at the front of her car, leaning against the fender. The roar of the pounding waves was soothing, primordial. *He wanted me safe. Maybe he does care more than he lets on,* she thought, then added, *Yeah, right!*

Everything seemed calm; a couple of families played on the beach behind her, and there was no sign of activity across the road. She inhaled and closed her eyes then opened them as she exhaled. She knew that vision of calm was superficial.

What? Her muscles tensed at the sound of someone running. She jumped when she saw a tall man with a frazzled expression race to the edge of the road on the other side of the highway. He kept looking behind himself while his backpack swung on his shoulder. He paused briefly searching the roadway for something. His eyes. His contorted features. She could feel evil emanate from him as he raced across the road and ran into the parking lot.

An engine started, and she watched two young women back their car out of a parking space. The man suddenly jumped into their backseat. *That's wrong. This shouldn't be happening,* she thought, and jumped back into her Civic.

Russell and Ha cleared the wooded area and looked around. There were no cars coming from either direction, but they couldn't see Dunne anywhere. The only movement was a car backing out of a parking space across the road. *What?* Russell turned to Ha. "Do you see that? That girl there," he said pointing across the road. "Her head, it's … He's gotta be in there."

"Yeah," Ha said. "You see him?"

"Naw, but something's definitely wrong." Russell waited until a car passed then started across the highway. He could see the top of a blond head above the edge of the rear window when the car turned. "Look. There. Someone's in the back seat. It's him." Russell and Ha started running toward the car.

"Get the damn car the hell outta' here, and I won't hurt her," Dunne growled from the back seat. "And, you, shut the fuck up," he said, jerking on the girl's hair again. "Stop your damn whimpering."

The car stopped and the driver shifted into forward.

"Move it. Floor it." Dunne yelled when he saw two cops racing across the highway. Then he noticed two more cops—no four, coming from farther away. "Shit!"

Sherrill started her car, took a deep breath, and shifted into reverse. *Please let this work.* "Please. Please," she muttered as she stepped on the gas pedal too hard, and her car jerked. She hit the brake then more slowly, more deliberately backed her car into the exit lane of the parking lot. *Please. Please. Please,* she repeated to herself then shifted into park, turned off the ignition, and set the parking brake. She crouched low and reached for the passenger door handle.

"What the fuck?" Dunne pulled on the brunette's hair again, and she yelped. "Why the hell'd you stop?" Dunne said. "Move it!"

"I, I can't," the driver said. "There's a, look, a car. It's blocking ... it's in the way." She looked at her friend next to her who was trying to pull invisible hands from her scalp. Both girls were crying.

"Ram it!" Dunne yelled. "Push it out of the way." He yanked on the hair again, and the girl cried out. Then he clenched his left hand around the driver's neck. "Move the fuckin' car. Now!"

Sherrill's hand was on the door handle when she felt a jolt. The car shook and her head slammed against the armrest. "Yow!" she yelled and pulled her body across the center console and parking-brake lever. Her car jerked again and moved sideways several feet. "What the—? They're ramming me." Her body was half on the floor and half on the seat and, afraid there'd be another collision, pulled on the door handle, and shoved on the door.

"Hit it again. Push it. Get the hell outta' here," Dunne yelled unaware of how hard he was pulling on the girl's hair or how hard he was squeezing the driver's neck.

The driver punched the gas pedal then her foot relaxed, her hands dropped from the steering wheel, and she went limp. The car hit the Civic again.

"Hell. Hit it again," he yelled shaking the unconscious girl's shoulder. "Push it, damn it."

Russell and Ha, guns drawn, caught up with the blue and white Chevy, its front bumper imbedded in the Civic's driver's side. Russell glanced at the Civic but didn't see anyone in it.

The two officers made eye contact before moving to either side of the Chevy. On a nod, as if they had worked together for years, they each jerked open a back door.

"I'll kill her. I swear," Dunne yelled still clenching the dark hair flowing over the car's front seat. "Let me go or I'll kill her,"

"Don't see how," Ha said through gritted teeth. "You move, and we blow your head off."

"I'll—"

"You'll do nothing except let her go, get out of the car, and put your hands up," Russell said, pulling his handcuffs out of his waistband.

Dunne glanced over his shoulder and saw the second gun aimed at him. His shoulders dropped, and he pulled his hand from the tangled mess of hair, shifting his weight to release the tension in his injured arm. He glanced around then leaned back towards Russell and kicked the opposite door with both feet. The door hit Ha's right cheek and then his chest. He fell backwards to the ground. At the same time, Dunne reached over his head, grabbed the door handle near Russell, and pulled it hard. The door hit Russell's gun, knocking it out of his hands.

Russell had been briefed about Dunne's injured shoulder but was surprised how swiftly he was able to move. Dunne scrambled out of the car with lightning speed and, meeting Russell face to face, drew back to swing. Russell head butted him then punched him on the chin. The two men tumbled to the pavement and scrambled for Russell's gun while punching and hitting each other until Russell's right fist caught him on the cheek with a strong swing and Dunne, stunned, hesitated. Russell hit him again.

Dunne rolled over giving Russell time to clamp a handcuff onto Dunne's right wrist. Russell held tightly onto the chain of the cuffs.

Dunne twisted, turning Russell over and ending up on top of him. With his right arm restrained, he pressed his left arm onto Russell's throat, but just as quickly, Russell jerked the cuff, cutting into Dunne's skin, and swung his right arm hard into Dunne's injured shoulder.

"Yeow!" Dunne's scream was ear-piercing. "You son'a bitch," he yelled and tried to hit Russell with his cuffed arm. Dunne couldn't move his arm far enough to connect with Russell's face, and Russell was able to roll on top of Dunne. Knowing he had to have complete control, Russell jerked his knee hard into Dunne's balls. Dunne yowled again, his resistance waning.

Russell could feel Dunne's energy ebb and—

Suddenly Ha was standing over his shoulder and yelling, "Hold it. Stop, you friggin—!" Blood oozed from a gash on his cheek, and his swollen right eye was already turning black and blue.

Russell yanked on the cuff and turned Dunne over. Ignoring the injured arm, Russell pulled both arms to the middle of his back and secured the cuffs. Russell wiped the sweat from his forehead, and his torn shirt was wet under his armpits and the middle of his back.

"You okay?" Ha asked panting hard to catch his breath.

Russell sucked in air over and over then said, "Better'n you," and chuckled as he straightened up and looked at Ha's face.

When Dunne had let go of the brunette's hair, she'd gasped with relief, and leaned forward as far as she could. Her hands went to her face, and she began to sob; her shoulders were shaking.

The driver's right eye opened a slit, and the corner of her mouth twitched. She blinked several times before glancing at her friend who was wiping tears from her cheeks. She reached out and put her hand on her friend's arm. The sobbing eased.

Russell, holding his gun on Dunne, opened the front door for the driver to climb out. She tugged on her friend's arm and they both scrambled out.

"Get away from here," Russell had said. "Officers, take care of these girls," he yelled to two officers who were approaching from across the highway, their guns drawn. "Take them where it's safe."

"You ... two ... okay?" one officer, panting and trying to catch his breath, asked the girls.

The girls looked at him, then at each other, and nodded.

One officer motioned his hand toward a picnic table near the edge of the parking lot. The girls grasped hands and ran to it and sat down.

The officer kept up and stood close by. "You girls all right?"

Through sobs, the brunette breathlessly gasped, "My head hurts ... my hair, but ... but I'm okay."

Her friend, coughing, nodded in agreement but held her hand to her neck.

Russell kicked the front car door closed. With two officers covering Dunne and two more appearing from the dense shrubbery across the highway, Russell helped Ha pull Dunne to his feet then Ha shoved Dunne against the side of the car. "Don't move."

Russell said, "We need to get a doctor to check the girls out, and you'll probably need stitches."

"Maybe. You'll have bruises, too."

"Yeah," Russell said rubbing his arm. He could feel the adrenaline leaving his body; his fingers were tingling. He took deep breaths, trying to relax. Dunne was securely in the hands of Ha and his men. The girls were safe. Russell looked around. *The car. Oh, my God! That's Sherrill's. But where is she?*

Sherrill, shaken, realized that the collisions had stopped. She rose and peeked out the window. The other car was surrounded with cops; all of them were holding guns. She could see the heads of two young women in the front seat then noticed the head of the tall guy who had run across the road.

She pushed the passenger door open the rest of the way and slithered out. Crouching low, she peered over the hood. She saw Russell wrestling with the large man and started toward the fight, wondering how she could help but did not want to leave him in danger. Within two steps, she paused. Det. Ha, pulling himself up with the bumper then the hood of the car, glanced at her. That look, with his swollen eye and blood trickling down his cheek, plus a quick wave of his hand stopped her short.

She watched spellbound as Russell and Ha gained control of the struggling man and latched handcuffs on him. *They got him! Too bad he's still alive.*

Sherrill took deep breaths, glanced around, and headed toward the picnic table where she saw the girls and a couple of officers.

Russell knew that Dunne was secure with Det. Ha and his men, but his mind was swirling and his heart pounding. *The car was Sherrill's. Is she safe?* He ran to the driver's side of the Civic and looked into the back seat then noticed the front passenger door was open. *Please.* It was empty. He sighed, stood up straight, and looked behind him. *Not there,* he thought then looked toward the beach. There were three women sitting at a picnic table. Their hands were shaking while they were talking and hugging. One officer was standing nearby, notebook and pen ready. The second officer was returning to the table with a bag of ice.

"Sherrill?" Russell yelled as he hurried toward the table. "Sherrill, your car— Are you okay? I was—"

"You *was* what?" Sherrill said nervously giggling and holding her hands together, fingers tightly intertwined.

He took long strides until he stood beside her. "Your car. It was—How?" He paused a moment, looked straight at her, then said, "What did you do?"

"Later," was her only response, and she clenched her hands tighter.

.

Chapter 85

"You're taking a different flight," Russell said as he cut into his teriyaki mahi mahi filet at dinner the next evening.

The sun was settling into the ocean; subdued hues of red and orange hovered over the horizon, reflecting off the few clouds hanging low in the sky. The breeze cooled the air to a relaxing temperature.

"What? Why?" Sherrill asked and took a sip of her Mai Tai.

"We've pretty much done what we can here. It'll take a few days, at least, to make arrangements to get him out of here. You should leave tomorrow, not be on the same flight with this guy."

"Are you saying it wouldn't be safe?" Sherrill smiled to herself. *Does he really care?* "He'll be in cuffs, right? And a couple of officers to help, right?" She thought for a moment then added, "Wait! You're not taking him back alone, are you?"

"Um, would you believe *yes*?" Russell took a gulp of his beer. "It'll be just me."

"What? How could they do that to you?"

"Budget. At least that was the excuse. Same excuse that sent me here alone." He shrugged.

"A set-up, I'd say. Someone back home doesn't like you."

"Aw, everyone loves me. Even you ... from the first day you met me." Russell grinned and stabbed a spear of asparagus and bit the tip off.

"Wow. A cop ... and delusional," she said and laughed. She pushed a piece of fish into her mouth. "Gosh, this fresh tuna is terrific," she mumbled. After a moment, she swallowed and added, "Hey, be careful. You've got a good dog to get back to; Shane would miss you, to say nothing about your two nephews." She stifled a giggle then looked straight at him. "And, this guy's no good. You could get—"

"Naw, I'll be fine. Those handcuffs are strong; he won't go anywhere. Besides, he'll be on a plane with no parachute." He ate a couple of bites of his fish and more asparagus then continued, "By the way, what were you thinking back there at the beach? You could've been hurt."

"Mmmfmffm," she sputtered, swallowed hard then coughed. "Thinking? I guess I wasn't." She coughed again. "He killed my brother. Two girls were in danger. He was getting away. I couldn't let it happen. I just couldn't."

"Well, don't do anything like that again." He looked at her and added, "It seems I'm telling you that over and over. Did you ever listen to your parents growing up? How did you make it through childhood?"

Sherrill, a tear forming in the corner of her eye, said, "I had a brother who took care of me," she said quietly, "a little brother who looked out for his big sister."

Russell took his napkin and dabbed the tear from her cheek. She didn't pull back or try to move his hand away. Russell nodded to the waitress and pointed to Sherrill's empty glass. She got the message and brought another Mai Tai to the table.

Chapter 86

The day Russell returned from Hawaii, he finished processing Dunne through the system and was taking a few minutes to clear his desk before heading for home. An officer plopped a manila envelope on his desk.

"Misdirected," the officer said. "Someone said you'd want this."

"Thanks," Russell said, tore open the envelope, and pulled the pages out. The letter on top said the materials were from the Sheriff's Department from Siskiyou County. He scanned it quickly. *Found red Mustang in the underbrush ... covered with branches ... Registered to Glenda Shore ... recent Humboldt State graduate ... moving to Portland, Oregon ... hasn't been seen or heard from since she left town more than three months ago ... no signs of violence.* He read the information again and glanced at the file folder under his lamp. *Sounds familiar. ... Like Christine? Naw.* He moved the letter to the back of the stack and counted six pictures: two of the Mustang's exterior, one of the inside of the trunk, and three of the car's interior.

Maybe I can look more closely at these tomorrow. He glanced at his watch. *It's late, and I'm exhausted.* He shuffled through the pages and was ready to stuff them back into the envelope when ... *What the—?* Russell sat on his jacket that was still on his chair, opened his lap drawer, pulled out a magnifying glass, and turned his desk lamp back on.

Sgt. Johnson walked up to Russell's desk. "Welcome back, lucky. Hawaii, huh? What a great place."

Russell shrugged.

"Did you ever finish reading that report of what Keno Lukin said on the way back from the search up in the woods?" Johnson asked.

"Not yet. Haven't had time. Just got back."

Johnson noticed beads of sweat on Russell's forehead. "What'd you find?"

"This picture," Russell said and handed Johnson the photo. "What do you see?"

"Inside of a car. Nothing special. Why?"

"Look closely," he said and handed him the magnifying glass. "There," he added and pointed.

"No shit," Johnson's jaw dropped open. "Just like—"

"Yes, shit," Russell said, reaching for the file under his desk light. The lamp tipped, and he barely caught it with his left hand before it fell off his desk. He stared at the file tab for a moment. "Cooper, Christine." *Christine, I've missed you. Hell, Shane's missed you.*

He took a deep breath, opened the folder, and flipped through to the fourth picture in her file, now dog-eared and smudged from nearly a decade of handling. "I don't believe it. What're the odds?"

"No odds on this one. It's the same," Johnson said shaking his head. "You really need to look at the Lukin report. Keno said the car he drove back had the same thing ... gear-shift knob is missing."

Russell's eyes opened wide. "No. You're lying. It can't be that ... that simple."

"Told you to read it before you left." Johnson went to his desk and picked up the Kevin "Keno" Lukin file. He pulled out a copy of the report and, back at Russell's desk, pointed to the fourth paragraph. "Right here." Johnson dug into his file on Dunne and pulled out a photograph. "Look here. Same thing. Unreal."

Russell swallowed hard and wiped his forehead.

Johnson waited for Russell to take a breath. "Besides saying that our boy Dunne killed Wanda Corbin, he said that driving the car back was hard because the gear shift knob was gone."

"Wanda, too?" Russell leaned back in his chair; the ubiquitous file folder in his lap was open to the picture of the interior of his fiancé's car.

"Yep, we've processed her son out."

Russell stared out the windows, seeing nothing. "It's the same bastard. It's him. It's ... it's Dunne."

Johnson watched Russell for a few moments before he asked, "What'll you do? Can we charge him?"

Russell sat silently. He closed the folder, shook his head, and said, "Maybe. We can try. Wanda? For sure. Christine's will be tougher. Never found prints. No evidence. Just like this Mustang here. But, but ... I don't ... he couldn't have ... must have—"

"Shows a pattern of behavior ... from way back," Sgt. Johnson said. "Could help with getting a conviction."

Russell nodded absently then tilted his head as he continued staring, at last understanding the answers to questions he had asked for nearly ten years. "At least I, er, *we* know. Finally." He looked at the folder in his lap, picked it up, and began to move it toward the base of the lamp. He paused, opened his bottom desk drawer, and carefully slid the folder amongst several other non-official file folders. He deliberately and slowly closed the drawer.

"Hey, man, you okay?" Johnson took a step back.

"Yeah," Russell said, then stood, picked up his crumpled jacket, and turned toward the stairwell. "I'm getting a drink. Coming?"

Chapter 87

Two days later, Sherrill had finished unpacking. The last of her linens fit into the closet in her studio apartment near Eureka's Sequoia Park and Zoo. The view from her kitchen window was filled with greens and browns of the stately redwoods that filled the park. She poured a glass of wine, returned to the chair that faced the television, and sat down. The call to her parents that she had made before she'd left to substitute in a third-grade classroom this morning was much easier than the calls she had made to them over the last several months.

Today's call home had only lasted a few minutes. "I've got to get to work, but, yes, Mom, they're sure they've got the right man. ... No, Mom, I haven't heard from Paul. ... Why would I? ... Dad told him? No! Why? ... I've been told it's difficult to get a conviction without a body." Sherrill inhaled. ... "Right, but tell Dad the police are convinced they'll get a conviction. Russell, uh, Detective Hurley said they're pushing for first-degree. ... No, that bastard denies everything, won't tell where Jeffrey is, where we can find him. ... I love you too, both of you." She convinced them that she was fine, had found a nice place to live and work, and would come home soon.

She was staring at the blank television screen when the phone rang. *Probably Dad, or maybe not; it's late back home,* she thought and picked up the receiver. "Hello?"

"Hi. Uh, busy?"

"Oh, Russell—no, just settling in." Sherrill had heard the hesitation in his voice and could tell that something was different. "Are you all right?" she asked. "What happened?"

"Did you watch the news tonight?"

"No. I worked all day. I'm still unpacking."

"Good. Well, we got some more help to convict that bastard, er, sorry, that, that, well, Dunne."

"What'd you find out?"

"It's not what we found out; it's what he did. He tried to escape."

"He what?" Sherrill sat up straight and stifled a yelp. "I thought that place was secure."

"Oh, yeah, you saw the inside of the jail, didn't you? Well, he didn't get very far. Yesterday, they searched his cell, and they found strips of sheets torn and tied together."

"What was he thinking? Was there any way he could have—?"

"No, no way. The windows are really small in the cells, and he certainly wouldn't fit through one, even if he could break the wire-reinforced glass."

"So that's it?"

"Well, according to the D.A., they can use 'attempting to escape' against him in the trial."

"Really?" She took another sip of her wine.

"Yep. It shows that he thinks he'll be convicted, shows that there is more reason to believe he did it. If he knew he didn't do it—well, most people would figure they'd get off, get let out."

"Wow. So that's good, then, right?"

"Yeah, but that's not all. While they were moving him to a different cell, he broke the chain part of his handcuffs."

"He what? You're kidding." Wine splashed from her glass as she put it on the coffee table.

"I know I couldn't break a cuff. Those chains are really tough."

Sherrill smiled at his unintentional rhyme then said, "Wow! Think what might've happened if he'd done that on the airplane."

"That's why I didn't want you on the same flight. Doesn't happen often, but once is too often."

Sherrill asked, "Did he get very far? Did anyone get hurt?"

"There were three officers with him, all big, over-grown apes who took him down in seconds. He got hurt worse than anyone else."

Sherrill sighed and sank back into her new, brown over-stuffed chair. "Good."

"Oh, we have some more news. Jake's innocent. He didn't kill his mom."

"I know," Sherrill said then reached for her wine glass and took a gulp.

"You do? How?"

"Um, well, I, uh, did a little investigating of my own. Sorry I haven't told you, but now I guess I don't need to."

"How'd you find out? What did you do?"

"Wanda's neighbor … across the hall. Bob somebody. He told me things he didn't tell the officers."

"Why?"

"Said he didn't like cops."

"No, why'd you go by yourself?"

"I wanted to find out for myself, wanted to try doing some investigating myself. So, who did do it?" She finished her wine and set the glass on the coffee table.

"Dunne."

"No, you're kidding?"

"Yep, it's true. Keno gave us enough info that we can probably get him for it. The District Attorney said he'd save that charge in case the jury gets stupid and doesn't convict him for your brother's." Russell took a deep breath and added, "We've got to talk about how you kept getting involved in the investigation."

"I guess I'm through with this case except testifying, but talking is good."

"How about dinner this weekend?" Russell asked. "Guess we can finally call it a real date." Russell had finally decided to tell Sherrill about his fiancé, her disappearance a decade ago, and now the connection to this case. *She deserves to know,* he thought, *and this week is as good a time as any.*

After arranging the time and deciding they'd go to O.H.'s Townhouse, a prime-rib restaurant with wonderful onion rings, she hesitated before asking, "How's everything else going? Any progress?"

"No, Dunne's still not talking, not giving any information. His arraignment's tomorrow, and that should go smoothly." He took a breath. "We need the name and address of the guy you talked to, Wanda's neighbor. Might not use him with your brother's trial, but need it anyway.

"Sure. But he says he hates cops and might not want to talk to you."

"Won't be the first time," Russell said through a chuckle.

"Your brother's case, well, the trial will be tougher without a, without his, uh, with no hard proof that your brother's, uh ..." *Shit, I can't even say it to her yet.*

"I understand. This is hard. Never thought about it from the cop's perspective before, but I see it now." Sherrill added, "What time's the arraignment? I want to be there."

"You sure? It will be—"

"Yep. I'm coming. Then I'll call my parents and keep them informed. They feel disconnected being so far away. They've talked about coming out here, but I convinced them there's no need, at least not yet."

"That's probably a good idea. They'll need to be here for the trial, though; they'll be called to testify ... you know, share how he always kept in touch ... that he would never just disappear. A family friend or two might be subpoenaed too. Things like that."

"Will they really have to? Isn't the evidence clear enough?"

"To us, maybe, but we have to prove it to the jury ... well, to the media and the public, too. Somehow we'll have to make Keno believable. Without him, we don't have much of a case. It depends on how much the defense attorneys are able to dig up on him, to discredit him."

"How hard will that be?"

"Unfortunately, not very. Keno's had quite a history up here. A real loser for years, decades.

"What'll happen to him?"

"Probably get off light. Without him, we wouldn't have Dunne. After that, it's up to Keno. Oh, by the way, two attorneys have volunteered to take Dunne's case. They think getting this scumbag off will make their reputation."

"Volunteered? Attorneys *volunteered* for real?"

"Yep. They deserve every penny we taxpayers won't have to pay them."

Chapter 88

Russell sat at his desk, working on his third domestic abuse case in the days since the lengthy trial ended. He was getting comfortable in his routine, even if it required writing endless reports.

"Did you hear?" a familiar voice asked.

"Maybe. Hear what?" Russell looked up as Inspector Devlin sat in the chair next to Russell's desk.

"There might be a glitch with the Dunne verdict." For emphasis, Devlin waved a file folder.

"What the hell? No way!" Russell's mouth dropped open. "Let me see that." He snatched the folder from Devlin's hand and opened it. He saw only a single piece of paper listing the jurors' names and contact information. Five names had check marks and a few notes jotted after them. Russell clenched his pen and glared at the inspector. "What's this mean?

"The District Attorney and I have been interviewing the jury members, calling them and asking about how it went in deliberations, trying to learn how to do things better next time." Devlin took the folder back.

"Yeah, but they got a *guilty* verdict—murder first." Russell punched the air in celebration. "So why call everyone?"

"Standard operating procedures—we usually do it after every trial, especially a big one like this." Devlin shifted his weight on the seat of the chair.

"And the problem is … ?"

"We stopped calling the jurors after the first five. Four of them commented that two members went into the restroom for half an hour. It seems that one woman was having a problem with agreeing to a guilty verdict, but when they came out, she was fine with it."

"Hell! They only deliberated three days. When did this happen?" Russell could feel his muscles tighten.

"Late morning of the last day. They had a final verdict within an hour."

"Coercion? You think?" Russell jumped to his feet and kicked the bottom drawer. "That'll mess things up, for sure." He sat back down when he noticed everyone in the room was looking at him. Russell threw his pen across his desk while his mind raced. "A mistrial? Hell!" He fought hard to keep his voice low and shivered when he thought how hard a retrial would be on Sherrill and her family.

"Don't want to think that, but they suggest we be there when they call those two ladies so we can all listen. The defense attorneys will be there too."

"Those jokers? Are they still trying to get money for defending that idiot?"

"Yep, but the judge ruled against their request late today. They volunteered *pro bono*, so it's on them." Devlin lifted the cuff of his jacket and glanced at his watch.

"Thank goodness something else went right." Russell chuckled. "When is this phone call going to happen?"

"Tomorrow morning. Nine sharp." Devlin stood and nodded to Russell. "You want to be there?"

"Wouldn't miss it," Russell said. He glanced at the clock and nodded to Devlin. "It's after five. Time to go," he said and shoved his paperwork into his top desk drawer, slammed it shut, picked up his coat, and left. "Hey, turn off my desk light, will ya?" he called over his shoulder.

Russell was at his desk nearly an hour early the next morning. His eyes were red from lack of sleep and, though tempted, he had not called Sherrill. *She doesn't need to know about this. A retrial would devastate her and her family.* He shuffled through papers, listed phone calls he needed to make, and watched the clock incessantly.

Devlin finally stepped off the elevator.

"You're late." Russell glanced at his watch. It was almost nine o'clock. "We've got to get going."

"What's your hurry? Sitting in the D.A.'s office won't change things." Devlin was carrying the same folder from yesterday. "We've got plenty of time. Elevator or stairs?"

"Stairs. I can't stand still."

"Welcome." The D.A. shook hands with Devlin and Russell as they entered. "The prosecutor and defense attorneys are already here." He swooped his hand toward the two men then pointed to two empty chairs. "Have a seat."

"What are the odds we'll have to go through this again?" Russell glared at the D.A. and shook his head.

"No idea," the D.A. and the prosecuting attorney said simultaneously.

"I've never known a trial to last so damn long," Russell said.

"Me either," Devlin said.

"Thirteen weeks? Piece of cake." The D.A. let out a hearty laugh and hung his suit jacket on a polished wood hanger.

"Just because you weren't the trial attorney and weren't there *every* day," Devlin said, then mumbled "Longest trial *I've* ever seen." He looked at Russell and whispered, "And the number of delays and petty objections, I'm surprised the trial *ever* ended." Devlin glared briefly at the two defense attorneys then pulled the page of names and phone numbers from his file folder.

Russell and Devlin sat in the two chairs near the D.A.'s desk. The two defense attorneys were already seated against the wall near the door.

Wipe those stupid smirks off your face, you idiots. This isn't happening because you did anything right for your client. Russell had hidden his anger at the two for the entire trial, but it was now coming to the surface.

"Which jurors are the two we're talking about?" Russell said aloud while looking at Devlin's list.

"Seven and eight," the D.A. answered. "Now, don't get too excited yet. The one who changed her mind, Juror Seven, was wavering for hours according to the others we've talked to."

"But she came out of the bathroom after another juror badgered her into changing her vote," the red-haired defense attorney said. His rumpled suit looked like it was made for someone two sizes larger.

"We don't know that yet. Don't jump to conclusions," the prosecuting attorney snapped.

Getting defensive, are we? Russell chuckled to himself. "Which are we calling first?" Russell asked and wiped a bead of sweat from his temple.

"Seven. She remained very quiet during most of the deliberations. Then we'll call Eight who was agreeing to a guilty verdict early on. Eight's the one who went into the bathroom with the undecided one." The D.A. dialed the number and pushed buttons to start the recorder and engage the speaker function.

Juror Seven's phone rang five times. The D.A.'s eyebrows raised when she answered the phone just as the answering machine started its greeting. His left hand had been hovering over the phone to end the call.

The D.A. told her the purpose of the call, "Just trying to touch bases with all the jurors and get their feel for the trial, their decision for the verdict." He started introducing the others in the room. "Besides the two defense attorneys, Mr. Char—"

"I'm sorry," Juror Seven said. "I don't have time for this."

"Would later today be a better ti—"

"The trial's over. My decision was made. I'm through with it."

"Yes, but we're talking to each juror to make sure everything went—" The D.A. tapped his pencil on his legal pad.

"Everything went fine."

"Do you have a problem with your vote?"

"Problem? Vote? You've got to be kidding. That son of a bitch is off the streets. That's the end of it." She took a deep breath then said, "I've already spent too much time on that trial. I'm busy. Don't have time to talk. Good bye."

The phone line went dead, and buzzing resonated from the telephone speaker.

The D.A. stared for a moment at the phone then disconnected the call with a firm punch on the red button. He looked around the room and shrugged. "Any comments?"

"Maybe we should pursue this further," the two defense attorneys said in unison.

"With her?" Devlin said. "What would be the purpose?"

"I agree with Devlin," Russell said. "I doubt she'll talk to anyone about this." He shifted his weight and crossed then uncrossed his legs.

"Perhaps you two could talk to her in person," the prosecuting attorney offered while looking at Devlin then Russell.

"Not yet, gentlemen," the D.A. said. "Let's see what Juror Eight has to say. If she's the least bit hesitant with how the voting went, then we'll do more follow up." The D.A. picked up his list of phone numbers and dialed Juror Eight's number.

Juror Eight answered on the third ring. Sounds of children playing nearby were heard before the "Hello." After a brief introduction of everyone in the room and the purpose of the call, Eight said she had time to talk. The conversation quickly turned to the deliberations.

"We all got tired of the defense attorneys with their non-stop and nonsense objections and the countless in-chamber discussions. We got bored with sitting in the waiting area for hours, for days, without hearing any testimony. My God, what was all that about? More than three months long? Oh, and we thought the prosecuting attorney was grandstanding ... like maybe he wanted to run for D.A. in the next election."

Everyone except the prosecutor chuckled.

"But what about the juror, uh, Ms. Downey, who was having problems with deciding?" the D.A. asked while frowning at the others in the room.

"Oh, Julia was upset for quite a while. She went into the restroom and didn't come out."

"Were there any deliberations while she was gone?"

"Uh, no, that would have been wrong."

"She's picking her words carefully," Devlin whispered to Russell.

"That a good sign? Or is she covering something up?"

"Wish I knew. Don't stress about it. Nothing you can do at this point."

Russell took a deep breath and said, "This is driving me crazy." He shifted his and stood up, nearly tipping his chair over.

The D.A. scowled as Russell started pacing.

"We could all hear her crying in there. I finally knocked on the door and went in with her." Then in a muffled voice like she was covering the mouthpiece, "Give that back to your brother," she said to one of the children.

"Do you need us to call you back la—?" the bald, overweight defense attorney started to ask then got silent when everyone else in the room glared at him.

"No, that's okay. With two kids and a part-time job, there really isn't a *good* time." They heard her chuckle.

"Okay, then," the D.A. continued. "How long were you in there? And what did you talk about?"

"We were in there quite a while since she was having a problem. She couldn't believe it."

"Believe what? That Dunne did it?"

Russell glanced at the two smug defense attorneys. He bit his tongue. *If she says that she had to convince that other woman, it's all over. Or re-starting.* He plopped down next to Devlin.

"You okay?" Devlin whispered.

"Not yet." Russell folded his arms across his chest.

The D.A. glanced at Russell.

"Yes, uh, no," Juror Eight said

"Could you please clarify?" The D.A. shrugged again. "Did you have to convince Ms. Downey that the defendant was guilty?"

Everyone in the room was holding their breath. The pause seemed to stop time.

"Um, well, really, the only convincing I had to do ..."

Russell clenched his eyes shut.

"... was ... well, she didn't want to believe that *anyone* could be capable of killing another human being."

"What do you mean?" The prosecuting attorney, who had been doodling on his legal pad, looked at the telephone.

Juror Eight paused for a moment then said, "That one human could cold bloodedly kill another ... with no real reason ... well, a reason like in self-defense or in war or something like that."

"Was that all?" the D.A. added.

"All?"

"Did you have to talk her into a guilty verdict? To change her vote?"

"Change her vote?" Juror Eight paused again. "No, not really. She didn't *change* her vote. She had avoided voting at all up to that point."

"Whew!" Russell breathed, and he and Devlin nodded at each other, smiles broadening across their faces.

Juror Eight continued. "She told me she thought Dunne had killed that young man. She was just having a hard time coming to terms with it, but she never doubted that Dunne did it."

The collective sigh from the prosecution side was audible throughout the room; the defense attorneys scowled silently.

The entire conversation lasted nearly thirty minutes and further questions brought the same replies, confirming what Juror Eight had said earlier.

As the D.A. thanked her for her time, replaced the phone receiver, he glanced at each face in the room. "Well, what do you think?"

"Sounds reasonable to me. There weren't any contradictions, and she answered the questions confidently," the prosecuting attorney said.

"Running for office, counselor?" the bald defense attorney asked.

"Uh, me? No."

Everyone chuckled again.

"Gentlemen," the D.A. turned to the two defense attorneys who were frowning and closing their faux-leather folders. "I don't think this issue will be a point in any appeal. Good luck with that since this is a capital murder case. Good-bye." He reached toward them but instead of shaking hands, opened the door and ushered them out of his office.

"Detective? Anything more? Inspector Devlin and I have several more jurors to call, and unless you really want to listen in—"

On cue, Russell said, "No, thanks," stood, nodded to Devlin, and followed the prosecuting attorney out of the D.A.'s office.

Now to decide whether or not to tell Sherrill about this bit of ... of tension. Russell headed back to his desk, phone calls, and ensuing reports. *Routine. Savor the routine.*

Chapter 89

Six weeks later Detective Russell Hurley was returning to his desk when the phone rang. He picked it up on the second ring and found himself talking to the Sheriff of Trinity County. After a few moments, he slowly hung up and went to Captain Reardon's office.

"Found him, huh? Trinity County? It's been what? Nearly a year?"

"Pretty close. Too bad these things draw out so long sometimes." Russell shuffled his feet.

"Was it near where that girl's Mustang was found?" the Captain asked while unwrapping a stick of gum.

"Nope. The girl, Glenda Shore, her car was in Siskiyou County. This site is in a sandbar along the Trinity River. Never found any trace of the Shore girl though … just like—"

"Yeah, I heard. Glad *you* got closure."

Russell winced at that word. *It doesn't change anything; it's still hard to accept.* Russell clenched his teeth and shook his head.

"What are you going to do now about Ms. Madison?" Reardon asked.

"Tell her."

"You sure you can handle this? Want someone else to do it?"

"Thanks, no. She needs to hear it from someone she knows. It wouldn't be fair to let her find out on the news or from anyone else. In fact I think I'll drive over to her place now."

"So, you know where she lives. Well, since the case is closed, I guess there's no problem, no fraternizing issue anymore." The captain smiled.

"Never was a fraternizing *issue*, Captain.

With a chuckle, Reardon added, "Good luck."

"Thanks." Russell returned to his desk, cleared the top, turned off his desk lamp, and picked up his jacket. The drive to Sherrill's apartment didn't take long enough; he'd rather that it would have taken days, but he was there in twenty-five minutes.

He knocked on the door of apartment 122. *Maybe she's not home.* He was ready to knock again, or maybe leave, when he heard the bolt turn. *Well, at least I'll get it over with.*

"Russell! What're you doing here?" Sherrill asked as she opened the door. She stepped back when she noticed the seriousness in his face. "What's wrong? Is everyone all right? Your brother? The boys? What's—?"

He took one halting step toward her and said, "Have you talked to your parents lately?"

"A couple of times a week. Are they okay? Have you heard from them?"

"No, not me. But I'm wondering how your folks are holding up." Russell had met them during the trial, and they were truly nice people, people who did not deserve to have their family torn apart ... of course, no one deserved that. *Why don't bad things happen to bad people?*

"What's going on, Russell? Why are you here without calling first?" They were still standing at the door; Russell was too concerned with the news to move any farther.

I can't put this off forever, he thought and took a breath. "Um, it's your brother," Russell said. He looked at her intense brown eyes and shrugged. "Can I come in?"

"Oh, sure. Sorry. What's happened?"

Russell motioned her toward the couch. "We got a call from the Trinity County Sheriff's Department." He waited until she sat down then he sat on the coffee table, facing her. "They found ... well, um, along a river, buried in the sand."

"Oh ... my ... God. Jeffrey? They found his, his—? What? How?" Sherrill covered her mouth with her hands and leaned back into the teal and beige striped sofa.

"You've got to keep breathing," he said softly as he moved next to her. "Yes, they found his body and, from what the deputy said, it happened just like Keno said."

"So, he was killed by that monster for real the way Keno said. Thank God the jury believed Keno and read the evidence right."

Might have been Dunne's comment, "What took you 'em-effers' so long?" that helped convince the jury members, Russell thought. *I almost laughed out loud in the courtroom when I heard that part of the testimony.*

Sherrill took a deep breath and let it out quickly. "Too bad the death penalty wasn't an option."

"You can thank the liberal, west-coast judges for that. That's the reason the District Attorney couldn't even *ask* for the chair ... or injections. But he'll never get out. Life without parole. L-WOP."

Sherrill looked at Russell. "It helped me make up my mind about how I feel about the death penalty." She paused and stared into nothing. "Why would someone kill just because ... well, for nothing. What a hateful son-of-a-bitch." She covered her face with both hands and sobbed.

Russell put his arm around her shoulder, pulled her shaking body close, and held her tight.

Chapter 90

Saturday morning, the next weekend

Shane lay on the kitchen floor, content that two people had taken care of his every need since last night.

Russell had his old, blue terrycloth robe on, and Sherrill was wearing one of Russell's flannel shirts. Over the morning's second cup of coffee, she looked at him and asked, "Can you take me to the airport a week from Sunday?"

"What?" Russell stood still, hands full of the plates and utensils from the kitchen table. "Not even a 'those pancakes were delicious, thanks' comment?"

"Okay, those pancakes were delicious, thanks. Now, can you take me to the airport?"

Russell glanced at Shane curled up by Sherrill's feet then put everything into the sink. He said, "Um, sure. I suppose. Where're you going?"

"Home."

Russell stopped short at that word. "Home? You're settled here, have a job. You're leaving anyway? I'll ... you're ... are you sure you want—? *Hell, close one door and another one* closes. *Getting shut out fast. Finally get answers to Christine's disappearance and brave enough to tell Sherrill, and now she's going home. Leaving. Damn.*

Sherrill bit her lower lip and said, "Paul was here this week. He heard that Jeffrey was found and thought I shouldn't be here alone."

"You're *not* alone."

"I know that. East Coast doesn't." She paused a moment. "Paul talked to my folks and our friends, well, to everyone back there anyway, and thought someone should be here to help with the cremation and arrangements."

"So, you're going home with your old fiancé?" *Guess it'll be just you and me again, Shane.* He patted his knee and said quietly, "Shane, come here, Shane." *Seems like you're the only one who sticks around,* he thought as he rubbed the dog's head. *'Dog' equals 'reliability.'*

Sherrill watched him avoid eye contact and smiled. "I've got to take Jeffrey home. Mom and Dad want to bury his ashes next to Gram and Gramps. Keep the family together somehow."

"I understand but I thought things were going great here. You said you've signed up for classes—"

"Yep, a criminal justice class at the community college ... be an investigator."

"You're giving that up?" He raised his arms in the air then folded them across his chest. He shrugged before dropping his arms to his side, and his shoulders drooped.

She paused to let him fret even more, reached for his hand, and smiled broadly. "Paul's not only my 'old' fiancé. He's my *ex*-fiancé. And my *never-again* fiancé. He drove here from San Francisco—heard Eureka was just a bit north." She laughed. "Then he realized it was a six-hour drive and isolated from the rest of the world. He stayed at a motel on Broadway then headed back Friday morning. Says he hates small towns; he'll never be back. Thank God." She took a deep breath. "By the way, I bought a *round-trip* ticket. Maybe you can drive to the airport again in two weeks to *pick me up?*"

"What?" Russell's stomach muscles relaxed. "Sure. No problem," he added and grinned.

"That's the reaction I wanted. We'll *talk* more later," she said, leaned across the dinette table, and kissed him hard on the lips.

Epilogue

I, the author, was a juror on this trial—the one who went into the restroom with the juror who was so terribly upset about a human taking the life of another.

The criminal, called Phillip Dunne in this book, is still in prison after being sentenced to seven years to life in prison, which has, so far, ended up being a life sentence. He was originally sent to Folsom State Prison near Sacramento, California and was incarcerated there when I started teaching inmates years later. He was transferred to another institution after I reported the situation to my supervisor. I never, *never* told anyone else working with me what the inmate's name was. I didn't want him to learn who I was and that I was working in the prison system.

He had earned his GED and had received some vocational training. However, his prison file of disciplinary reports filled three cardboard boxes, proving that, though he had received some education, he had not learned much about getting along with others.

I had two young children at the time of the trial and relied on friends and family to take care of them while serving on the jury. My $5 a day payment, plus mileage, paid for a large party as a thank you for all their help.

My husband had saved the many weeks of newspapers since we were barred from reading or listening to radio or watching television reports about the trial while it was going on. Reading the newspaper accounts after the trial ended made me aware of what all my friends and family could not discuss with me while I was serving. From those articles, I learned details that were not allowed to be presented during the trial—for fear that we jurors might be swayed by hearing that he was suspected of killing others besides the victim (called Jeffrey Madison in my book). Nor could we be told of his prior convictions.

Traumatized? Bothered by hearing all the terrible things we heard? Definitely. That's why I had to write this book. I still have those newspaper clippings.

I added the romance between the victim's sister (called Sherrill here) and the detective (Russell) to add a positive aspect and allowed the snitch (Keno) to give comic relief. Other characters and victims (Wanda and her son, Glenda, and Christine) were added for the purpose of telling the story.

Most of the story is true: the young man disappeared; the car was dumped in the bay; the jailhouse snitch helped with clues; the hypnotist was called in to jog the snitch's memory; the car's contents were strewn about the redwoods near the California-Oregon border; receipts were found that helped retrace the victim's steps; the murderer tried to escape to Hawaii where he was caught; he really did say, "What the f... took you so long," when the Hawaiian police finally arrested him; the girlfriend sat through the trial behind the "suspect"; the trial proceeded and the verdict was rendered without the "benefit" of the victim's body; the phone call to me was made after the trial; the victim's body was found near a river, uncovered by a foraging animal; and, devastation was felt, is still felt, by victim's family living without their son and brother.

All members of the jury were pleasant and ranged in age from the mid-twenties to retirees. We did request a few clarifications during deliberations but did not have much problem arriving at a verdict. Two alternate jurors were seated, but, somehow, all twelve of us on the original panel made it, unwilling to relinquish our positions.

Thanks to my friends Sandy, Kathy, and others I've undoubtedly forgotten by now, and to my husband and my parents who are no longer with us, for all their help during the trial.

From the *Times-Standard*, the newspaper of Eureka, California

August 23, 1977
"The prosecutor called ... [the] murder 'a very serious, cold-blooded, heinous crime (and) a very [b]ase antisocial cowardly act,' just before [the] judge ... pronounced sentence."

"... [the killer's] trial was one of the most unusual, most expensive and longest in Humboldt County history. Local attorneys said convictions in murder cases where no body has been found are very rare."

September 8, 1977
"The body of a 22-year-old ... man was recovered Wednesday from a makeshift grave near the Trinity River, almost one year after he was murdered ...." [and about six weeks after the trial ended.]

September 13, 1977
"A letter of commendation was presented Monday to ... , [the] chief district attorney's investigator, for his efforts in the recent murder trial. ... [He] worked for nine months gathering the evidence which convicted [the murderer] of first degree murder of a 22-year-old ... man.

17666498R00138

Made in the USA
Lexington, KY
21 September 2012